Mum and William Wordsworth

Julie Kennedy

Published in 2013 by FeedARead.com Publishing – Arts Council funded

First Edition

A CIP catalogue record for this title is available from the British Library.

This novel is a work of fiction. Names and characters are the product of the author's imagination and any resemblance to actual persons, living or dead, is entirely coincidental

Acknowledgements

I wish to thank all those who have helped me with this book, especially Fred & Alan Seaton for their invaluable help with the publication. Thanks to the previous Scottish Arts Council for a New Writer's Award and to Cill Riallaig in Kerry where I spent some time working on the book. And all those who encouraged me at different stages of the book, particularly, Doctor Willy Maley of University of Glasgow, a guardian angel of new writers. I wish to thank Evie Wyld for feedback on an earlier draft. I also wish to thank all my friends for continually asking me when I was going to finish this book so they could read it. Thanks to Kenny for putting up with my tapping away in a corner for years and my sisters and brothers Kay, John, Christy, Brian, Anne-Therese, Marie and Trisha for inspiring me to keep going. Thanks to my friends Jane and Tommy Kirkwood for their support and hospitality at Carbeth. I acknowledge my debt to the words of William Wordsworth and the quotes from his poem '*Tintern Abbey*,' used in the book; words that moved me to feel something so strongly, I never forgot it. Also to my first great teacher, John Dougan at St. Matthews Primary. Finally, to the people of Craigneuk, Wishaw for the help along the way.

To the memory of my mum and dad,

Joan O'Connor and Benny Smith

and my beloved brother Brian.

'…………………………And I have felt

A presence that disturbs me with the joy

Of elevated thoughts; a sense sublime

Of something far more deeply interfused,

Whose dwelling is the light of setting suns,

And the round ocean and the living air,

And the blue sky, and in the mind of man:'

From 'Lines written a few miles above Tintern Abbey On Revisiting

The Banks of the Wye During a Tour,'

by William Wordsworth

(July 13, 1798)

PROLOGUE

Ma name is Erin McLaughlin, ah'm fifteen. The poster of The Police looks out at me an ma Aunt Geraldine who is aged forty three an disnae see Sting wi his leather jacket over his shoulder, blonde hair sticking up at the back of his head like a halo. She sees a room full of mum's clothes to be packed away.

'This is yours,' gien me the weddin ring. It feels heavy.

'Eldest girl.'

Like a coronation with bin backs scattered about the carpet for an audience.

At first the ring nips ma finger. Ah've fatter fingers than mum had. New stuff about her. Another useful fact.

'Now, is there anything in this bag of clothes that ye'd like to keep, Erin?'

We were never allowed in her room, never mind the wardrobe but now ah can have anythin ah want. Keep expectin mum to come into the room, hit me over the head for nosin about her stuff.

'Did she not leave us a letter or somethin?'

When ah try to take it off, gets stuck across the knucklebone.

'Shite.'

'Your mum was too sick to write letters, pet. A ring's much better.'

The uncles are at the pub but she never went, she stayed to do this. Tidy up the clothes.

6

Too tired to argue.

'Don't want it.'

'It's a mindin. One day you'll understand. Trust me. Anyway, you've got your memories. Remember the nice things, dear, that's what's important.'

Any minute now it'll be *God works in mysterious ways.*

There is somethin ah want but don't know what. Ah know ah don't want only the nice things. Nothin in that bag cos black bin bags are for left over food an other rubbish for the bin.

'You can keep the clothes.'

Mum would haunt me if ah wore her stuff.

'Well, I always admired that velvet skirt. Your Aunt Mary would like the fur jacket.'

Careful not to grab.

Aunt Geraldine looks nothin like mum; she's heavier, in low- heeled shoes an her hair is brown, no jet black. Ma hair is darker than Aunt Geraldine's but no as dark as mum's. Ma hair's short from mum always makin me get it cut cos she was terrified of nits, them spreadin lik wildfire in her house. All of us, lassies an laddies, have bowl cut hair. Ah'm lettin mine grow long now, Dad won't care. Ah've green eyes from his side of the family, a light shade of green, that ma best pal Sally says are cats' eyes but real cats' eyes are yellow an mine don't glow in the dark. Folk say ah look lik mum but ah don't see it, only that ah've got her mouth an her smile but she's taken our smile with her, wherever she's gone. Everyone else in the family has a pointy chin, more lik our dad.

Could still ask Aunt Geraldine to stay for a few more days; the funeral was yesterday; her an ma uncles are gettin the boat back to Ireland first thing the morra mornin cos they've farms to run, sheep to shear an cows to milk.

We'll be on our own soon after it bein so busy wi people in the house, us, makin sandwiches and cups of tea. The funeral is over an now we're clearin her things away, nobody says it but they expect us to start getting back to normal, whatever normal is.

'Why did ma Aunt Mary not come to the funeral?'

'You'll have to ask her, sweetheart. She said she couldn't face it as if anyone could right enough. Still, she's taken your Paul for a while. Poor Paul. That'll help your father. If only he'd let us take the wee ones with us.'

Over my dead body.

He'll never let them take the wee ones away.

On the flat roof of Rooney's shop across the road, some starlings have a wash in a puddle then shake themselves out. Reminds me of our Paul

'It's okay to cry.'

And then Aunt Geraldine has that look when she's desperate for a fag, turning quickly away, head inside the drawers, hands sortin out blouses and underwear. She fills a half a bin bag then moves on to the white wardrobe that dad built up from flat packs from MFI: a bit wobbly and caved in at the back.

Clears all the spaces of mum's stuff in twenty minutes. Everythin has tae happen so fast. It's the first time she's been in those drawers yet she acts lik they were her drawers. Her stuff. No lik me, sittin on the bed pickin bits of the bed- spread, heid still fuzzy lik ah've only

8

wakened up or ma heid's stuffed wi bits of bed-spread: Straw Man out the Wizard of Oz. Wool Girl fae Wishaw.

'And Erin…'

'What?'

'Try not to have your head in the clouds my dear. Your father needs you now.'

Stratus, Beaufort, Cumulus, Cirrus, Nimbus. Clouds are whitish parachutes that take me away from here.

The phone goes later. Aunt Mary.

'I'm sorry I never made the funeral, dear. How was it?'

Steak-pie, potatoes and vegetables at the British Legion. A picture of the Queen starin down at us.

How does she think it was?

'Well Paul's fine. Your dad was right to send him back with your uncle. Come and see us soon, Oban's not that far.'

Only one hundred and fifteen miles away.

He has blonde hair an blue eyes, our Paul; he even looks like the golden boy of his Player of the Year statue. Has a hole in his heart: his only mistake. Never thought about it at the time but cannae remember seein him that night when him an dad came back from the hospital. The morning after we found out, met our Simmit, on the stairs:

'Do you want me to make yir breakfast?'

'Shut-up, you. You're no the mum of the house now.'

Then ah knew Paul must have told him an Pinkie as well.

Did she say any last words so that we would know what to do? How to go on? Always thought there'd be time enough to ask him properly. Never thought Paul would go too.

'Ye'll be glad of that ring one day. Take good care of it, will you?'

'Okay,' ah say to ma aunt.

Later, find the black bin bags Aunt Geraldine has tied at the top: one bag each for mum's sisters. Drag out the fake fur coat with suede patches on the elbows and put it on. Its warm inside the coat and in the mirror ah look lik Marc Bolan's wee sister. The coat smells of mum.

After a while of sittin on the bed, take the coat into our room and hang at the very back of the wardrobe ah share with ma four sisters: our Anna, Elaine, Lizzie and Annemarie. Now, the coat can watch over us from the back of the wardrobe, look across the wee dresses and lassies' coats. There's a half a bottle of Coty L'Aimant tucked away at the back of the wardrobe. Wonder how that got there?

ONE

1

The words of Wordsworth's poems are dead old fashioned. Ah'll never get what he's on about.

'The day is come when I again repose

Here, under this dark sycamore…'

Who talks lik that?

Mrs. Kelly, ma English teacher, says that the natural world was his religion. It's hard to understand when ye're brought up Catholic. Mrs. Kelly says ma poetry is very dark. She called me outside the class on Monday.

'How are thing at home, Erin? Are you coping alright?'

She's got red straight hair an she's expectin a baby. It's no really showin yet but she told the class she wouldn't be here after the summer; goin on maternity leave then. Hope she disnae go for good after the baby is born. Focused on the poster of Albert Einstein behind her in the corridor, his bushy eyebrows. Thank God dad disnae have dead bushy eyebrows.

'Fine, miss. Ah wasn't close to mum. Ah'm closer to ma dad.'

Mrs. Kelly gave me a look, as if she was seein me for the first time. Don't know why ah said it. Weird soundin but still true. Ah can say stuff now mum isn't here.

'It's just your poem, Erin. It's so dark.'

Every Tuesday, last two periods is English. We're studyin people called 'The Romantic Poets.' At first the boys went:

'Ah naw, miss. That's lassies' stuff. Fallin in love an aw that.'

They thought it was about romances an folk snoggin, none of them wanted to listen to that in broad daylight especially from Mrs. Kelly. That's probably what people mean when they say that lassies mature earlier than boys. Last week the class had to write a poem about nature. Wrote about a beautiful, golden eagle soarin above the steelworks, right in the middle of enjoyin bein an eagle it gets shot by someone and dies; in the last verse rats are eatin the carcass. Didnae know what to say to Mrs Kelly. Ah wis dead chuffed about usin 'carcass.'

There were loads of staples on the carpet tiles. That'll wreck the hoover, ah thought, an prayed ah wouldn't get one of the voices in ma head, look like a right eijit. Cos even if ah didnae say anythin, ma eyes would go funny, the way it does when ye hear a voice in your heid. While Mrs Kelly waited for an answer ah was wonderin if she'd shown the poem to other teachers in the staff room an was ah up there wi first year boys who write in their jotters: 'teachers must die.'

'Well, if you ever need to talk or anything. Okay?'

'Thanks, miss.'

'How are you getting on with your poem for your class talk?'

'Fine, miss. I'm doing *Tintern Abbey*.'

'Oh, that's far too long to remember. Just do a verse, okay?'

'Yes, miss.'

'And a one minute introduction. Most of the class won't have heard of that poem.'

2

That night when the rest are in bed ah'm doin ma homework in front of the fire an dad has the telly on.

'Dad?'

'What?'

'How did you an mum meet?'

'What? You're no real, Erin. Don't ask me daft questions, ah've enough on ma plate.'

'But...'

'For God's sake.'

'It's only a question.'

'Ah'm warnin you, Erin. Don't start....'

Always the same. Only yesterday he couldnae find a clean cup for the tea cos aw the cups were in the sink, every cup in the house wis in the sink. Can you believe it? Can you? People don't. He tells Azir, the Pakistani man in the shop, when he goes for the paper; he shakes his heid. Do you know what he did last Thursday? Put aw the dishes in the sink. That'll teach us. If we want to eat then we need tae clean every dish in the house. That's the only way we'll learn. The hard way. The only way. Right?

'But we never asked tae be born,' ah say.

Wouldnae hit me but says ah deserve a slap for unadulterated cheek. No respect, that's all he asks for a wee bit of respect. And cleanliness is next to godliness so it must be good? But if ye're cleanin aw the time ah wonder how could that be godly? Sometimes, think he hates

14

us, it's scary. He thinks we killed her cos she was always runnin after us. If she'd not worked as hard maybe. Never gave her a minute. Wouldnae let her sleep. No wonder he takes Valium. No wonder the doctor writes out wan ae they thirteen-week prescriptions. Sign your name on the dotted line. Jist need tae phone. The doctor knows the score, even the doctor knows.

Stare at the brown carpet, at the patch of stickiness that one of the boys brought in on their boots. Can't get it off; ah've given up even tryin.

'Ah mean that was just stupid, paintin the livin-room pink for Jesus sake, Erin. Why don't ye think before ye act? Tell me why?'

Because there were a year's worth of scribbles and marks on the wallpaper.

Upstairs, behind the three doors of the upstairs rooms, all ma brothers and sisters are sound asleep. The sound of them is breathing and snores as well. Dad and me lik two ornaments either side of a mantelpiece.

Maybe, if ah painted the place again, it would cheer everybody up. She'd been gone nearly six months. It won't bring her back. Nothin will bring her back, of course, ah knew that.

***

Planned it at the start of the week when dad was goin to visit our Paul in Oban. Paul's got his own doctor now and dad went to meet him. Coloured paint is too dear but white emulsion's quite cheap. Still, what would be the point of white wi all of us? Lik a white suite, askin for trouble.

Woolworths sell tubes with colour that you add to emulsion. That would do. Once they were aw in bed, ah could start paintin but that was the night took ages to get our Lizzie to bed cos of bad dreams.

First, squeezed the contents of the tube into the big paint tin, stirrin wi an old wooden spoon. Raspberry jam sauce to white cream makes raspberry ripple. Mine's a cone, what's yours? Nougat or an oyster?

Pinkie was up watchin snooker.

'You must be jokin,' his finger was a pool cue pointin at me when he said 'you.'

First slap of paint already on the wall. Couldnae turn back. It felt good.

'Ma da'll kill you. Bright pink, Jesus.'

Went to tell Simmit. Two of them are best pals since our Paul left.

'No he won't.'

'You're mental,' Simmit, our clerk of works inspected the walls then he went back upstairs to examine his plukes in the bathroom mirror.

Later, Pinkie tried tae help wi the paintin, kept splashin bits of pink on the skirtin boards, makin more work for me. When even they were sleepin, painted through the night; at first, tryin to spread the paint in the same direction but after a while didn't care as long as the wall got covered. Just slapped it on.

People think it's all bad stuff when ye're mum dies but there's no many lassies ma age get to paint their livin room their favourite colour though the room seemed a lot smaller when ah thought the idea up; took ages to paint one wall. When ah did one, couldnae stop.

Remember the skirtin.

We've had every different type of wallpaper on our walls; washable vinyl, white woodchip. Always have fancy wallpaper on the wall with the fire, cos that's the wall the chairs face, plainer stuff everywhere else. You can never change where the suite is cos the visitors couldnae look at woodchip.

Helped mum when she was paperin and paintin, usually, the doors. White gloss paint an the skirtin boards as well, which by the way ah hated. The last time was a year ago when she first was in hospital; now, our school clothes get shabbier an no adults notice or if they do, don't say. Worse than paint on a wall fadin, nobody knows what's goin on inside anybody else.

Till half past two in the mornin, till ah'm dizzy wi fumes. At the end, put the Sacred Heart picture up again, his plump red heart set in a background of candy floss. Red and green should never be seen but nobody said anythin about red and pink. When ah finish, ah'm nearly sleepin on ma feet. One last look. The place looks that new way again. Forgot turpentine for splashes but so there's pink on the white skirtin.

Soak the brushes in turps.

Come back to that when ah get up. If ah inhale any more fumes, ah'll be high as a kite, higher than him.

That night bein a good farmer, take the sheep in ma head out the pen, line them up one after the other and start tae count till the sheep are pink. Finally, sleep great from fumes and tiredness. Me an the pink sheep are high on paint, runnin up the mountains. Next day up early to get the turps. The man in the shop gies me a funny look. Thinks ah might drink it but he still sells it to me.

***

17

He was only in the door. You could still smell the paint: a slightly brighter shade on the wall than it had said on the tube. Fluorescent.

'Wait till ye see what she's done, dad. Wait till ye see.'

'What's she done this time? Ah'm hardly away a week. Tell me, what's she done?'

Nothing about how the dirty smudges weren't there, right below The Sacred Heart and the one over at their wedding photo. And the scribbles Annemarie did with coloured pencils, all gone. Nothing about that. And no drips on the skirtin boards now even the ones our Pinkie made, wiped those clean with the turps, nearly took ma skin off. Nothin about any of that. Only...

'Jesus Christ, it's pink. What've you done?'

'What's up wi pink?'

'Da, tell her,' Simmit's at his side.

'Tell her, tell her. It's a lassie's colour.'

'But it was horrible. Even you said that Pinkie. And it's no been done for a year. Surely, ye can see the difference.'

'Aye, ah can see a difference. And anyway, where'd you get the money to buy paint?'

'Ah saved.'

'How? How did ye save?'

Stayed calm.

'Ah saved from the messages money.'

His forehead, all wrinkled up as if his anger pushed against the surface of his skin an any minute it'd burst out into the room, splattin all over the pink livin room walls.

Simmit was grinnin, big style.

Turncoat.

'You spent ma money on pink paint without even askin. Whose house is this? Whose? Is it yours or is it mine?'

As he got louder, a sort of amnesia came over me, about how words connected, joined into sentences and even worse how individual letters make words.

'It's our house as well,' ah said.

And it is.

'Your house. Is it? Do you pay the bills? Do you pay the rent?'

'We don't pay rent. We get housing benefit.'

Should have shut up but remembered how to talk.

'We cannae live in the past, dad. We've got to freshen the place up.'

'Would you listen to her? Would you?'

Next door definitely heard. They'd probably turned down the telly right in the middle of Coronation Street. A real row with people you know is always better than a made up one. Simmit's rabbit nose twitch started, scrunchin lik mad. Poor Simmit. He disnae like shoutin.

'A pink livin room. We'll be the laughin stock of the place. Another one of your daft ideas.'

'It's ma favourite colour.'

'Well, that would explain it. Your favourite colour. Have you no common sense? No brains?

'Your mother was right. Head always in the clouds. You'll never change.'

There are lots of good things about pink: the colour of sunset over the steel works when the sun's burnin red an sinkin below the skyline even though the place smells of rotten eggs lik the world's just farted.

Sulphur dioxide. The wee hamster we once had was pink, especially his stomach. Sticks of rock are pink, when ye get them from Blackpool or Ayr when we're pals go on holiday and when ye lick it for ages ye get a pink tongue.

'What will ye do, Dad?'

Simmit was back on the stronger side again. The wimp.

'Ah'll just have to paint over. Right here an now.'

'Ah don't suppose there's any money left?'

'No,' ah lie.

'Might have known.'

Then he was straight out the door again, his bag still lyin in the hall.

Honestly, Erin. You're supposed to help your father.

When dad came back, he was carryin two tins of paint; Mr. Wiley from Hazel Drive was with him. He does all the homers around here: cheap as chips.

'Here it is, John. Can ye do anything with it?'

Mr. Wiley has stooped shoulders that make him look as if he lifted them up one time to hold up a ceilin that he was paintin an his shoulders got stuck.

'What do ye make of it, John? Eh? Eh?'

Mr Wiley ran a hand across the surface, took a few steps back and looked at the walls for ages. His face had white flecks of paint.

'It's no that bad, Joe. Quite an even spread. You'll be comin to work for me, hen.'

Winked.

'Very funny, John. That's hilarious.' Ma dad shook his head, lookin around the room, still tryin to enlist the support of everythin that

20

moved even everythin that didnae, even the switched off telly and the couch and the chairs and the cat's basket. At least the Sacred Heart stayed stum. No miracles, talkin pictures sayin, *aye right, Joe.*

Hours later, ah could smell the fresh paint from upstairs. Sneaked down. No even proper brown; the livin room looked even darker.

'Right, that'll do us for a good few years,' dad said. Much calmer. 'Is that no better?'

Nobody answered. Nobody knew what to say. How could it be better? What a daft question.

'See what you caused?' Pinkie said.

At least ah got it painted even if it is mustard now. A horrible shite like brown.

***

That's his life, cups ae tea and valium. Feels drunk when he's no been drinkin cos ye know he hasnae touched a drop since she died. No a single drop. Must be the pills, sleepin tablets to help him sleep otherwise, hell on earth. He gets drowsy. Tell him he talks dolly dimple. Later, when he's calmed down, he says ah can stay up and read. Sometimes, he goes out for a walk an marches from our house right up to Newmains an back.

Walk the open roads, find freedom of mind.

Make sure the wee ones have got clean clothes for school.

Somethin mad in him makes him walk, maybe, it's the same madness makes me paint an that made Wordsworth walk too. At least when ye walk ye're alive. At least when ye paint ye're alive.

'What ye readin?'

'Wordsworth. Poetry for English.'

It's actually a poem about tortoises havin sex by D.H Lawrence; found it at the back ae the book the teacher gave our class cos we're top section; it was supposed to be for Higher English.

'Poetry? Ye must get ye're brains from ye're mum cos it's no fae me. Wish ah'd stuck in at school but me, thick as shite. Did ah ever tell ye that at ma school the boys went in the mornin an the lassies went in the afternoon. Whit kind of a school wis that, hen? No wonder ah cannae read an write.'

'How come?'

'Aye, how come? You stick in, hen. That's the only way out.'

He's always goin on about getting out lik we're in a big dark well and school is a rope that ye grab on to, haul yourself up and away. But he's lived here aw his life so maybe it cannae be that bad.

'Dad, ah'm leavin school,' thought it would be hard to say but after the paintin is isn't.

'You're what?'

'Ah'm leavin this Christmas. Mr. McKay said a while ago, ah should. About time.'

Mr. McKay, the next door neighbour says he's gonnae tell ma dad ah should leave, to help in the house.

'That'll be fnn right. Your mother would turn in her grave. What does he know? Auld hen-pecked, himself.'

He's quiet an ma dad's loud. Don't get on except at New Year when everybody's best pals round here then it's mum upstairs sayin a decade of the rosary at the bells before they are in and out the neighbour's houses, bottle of whisky under their arms.

'Naw, we'll muddle through this. Jist as long as we have a system. System's are everythin. In the army when ah did ma National Service, they had systems. Ye made ye're bed an it got inspected. Polished ye're boots or ye'd get court marshalled. If ah can get a few goin here. If you help me, hen, we'll be fine, don't mention leavin school again.'

Gas fire hisses as if tae say, *aye right.* Two orange panels glow orange, blue flames at the edges. His feet are on the fireguard. It's nice to see him dead relaxed. Upstairs everyone else is sleepin. When he goes to bed, ah'll turn the fire up, get the heat from three panels until ah feel ma face burnin.

'Dad, can we go to The Falls of Clyde for a drive?'

'Where is it, hen?'

Don't know exactly but Mrs. Kelly says Wordsworth went there.

'Near Lanark ah think.'

'Mare petrol. We'll see.'

'It's for school, for the poem ah'm learnin. Remember, ah told you.'

'Now, be a good girl. Try not to do daft things, lik that paintin carry on. Ah'm away tae ma bed. Make sure ye put out the lights. Anybody comes tae the door, we're no in.'

Poor dad, cannae cope bein the man of the house. He needs our Paul. Another man about the place. He misses talkin about football, watchin Paul playin for the school team. Up at the mantelpiece, lifts one of the medals Paul won, after a while lookin at it in his hand as if dad cannae work out how the medal got from the mantelpiece to his hand.

23

There's a big brown mark on Wordsworth's forehead after dad throws him out. Did he ever see his life comin down a stair; the way ah saw mine tumbling down? That his poems should end up in a puddle at the bottom of our step, three days after ah painted the livin room pink. Ma dad didnae know, of course. Didnae realise it was Wordsworth in the bag: his long, black coat, hand on his foreheid like his thoughts hurt and his eyes lookin down tae empty space. Bet folk said he had his heid in the clouds. Photograph on the front cover was soaked and that was bad enough, but the English jotter ruined as well an Mrs. Kelly's pencil lost in grass that ah was supposed to bring back. She writes your name in a book if you don't bring your own pencil. Three times then you get a letter home.

Maybe, dad's right. *Ah'm a dirty, lazy so and so* an maybe it is his way or the highway but the way the bag opened at the top of the steps an everythin fell out, tumblin down the stairs in slow motion time. Agnes, our neighbour, of course, was out on her step, spied me on the ground gatherin the books up, and a bus passin an people that disembodied way they look when ye can only see their heads an shoulders. But they could see the whole of me: the rubbishy stuff, bits of sweeties that got stuck in corners of the bag from months ago an a dirty hankie suddenly dislodged by the impact of tumble.

It would never have happened if mum was here.

Crawling about in the grass, gathering the books up, couldn't understand why dad was always telling me to be good at school but then he was shouting at me for reading all the time and why wasn't ah cleaning the place rather than reading school books. His nerves make it happen.

Sneaked the books upstairs. Downstairs, he kept goin on about the mess an books lyin about but it was only school books an books from the library an it's no as if we have special places for books in our house, only the drawers for the clothes.

And all the time, Agnes' sweepin brush scrapin steps in the background. She'd make a great private detective, always doin her nosy. Ah stayed on the ground till the brush stopped. When ah stood up, ah'd squashed a worm with ma knee. Had to rinse the tights out for school next day.

There is a whole world out there.

Wordsworth went travelling around the place, writin poems about beggars an farmers. For enjoyment. Thought about how the walls were pushing in on me, an how there were eight of us now with Paul gone, and how there had been ten when mum was alive, and ah could count our names on two hands.

It was Paul's idea to gie everybody a day for the telly, the eight of us no countin mum an dad. The wee ones had to share Sunday cos nobody else wanted it. Paul took Saturday cos of Match of The Day. Ah was happy cos ah had Friday for Cracker Jack.

CRACKER JACK.

If dad wants to watch somethin then he never bothers whose day of the week it is or that we have a system. Even though he's always goin on about his systems. If there's football on a Tuesday, tough luck. Now we're two less an the system disnae work cos

25

nobody is Saturday, cos Saturday was always Paul. Not only that, how it all really got worse after our Paul left. Decided ah would never ever get any answers at home. It would soon be the September holiday weekend. Go then.

4

The mornin ah leave home, our neighbour Mrs Simpson has a new sign on her gate: Dangerous Dog- KEEP OUT and the Polish brothers next door have cut their grass, garden full of buttercups and daisies wi heads chopped off. Bee hedges that run the full length of our block have been trimmed, though the tops are flattened now, bees still sing inside as if the whole street is singin. That makes me sad to leave. In another month, there'll be birds nesting in the hedge, a different kind of song.

Don't look in the direction of windows. Last thing you need is to catch somebody's eye.

Heid down only the grey pavement and tarred roads wi white chips to look at until no danger. Don't see patterns in the clouds this mornin, that the sky is blue with a grey shaped whale. Three big towers of the steelworks, behind me: see –no- hear- no -speak no- but- smells evil. A blackbird falls out of the hedge, panics when it sees me, scurries away in front on the pavement. Can't find a way back in.

'Ah'll no touch you,' nearly say out loud; how daft to speak to a bird in the street. Finally, the blackbird sees a gap in the bottom of the hedge and disappears.

Dad will be up first. Then our Simmit- so called because he used to play outside in his vest- back from his paper round at Rooney's shop on our Anna's bike. He'll start the toast goin for him an dad but the smell will waken up our Annemarie, Lizzie and Elaine and he'll never get any toast himself till he's fed all three of them. Pinkie -so called

27

cos he was the size of a Pinkie when he was born- puttin on our Paul's Bob Marley records. Our Pinkie's turn now for a Bob Marley phase. Up full bung. *No women no cry* right through the house. Anna will be last up; think ah'm already away to Drew's for the long bank holiday. She'll complain that once again, she's left with the housework until she realises she has our room all to herself. Imagine her stretchin in the bed, the luxury of space and bed covers with nobody pullin them away from ye so ye end up freezin durin the night, never gettin a good sleep. They all knew ah was goin to Drew's but they didnae know it would be first thing, only dad knows that. Told him last night, when the rest were in bed.

'What you goin at the crack of dawn for? That fella's mother will be heart sick of you. Wait till the afternoon an ah'll run ye there in the car.'

'No, dad. She wants me there early cos Drew's sister is goin to a weddin an we've to help wi the weans when they get up. It'll be fine.'

'Have ye no enough weans here to help look after? Honest to God, charity begins at home.'

'It's no charity. We're getting paid.'

Makes a grunting sound. Sometimes, he just gives up. Thank God for me.

'See you Saturday, at our Karen's then? '

On Thursday, Drew walked me to the bus stop after school.

There was a group of boys already there, aw grinning at us.

'Hiya, Drew, is that the burd?' one of them shouted.

He wouldn't kiss me now.

The boys turned away from us when two girls from the year above walked towards them from the underpass. The girls were giggling loudly. The sun had come out, just in time for the long weekend. It's great when it does that on a Friday.

'Sorry, ah cannae. Ma gran in Ireland's sick an we've got to go over to see her.'

'Och, that's rubbish…ah mean…'

'Ah know, but she is ma gran. Ah'll be back on Monday night.'

Never thought ah could be such a good liar.

'That means ah'll need to babysit on ma own then. Wee Daniel an Mathew were looking forward to seein you.'

'Sorry. Tell them ah'll come over next weekend.'

Drew's cow's lick of blonde hair that falls over one eye so he's always has to sweep his too long fringe back with his hand. When he talks to me, only see the one blue eye, have to stop maself reachin over and sweeping the hair back so ah can look into both eyes. Sometimes, cannae believe Drew is ma boyfriend. He's one of the best lookin boys in the year an he usually disnae go for brainy girls. When he first came to our house, he said how lovely mum was wi her dark curly hair. Ah was mortified that he might fancy her but then he said that ah looked dead like her and ah guessed that was a third year boy's way of sayin ah was nice too.

'How much do you like me?'

'As much as Debbie Harry,' he says.

'Liar,' ah say back. We both laugh.

'Abba's better.'

'Souper trouper...' sing down the phone to annoy him.

'Come any time, sweetheart,' Aunt Mary said, last time we spoke on the phone.

Figure she owes me somethin big, after not commin to mum's funeral an then takin ma brother away. Always been the ten of us in the house. If we cannae be ten, the nine that are left should be together.

That's right. One for all and all for one, remember?

The Ten Musketeers. Aye.

Couldnae lie to the three wee ones though. If Annemarie, Lizzie or Elaine asked me straight out could they come to Drew's, didnae think ah'd be able to ever get away. So that's why it has to be early. Phone dad when ah get on the road, gie him a bit of made up news about goings on at Drew's sister's house to keep his mind at rest. There's racin on the telly today so that will keep him occupied, starin at the screen until his horse comes around the bend, then he'll be up at it, holdin back the other horse wi his hand, as if he could hold them back in real life. There'd be teenagers would leave home for just that.

Pray to God he disnae decide to phone Drew's house but he's miserable about the phone bill bein too high: probably be put off.

Under the bridge pigeons are cooing, wish ah had a hood in case ah get a head of bird shite. That would be aw ah needed. Ye cannae really keep a low profile then. Their cooing is like a voice tellin me to stay, that this is hooooome...hoooome.

Talkin birds again, bad enough wi human voices in your heid, without the animals getting involved.

Past the steelworks canteen where dad gets a cheap lunch after his walk, towards school, that's me officially in Motherwell cos houses have started again. Half an hour later through no man's land between the steel works endin and Motherwell startin then at the school gates. On the other side of the road is the bus stop for goin home; turn away from the wide road lined wi big trees, an houses on either side. Three years of secondary school, three years of waitin for a bus; mad crush when it comes, everybody pushin to the front desperate for their dinner, till the driver shouts:

'That's enough, Jesus Christ,' under his breath, foot touching the accelerator even when they're not all on. Sometimes, he starts drivin away with a boy's blazer stuck in the door. That's a laugh. No, if you're the boy.

By the time ah get to Motherwell train station, feet are sore, start of a blister comin on the ball of ma foot.

You should get a plaster.

Tights will soon dry in but the cold of early morning makes me shivery.

You'll get a chill from that.

Hears the voices more and more but sing to drown them out. La la la la...

Got Paul's old sports bag; he threw it in a cupboard, along with the coats, two sweeping brushes and a broken hoover. Travelin light: spare jeans, a thin jacket, a jumper an a kagool for emergencies; hated leavin behind the curlin tongs Uncle Tom bought me but took our Anna's eyelash curlers instead: revenge for her callin her a prostitute. Anna

31

disnae even know what the word means, heard it from lassies at school who were talkin about some woman in our street.

Salmon paste sandwiches an a half bottle of diluted orange in case ah get hungry. Hope the pieces don't go to mush. Tucked in the pocket of the bag, peach lip gloss that doubles as blusher; spare knickers an one pair of socks; school library book about Wordsworth's poems, due back next library period. Mrs. Kelly gave me it to help wi the talk we've tae give to our class. Mrs. Kelly's right, *Tintern Abbey* is dead long but picked it cos of that: nobody else will touch it. They'll all be gien it 'I wandered lonely as a cloud'…bla bla.. Only trouble is, don't really understand it maself but, maybe, this is no a test of understanding as long as ah can learn a bit off by heart, ah'll get to go on the trip to New Lanark. Still, the book's dead heavy, cannae leave it though. Mrs. Kelly will go mental if ah don't do the work.

5

The man behind the glass partition throws change onto the metal tray. Coins ring on the surface of the drop that bevels like the sink in the kitchen. Dishes bein thrown in, plate against metal: clink.

'That'll teach you to wash the dishes when you're told. If you're hungry, you need plates.'

'Platform One, in ten minutes, hen.'

'Where's Platform One?'

Face nearly touchin the glass. Hairs in his nose, his right arm points in the direction of a stairway cannae see cos of a door.

'See the stairs, hen?'

'Aye.'

'Go down there. That's Platform One. Awright?' Already, lookin over ma shoulder to the person behind.

At the top of the stairs, there's three possible directions, makin a cross -roads, but the man said straight ahead. Smell of wet paint lingers in the tunnel that leads to the platform. Tunnel's made from perspex; shadows become passengers when ah pass a real glass window. Down the stairs, leadin to the platform, a smell of pee like somebody's dog's been let loose or a drunk strayed here durin the night. Railin is icy cold, paint chipped and dead rough under ma hand.

Check ma ticket. Money left over for food an the connection to Oban. First, get to Glasgow and then another train to Oban. One hundred and fifteen miles, ah asked ma Uncle Jim. At Aunt Mary's there's a river wi some boats, an then a big hill. Remember turnin off to a street lined wi trees an us walkin to a gate then a house with a red slate roof, white stones in the garden an smoke from the chimney.

Ah've got on mum's lilac top under ma black jumper. She used to gie me a loan of it for school cos lilac an purple are our school colours. But it's mine now.

The track leads into a tunnel, a black empty eye that stares back giving nothing away. A man in a suit, reading a paper, perfectly polished brown shoes, the way ma dad likes his shoes tae be: 'Cherry Brown,' written on the tin, the sweet smell, and the money in your hand when you've polished them till they shine.

An old woman sits on a bench, watchin the tunnel like any minute the answer to the whole of her life will appear. From the platform you can see onto the tracks were the wind has blown pieces of rubbish: an empty pot noodle, crisp packets. Ye can smell the pot noodle: a scent of chicken stock.

'It's supposed tae be on time,' she says, suddenly, takin it personally.

Could be talking to herself. Not me for a change.

We'll all be old one day.

'The man said ten minutes,' ah reply.

'Aye, they tell ye nothing.'

Try to read a bit of *Tintern Abbey* to get ahead wi ma schoolwork but the breeze keeps blowin the pages shut. The drop down into the track makes me feel dizzy. Top floor at school, in geography class when you can see the whole of Motherwell and Wishaw from up there, a sprawl of houses, sky-line broken by the high-rise flats in Muirhouse, the blue cooling towers of the steel works, bullying everything in sight. When the teacher leaves the room, Drew hangs out the window aimin his spit

34

at the ground or at one of his pals. Dead funny, especially when he hits someone.

This waitin, slows me down. Any minute now, dad will appear. Wish the train would hurry up.

Suddenly, a pigeon flies out the tunnel, landing on the ground, red eye flickerin in its head doin half circle turns. The place is freezin. Wish ah'd put another jumper under ma coat and nicked our Anna's clean tights stead of these wet ones.

Best to dry them on the washing line.

Ages an ages of lookin into the distance until beyond the tunnel, the grey snake of the train appears at last twisting and turning across the lines. Then it disappears inside the tunnel becoming a murmur like a sound inside a belly when it's period four and the bell won't go for another twenty minutes and you have to concentrate or you might faint.

You should have had a breakfast.

Have one of your pieces soon.

Ah will.

 Doors open, suddenly. Beeping sounds, a man leaning out a window.

'Hen. Are you getting on?'

Could be goin on ma holidays to Ireland. Except there's nobody else with cases an no weans greetin that they don't want tae go.

Big gap between the step an the platform, dark and deep, that you could step into as part of a dream, yes, you could easily miss it and fall onto the track. Across, on the opposite platform, people watchin our train pull in. One person seems familiar, a woman in a beige raincoat, her well-cut, short black hair, shoulders held back.

Standing straight gies ye good posture.

Don't slouch or ye'll have round shoulders for life.

How do ah walk then?

Stick your chest out. See.

Doors close abruptly, engine cranks into gear. Movin away from the platform, the stranger turning to stare back at me. When ah look again to check, her smile is turned upside down.

'Hen, ye'll need tae make ye're mind up

Enough that you are free.

Watch the step up, it's high.

One foot then the other an ah'm on.

Our Paul's interest in birds started when mum bought him the red binoculars for Christmas: red plastic an ye couldnae see farther than the fence at the front of the house wi them. It was funny seein the faces of people on the buses that passed right in front of our window cos we live right at a bus stop.

'Whit ye getting him those for? The boy'd be better off wi a fitbaw,' dad said.

It's no as if it was a toy hoover or she was sending him to the tap dancin in the community centre.

Paul learned aw the names of birds out a book he got from the library. Wrote them down in a jotter mum bought for him. Birds in Scotland are only ever the same kind: wee, an grey or black, or big an grey an black. Once, soon after he got the binoculars, showed me a picture of a pair of African Lovebirds in his library book.

'*Mostly green, orange upper body and head, blue lower back and rump and red beak,*' the book said.

'Saw one the other day,' Paul said.

'No, you never. It says in the book that you only get them in Africa. Here's too cold.'

'Ah'm tellin ye ah saw one. Maybe, it was flyin off course or somethin. That sometimes happens.'

Totally serious.

Decided to play along.

'Really, that's amazin. See the next time ye spot one, gonnae gie me a shout?'

'Okay.' Dead chuffed.

'Do you ever wonder how birds can fly?' Paul asked when he'd had his library book out that many times, the woman behind the counter said the next time she was gonnae charge him the price an just let him keep it.

'Listen tae this,' held the book up in front of him as he read.

'Lift.'

Long pause. Looked at me.

'What? For God's sake hurry up.'

'The fundamentals of bird flight are similar to those of aircraft. Lift force is produced by the action of airflow on the wing, which is an airfoil..'

Another pause for effect. Maybe, he was finished. No chance:

'Gliding.'

Deep breath. This was gonnae be long.

'When gliding, both birds and gliders obtain both a vertical and a forward force from their wings. This is possible because the lift force is generated at right angles to the airflow, which in gliding flight comes from slightly below the horizontal (because the bird is descending). The lift force, therefore, has a forward component that counteracts drag.'

Really hoped that he was reachin the limit on the number of times ye could borrow one book. There must be a rule about it. A big fine. That's what he needed.

Funny though, a Lovebird stuck here wi our weather.

'It'd miss the big, red exotic flowers of its own country,' Paul said.

'And flyin over camels an blue sea water an always the sun beatin down.'

Gied me a look lik ah've taken it too far.

'Don't tell Simmit and Pinkie, ah said it. About the Lovebirds.'

'Why not?'

'Cos they'll slag me off. Think it's for lassies.'

'Ah'll only mention that you saw a dirty lookin, big Scottish crow.'

'Aye, they'll be fine about that. Anybody can see them even our Pinkie an Simmit.'

Our Paul had a Bob Marley phase when he was eleven. Cos he could get his LP's from the library. Every Saturday morning our whole house got wakened up to:

'Exodus, all right! Movement of Jah people'

Knew the sound track off by heart: No Woman, no Cry from the boys room, along to our room.

Couldnae get back to sleep, an spent most of bein thirteen tryin to work out what did the words mean: if he disnae get a woman, he'll cry or if he disnae have a woman, then there's no one to make him cry. Asked Paul once an he just shouted BABYLON into ma face.

'Open your eyes and look within:

Are you satisfied with the life you're living?'

Wished to God, then that Paul was the boy who liked birds again instead of a eleven year old, nearly a teenager who was turnin into a football playin maniac reggae freak.

***

39

He was born two minutes into the first of January 1968. The local newspaper came to the hospital the next day to take their photographs, him with mum. The headline read: 'FIRST BABY IN MOTHERWELL.'

He was their first son, after two lassies in a row. No one thought it would never happen, and then there he was a blonde haired, blue eyed boy.

When mum was in hospital havin the baby, dad stayed off work, cooked me an our Anna eggs wi toast soldiers for breakfast an told us stories about his job drivin lorries all over the country. The house felt different, much quieter, as if it was getting ready for the noise of a new baby: the upheaval to our lives.

Every year for six years a new baby came along to come between Anna, me and mum.

'I don't have favourites,' our mum always said when me an Anna asked her.

She said it but we didnae believe her.

One time, overheard her talkin to a neighbour when she took the new baby out for its first walk in the pram:

'I really wanted a boy this time.'

She must be fed up wi lassies then, ah decided. Fed up wi Anna an me. After Paul, she had another two boys in a row and then she said next time she was expectin:

'I'd love another girl. Three of each would be nice.'

Then even Paul could think the way ah used to think but never asked him if he did.

When she was expectin the youngest two, after our Elaine had been born, she would say to people who asked her what she wanted this time:

'Only for it to be healthy.'

That's what happens in a big family, there's so many already of boys and girls, in the end the person havin them already has every type they want. Even when the other babies were born, Paul got to hold her hand, he still got lifted, even when Simit came along an really it was Simit who was entitled to be lifted cos he was the baby. Growin up, Paul was good at school, though not as good as me but he was better than me at any kind of sport: football, specially but even tennis and golf. He still wins stuff that matters, medals and cups wi golden boys on top. Ah get good report cards for readin an writin but mum says ye could be too smart for your own good. She never says that about bein good at sports. Ye could never be good enough at that, especially, a boy.

Paul keeps his fair hair as he grows up, an that makes him stand out from the rest of us who are mostly dark haired, apart from Anna, but even she is darker than Paul.

Ah remember how he liked to line up bread he'd torn up from the last slice in the loaf, line it along the windowsill of the boys' bedroom and wait for the birds to come. He would watch them, little bluetits and blackbirds, fat, grey pigeons wi pulsin purplish throats. Mum must have known he did it cos one time a bird shit all down the windae but still she never made a fuss, just got a bucket of soapy water an a long brush and cleaned it off before our dad came home from work.

If that was one of us, she'd have killed us.

Ah just couldn't find anythin to prove he was the favourite even though ah'd ask her:

'Is Paul your favourite cos he's the oldest boy?'

'I don't have favourites. Everyone of you is equal.'

And to prove it she would give us exactly the same amount of everythin, food, sweets and money; when there was any money to give out.

The mornin he got the binoculars, ah got a doll and a watch. He was eight and ah was ten. A gold Timex watch wi a black strap. We sat out the back step in December, watchin birds nestin in the hedges, landin on the grass for the scraps of bread we'd thrown. Kept askin him:

'Guess what time it is?'

'A hair past a freckle?'

'Ha, ha. Turkey time.'

For a while after then, it was good havin someone to mess about with about birds an stuff. Ah was always readin books an that made me good at makin games up. He liked that about me, that ah could think of a whole story about us bein robbers on a stake out an make ye believe it was true. But when Pinkie and Simmit started to get older, the three boys became a team an aw made their own friends. Other boys didnae want them trailin a sister about wi them an ah couldnae play football anyway so wasn't any use. They got too old for stories an daft games, an Paul was too old for lookin at birds through red binoculars.

'Can ah have them?' ah asked one day, when the sun was shining and the back green and hedges were full of birds.

'Aye, take them. Ah don't care,' Paul said, tyin up his football boots.

'Ah could play football, if ye'd give me a chance.'

He laughed at me:

'Ye're a lassie. Leave us alone an play wi your dolls.'

7

Crawl out Motherwell station, gradually pickin up speed until views of sides of garden walls, different kinds of trees. Didnae know we lived at the edge of a forest, big swoopin view of a river that ye only see fae a train. About time ah got away, otherwise, might never see anywhere. High up above two arcs of a bridge, and below, the water: must be the Clyde. There's the sea where Paul is livin. Mrs Kelly said Wordsworth visited Scotland on a walking tour in 1803; he went to the Falls of Clyde in Lanark; only ten miles away from here but ah've never been there. He was from another country and walked all over ma country an ah've never even heard of half the places he went to. He went to Glasgow and up to the mountains of Glen Coe, went along Loch Lomond to Inveraraghy in an Irish jaunting cart with his sister and another poet. The other poet didnae make the full trip cos of the Scottish weather. Must've thought he was goin to Tenerife. The train to Oban goes through that bit of the country so maybe ah'll see some places he went an that will help me wi ma talk. Mrs Kelly says we've to introduce our poem with a few useful facts. So, need to find some useful facts about Wordsworth and *Tintern Abbey*. Only one minute though. Drew's sixteen after the summer, leavin school at Christmas. for an apprenticeship as a trainee welder in the steelworks. If he comes to New Lanark that will be his last school trip. We'll only get to go if we pass our project. We'll get a new topic then.

Open ma book at the poem. It says: '*Lines written a few miles above Tintern Abbey, on revisiting the Banks of the Wye during a tour.*'

This is a tour, not only walkin but a train as well.

'....... *Once again*

Do I behold these steep and lofty cliffs

That on a wild secluded scene impress

Thoughts of more deep seclusion...'

Cannae be bothered wi this. If he was lonely, he should jist say it.

Back to lookin out the window. Branches trail sides of the train, making a scrapin noise but not unpleasant lik fingers down a blackboard when the teacher's out the room. Faster and faster until the landscape opens into miles of waste ground: an old crane an broken railway lines branchin out in all directions but the lines are rusty an the railway trucks havnae moved for years. Never been on a train on ma own, only with the family, goin our holidays to Ireland. The best bit is- was- when we used to play chases an run across the connectin bits of carriages, where the floor moves an gies ye a shake, parts of the train could come apart. Then you'd be flying through the air. Fly like a bird into a field between Dublin and Kerry; or stand wi the window down, breeze whippin your face till another train speeds past, nearly taking your head off: ye're in Doctor Who's Tardis, space and time fast forwarding, fast forwarding, field after field after field. Still, not there. Apart from after aw the travelling, dead on our feet but waken to the smell of burnin turf, her an ma auntie laughin. Apart from that. And the worst bit when she's no paid the fare for at least two of the younger ones and we've tae put coats over them to try to make them under look under five. It's no that easy. Ye cannae make somebody's legs shorter. At least don't have tae do that ever again, waitin until the

45

conductor gets suspicious and they ask what age someone under a coat is-they're telt tae act like they're sleepin. Only she said it wi confidence that somebody aged seven is four; didnae even care that the conductor smirked when she said it lik it was a natural part of the holiday experience.

Shhh, don't move. And remember you're seven.

Check ma ticket.

A face stares back at me: white-faced lassie ah don't recognise, purple bags under her eyes. At least ma hair is getting long now, nearly level wi the bottom of ma chin, growin in its own direction, wild an curly. Smile and the lassie smiles back.

You need a bit of rouge.

Rub some red lip -gloss on ma cheeks.

A window flies open, the carriage erupts with the sounds of wheels on the track even louder, screamin in ma ears lik a loud passenger, until the old woman complains of a draught. A man looks up from his newspaper. Goes over an closes the window.

Dark suddenly, when we enter a tunnel; can close ma eyes and feel the peace of it but then it's bright with sunlight again and the red bricked walls skiffing past to the constant rhythmic sound of the wheels on the line. Finally, ah'm doin somethin instead of life just happenin to me. Grabbin that rope an gettin out. She got out of Ireland when she was young. No work. Ah'm followin in her footsteps.

'O sylvan Wye!'

O Clyde tell me what to do. No answer, only the sound of train wheels on tracks, train wheels on tracks…

Don't know how ah can ever be free when ah've a family to think about, when everythin is upside down in our house.

Trees start to seem like people with faces, our Annemarie's face, ma dad. Fix on the way sun makes leaves dance wi light patterns and if it was a tune it would be Radio One first thing in the morning, us gettin ready for school to 'Going Underground,' by The Jam. Simit an Pinkie poggo to the beat, right out the door. Just a dream of it.

A fox lounges on a piece of bare ground, sun-bathin. The train disnae scare it. Brown with patches of black. Wish ah could tell someone: Look, look. A fox.

The other people don't seem to see it or if they do don't think it's that interestin. Our Annemarie would love that, a fox right there before ye're very eyes. Between Motherwell and Glasgow. The old woman yawns; at the same time, the doors of the train open for a stop as if the train is yawning too.

Bet that fox has a family to think about, disnae just lie about in the sun aw day.

Take out ma salmon paste pieces an start tae eat them an the man looks up from his paper. This sick feelin in ma stomach aw the time as if ah'm hungry but food disnae take the feelin away.

'You havin a picnic?'

Remember, don't talk to strangers.

Don't know what to say anyway, so jist keep eatin, wash the food down wi a drink of juice.

Before ah know it the train is crawlin into a glass roofed buildin, high beams intersectin, gies the impression we're aw trapped inside a metal cobweb. And where's the big spider waitin tae catch us? Big, beady eyes.

Dead slow for ages, then a platform at the sides, pigeons flyin through gaps in the ceilin.

Beep. Beep. Beep. Glasgow Central. Glasgow Central.

Where to go, what direction? Join the flow of people, follow the other passengers towards the turnstile, to a man in a navy uniform, wearing a blue cap. Takes my ticket with a tanned wrinkled hand, disnae look at me until ah ask:

'Can ye tell me how to get to Oban, please?'

'Oban? Platform 3 but check the board, hen. Ah'm a bit busy here. Tickets at the information desk,' reachin out his hand to the old woman ah spoke to at Motherwell. She's still rummaging in her bag for the ticket. Disnae look good.

A gigantic noisy place. For a minute wonder, should ah turn round an go back home lik this is kid-on runnin away. All the people off the train have disappeared out the exits: all with some place to go.

Don't be afraid of your freedom.

This is isn't about ma freedom. Ah'm not afraid.

That's right, Erin, concentrate.

This time it's for real. Ah know what ah have to do. Get Paul home.

Mind your bag. There's thieves everywhere.

In the middle, a big clock hangin down, people standin under it. Every few minutes one of them looks up an smiles, an then they're walkin towards someone walkin towards them. If ah stand for a bit, someone will come and meet me, tell me what to do next.

The numbers are Roman numerals like in our Latin book: Ecce Romani. Massive hands. In the background, a train roars to a halt. All the other sounds rush in: constant burr that ah don't know what from, click click of a woman's heels, everyone's faces engrossed in where they put their ticket and will their train be late.

A man's voice announces train times over a tanoid and people stare at a big board wi destinations constantly changin. If only ye could pick a new life like that, climb out ye're old life wi your rope and then decide what's next cos ye liked the sound of the place or ye'd read it in a book.

Pigeons, low fly through the station, headin for the bits of sandwiches, tomato sauce on their claws, makin people duck. Their pigeon heads bob madly, all business like, struttin ladies on a shoppin trip, dead bold, right up near ma feet. If they were upright they'd have their arms folded, a piny on, gien ye a row for no helpin wi the dishes an they're everywhere people are, makin an upside down shower, scatterin from the feet of office workers headin for the way out.

An old man and an old woman wi a stick, hug each other.

You need to stay strong for the rest of them.

God sake. Better pull maself together.

Sounds seem to come no right at you but take a detour, towards the glass roof first like being under water, people, above, shoutin to each other from divin boards or the guards yellin to folk in the pool. And then ma dad in ma head sittin in the café at the swimmin baths, wavin down to us.

'Look, look at me on the top dale,' one of us shoutin up to him.

Three in the wee pool, five in the big pool.

Wonder will he get himself a sausage roll.

He has to keep movin his chair to wave to us all.

And he's smilin even though he looks drowned in his parker wi the big fur hood an he probably cannae hear us cos it's double-glazin in the café.

At the information window, a woman with dyed blonde hair that looks like yellow sheep wool tells me the price of the fare to Oban. Didnae think it would be that dear. If ah buy a ticket won't have much left.

'C'mon, hen. What's it to be?'

A queue behind an you can feel the angst, all waitin for me to make up ma mind.

Hurry up. Hurry up. God sake. Tch tch.

'Ah'll think about it.' It seems dear. Maybe a bus.

'Okay, hen, gonnae move, there's a queue.'

Spot a free space on one of the benches in the middle of the station near the clock hangin down. A man wi a skinhead on the ground, black dog tied to a bike pole with a tatty lookin rope. He's sleepin an the dog's got its eyes closed too. How can they sleep in all this noise? There's a lassie down a bit from the man; she's a few years older than me. She's sittin on the ground too, a black bin bag at her side and what looks lik a tobacco tin for collectin money. Around the station, people walkin that fast, ye're mind disnae get a chance to fix on anything, you can't catch anything and everything you could hold before is water in ye're hands. Take ma book out ma bag cos don't know what else to do. Maybe, if ah pretend ah'm reading, can sit here for a bit while ah decide what's next about the train an that.

'Hiya, hen,' a voice says. A hand between us on the seat. Looks a lot older than dad. The man has longish, grey hair, a bald patch, and he smells fousty like his clothes have been hangin in a damp wardrobe.

'Hiya.'

Don't talk to strangers. How many times?

Doesn't look straight at me, not at my eyes or any part of me lik this is a spy film an we're meetin up to exchange important information.

Then he looks at the words of a poem on the page of ma book.

'Underneath what grove shall I take up my home…'

'What you doin on your own? Busy place like this?' Eyes wander first to the ring on ma finger, to ma ankles then rest on the smudge on ma ecru tights. Anna, ma sister, likes American Tan but ah prefer the lighter colour, only trouble is shows the dirt dead easy.

Always wear clean underwear in case ye get knocked down by a car.

Don't smile at strangers.

His eyes are too bright.

Mouth open but no words come out.

'Hey creepy features, that's ma pal. Beat it. Leave alone, now. Ah'll set the dug on you.'

She's standin in front of me, hands on hips, talkin right at creepy features. It's the girl wi the the plastic black bag. The man spits on the ground. She's tall and skinny, taller even than Drew.

'Hiya, Donna,' he says. 'Fancy meetin you here.'

51

'Fuck off, arse hole. Ah'm callin the polis if you bother me or ma pal again.'

There's no need to swear.

It's as if ah've walked intae their conversation. Only thing is how do ah get away? Don't get the chance. She takes me by the arm, pulls me to a standin position as ma book falls to the ground. Pick it up and shuv it in ma bag.

'Stop…ah…'

Erin, what did I say? Don't go with any strangers. Why don't you ever listen?

She's the weirdest dressed lassie ah've ever seen. Black lik boot polish hair wi blue streaks through it. Pale skin makin her brown eyes seem even browner, a tartan mini skirt over ripped, black tights an her jacket sleeves cut short to show a tattoo of stars around the tops of both arms. The half jacket is the exact same blue as her hair wi safety pins pierced over it, the kind ye fasten a baby's nappy with. If the pin opens, she'll get a sore one. And there's a smell from her as well, same foustiness as him: the smell of wearin clothes ye found in a bin. Ma arm is dead sore. Don't feel like tellin her though, the way she's nippin lik it's me got the safety pin burstin open on ma bare skin.

'Let's get away from that creep,' noddin in the grey head's direction. He seems a lot smaller now he's sittin down an we're standin, especially cos she's so tall. Then in the same way ah take our Annemarie's hand, she pulls me away.

Disnae let go off ma arm until we're at the other side of the station.

'Hate ones like him. Yeuch!'

This is the first real punk, no jist telly, ah've ever seen close up. Anyway, who does she think she is? Dragin me lik a wean towards the exit, disnae even bother to check if ah agree wi this. Up close there's a tiny hole in her nose were a nose ring should be.

 Ma knowledge of punks so far: they drag strangers for no reason, they love music without any tune an they assault each other on the dance floor. Dad says when there's punks poggoing on Top of The Pops:

That's no dancin. That's jumpin up an down an makin an ejit of yourself. Gime ball-room any day. That's dancing. Come Dancing on a Thursday night. Bla bla. Gime the moonlight…gimme the sun….

'You're hurtin ma arm. Let go.'

'Not until you're away from him, there.'

Safer bein kidnapped wi somebody nearer ma own age.

'C'mon, sit, keep an eye.'

Plonks herself down on the ground, black bag tied at the top. Still manages to keep the short skirt in a lady like position even wi her long gangly legs lik she's done this loads ae times before.

If you sit like that, everybody will see your knickers. Sit up straight.

Ah can hear leaves rustling. That's the sort of thing would bring her back.

Fag buts, bits of food etched on the floor.

Gies ma ecru tights an ma green gypsy top wi the flowered embroidery around the trim, a long, long look. A look of disgust.

A train screeches into the station.

Aunt Mary will scrutnise ma clothes, dirty marks on the tights.

'So everythin's been let go since their mother died. Well, did you see Annemarie's collar?

'Sorry, what did you say?'

The lassie is lookin up at me as if it's ma turn to talk.

'Hey, the lights are on but there's nobody in,' she says to herself.

'Sorry, what?'

'You're a bit jumpy. That's all. Have you never seen a train before? Sit down, c'mon.'

No way. We watch people rushin backwards and forwards. Disnae say anythin for a bit. Try not to stare at the wee scar on the left side of her face.

'Ah'm visitin ma aunt. Don't want to get messy.'

Nose scrunches up.

'You're funny, hen.'

She says 'hen,' lik ah'm ten years younger than her.

A bit of dirt never did a child any harm.

Crouch on ma hunkers, no touchin the ground. Punk girl grins, satisfied, no insult taken.

'What's your name?'

'Erin.'

'Your real name?'

'Ah've only got one name. How many names have you got?'

No answer. Looks into the distance.

Watch the man get up an walk across the main waitin area in the station then disappear down the exit stairs.

'How do you know him?'

Awkward silence.

She keeps lookin around, checkin whose behind us.

'Are you s'pectin somebody?'

'What do'ye mean?'

'Jist, ye're a bit jumpy now. Is everythin okay?'

Up close the lassie's skin is yellowish.

'Any fags?' she says, throwin me a deafie, first about the names and now, two can play at that game.

'Naw.'

'Nae luck then.'

Bites her thumbnail.

'Ah could eat a horse but. You hungry?'

Still, the pieces didnae fill me up. Feels ages ago since ah ate them.

Can't do anything on an empty stomach.

'Starvin.'

'C'mon then.'

Stands up, straightenin the tartan skirt, wipes dust off the bum then walks towards this woman: a complete stranger. As the woman goes to walk past, punk lassie says somethin, holdin her hand out at the same time. The woman pulls her brief case closer, gien her a dirty look an marches past. Punk lassie makes a face behind her back an it's really funny, the way she takes the Micky, nose in the air. A right one.

'La dee dah dah.'

When she goes towards a bin an starts rakin about lik a down an out, not cool, a real punk: no that's not trendy, only embarassin. Ye can catch stuff from bins. No matter how hungry ah am, ah'll never eat out a bin.

Her hand brings up empty crisp pokes; squeezes the bottom to see if there's any crisps left.

'Hey, you.'

The brown eyes remind me of the dates ma gran likes to eat.

'Ah've got some money. Ah'll buy us somethin to eat if ye like. You can help me find ma bus, after.'

Need tae eat anyway.

'You've got dosh?'

Another stare that lasts for a while before breakin into a big smile. Cool, young punk again, who'd never stick her hands in a dirty, old bin.

'Well, ah've got ma fare. And then a bit...'

Don't tell everybody your business, Erin.

Fiddlin wi one of her safety pins; tights so ripped, the tears'll meet and divide into two, leavin her wi black nylon socks around her ankles.

'Gaspin for a juice an a poke ae chips. There's a place ah know across from here. Just wait there a minute.'

Goes back over to the man with the dog, lifts the tin, pats the dog on the head.

On second thoughts, don't know if ah should. She's a bit...loud. But ah'll be hangin about this place on ma own an it disnae feel safe.

'Well, let's go then.'

Ah'll go an get something to eat to keep me goin, thank her for helpin me then ah'll leave.

That's right. You don't have time for this.

On the destination board, the train to Motherwell leaves in ten minutes. If ah got that train, ah could phone fae the station. Be up the

56

road in ten minutes. Nothin's changed though. Back to square one. It's settled, anyway, ah'm goin with her for somethin tae eat and then ah'm goin to the bus station.

A step towards freedom.

Erin, remember why you're here.

Ah've got time.

'What did you say, hen?' she's lookin at me.

'Ah never said anythin.'

Gies me a strange look, stares at the ground.

'C'mon, follow me.'

We turn away and walk in the opposite direction from the Departure Board.

'Watch it you,' a woman rushing to catch a train, shouts in ma face.

Keep an eye on your bag, it's all thieves here.

Metal spikes below the roof on the tops of the station wall, a defence against those pigeons. The lassie dodges the crowds like one of them dodges the spikes, pullin me by the arm behind her. Me, that's always got someone else by the hand, bein dragged by this lassie ah don't even know. No sure ah like it but dyin to ask her what she's got in the bin bag though somethin tells me don't get personal yet.

'What you doin smilin at complete strangers all the time?'

'That's what we do were ah come from.'

'Where's that? The Olden Days.'

Erin, this girl is no good. Taking the Lord's name in vain.

'Don't make it so obvious.'

'What?'

'That you don't belong, it's so obvious from your face.'

It's the only face ah've got.

A group of lassies and boys about ma age and older, inside the station makin a noise. All dressed in black, clothes from charity shops. Punks like her. In their own world of ripped clothes, smokin fags, ignorin everybody but themselves. Must be great to put two fingers up at other folk's borin rushin about, goin to work an school, feelin you're better than them. Wearin clothes that make ye stand out. Only thing is they look a bit miserable lik bein a punk is deadly serious.

'Do you know them?'

They all turn, start loud laughin at a litterbin on fire. That's better. At least they're smilin.

'Aye, they're posh kids. Come in to the station to hang around lookin cool then mummy or daddy comes and picks them up in a big car as soon as it starts to get dark. Let's go the opposite way, don't want to have to talk to them.'

Outside the café a bundle of rags is sleepin on the pavement next door to a shop that says: PAYDAY LOANS.

'Smelly Sammy, should lock him up for good,' she says as she opens the café door.

But deem not this man useless.

There but for the grace of God...

At least the voices agree.

Our hamster was called Sammy but don't say that out loud in case Donna, bossy lassie, laughs at me. We fed him cotton wool to watch his cheeks blow out then one day he stopped breathin. Mum tried to revive him on the fire –guard like he was a wet sock drying for school.

He lay lik that for ages and we had to hide him from our Annemarie because she loved him to bits. The sock never woke up.

The owner of the café recognises Donna when we walk through the door:

'Hiya, pal. You lookin after yourself?' A wee light pat on her shoulder. Shop's empty. Two lines of tables attached to the walls on either sides. Painting of a forest wi sunlight floodin through and a sign that says: 'No toilet here.'

'Ah'm great, Marco. This is ma pal, Erin. She's a tourist from the countryside, visitin the big city.'

The man grins at me. Nice, white teeth.

'Don't let that one get you into trouble, hen. You listen to me.'

'Aye, very good, Marco,' Donna buts in.

'Any chance of some ginger and a plate of chips to share?'

'Any money Donna? Or are you playin on ma good nature again.'

'No the day, Marco. Ma pal, here, Erin, is payin. It's ma birthday.'

'Very nice. Happy Birthday, hen. Away and sit down and ah'll bring them to you. No harassing ma customers mind.'

You don't have time for dithering, Erin. Remember, Paul.

Somethin to eat then ah'm on ma way.

Find a cubicle wi two benches facing each other. Dried brown sauce on the table. Hope he wipes it before the food comes. Disnae take much. Donna puts her feet up on the free seat beside her. Nice havin some company but, cos ah thought ah'd be on ma own the whole way. Wonder what they're havin for their dinner at home. Friday, so it'll be somethin nice. Fish fingers an beans. Don't want to start missin them too soon or ah'll never get away.

Make your bed an lie in it.

Marco brings the chips, hot and steamin, smellin delicious.

Donna wolfs the food, disnae speak.

Put ma fork down.

Awkward silence.

The hole in her nose looks a bit scabby, like it's been infected.

'How many sisters and brothers have you got?' ask her, tryin not to stare.

'None. Only little old me.'

Dip chips in the tomato sauce. Delish…

A room to yourself and never havin to share with sisters and your birthday the only one, apart from ye're mum an dad's an that doesn't count. Aw that space.

'You're lucky.'

'Don't think so, hen.'

Says it so sure. Looks up from the chips, a trail of tomato sauce on her chin.

'How'd you like if the pressure was on you aw the time?'

Now, she's starin at me, waitin for an answer.

Cannae even imagin it.

'See what you mean. Never thought of it lik that before. You've got sauce on your chin.'

Wipes it away wi the back of her hand then rubs it on a dirty hankie that she takes from up her sleeve.

'Load of crap all of it.'

Don't disagree though no sure what she's talkin about.

'Ah'd have liked a sister though. Somebody's clothes to nick an somebody tae cover for you when ye need it.' she says.

'It's no lik that wi me an our Anna.'

'Who's Anna?'

'One of ma sisters. Next one in age to me.'

Nearly show her the eyelash curlers but on second thought, leave it. She might take them off me.

'Next one? How many've you got?' Donna asks

'Eight all together. Four sisters an three brothers.'

'Eight. No wonder ye're on the streets.'

'What makes ye think ah'm on the streets?'

She points at ma bag:

'That, an your face.'

Eat the chips an don't say anythin.

Sarcasm is the lowest form of wit, Erin. Ignore her.

'So, where's your bit?'

Gies me a look as if ah'm daft for askin.

'Where do you think?'

'You said you didn't have brothers and sisters but you never said anythin else.'

She looks outside.

'Ah jist doss on other people's couches.'

Pulls her long legs towards her, stares straight at me cos now it's ma turn to be under the spotlight.

'So, what really brings you into the big bad city, kid?'

No in the mood to tell the story of ma life, everybody knowin ye're business. Everybody lookin at you as the poor McLaughlins who lost their mother. Like we're somehow soft in the head, that we lost her deliberately; all went to the shops an now we cannae find her cos she's wanderin around the frozen food section: cannae remember how to get back home.

Bit of a cheek but, her callin me a kid when it's ma money buyin the grub.

'One of ma brothers is stayin at ma aunt's in Oban. Ah'm goin to bring him home.'

She whistles. An impressive whistle for a lassie.

'A kidnapper. Get you.'

Hardly, he's ma brother.

'How long's he been away?'

'About six months.'

She nods her head in a no, whatever that means.

'Sounds he's gone for good to me.'

Don't listen to her, Erin.

It's hard the way she says it though.

She scratches the outside of her nose.

'Afore you go, you an me could hang around today.'

Don't have time.

That's right, Erin. You don't.

Don't know how to tell her, she seems to have latched on to me.

We've nearly finished the food, as soon as she finishes her drink, ah'm off.

Least ah won't have tae listen to this much longer.

Donna takes along sip from her Irn Bru until her top lip has an orange fringe.

The brown eyes don't laugh though, staring out from under her heavy make up, weighing everything up. Not sure if she's weighin up ma situation or her own.

'Are you alright? Ye look a bit funny.'

She puts her hands out in front of her, stretches her fingers.

'Owe some guys money an ah don't have it yet.'

Don't ask what she owes it for.

'How much?'

'About twenty quid.'

'Sorry ah don't have that.'

'Did ah ask you for money?'

She's almost spits it right into ma face.

Put a hand up.

'Ah'm only sayin.'

'Ah know. Didnae mean that, pal, only it would be good to have someone about till ah work out how ah'm gonnae pay it.'

'Can whoever you owe it to, not wait?'

'S'ppose they'll have to.'

Fiddlin wi one of her safety pins, tights so ripped, the tears will meet and there'll be strips of nylon were tights should be.

Now, the street outside is quieter like the crowds in the station didnae exist. Somethin else, there's no trees in the city centre, no green. No that we live in the country lik ma gran in Ireland wi fields an cows an sheep but our five apartment has a big garden at the side an the streets of our scheme are named after trees and plants: Laurel Drive, Broompark Road, Hawthorne Quadrant, Myrtle Drive.

'We're all the same, pal. A story to tell. Anyway, good chips.'

She's grinning again. Gave me a bit of a fright there but everythin seems fine now.

'Not bad. They could have done with bein in the fat five minutes longer.'

'Check you out. That's a good one. Did you study chips at university or somethin?'

'Used to work in a chippie on a Saturday. Got a degree in fryin.'

'My God, ecru tights girl has a sense of humour.'

Donna leans over her plate; stuffs a corner of roll full of chips into her mouth. Some of them spill back onto the plate. Then, she gets red sauce on her tartan skirt.

'Shite. Hate when that happens.'

Lift ma roll up to take a bite of mine. Soft and the chips are hot an soggy; smell of frying from a little doorway, behind the counter. The man has a radio on, an old Frank Sinatra song. Dad loves his music; he sings in the bath: *Gimme the moonlight…gimme the suuun…* And he's really good. *That's why the lady is a traaaamp:* this big generous soundin voice booming through the house. Right now, ah'm happy lik he's happy when he's singin. Soon, finish eatin then ah'll go to the bus station, catch the bus. Won't be long till ah see Paul. It won't be long till ah start to get him back for us. If ah knew the words to the song ah'd join in. Ah'm goiinn to Obaaaaan…

8

Anna is obsessed with smells: her own skin, includin feet, her hands after she's helped peel the potatoes, vanilla from helpin bake cakes at the weekend, a clean smell of Saturday night after a bath, talcum mixed wi soap. Tells everyone she's going to work for Chanel when she grows up.

'You don't even know what Chanel smells like. It's no Coty L'Aimant,' Erin says.

'Shut-up, you. You're just a prostitute,' although not quite sure what it means.

Anna's nose can pick up the difference between their mum's Coty and Agnes' Cacharel. Agnes, their neighbour is their mum's best pal.

Their mum shows her an Erin how to make scent from big, fat roses out the back green. They only have old medicine bottles: dark, brown glass. Stuff rose petals through the neck of the bottle then add a small amount of water. Wait for a couple of hours.

'It smells lik penicillin,' Erin says.

'We need to give it more time. Perfume disnae just happen,' Anna's delighted they're doin somethin she likes for a change.

It's the smells Anna misses most: coming home from school and dinner being cooked; soup disnae really have a smell and burnt mince is the smell of burning. Their mum's cooking smells made her want to eat. It's Anna that looks for smells more than anyone: talcum powder and musk smells of hairspray and furniture polish. Smells they don't have in their house, now.

She was never first in the family to do anything except break a bone; second born, second to start school, second to make her communion. To look at them, ye wouldnae think they were sisters: Erin's dark, thick hair and green eyes; Anna's lighter, blondish hair and brown eyes, her long eyelashes always curled upwards since she got the new eyelash curler. Except for the time when she first got it, was learning how to use it and ended up pulling all the eyelashes off her lower lid. Took ages to grow back.

Erin's always beem weird, she thought. When they were a lot younger, they were playing with a lassie from a couple of streets away who had a room to herself, a space hopper in the garage and her own record player. The records were red plastic with a yellow label in the centre and black words written across: KC and The Sunshine Band or Marmalade. It was a rainy summer's afternoon, the three of them in the other lassie's bedroom, exhausted from dancing to Sugar Sugar Honey Honey. Erin turned to her pal and started this story about how she'd been abandoned by her real mum and dad, a gypsy princess and prince, and adopted by their mum an dad an how none of them, Anna included, were her real brothers and sisters and somewhere in the world her blood family were regretting they'd given her up. Scary thing was she seemed to really believe it as if right from the start she'd decided she was different from everyone else an was forever tryin to invent a story tae explain it. The funny thing was she made Anna half

66

believe it too, the way she described the camp fire at night, the sounds of the adults breaking bracken underfoot as they gathered kindling, an the scents of the different types of branches, aw mixed together, an how the grey wood smoke was always getting in her eyes. And how the gypsies wrapped her in the skirt of a wedding gown that her real mother had worn an carried her one night in winter with the rain peltin down an left her lying on their back step. And why did they pick that step, Anna asked tryin tae get her to admit the lie.

'Because your real mum'- my kiddon mum- yes, she actually said it- 'Was always kind to strangers. Mind the time she took the old tramp into the house an fed him our dinner when we were at school. Ah swear to God on my life.'

And that made Anna think she must be right or mad or desperate to convince herself that cos they didnae have a room to themselves or record players, there had to be something else that made her special. Didnae push the point because she could kind of understand that; still was shocked that her sister, real or not real, could swear on her life for dramatic effect. But it seemed to get worse. People in Erin's class told Anna that her big sister was always makin things up like on school trips if the bus went into a strange area, she'd be pointing at houses, sayin her auntie lived there. All their aunties lived in Ireland except Aunt Mary in Oban an their old Aunt Maura who lived wi their gran down the road from their house, so that didnae count.

If she was from gypsies that would explain why Anna felt no connection with this dark haired girl and it was only a coincidence she looked like their mum.

After they got caught shop lifting, Erin gave up her wild gypsy ways, trading them in for jotters with gold stars an privileges like being the cupboard girl who got to spend whole days in the teacher's cupboard tidying it up. Her head was still full of lies but she wrote them down now, an the teachers gave her a tick an a 'very good,' in every box of her report card. Anna was always behind in that particular race.

But Erin had never broken a bone and even though Erin caused Anna to get one, she was still glad that she had that one over her.

It is really Erin who causes the broken bone, telling them about the playing cards, the words like a challenge to find them. That's her style, getting someone else into trouble.

'She bought them today, for the journey. In Woolies. Ah was with her. Comics and cards to keep us quiet,' Erin said to Simmit the night before they left for their fair holiday to Ireland. The rumour travelling lik Chinese Whispers through the house, Simmit tellin Anna and she passing it on to the other two laddies.

'Where do ye think she put them?' Pinkie, always first for an adventure, his blue eyes bright at the prospect. You'd think he'd have learned his lesson from the time he and Simmit were playing soldiers and he got the soup pot stuck on his head then he was running around the living-room like a headless chicken. Their mum took him to Accident and Emergency and he had to get the pot cut off. The doctors couldn't stop laughing once they did the operation, even offered him two halves of the pot as souvenirs.

'In the wardrobe, probably. You should look in one of the pockets.'

Later, they'd all had their baths, the mirrors steaming from the heat, wet towels hanging over radiators and Anna's skin still red from the water. Everything is ready for the early rise in the morning; the three younger ones already in bed, the curtains drawn on a summer's evening. On the floor of the living room, two big cases with all the clothes; the blue one, they use every year, a label around the handle from last summer. The suitcase is shabby looking at the front but it still locks and can hold loads of stuff. Their tickets are in the bowl in the kitchen so their mum and dad can read over them time and time again before they put them in their mum's brown handbag. Anna isn't really lookin forward to the long journey but she's dying to see the Irish cousins again, curious to see how they are different or the same, amazed that these strangers can have her brother's eyes or her sister's mouth; neither, is she lookin forward to avoiding the sheep dogs on the farm but she's excited about their uncle shearing sheep and being able to run down a field without stopping.

'Let's go look for the cards,' Anna has a plait in her hair, so her hair will come out in ringlets in the morning. Erin says out the corner of her mouth, she is going to watch Val Doonican and that she doesn't want to come upstairs and look for the cards. She's getting quite boring actually. All she can think about are books and daft boys.

Upstairs, the others sit on the big bed, discussing the best way to find their prize.

'Let me go,' Pinkie is getting to the age where he wants to lead and not be the one always doing what his older sisters tell him.

'No, ah'll do it,' she says, knowing that whoever secures the deck will have increased power during the holiday fortnight; who to allow in the game, who to exclude.

Inside the wardrobe it's dark and fousty smelling. Sometimes, their mum buys things an doesn't wear them for years, not like their da who has one suit and a few nice shirts for going out on Saturday night or mass on a Sunday. She nearly trips on a long crushed velvet skirt and has to bend to lift the hem away so she won't tear it. Inside every jacket and coat pocket yield bits of non descript fluff, and one ten pence in a coat but no cards. Until, right at the back, their daddy's Sunday suit and the scent of his aftershave, the shiny silver coloured suit that they often raid for money when he's had a few pints and thrown the change inside. Anna knows the cards are in that pocket from the feel of the surface of the material. She imagines the smiling Queen and the daunting King and the silly Joker with the daft hat. She has to trudge deeper, deeper into the blackness of their kingdom, like a blind person with her arms stretched out, trying to decipher her route by touch. Someone closes the door for a laugh and although it was dark before now it is completely black and clothes are covering her face, making it harder to see. She panics, can't breathe and the more she tries to get out, the more trapped she feels, shouting and banging on the side of the wardrobe, until after ages, a rectangle of light appears again where the door must have been all along.

'You eijit,' she aims the insult at Pinkie, who is lying back on the bed, acting all innocent. As Anna steps onto the carpet, she feels a movement behind her, the wardrobe starting to topple like a great

70

brown mountain falling, that mountain where her granny in Ireland lives, the one that isnae on the map.

'Help, you lot, help.'

But they don't have time and the only thing moving towards the wardrobe is her white arm with the love beads around the wrist. And how can she stop it? How she can hold up a mountain with one arm? The pain makes her faint and she thinks she's dying as she falls to the floor and the others disappear and the room disappears and then there is nothing only the pain. Next thing she remembers is wakening up at Law Hospital, her mum's hand with the wedding ring on her finger and the gold watch for nights out around her wrist. She's holding Anna's hand, sayin it's going to be alright and not to worry and how she's been a good girl to waken up. Later, they tell her how the bang of the wardrobe made the ones downstairs think the ceiling was caving in and that their mum came tearing into the room, knocking the ironing board over, all the clothes for the morning landing on the floor. She could imagine Erin sitting on one of the comfy chairs, turning down the telly, straining to hear the sounds from the room above, stayin out of the way in case she got implicated.

The last time Anna was in hospital was when she got her tonsils out.

'Look at the wee animals on the ceiling and count to ten. One, two, three….The nurse in the operating theatre said. She never reached four that time and when Anna opened her eyes, she was in bed and a dinner lady comin towards her with the biggest plate of ice cream she'd ever seen. This time no ice cream but a wee plastic bangle around her wrist and her name on it and a chart at the end of the bed that her mum got up to read. Anna's other arm feels ten times as heavy from the plaster stookie. No one in their family has ever had a stookie before.

'You can get your brothers and sisters to write on it,' a nurse with curly blonde hair says.

'You could have done yourself a worse injury, all for a pack of daft cards,' their mum says, recovering from the earlier shock and scowling at her before turning to smile at the nurse. Still, Anna is enjoying the prospect of everyone clamouring to write their names, all her cousins and the laddies, and of course, their Erin. Their mum can only be annoyed for a wee while and then she's glad nothing worse has happened and that they never missed their holiday. She'll have her few drinks tomorrow night in Killarney, waiting for their uncle, and be sitting at their granny's range, within a few hours of that.

Next day on the boat, sitting at one of the tables, Anna shuffles the cards slowly with her one good hand, while the rest of them wait and wait for her to deal.

9

After Donna an me have finished the food, nothin to do but watch the pavement as the man Sammy reaches out his tiny hamster hand from his bundle of rags to people walkin past. People don't beg in Wishaw, it wouldn't be allowed. Two coats and long trousers trail on the ground like a hamster tail behind him. Now and then a person bends towards him, puttin money in the wee tin mug. Sammy looks up. Tiny red hamster eyes. He hasn't shaved for ages an you can't tell if he is old or middle aged or young.

'So what's your plan, kid?'

The glory of the open road.

Don't listen to that talk, Erin. Remember, Paul.

She points her last chip at me, sauce drips onto the formica table.

Rather we ate quickly. A bit scary this one when she puts on the shouty shouty voice. Don't want to miss ma bus.

'Told you, Oban. Need to get a bus. Where would you get a long journey bus here?'

Would like to tell the girl about the great cakes ma aunt makes, chocolate sponges wi melted chocolate on the top, coconut cakes, apple cakes with the sweetest apples in the centre but she might laugh at me, getting excited about a few daft cakes. It's things like baked cakes ah miss but.

'Buchanan Street. All the long haul buses go from there. Can walk there together if you like.'

'Okay. That's great.'

Wonder how she ended up homeless. Don't want to scare her away wi too many questions an ah'm not sure ah want to know, not really. Got ma own troubles to think about.

The man, Marco, brings us two Cokes.

'On the house, Donna. Happy Birthday.'

When he's back behind the counter, ask her.

'Is it really your birthday?'

'Jesus Christ.'

Definitely positively glad, didnae mention ma aunt's cakes.

Then before ah tell her to stop swearin, singin comin down the street:

'HERE WE GO…HERE WE GO… HERE WE GO.'

Loud enough for us to hear inside the café.

'Shite. Of all the places…'

Four of them, boys bumpin intae the other; pretend fightin.

Donna ducks under the table.

'Do you know them?'

A hand whack across ma knee, the fright making me jerk ma leg upward towards the table for a second whammy across the bone.

When ah jump intae the aisle the man, Marco, is all attentive.

'Whit's up hen'?

Donna's still under the table.

'Ah'm fine. Hit ma leg by mistake.'

' Lookin for money ah've dropped, Marco,' Donna shouts up.

Shrugs his shoulders then he's away towards the till again.

Need to duck under the table as well to have a conversation wi Donna.

'What was that for? '

'Shhhhh. Those guys out there are nutters. Ah was tellin you about them earlier.'

Must have been when ah switched off.

Get up cos keep hittin ma head; anyway, want to see what happens.

'Ah've had a few run ins wi them. They don't take prisoners. For God's sake don't draw attention to us.'

She's changed her tune.

'What about Sammy?'

'Forget about him. He's well used to this. Believe you me.'

Marco walks quietly to the open door, closes it over; now, he's smilin at me as if this is an everyday occurrence.

'Don't look so worried, hen. Just those fellas makin a racket.'

So, ah wonder why is he closing the door? Turns the volume up on the radio.

'Look at the auld guy, lads. Let's have some FUUUNNN.'

One of the them, a skinny guy wi a clapped in face same as when ma granny takes her teeth out, goes to the start of the alley across the road. Has his back turned but it's obvious that he's peeing into the bottle. Look away in case ah see the bum. The red tracksuit seems out of place in a street where everything is grey. Sip the ginger then when it's safe, look again. He's still sleeping, or, at least, it looks that way though a woman is dragging a board advertising a hairdressers along the same side of the road, makin another sort of racket. When she sees the laddies, she turns and crosses to the other side, the big board on wheels, rattlin behind her. Now the street has emptied apart from the old man: Sammy, and them.

'Waken up. Waken up. ARE YOU A DIRTY OLD HOMELESS MAN? HOME...LESS... At first it's me screamin the words inside ma head but then the words are outside and loud and nasty soundin and right in his face, as one of them, one with beige stapress is right up front of him. In his face. He's a roll of fat around his stomach; his trousers are too short. Fat Boy. Burgundy doc martins with yellow laces.

'Get up, old man.'

Nothing happens. Marco has the phone in his hand, he's speakin but it'll be too late because Sammy is a shape made of rags. Doesn't move. Maybe, thinks if he just stays still then they might think he's dead and leave him alone. Like Sammy the hamster but pretendin. How can people give up like that?

'You're smelly, old man. Aren't you?'

God sake. Even if he is. No need to say it.

'Any spare change?' the man says.

Shut-up Sammy. Keep actin dead. But he ignores the fat guy holdin the bottle above his head. Brave but kind of stupid as well.

'Shouldn't we do somethin?'

'Awright, Joan of Arc. Could have knives or anything. This isnae the countryside now. As ah say ah know them, get it?'

Why does she keep goin on about the countryside? Who does she think she is? Wishy's better than this place anyway, men lyin in the street, people wi pee in bottles.

'Well, if you know them can you not ask them to stop?'

'Stop what?' Ah can't see. What's happenin?'

Then, she actually crawls along the floor from our seat to the back of the café. Marco looks up sees her, shakes his head. She's moved her seat so she can't be seen through the window.

Now, she's seein everythin in the mirror, careful not to look round.

Sammy doesn't turn his head away while the loud, fat one pours the pee over his face. It seems to go for ages, the yellowness pourin from the bottle. Poor Sammy the hamster, Sammy the homeless man.

Look out for a bit until Marco unlocks the door again to let another customer in. A woman and man are walkin past the window, hand in hand. She sees Sammy and steps to the side of him. You can almost smell him from here. Donna's disappeared, gone out the back of the cafe.

Eventually Marco goes outside, carrying a towel. Ah follow him.

'You awright, pal?' Marco on bended knee, wipin his face with a dry towel. Ah like Marco, he disnae cough lik there's a smell an the air fresheners needed.

The man nods and turns like he's turning in his sleep, bottle of cider under his head for a pillow, Marco's towel for a blanket.

'Do ye need any help?'

'Have a nice night son. Have a nice night.'

'Ah will, Sammy. Don't you worry. Don't you worry about a thing.'

'*His little, nameless, unremembered, acts*

Of kindness and of love…'

The words from the poem come from no-where. Now, ah'll think of Marco with the towel and Hamster Sammy to help me remember the lines.

77

***

'Who were those boys? How do you know them?'

Ask her as we walk to the bus station.

'What boys?'

'The ones, at the café.'

'Forget it, kid, will you. Ah've other things on ma mind.'

Must be the money she owes.

'What's this?'

Donna grabs ma poetry book that's stickin out the top of ma bag.

'Book for school. Supposed to be learnin a poem.'

Turns over the cover, gies me it back. Shakes her head in total disgust.

'Have you no pals an that's the real reason you're runnin away?'

Now, she's getting on ma nerves.

'Ah've got a boyfriend called Drew.'

Shakes her head in a *yes* way.

'Now, that's interestin.'

10

Mrs Kelly is always talking about local history even though she's an English teacher. She took us to The Mitchel Library. There was stuff there you couldn't get in our own library. Mrs Kelly said the study of history was the study of past peoples. Our mum wasnae interested in local history.

'Ye should be studying Irish history, that's your history.'

But we live in Scotland and Ireland isnae the project. It isn't local, local's where you live.

'Ye're Scottish, hen. Don't listen to your mum. That's your history,' dad said, lookin up from the Daily Record.

Wish they'd make up their minds.

'Take all the time ye need, hen,' the woman in the Mitchel Library said.

The library was dead big. The woman behind the desk gives me a book about Lanarkshire. Ah looked up our town; one time, a wee village with flax in its fields. The pits started then and Irish and Polish came lookin for work. There was a photo of a man, a woman and six weans, standin outside a house shaped like a beehive, no windows. Mr. Twaddle the history teacher says people where we live still live in caves. That house looked like a cave. Mum said Mr.Twaddle wouldnae know his arse from his elbow and no to mind him.

'What ye doin standin in the pitch black? Come in. Ye'll catch your death.'

Ah was standin on the step at the front door looking at the steel works.

'That's what history's for,' said Mrs Kelly said 'to put you in touch with the past.'

'Miss, is that what Wordsworth is goin on about in *Tintern Abbey*?'

'Well, in a way, he's talkin about his own past and his feelings about a particular place.'

'*Tintern Abbey*,'

'Well, yes. And really what it represents. That's your homework, remember.'

'Yes, miss. Learn the poem.'

'It's in the notes.'

At night they're all around me, the people crowded in wee houses an, sometimes, can hear their voices, weans playin in the streets and lassies and laddies ma age helping at the mines, seperatin good coal fae bad, goin home at night to their bee hive houses wi no windows; dark inside like bein down a pit.

'You're part of a long line that goes back to the worst housing in Scotland, and another line back to Ireland.'

The way Mrs Kelly says it like it's somethin really great. Somethin to be proud of. Awright for her though, she lives in a bought house miles fae here.

When ah tell dad he says.

'There's nothing wrong with our houses. Those teachers are living in the past. We've good, big house here.'

We have too, with our new central heating. So take that Mrs Kelly and William Wordsworth and smoke it in your pipes.

11

'Bet boys go for lassies lik you, high cheekbones, skinny wi those big eyes, all that mad, curly hair. Only trouble is they'd worried they might lose you down a crack in the pavement.'

Bursts out laughin. No point in startin a fight. Won't need tae put up wi her for much longer.

'Have you got a boyfriend, Donna?'

She disnae look at me:

'That's for me tae know an you tae guess.'

That means 'yes,' cos ye'd obviously deny it if ye hadnae.

At the station ah go up to the wee information windae. There's a German man in front tryin to get information about buses to Inverness. He has so many questions for the man servin, the man has to ask the German to step to the side so he can serve other customers and then come back to him.

Me next.

'Mister, when's the next bus to Oban?'

Another man, carrying two mugs, puts one of the mugs down on the desk beside the one serving me. The mug says:

'Caffeine Addict.'

Takes a big slurp before speakin.

'You've missed the afternoon bus and there's none the night. Saturdays, there's an early evening special, hen. No a Friday. Check the timetable on that wall. It tells you there.'

The man points towards a white square attached to a wall, opposite the kiosk. He has a tired lookin face, his hair the colour of a dried out mop. The city makes everyone look so grey.

'Eh, let me see. Aye, two o'clock. Ye just missed it.'

Ah took ma eye off the ball as ma dad says now the game's over for today. But ah don't have time. Ah've only got till the end of the weekend an ah'm nowhere near Oban. Only travelled about seventeen miles. Nearly lost a whole day.

 Donna's waitin outside wi the other people, aw waitin for buses, bags at their feet. She picks chewing gum off her shoe. God, she's so disgustin.

'Right, are you sorted? Is this the big goodbye?'

Imagin the journey back, goin to the kiosk and buyin a one way ticket to Motherwell. Ah'll have failed, failed to get to talk face to face to our Paul.

'Ah've missed the bus. There's none till the morra mornin.'

'Sorry, pal. Will you go back to that mad Wishaw place?'

Wi ma tail between ma legs.

You need to get Paul home. Everyone makin a fool of me, takin my own children away.

'Could ah stay wi you for the one night? With one of your pals. Don't mind a couch.'

Makes sense. Be in the city near the bus station so would be dead easy in the mornin. It's a pain that ah'm wastin a day but ah'd get tae see where she lives an maybe ah can help her think of how tae get the money she owes. After all, did save me from old letchy features at the station, earlier.

82

Donna starts tae examine the soles of the other shoe but there's no chewin gum there.

'Donna?'

'What?'

'What's up? Ah'll be no bother. Afterall, ah would have caught the bus if ah hadn't gone wi you.'

Shakes her head, glances at me; biting a bit off one of her nails, spits it onto the ground.

'So, where do you think ah live? Where do you actually think ah live cos this should be funny?'

'You said you stay wi pals, on their couches.'

Her voice is softer when she answers:

'Ah'm no sure. You're a bit...'

Ecru tights, gypsy top. She can be very narrow minded for a punk.

'You'd not...fit in...'

'It's only one night. Ye're sort of responsible for me now.'

Smile an she smiles back then goes quiet again. When ah stand, Donna stays sittin, still not speakin so ah take it that's the end of the conversation. On ma tod again. Okay.

The solitary life begins...

Don't want the solitary life. Want ma brother back.

'Ah can get us some place. Only, if you do as ah say. Don't blab about your age for starters. You in or out?'

Never slept away from ma own house before unless at gran's on holidays with the whole family or at Drew's sister's house.

'In. And don't worry about ma age. It'll be fine.'

'Naw, don't say it'll be fine. Say you'll do as ah say.'

83

'Okay, ah will.'

'First, we'll need tae get you some make-up. That'll add a few years on. You need somethin to tie that mad hair back. Once ah'm finished wi you, you'll even get intae the dancin without ID. Some mascara, foundation and a bit of lippy. Wait outside this shop, ah won't be long...'

Flexes her fingers.

'Hope ah havnae lost am touch. If ah come out runnin, jist go lik the clappers an ah'll meet you back under the big clock at Central Station. Okay?'

'Okay.'

She disnae need tae explain.

Knew our Anna's eyelash curler would come in handy.

The housing department in the city centre is a big, old lookin, red building; ten minutes walk away from the station. There's a plastic sign on the door says 'lousing department.' Somebody's made the 'h,' an 'l' with a black felt pen. Feel a scratch coming on.

A man with a moustache is sitting at a desk, newspaper open at the sporting pages. He has a khaki coloured shirt on to make him seem official.

'Can ah help yeez? Looks us up and down, especially Donna's ripped tights and the safety pins.

'No, you again.'

'No, you again,' Donna says back.

84

The man stands up, the chair squeaks across the floor as he pushes it away.

'Same right as anybody to be here.'

They're eyeball to eyeball now an Donna has lifted herself onto her toes to look taller than she usually looks. He's wide, sticks his chest out as if that'll scare her.

'Ye've no right havin a go. Us only walkin through the door, mister. We're homeless an this is where homeless people go.'

'Don't want any more trouble from you,' he shouts, up close there's spit on his moustache.

'Not lookin for trouble, only somewhere to stay. It's you lookin for trouble. Ah never said a word.'

'It's no ma fnn job to take cheek from the likes of you.'

'Your job to give us a place but.'

'It's their job up the stairs. Any more trouble, you're barred.'

Sits back down, turns a page nearly ripping one as he does it.

Donna makes a face at the CCTV cos he's looked away. We both start to climb a flight of stairs that lead to more stairs, never-ending stairs and corners until we're at the top floor. Donna opens glass doors. We walk in. Place is bedlam: weans crawlin about the floor, one needs its nappy changed. The adults look in a daze and it's me has to grab a wee boy crawlin to the glass doors that lead to the stairs.

We go to a plastic mouth on the wall and its tongue spits out a ticket with a number.

'That's our turn,' Donna points to the green panel of numbers above the main desk.

There is a row of three glass cubicles that people go to when their number comes up. The boxes are sound proofed; try to read bodies and faces to pass the time.

Donna holds the ticket like we're in a raffle for a new life.

A bald man, his head covered with tattoos storms out one of the boxes.

'Waste of fnnn time, comin here,' he shouts to all the people waitin.

We're all glad cos our turn gets nearer the quicker they are in and out.

The light changes to our number. Donna leads the way.

Inside the box, there is one red plastic chair on our side: Donna sits down.

 She's the main applicant for the homelessness application. That's probably why she gets the chair.

The other side is a woman with straight blonde hair and pink varnished nails. She has dark brown foundation on. She knows Donna.

'You chucked out, again?'

'Fraid so. This is ma wee sister.'

Donna says our mum an dad are alcoholics an they've been on a bender night an day for a week.

'Any other kids at home?'

'No, only us. They two can kill each other, all we care.'

Dad hasnae touched a drop since mum died. Can hear him sayin it in ma head an ah'm scared ah'll blurt it out.

Lies about our ages. She's eighteen. Keep ma fingers crossed behind ma back.

All this for one night.

'You'll need to see social work stand by in the morning. They're busy with a crisis just now.'

She hands Donna a page with writing on it, a list with bed and breakfast places and at the bottom of the page; it says there's some limited camping available at Strathclyde Park but that means being accepted by another Authority. That park's only three miles from ma house. Why would ah go through all this to end up there in a tent, a good bed up the road?

Cannae blow the cover though.

'You need to give us some place the night. It's our rights. While you're sorting it all out, a proper flat.'

The woman's eyebrows go up as she sizes Donna up. She looks over Donna's shoulder: the big bald man is back in at the reception desk. Picking up the phone, she disnae speak to us while she waits as the phone rings at the other end.

Could be anybody she's phonin, us sittin here.

She asks down the phone if there are any spaces for two female youths.

'Is that all?'

She looks at us, shakes her head.

'Hold on a minute, ah'll ask.'

She puts her hand over the mouth of the reciever.

'All the places for younger people are full. There's places at one of the hostels down near the station. It's not supervised though the same way and you'd be in with older people as well.'

'S better than a tent though.'

That's the main applicant decided then.

'They'll be over later.'

While the woman goes away to type a letter Donna says she knows the hostel, she's stayed there before. It's not too bad. Not dodgy or anythin, one of the best in the city.

Outside the people are starin at us, starin back at them. Donna does a thumbs up to the baldy man an he turns away from her. Inside the box, we're trapped like two fish in a fish bowl.

When the woman comes back she gives Donna the letter and a compliment slip with the time of the appointment with a social worker the next day. It's late on in the afternoon. Ah'll be well on my way to Oban by then. Wonder what story she'll tell them about her wee sister then?

12

The railway bridge covers the street, dark like in a room when somebody turned the light off.

The entrance to the hostel is a small, double doorway with a buzzer and an intercom. One of the doors is open. Before you go through the door there's a smell of beer and pee. Ye couldnae be fat and get through. Big fat tumshie. Move your bum. Some of the windows in the buildin next door have a single, dirty curtain tied in a big knot. A few of the windows are lying wide open but there's no one leanin out. Donna's takin the lead, remindin me for the millionth time that ah'm a different age.

Play follow my leader behind her an get ready to take her cue.

'Ah'll do all the talkin and mind, you're seventeen if anybody asks.'

Ma eyes feel they'll stick together, aw the mascara she's put on me an the foundation too dark for ma skin. Ah look orange, and that's no great if ah'm no supposed to attract attention. Ma hair's tied so tightly back wi the bauble that ma eyes sting. Still, she's right it adds at least two years to me.

Inside the buildin, a wee window and a sign: RECEPTION. A woman with short, brown hair sittin at a desk. She's wearing a flowery dress. Behind her the wall is covered with flowery wallpaper so it's hard to tell where she starts an the wallpaper finishes. She's watchin a screen with loads of squares, only views of corridors, one screen wi a big room, rows of chairs and a snooker table in the middle. Donna goes straight up to the counter.

'Well, well, Donna. We've no seen you here for a while. Thought you had a social worker lookin after you?'

Breathe in get ready tae push ma chest out a bit though there's no much tae push out.

Don't walk wi round shoulders or they'll stick like that for life.

'Housing Department were choka so they gave us this letter. They're tryin to get us a flat but it's goin to take a few days. They phoned.'

Any minute now. Any minute, an she'll see me. She stares at Donna; looks as if she disnae even half believe her story.

'Always passin the buck that housing lot.'

Donna pushes me gently towards the desk as the woman takes a while to stand up.

Ye have to speak through a grill in the glass and ye're not sure if the words get through.

'Swollen ankles,' she says, a film of blonde hair covering her face. In the sunlight, it would light up.

'This is ma wee sister. We need a place for the night till our appointment the morra.'

Mrs. Flowery Dress gives me a long, searching look. That's it. Disappearin ink wearin off.

'You look young, hen. What age? We don't like young ones here. There's special places for your age. Nobody telt me she was commin. Are ye sure ye didnae see the social work? You know it's mixed?'

She's holdin me right up tae the light of her gaze now.

There's keys on a board with numbers and hooks beside the numbers an all ah want is to have a key for myself; to feel one in ma hand and to know ah don't have to go home because ah missed the bus. Ah

90

wonder if it's like the hostel Drew told me about and ye have to do jobs like sweep the kitchen floor in the mornin. Bob a job. Thank God ah don't ever have tae go round doors in the street wi Our Simmit sayin that: Bob a job.

'Listen, son, there's a tin ae beans. Forget about the job.'

Anythin to get rid of us. Word must have got out about the time Mr. Reynolds asked us to cut his grass an Simmit, daft eijit, cut the heids off the pansies. Orange, red, yellow. We tried to hide the evidence in a bin but when ye looked at the garden, the colour had half disappeared. Anyway, it was a lot quicker getting stuff after that.

'Seventeen, are you sure? You're awfie wee for your age.'

'She is, everybody says that. Listen, social work stand-by telt us to come here. We could always bed down near the station or under one of the bridges…'

Under one of the bridges.

'No…no….it's just ah need to make sure ye're getting the support ye need. We'll need tae get details once ah'm organised wi the rest of the residents so ah can do the paper work. It's aw paperwork these days.'

Next minute, skinniest woman ah've ever seen, made skinnier by the track suit that disnae fit, walks past an nods at the woman at the desk. She looks at first lik she's smokin the end of her finger but it's a wee end of a roll up. Drew says his mum says ah'm awful skinny, jist flesh an bone. Ah don't say, she's awful old lookin cos ye're no allowed to speak ye're mind when ye're a teenager even though folk can say you're wee or skinny or pretty or anythin.

Donna gies me a kick an ah kick her back. Hard not to laugh cos she's makin faces again behind their backs.

'Right, Doris. You know the rules.'

The woman called Doris goes to the front door, throws the fag end down an twists it wi her heel. Ah thought only film stars had names like Doris. Even the way she twists the heel intae the fag, that's straight out a film. Our Annemarie thinks Doris Day is a holiday like Christmas Day. She's no seen Calamity Jane. Ah wish ah could tell Donna that but she'd say it was daft. That's about five things ah've no been able to say.

Doris' face is caved in like the fatty part of her cheeks has been sucked out, she has tiny feet for a woman an her dark hair is straight and her face is pale.

'Junkie,' Donna whispers to me.

Ah look at ma feet.

'And where is it you lassies are from?'

The woman wi the pen eyes us, the two of us, we're no there yet. No there yet.

'Castlemilk. Both of us. You know the houses that are commin down? Waitin for a decant.' My new voice. Ma new big sister.

Blood is thicker than water.

One day won't make a difference. Ah'm still goin.

She said 'us.' She said 'gettin us a flat.'

'One night. But ah'll be checkin wi social work in the mornin. Don't want any hassle. Ah've enough bother, aw they daft men an Doris, last thing ah needs is mare trouble fae social work.'

She writes somethin in a black book. Still tryin tae look taller, standin on the balls of ma feet. Donna draws me a dirty look so ah come back tae earth. Ye cannae keep that up, afterall.

'Any valuables. Your own responsibility. We advise you to look after them at all times. So where have you been stayin?'

'Ah've been on a cruise, that's why ye've no seen me. But ah'm back in the country again.'

Donna's got a big grin on her face. This isnae the time be a right pain in the arse.

'Do you want a space or not?' The pen above the book, our names not written.

'Sorry. Course we do. Ah've been sleepin on ma pal's sofa and she's...this is her first night...'

Just then a man and woman come in. That'll do. Nice distraction from the pal wi the big mouth. Thank God. Donna's gob nearly made the pen stay above the book and that would be it then. Ah'd have tae phone ma aunt or maybe phone ma dad an just admit the whole thing.

'You lassies, wait a wee minute. This won't take long.'

'Shite,' Donna says.

'We were first. Oh naw, her.'

Small world for a city.

The woman shuffles up to the desk. Flowery Dress looks up.

'Okay, Rosie?' Her voice softens.

'What happened to your eye, pet?'

The other woman lifts a skinny hand to a purple eye, a look on her face lik she disnae know or has forgotten what made it lik that. Maybe she was born that way. But ah don't think so the way Mrs. Flowery Dress is shakin her heid, starin at the man beside her lik he's a piece of dirt dragged in on somebody's shoes. It's funny she seemed quite hard,

Mrs. Flowery Dress, when she was talkin to Donna and the other woman but now she's dead nice. Maybe she's no so bad after all.

The man coughs. The man waits.

'Ah walked into a wall or somethin. You know me. Always getting intae daft scapes.'

She lifts her hand to the eye again, pattin it gently. Ah've never seen a real black eye before. The colours are lovely, a kinda greeny brown, a pattern lik a swirly carpet.

The beauty of a sunset.

Donna's pointin tae her wrist as if despite the fact we've no got a watch between us, we've still got a shedule.

'Hiya, Bobby. You're awfie quiet. Don't suppose you know anythin about it?'

Mrs Flowery Dress waits for the man to speak.

'Me? No way. If she says she walked into a wall then that's what happened. She's no the full shillin, ma Rosie. Are you sweetheart?'

'You better be lookin after her, Bobby. Any trouble and you're out.'

'Aye, nae bother. We're sorted me an Rosie.' He puts an arm around Rosie. She leans into him, smilin up at him like you only see in films, lik the couple in mum's favourite film, Love Story, before the woman gets sick. Except for the black eye on her an his yellow teeth, they don't belong here, not here in the West of Scotland. Even ah seem more worldly wise than she does.

'We're in love,' Rosie says.

'Pass me the sick bag,' whispers Donna, too loud.

Mrs. Flowery Dress throws a key on the counter. She's heard her.

'You know the rules. The Sally Army café is open in the mornin if you want somethin to eat. We'll have some soup in the dining room later if you're hungry. Aye, an Rosie an Bobby are next door. Any nonsense just let me know. Now what was ah sayin...aye valuables.'

There's nothing in the bag worth stealin, a few clothes, that's all. The only thing ah have of any value is mum's weddin ring. Ah never take it off. Don't think anybody here will be interested in pinching ma Wordsworth book. They're welcome to it. See how they get on learnin *Tintern Abbey.*

13

He met the doctor in Oban himself, went there for a few days and stayed at Mary's place.

There were boats in the harbour.

'Could get on one of those,' he thought.

'Is it normal for a boy to stop talkin, doctor?'

The doctor was a wee Malaysian wi a constant smile.

'It can be a symptom of trauma. He'll be fine. Paul just needs some space from the family and time.'

'Who doesn't?' Joe nearly said.

Her family had already offered to take the three youngest back to Ireland an her oldest brother had said the two eldest lassies could stay wi him an his wife. They already had four girls so two more wouldn't make much difference. Even with the car it would mean a day of driving and a two and a half hour boat journey between them. He'd put his foot down, knowin she would have hated them aw to be split up but he couldn't stop Paul goin. That was only a three and a half hour drive away. Anyway, there was no point when he wouldn't talk to anyone. Still, he wishes it wasn't Paul who has gone of all of them, his eldest boy, the one he feels most comfortable with. The other two boys are that bit younger an don't appreciate the finer points of football, that the team needs somebody that can break down a defence or somebody to dig in. They two stare at him lik they havnae a clue but Paul would get it. Paul's a great wee player; an he can talk to him. Boys are so much easier than lassies; he stops himself thinkin he wishes it was one of them.

Later, Joe was thinkin he'd give Mary's place a ring an see if the boy is ready to come home. Mary said the doctor said he'd not to put pressure on Paul, that he has some kind of stress disorder, after his mum. Joe isnae so sure. Paul should be at home but no one else seems to agree, none of Eve's brothers an sisters, an he isn't in any fit state to take them all on. Eve would haunt him if she knew he'd agreed to let Mary take the boy but what else could he do? After that thing at the funeral with the cross, in front of everyone. There are too many of them, that's the bottom line an he needs the help.

At first he's on top of things, rises early in the morning and gets them out to school. The house is so quiet when they leave, he goes for the shoppin to get out for an hour, tries to get away from the house and his thoughts. Everyone he meets asks:

'How's it going, Joe? How you all doin Joe?'

It's exhaustin, answerin the same questions.

He has to make the money stretch when he goes down to half pay and then the pay stops and he only gets benefit. There's no money for fancy clothes or things for the house but really only Eve bothered about that.

It's tiring tryin to think up different dinners every day: mince, stew, soup.

Soup is easier, easy to make and cheap. Open the tin, heat it up. Open the tin, heat it up. They'll always have meat at the weekend but young weans don't need that much. The afternoons are the worst, the hours before Annemarie, his five-year-old, comes home. Four hours when the messages are done an the phone disnae ring an the house is silent apart from when he puts the heating on and the system clicks and burrs to its own tune. He tries to keep the place clean, washin the dishes after breakfast but it's non-stop, thankless. There are so many of them, so many dirty plates after they aw eat an he disnae even go near the bedrooms. As long as Erin an Anna take care of the rooms upstairs, he'll manage wi the shoppin an the bits of cookin an the discipline. That's the system. It works for a while but only Anna does any housework. Erin has her head in books upstairs after school, always studyin for this exam or that one. He likes that she reads, likes that she's smart but there's a limit to how much readin's good for a person.

At first he lets it go but then he can't stand the mess an tells her to clean up her own room, put the cloths away. Half the time, she looks at him like she's in another world an once he overheard her on the stairs, it sounded like she was talkin to herself. That's aw they need. Him and her for the looney bin. Someone has to keep on top of the mess or they'll all go under. Joe hates the thought that he'll have to live in a dump for the rest of his life. Durin the day when they were aw at school, he went into Erin and Anna's room. Anna's been complaining about Erin bein untidy an she asked if she could have the room to herself and Erin could move in wi the other three lassies. Honest to God, it's lik havin to chair The United Nations, Joe thought. Right enough, there were clothes an books aw over the floor, he couldnae see the carpet for them. Just because there's no mother disnae mean the place can go to rack an ruin. He decided to teach her a lesson an would

98

have thrown the clothes out the windae but the windae was stuck shut. He met her at the door when she was commin in from school. She looked surprised to see him, specially when she saw his face and that he was mad. Mad out. He grabbed her school bag an threw the whole lot back down the stairs an onto the grass.

'That's the teacher's books, you'll need tae explain to her.'

Bold as brass.

Joe followed her out; accidently stood on a book wi a picture of a man in a frilly blouse, his hand on his heid. The boot print was aw over his face.

When she looked at him it was hatred in her face, aw for a daft schoolbook. She needed to learn a lesson an maybe the next time he told her to tidy her room an help around the house, she'd do it.

He wondered was it his fault Eve got sick? Maybe, if she'd not had so many weans but she wanted a big family. She always said that. And he would have been okay if they'd taken precautions, but no her, everythin had to be always right. Maybe, if he'd stood up to her more when she first said she was going out to work on the wards two nights a week. Maybe, that's what killed her or weakened her.

Why did she leave him wi aw this? She's okay: well out of it. He's the one wi all the worry. Goes walks tae take his mind off things: bills an that. There's that many things to pay. And how can he keep up wi clothes an food an lights an immersion heaters on and a tumble drier in the summer? See they lassies. And why did she buy a tumble drier an leave him wi the bills an that big chest freezer as well? Costs a fortune tae fill it. He wis workin then. Invalidity cannae pay for all that. Social security cannae keep up wi it.

Mornin, noon and night, lights on, washin machine goin, that gas fire blazin. They don't realise, think money grows on trees. That tree oot the back. Think there's money hangin fae the branches that he goes oot when they're in bed: rakes it aw in; he doesn't know how she managed. He's a man, for God's sake.

At night Joe goes for a long, a very long walk. Some nights as much as three hours. Fresh air. Nothin like it. Ye cannae beat a dose of fresh air.

They're alright watchin the telly. He'll get back and they'll aw have the tea and biscuits. Erin's upstairs studyin. He'll bring the fire down, later.

God this is good, he thinks. This is the best: fresh air.

Maybe, he'll sleep the night.

For miles, walks himself to a place called Exhaustion, walks himself out of his thoughts, walks so he is too tired to think. If he can't sleep he can always some pills.

14

Away from the desk, Donna pushes open a door: 'FOR RESIDENTS ONLY.'

'Well, come on. What you waitin for?'

'Ah'm dying for a fag.' When we're out of earshot of Mrs Flowery Dress.

Hope she's no gonnae try an make me smoke.

We keek into a room done up lik a chapel, an alter and chairs in a row. This place cannae be that bad if they say prayers in it. But the walls are school white, worse even. At least, there's paintins on the walls; could be that shitey brown colour ma dad's painted the house. We turn a corner and there's Jesus on a cross, suspended in the sky, gazing down a group of fishermen. Sometimes, it's as if Jesus is followin me everywhere ah go. He's in the livin room above the fire, now he's here, always starin.

One door in a corridor of doors leads to a room with four beds. It's like bein on a campin holiday, small single beds in the same room.

'Take that one,' Donna points to one near the window.

There's a lot of wee paintins on the walls, paintins of bowls of fruit an flowers but the colours are too dull or too bright or the fruit is nothing like the fruit in real life.

'The dossers' art work. Crap, isn't it?'

'Is that supposed to be apples?'

The fruit in the fruit bowls on the wall look caved in, apples made of plastic that have been punctured.

'We'll have company for the night. Let's hope they're not nutters. Nothin worse than that.'

'Donna?'

'What?'

'What did Rosie mean she'd walked into a wall?'

'You're not serious are you, country lassie?'

It's like the answer is near but cannae quite find it.

'Bobby beats her up. That's what ah was tryin to say. Walked into a wall, ma arse.'

'It means, mind your own business. He's ma man an ah'll do what ah like.'

It's no as much fun as ah thought it would be. Livin in a hostel. Rosie wi the black eye, them next door, her wi that man. Four walls and a door, that's a lot of bumpin in to do. Ye cannae help wonder about it. Ah wouldnae like to live here aw the time, ah'm glad ah'm no Donna or Rosie. But that makes me think about who me is. Donna lifts a paper that somebody's left on the bed an starts readin it so ah take out the only thing ah have to read:

'William Wordsworth Selected Poetry.'

'*The sounding cataract*

Haunted me like a passion, the tall rock,

The mountain, and the deep and gloomy wood...'

Makes ma brain sore tryin to understand what he means.

'Cataract,' was what ma gran in Ireland had in her eyes, that she had to go to Cork Hospital for but our English teacher told us it was also a waterfall. Haunted by the sound of a waterfall. Don't really get it, but feel excited when ah read it.

'Oh for God sake, who is that guy?' she's pointing at the cover of ma book.

'It's William Wordsworth. He wrote the poem ah'm learnin for school. Told you.'

'Well, ah cannae look at him. He's dead ugly.'

She leans over, grabs the book and shuvs it in the bin.

'Sorry, pal, ah jist cannae look at him'

Then she goes back to reading her paper an ah'm left starin into space.

After a while she says:

'What's up?'

It's weird, one minute she's slaggin everybody of, including Wordsworth who isnae even alive an the next she's dead nice. It's hard to figure her out.

Ah miss Lizzie an Annemarie's scribbled drawings on the walls. Ah even miss dad's dinners, soup the loup, big plates of pan bread, Ambrosia Creamed Rice and strawberry jam, mince and beans mixed together. Craigneuk chile con carne. What's the point dirtying two pots, he says. It's aw goin the same way. His way or the highway.

'Nothin.'

'It's no that bad. We'll go for a walk. Show ye the sights. How does that sound?'

'Great.'

Listen. Everything quiet. No movin walls.

When she dozes off, ah'll get Wordsworth out the bin.

***

103

Later the skinny woman from the front desk comes into the room carryin a black bin bag.

'Hiya, flat mates. Any smokes?'

Glad there's someone else in the room now, she can talk to Donna. Get inside the bed, pull the cover over ma head.

'Here, ye can get a draw of this one.'

'Was it something ah said?'

Donna pulls the cover off me.

'You're lucky her downstairs let your pal in. She looks about ten. What's the story wi you, hen?'

Why not say ah'm wee? You're dead wee, hen. For your age. For any age. How would she feel if ah started tellin her what ah thought about her? Och, missus, what happened tae you? Did you smoke the fatty part of your face away or something?

Doris leans into me when she speaks her breath is heavy wi the smell of Embassy Regal.

Take a deep breath an try to not make it obvious. Mum used to smoke the blue packet when she was short of money and the red ones when she was flush. Her whole body seems to be shrinkin away from her but she cannae be sick cos she's buzzin around the room, lookin under the beds and checkin in the drawers of the three wee cabinets.

'She's with me, Doris. Ma wee sister, come to find me.' Donna says.

'Well, she disnae look like you. She looks too pale.'

'There's a lot of things you don't know about me, Doris. A woman of mystery, that's me.'

'Aye, right, very funny. Anyway, can't stop. Places tae go, people tae see.'

After she pushes the bin bag under one of the three beds, she's off out the door.

'Love ya an leave ya.'

Donna and me lie back on our beds.

'Her breath's horrible, isn't it'? she says.

'Aye, stinkin.'

'Venom Breath, we'll call her.'

'No to her face,' ah reply.

'Let's have a look at her gear.'

Donna goes under the bed, pulls out the black bin bag.

'Don't think you should do that.'

'Och, don't be such a baby; she'd do it wi our stuff.'

Donna empties the bin bag onto ma bed but it's only raggy lookin clothes an a few wallets an old womens' purses and some cheap make-up. She holds up half a bottle of red nail varnish.

'Result.'

Then she goes through every wallet an purse but only finds receipts and one photo of a young lassie that she passes to me. A girl about five in a school uniform: big, cheesy smile and a yellow hairband. When Donna loses interest, ah place the photo inside the wallet again so she can be seen when ye flick it open. Throw all the clothes and stuff back in the bag an put under the bed.

'Hey, waken up.'

Donna is duntin me on the arm. Ah must have fallen asleep proper this time.

'Are you hungry by any chance?' She's got that ah need food look about her. Suppose, it's been a few hours since the café.

'Aye. Are ye thinkin about the soup?'

Ah'd like to pull the covers over ma head. Wish she'd go away. Wish she'd leave me alone. That everybody would leave me alone.

'Three days old and diluted. You've got to be joking mon amigo. No way. Ah've got a better idea.'

Giggle our way through every big department store in the city centre until hunger kicks in even worse. Starvacatin. Calculate in ma head that if we spend more money on food, ah'll start tae struggle to get any further. That's if ah pay an ah cannae see any signs of money from Donna.

'What's up wi your face, hen?'

'Nothin. It's only…well. Ah still need ma fare for the morra, for the bus.'

'Och, the morra's ages away. You need a fag. That'll sort you out. You worry too much.'

'No ta, ah tried smokin when ah was ten an it didnae agree wi me.'

'Ha, ha. You're a scream. The way you talk. Sometimes, you're straight out a film. Don't worry, got an idea. Follow me and learn.'

It's dead nice havin someone else take the lead aw the time but ah still don't know anythin about Donna. Every time ah'm about to ask her something about herself she seems to sense a question commin, finds a reason to change the subject. Is it to do with Liver Spots at the station? Or is it the reason she has no family and no proper home? Maybe, she's sensed ah don't want to talk about stuff and we've made a kind of silent pact without havin to seal the deal in words. Ma lips are closed. Shtum.

At least ah've got somewhere safe to stay an ah know where ah'm goin in the morning.

To get Paul.

We're at the swing doors of a big department store. Inside, zigzag through aisles, avoidin shoppers. Donna knows where she's going as per usual. And, well, ah follow as per usual. She takes me to the third floor, into the restaurant area. It's busy. Smells of cookin food make ma stomach go ahhhhhhh like out the Bisto advert when the woman carries the big roast of meat past the family. You can smell it through the telly.

Find a seat near the entrance while Donna asks for a menu.

'You girls eatin?' A tall woman with a yellow apron asks.

'Yes, Mrs. A birthday treat.'

'That's nice, hen. Gie me a shout when you're ready,' as she turns to the pile of dirty plates at a nearby table.

'But Donna…' A hand up to stop me even startin. Ah'm too hungry to argue wi her. We choose two chips and sausage. Chips, again. Our Annemarie would love this. And Cokes. There's a young mum wi a baby in a high chair and an older woman at the next table. Keep ma voice down but the baby is playin up, hittin a spoon on the tray of its highchair.

107

The small scar on Donna's left cheek is a finger mark but the print never settles into her old skin.

'So, what's your idea, then?'

'Are you fed up wi me already? Thanks very much.'

'No, it's no that.'

It's hard tae tell her the full story.

The woman brings the food and we don't speak while we're eatin.

'Maybe, when ye get your flat ah could come and stay for a bit. After ah get get ma brother back, that is.'

'Aye, be great.'

'And ah'd bring Drew. Would that be okay? Or maybe one ae ma wee sisters?'

'Bring the boyfriend. Don't want greetin weans. Might cramp ma style.'

The baby at the next table is happily eatin its food now. We eat our chips in peace.

'That ring on your finger. Whose is it? You're a bit young to be married or are you hidin something?'

Good gold. They didnae skimp.

'Ma gran that lived in Ireland. She died an ah got the ring.'

'Geez it, will ye, to try on?'

'No, ah'd rather you didnae.'

All ah've got of her.

'Pardon me for askin.'

'Look, okay. Ah've been wearin it for a long time. It sticks when ah take it off.'

'Calm down, just want to try it on. You'll have it back in a minute.'

Too tight for Donna; cannae even get the ring past the top part of her finger, at least ah managed tae push it down on mine. Throws it up in the air towards me an as the baby sees the ring in the air, reaches out to grab it as if it really could from that distance. The two woman look around as ah'm closing ma hand over the wee gold circle.

'You know if you're stuck for money you could always pawn it. You'd get no a bad wee price.'

'No, you're okay.'

Slip it onto ma finger. Fits me now. Doesn't feel as tight as it did.

'Please yourself. Ah'm only sayin… Right, now when ah say go, you stand up an head for the toilet, okay?'

'But ah'm no ready.'

'Just do it, doll. Okay?'

Doll's worse that hen. Hello Dolly, well hello Dolly. It's so nice to have you back where you belong. Ma daddy loves that film.

'And what then?'

'Never you mind. When you're finished, walk straight out. Ah'll still be here but don't look in ma direction. If there's anyone watchin you then go right back in. Kid-on you've left something. If the coast's clear, walk out, down the stairs and ah'll meet you at the big statue we passed earlier. Okay?'

'Donna, is this some kind of detective movie? Cos you're talkin kinda funny.'

'Mush. Hurry. You want to keep your money, don't you.'

She's right. This will cost a few bob and if ah have to pay well....Might leave me short for the fare to Oban. So, we've eaten the food and we've no money to pay and now we're leavin. Ah knew that's what she meant. Ah must have done. That's how she got the make-up. That's what she does. She steals. No matter how hard ah try to keep away from stealin; ah seem to always end up doin it and this time we really could get caught.

'Okay.'

15

'Da, she needs a shirt. Ma mum…'

'Erin, don't start.'

His eyes fill up with tears an ah have tae look away. God, wish he'd pull himself together. Ah know ma mum's no here but this is doin ma head in. It's no him that's dead; it's no us. Exhaustin, havin tae tiptoe around him. *Get up,* mum would say. *Get up and do a bit of housework. And you, Erin, go and get your sister a proper shirt for startin school. Just cos I'm dead, doesn't mean you all need to give me a showin up.*

'Anyway, can she not wear Lizzie's? Ah've enough on ma plate.'

He disnae get it. Never went shoppin for our clothes in his life. Ah don't think he's even went shoppin for his own clothes. Shakes his heid. He's got a beard now, a gristly, red beard. His hair grows wild, aw stickin up an curly; one day a bird'll make a nest in that heid an fly right out. He wears the same jumper every day: a big, chunky, colourless jumper. An it smells.

'Everybody wears a new shirt when they first start school. It won't be dear. Ah'll go somewhere cheap. Anyway, Lizzie would need a new one then.'

'Jesus Christ, will ah ever get any peace?'

He unlocks the cupboard in the lobby where he keeps the valuables: social security money an chocolate biscuits. One day he's gonnae pay a bill wi a Penguin. A rustle of the packet, brings us runnin from aw corners of the house. In fairness, everyone always gets equal, those

Pennywise, you can get five each. They're not as satisfying as a right good proper chocolate biscuit with its own wrapper. The money's there, in the dark. He reaches in. There are empty boxes wi old photographs and important stuff: mass cards and insurances. Its aw mixed together in the dark, we're no allowed in.

'Right. Right. But it better do her all year, do you hear me?'

'Aye, it will.'

'We have to tighten our belts, Erin. Do you know how much we get? It's not much.'

'Ah know. But there's enough for one shirt.'

Gies me three pounds. This is Monopoly an ma da's the banker but then it hits me that we're actually poor now an there is no point arguin. When ah started school, getting the uniform was a big occasion. Ah actually got measured for a blazer, made up specially for me and two shirts for when one was in the wash. And the woman in the shop said my God is that your eldest startin school.

Aye, they don't be long.

Mum eyeing up the hem of the skirt to make sure it was perfect.

'Indeed they don't.'

Dad turns away, towards his room, leavin me to put the lights out. Listen for the rattle of the Valium tablets being shaken out onto his hand and the gulp of water; the miracle mix that will help him sleep. Rustle of biscuit papers, rattle of pills.

Find God in nature and in your own mind.

Well, that's the daftest thing ah ever heard when ah read that's what they Romantics thought. That God could be in a tree or the sky or a pigeon or me. Ah think Wordsworth was a sort of lunatic to think that. Ah can imagin me suggestin that to ma dad.

'There's nothin. Nothin anywhere,' he'd say.

Only, silence broken by the rattlin of pills.

***

After dinner, Joe was lookin forward to a sit-down wi the paper and a bit of peace. Few hours of the box then an early night. Hoped Eve had the place cleaned up. He hated an untidy house. Got it from his mother. He'd never really got used to it, the amount of clothes and stuff that weans generated. The smells: milky smells, and shitey nappies and now they were older, the sweaty smells of them all together. Okay, there were ten in the house but ye'd think there'd be more order, that she'd have a proper system. Sometimes, he longed for the army, everything neat and folded. Ye had to be tidy or ye got court marshalled. Didnae have a clue when he first joined but an ex-convict from Dundee showed him how to make the bed, the way the sergeant liked. Nobody ever bullied Joe wi him about an he'd some great stories about his days in the jail. Whatever happened to the big black fella: their scout in Egypt, Joe wondered? There was a photo of the three ae them in the biscuit tin. He'd look that out one of these nights.

It was his mother's voice he heard as he came through the door. Christ, what did she want? He hoped her and Eve hadnae been fightin again. Him in the middle as per usual. Last time, Eve kicked her. Took them years tae talk again. He wasnae in the mood for a house full of women.

Maura, his aunt, and his mother were drinkin tea. She still had her hat on. No stayin then, that was good.

'Is that you, Joe?' Eve was cookin in the kitchen. From out the back, yelps and screams of weans. He closed the window. As long as they stayed out, till he had his dinner. Later, he'd be in better nick.

'What's up?' Eve had taken her apron off. Usually, he had a quick wash before the tea. There were showers at work but he liked his own bath. Now he'd have to stay and talk, feelin manky. Why did women always want to talk? He never understood it. His mother was resting back on the couch, like a cat that's tired out purring. He knew what she was thinking when she looked around the house at the walls with weans' hand-prints on them, or the doors with blisters of paint burst and picked; no matter how Eve cleaned they were always behind her, messin the place up. He could have done better, she'd say: all those weans, the family business. She'd had high hopes for her only child. Kept him in short trousers till he was fourteen and never got his curly hair cut so he looked like a girl. Never forgave her for that. Annemarie was glued to Maura, gibberin about some cartoon. Thank God for Maura; she came over a lot to help Eve wi the weans.

Eve was perched on the edge of one of the comfy chairs.

'Good day?' she said.

'Aye, no bad.' It was their nightly ritual.

He started to lift the paper, hopin they'd gie him ten minutes.

'I've a thing to ask ye Joe?'

Although she had her apron on, he could see her figure underneath. How the hell had he been so lucky? Even after aw they weans, she was still beautiful. Those eyes that knew everythin about him. She didn't look at him that soft way now. Not as much. Too busy wi the house and stuff, more like a pale statue watchin him from a distance. Had he made her into a statue? He didn't know. She was the one could have done better.

In his own chair, he was the man of the house. Sometimes with Eve, it was hard to feel that way. She did everything about the place, took his wages on a Friday; he was happy enough to get a bit of pocket money for a bet. You couldnae feed seven weans on thin air. Maybe she was expectin again? The thought of his mother talking about them havin sex, mortified him.

Through the open window, the sounds of cars up and down the street. Dogs barkin.

'What is it? The suspense is killin me?'

'The hospital's lookin for part-time nurses. I've got a chance of a few shifts. Nights. It would take the pressure off you and the weans always need things. Maura said she would help. Won't you, Maura?'

Margaret didn't volunteer.

'Who'll keep the place tidy? Who'll make the dinners? No way, Eve. Don't you think you've enough on your plate? You've got seven weans for God's sake.'

'Please, Joe. Ye wouldn't notice a difference. Two nights. The money's great.'

She ignored 'you've got seven weans.' Was used to hearing it, that she was the one wanted a big family. Sometimes, it seemed they had been having the same row for years. Could turn a tape on with her answers. Not this time. She'd made up her mind.

'Let her go, Joe. All the married women are goin out to work now.'

Margaret's health wasn't as good as it had been. She'd rather not get involved but she knew what it was like, wantin to work, wantin to get out in the world a bit. Sure, wasn't it 1975. Not like when she was young. As long as they didn't expect her to run after that squad.

'She could do it for a trial run. See how it works. No harm in that, is there? Really it's none of my business. Do what you like.'

Eve couldn't help drawin her a *don't you dare back out now* look. She hated depending on her; it had cost her a dear sultana cake to tempt her up the road to their bit.

Joe was in a corner. He was workin all the hours God sent; a few extra pounds would do no harm. On the other hand, if she couldnae cope, that would be the end of the idea for good. If he said no, she'd take it out on him some way, not speak for days or weeks. That would be worse. Her body a statue, her eyes hateful, her words full of spite. He'd look stupid, if she went anyway. Maybe if he agreed, things could be good again between them but there was no way he was turnin intae a nancy boy, doin women's work, no way.

'Well don't blame me, if you're tired. If ah hear anything about you no bein able to cope, it stops without an argument. That's aw ah'm sayin. Cannae say fairer than that.'

Now she was smiling and he liked it when she smiled.

***

Eve got up to make the pieces; yawning in the kitchen while Joe was getting ready for work. She was back in bed by the time he left, easier now with the gas in the mornin, used to be one of them had to light the

116

coal fire first thing. He didnae miss that, cold mornins, carrying buckets from the shed out the back and his hands always black from the coal. He was lucky. Away to work, before they were up for school and Thank God; he'd go dolally aw the mess, weans clothes an shoes, trip an pick: a bit of a doll or some toy. Why did she let it get that way, he'd never know.

Joe's flask was warm. His piece, chopped ham and pork, in his other hand. A short walk to the steel works. One of the gaffers, from the south side of Glasgow had two buses and a walk. This time of the morning, you'd see them, lone figures, heads bent, heading in the direction of the three blue towers dominating the skyline. Sometimes, there'd be a roar from the furnace, flames rising and emergin like a fire genie licking the rim of the tower, subside again an disappear. Hell on earth, inside the furnace, molten pig iron bubbling and simmerin like a volcano, biding its time and men in brown overalls scrutinisin the Integration Timer for the perfect temperature. The melt had to be right. Too much of a boil and you took away the strength, too little, the steel wouldnae be any use either. Twenty years and hard to remember, it had all been fields before. His own da had an allotment, protesting against the steel works, him a miner as well, organisin a petition to give to the big iron and steel company. The local paper reported the demonstration to the council offices in Motherwell but the council didnae even meet their delegation. Nobody cared about fields and bits ae trees, it was work people needed. His da used to spit into the fire and say how one day they'd regret it when the air was rank and the sky disappeared. Other men thought he was off his heid but he was right in the end about the sky though they did get beautiful sunsets, pink skies

117

at night from the gases. Still, it was good to have work. His mother was always talking about the Depression when the miners didnae work an she served soup in the street, they'd never had times like that, his generation. The workin man could buy anythin these days: tellys and some people, better off right enough, fridge freezers and phones.

Joe liked the early morning, curtains drawn, dawn air settling itself lik a heavy jumper about his shoulders, sunshine and dew on the wee bits of grass in front of houses. Hardly a sound except for the birds, aw excited that the light was back. The sunshine seemed precious when he knew he'd be inside for a double shift and the air was fresh and even the chill was a delight.

Joe could think when he walked. He couldnae think, sittin down, as if the thoughts got stuck cos ae lack of circulation.

The big blue gates were open for the coal lorries. He took the path, towards the strip mill.

'Macaroon bars, mister?'

A wee scraggy boy about Pinkie's age, was lookin up at him, laden down wi brown boxes. Ye got everythin in there: chocolate, cigarettes. God knows where it came from. Ask no questions.

'Naw, son. No the day. Are the schools off the day?'

'Naw. Dead cheap, mister. Ye sure?'

'Here, let me see.'

A bit early for sellin macaroon but the early bird an aw that.

A row of six in a box.

'How many layers, son?'

'Three.'

That's eighteen, that's two each.

'Gimme a box on Friday.'

'Thanks, mister. Ah'll be here.'

The boy was wearin the same black donkey jacket as Joe: payment for a box of those macaroons. That reminded him, Erin was lookin for one but Eve would go mad if he took anything without payin.

'Did you hear about the accident, mister?'

'Naw, son. What accident is that?'

Joe had only been there a couple of months. He was a driver for a small haulage company who'd laid him off for a few months when business was slow. His pal, Marty, got him the job.

'A guy fell from one of the towers. Young laddie.'

He spoke like a man but looked like a boy.

'That's bad, son. Naw, ah didnae hear.'

'Ah'll see ye Friday wi the macaroon bars.' Joe wondered who the boy's family were and did they know he was selling stolen stuff to steel workers.

Marty was already in his overalls. They need to be covered or the limestone got everywhere.

'Hiya, Joe. Nice mornin. There's three cars on the line. Did ye hear about the accident last night?'

'Aye, ah just heard. Who was it? Anyone we know?'

'He comes from Branchalwood Drive. His da's big George Findlay. A young man, Joe.'

'Any weans?'

'Naw, single.'

Joe shakes his head and Marty stubs his cigarette out on the ground.

They walk from the shed at the back of the yard to the pile of limestone. Their job is to fill the waiting trucks.

'What's new?' Marty asks, bending his back, to shuvel the first scoop of limestone.

'Och, nothing much. Eve wants to go out workin. Women these days, ye cannae be up to them.'

'Has she not got enough to do, lookin after aw they weans?'

Marty had a soft spot for Eve. He'd never married, although, she'd tried to fix him up a few times.

'It's good money, Marty. She's talking about a couple of nights.'

'What next, eh? Soon, they'll be sending women an weans down coalmines, again. How's ma goddaughter? Still as brainy?'

His main duty had been to buy Erin an Easter egg every year. It should have meant she got one more but Eve didn't buy her one because it wouldnae be fair to the rest. It was nice of them to ask him.

'Aye, reading aw the time. She's started a wee Saturday job in a chippie in Wishaw. Money for clothes.'

'God. What did ah tell ye even the weans are goin out to work.'

Joe was slower than Marty, not used to the hard physical stuff. He was hoping his gaffer from his old work would give him the shout to come back. Rather be driving any day than breakin his back, shuvlin this shite.

'So, what did you say? About Eve?' Marty asks, waiting a reasonable amount of time so as not to be nosy.

Quite a few of the lads had wives that worked: cleanin mostly, or workin in a shop. Eve always said she'd go out nursin again when the weans were up. She'd been training when they got thigither, when she

120

was nursin his da. She'd cried, at first, when she told him she was expectin an he said what's up an she said, it's all been a waste, all the trainin and learnin, an he said, no, you can always go back to work. Never thought she would.

'Ah'm no sure. Ah don't want her over doin it.' Joe was already thinking about when Marty would call the first break. They had strong black tea in their flasks and the thirst was on him.

'Aye, right enough.' Marty was never a man of strong opinions. He liked to spend all his wages in the pub, play cards and have the odd fight with his brothers. Three of them shared a house. None of them married.

'Ah'll probably say it's okay. Ah mean to be honest the money would come in handy.'

'Ah'll bet.'

'Never thought she'd take me at ma word, not after aw these years. But as long as the housework's done an the weans kept awright, ah cannae see the problem. Let her work a few nights a week; she'll be tired right enough, an ah'll have to say ah telt her.'

Marty was always the quiet one. They'd been hell raisers in their youth, travelling to the dances all over the country: Glasgow Plaza, The Hamilton Palais. Marty tagged along. Joe was the one had all the flash moves: a real dancer in his day.

'It might do her good. Getting out the house, a bit,' Marty says.

He phones up to the office.

'One truck, ready.'

The word comes back: 'Fill the grey lady up, then drive her.'

121

'He must have died right away. What do you think?' Joe was looking up at the cooling tower.

'Ah hope so,' Marty replied. They sit on a wee bench inside the shed, drinking their black tea, Marty lightin up another cigarette.

'Twenty-seven. That's aw he was.' Marty had worked in the Craig all his life. Joe didn't speak right away in case Marty was thinking it could have been him or about other men who might have gone that way. Instead, he sipped at his tea; hoping things in the haulage trade would pick up soon.

***

Annemarie is still half-sleeping when we get on the bus. She has the whitish crust at the corner of her eyes. 'C'mere.'

Have tae help her pick it out so she can see. That's better. Ahhhhh. She squirms; grey-blue eyes follow ma hand.

'Can ah get sweeties?' She has a duck tooth at the front, her baby teeth refusin to fall out.

We could walk to the town but with Annemarie in tow it would take aw day, the way she has to tight rope walk on every single low wall, pick up leaves and dirty stones an jump over cracks in the pavement in case the devil gets her. God before the devil. One, two three. Big jump. We'll never get to Wishy market, this rate. There's a man lives near us, wipes the walls with the sleeve of his jacket. Somethin happened when he was in the war but no one knows what because he disnae talk any sense. Must have jangled him up. A big fright. Ye can't stop yourself starin as he gets ready to wipe the wall wi his sleeve. Ah

122

wonder what it feels like to take a nice clean sleeve and make it dirty like that. Hope our Annemarie disnae end up lik him. Sometimes, ah like to pick leaves off the hedges when ah'm out walkin an pick the green away until only the stalk is left lik when ye pick aw the chocolate of a Club biscuit an line it up on the wrapper so ye eat the chocolate in one go; well, it's only a habit but when does a habit become something that makes other people think ye're weird? Everyone knows that man about here but no one ever gets in his way, no one gies him a hard time about bein daft.

Eventually, have to drag Annemarie all the way, her complainin about her legs being sore an can she sit down for a rest.

'Ye'll get sweeties if you behave.' Annemarie looks up, gies me one of her big grins, the front tooth curled over the bottom tooth. Everything about her seems tiny, the white teeth, her small hand on the railing, the way her legs dangle from the seat. Every part of the bus rattles so Annemarie has to lean forward an hold on to the rail. The roof's made of material that looks like old stained carpet above our heads. The yellow strip light is on full bung even though its morning makin other passengers have grey lookin skin: a man with the start of a bald patch an dandruff on his shoulders; a woman with black roots growin through dyed blonde. We look out the dirty windae at another bus. The passengers are framed by the square of their bus windows; same way we must look to them. Bein on a bus without mum is weird but it makes me feel close to her, takin Annemarie for her first school shirt; she would have organised it by now. She wouldn't settle for a market stall either. Ah can hear her naggin me an ah tell her to shut-up. That's one good thing about talkin to someone who's dead. They cannae gie

123

ye a slap across the face for bein cheeky. Annemarie leans her head against ma shoulder. Ah feel for the three-pound notes in ma pocket, pushin them further to the back. Gie her a shake. She stifles the start of a cry- baby moan when she sees ma face. She's a good girl, really.

We get off at a stop quite a distance from the market, at the start of a hill, leadin into the town. There's no shame in a wee walk.

Exercise is good for you.

'Why do we have to get off? It's miles away?'

'Cos we do. C'mon, you were doin well, Annemarie.'

Gies me her hand, we dawdle up the hill, stoppin to look in shop windows, admiring the mannequins with ladies dresses or giggling at the bare naked ones. There's a fish and chip shop half way up the street. A lassie inside butterin rolls same as me when ah had ma Saturday job. Imagine ah walked in there and she became the me ah used tae be. What would that be like? Science fiction. That's the kind of thing ye could make a film about. The smell of chips sizzles in the fresh brown oil, wafting through an open door. The pavements have bits of chewin gum and stamped out fags, stuck to them. Ye have tae watch ye're feet for dried dog's shite as well. Annemarie's hand pulls away from me.

'Look, look.'

The absence of her hand gies me a right fright. Automatic pilot mode. What if she walks onto the road? What if she falls? She's dodging through people, headin towards the window of the biggest store in the town. Right enough there's a display of school uniforms. The small mannequin is wearing a brown wig and a uniform with Annemarie's school colours, ma old primary school. If we could make her look lik

124

that lassie on her first day at school. If only...But it is a dummy and it does have the same daft look on its face as the lassie on the test card last thing at night, sittin in front of a blackboard wi a clown at her side. Though she should be in bed at her age instead of playin o x o.

'That's where ah got ma other things, Erin.'

'That's right. Ah got ma first uniform there too.'

'Did you?'

'Erin?'

'What?'

'When's ma mammy comin back?'

Ma mouth must be open lik a gold fish but no words come. O. Waitin, lookin for an answer. Lookin through the O window in Jackanorry.

'Ah told you, Annemarie. Remember?'

She kicks the wall and a woman passin turns an gies us a long look. Ah'm mortified when Annemarie sits on the pavement, leanin against the store wall.

'You said she went to heaven in taxi but when's she comin back?'

Ah could make a joke about when the metre runs out but Annemarie won't get it. She's never actually been in a taxi, only seen them pullin up at other people's houses in the street. Everybody's got questions. And nobody has answers. Not even me. And it's funny cos ah'm mad at ma dad for no tellin me about mum and stuff but here's me makin up stories about taxis that go to heaven. That really would be some fare. Ah don't care. She's too young to hear it and ah'm too young to say it the right way.

The market's down a muddy lane that leads to an opening were the stalls start. The first one is the biggest; all kinds of shoes an boots an ladies bags an schoolbags as well. The woman serving wears gloves wi no fingers that must be cos she's outside in the cold aw day either that or she couldnae afford the ones wi the fingers. She holds her hands round a white polystyrene cup, steam risin from the cup warmin her hands an when she lifts the cup, warmin her face too. Edges the cup to the tips of her fingers. Ohhh. That feels good. Annemarie starts tae touch the strap of a school bag an the woman looks at us if she's decided we're gonnae nick it.

'C'mere. Don't touch.'

Ah take Annemarie's hand cos if ah lose her here ah'll never find her. Walkin deeper into the market, crowds of people walkin past stalls, carrying us along. Food stalls wi home bakin an sweeties, jewellery stalls wi cheap watches an bracelets; big metal wrist bands in velvet cushioned boxes. There's clothes stalls sellin ladies dresses an tops but we have tae walk for a while before we find one sellin childrens' things. Right at the back of the market, when you are on the way out again, Annemarie spots some school blouses hangin up on a rail above a stall. The hand written sign says: £1.99. Ah reach over an feel the material. It's thin an nylon. Ah can see ma fingers through it. The man is watchin me, an oldish man wi big lines carved into his face. Would it bauble up at the first wash? That's the thing about cheap stuff. God, ma mum would be proud that ah'm havin all these domesticated thoughts instead of bein Head in the Clouds. She did Domestic Science at school. Now, it's Home Economics: how to make toast, scrambled egg and white sauce. In mum's school she got every possible kind of housework lesson taught. Not once, did the teacher ever show us how to make a bed.

'What do you think Annemarie. Do you think it will do?'

'Annemarie doesn't like it.' She has a habit of talkin about herself as if she's an actual other person. It's weird. Ah have to do a sort of double take, to check there's no a wean missin.

She gies me a long look. Disappointment. God. What am ah supposed to do?

She's small for age but she might grow fast an then it would be too small. Better get a big one to grow into.

'What size you lookin for, hen? Is it for you or the wee lassie?'

He's got a brown faded leather money purse around his waist an he's got a fistful of fivers that he's countin on top of a pile of girl's grey skirts.

'Aged five to six, mister, please.'

'Right, hen. Colour?'

'Green.'

'We've no green but we've white an grey. Any good?'

The shirt he hands me is white, in a plastic bag, not folded over cardboard so that when you open it you know you're the first to hold it an the creases of the card advertise its newness to aw your pals.

Nylon collars fray easily.

Annemarie looks disgusted at the shirt.

'Annemarie wants green. Ma mammy said ah could get green.'

'Can ye hurry up, hen. Ah'm just about tae close for ma tea.'

He's startin to roll a polythene cover over the clothes on the table.

'It's okay. Ah've changed ma mind.'

'Please yourself.'

He pulls down a plastic sheet separatin us from the stall an suddenly he disappears.

'Ah'm hungry, Erin. Can us get hot dogs?'

'We'll get something tae eat soon. But, first ah need tae get you a shirt.'

'But the man's closed. Where will we get me one?'

'C'mon. Let's go. Ah've got an idea.'

It's lunchtime when we reach the library. Annemarie settles down in the children's section, near the books with big writing for shortsighted people. Get her to sit on one of the low plastic green chairs. Don't mention that ah hear her stomach rumbling.

'You wait here. And don't speak to anyone. Don't speak to strangers. Remember. Ah'll be back in ten minutes.'

She looks so small in a small chair. Maybe, ah shouldnae leave her but cannae do this wi her in tow. The woman at the desk is grim and unsmiling, watchin us over the rim of her half moon specs.

'Here. Read this.'

A book about cars.

'But Annemarie cannae read.'

'Then look at the pictures.'

'Ah don't like cars. Ah like dolls.'

Tiny Tears. Her baby. Give her a drink of water an she wets herself. Thank God ah'm a teenager.

Along the aisles, search for something to amuse her. Anythin for a bit of peace. Find a hard backed Beano and a Twinkle. She loves Twinkle. Twinkle Twinkle little star. That'll do nicely. Her lip trembles an ah cannae see the duck-tooth.

'What's up?'

'Ah wanted Hansel an Gretel. Ah tolded ye that.'

The woman at nursery read her it before she started school. Annmarie loves the bit about a house made of gingerbread an the whole world turned to sweets: birds and trees. She'd eat the lot.

It takes me ages tae find the fairy tale section.

'There, now, milady.'

She grins again. Ah love our Annemarie when she smiles.

'Now remember don't talk to strangers. If ye talk to anyone then the bad man might get you.'

'Erin?'

'Why do ah have tae stay here?'

She's like a book ah'm handing back. They'll check the stamp an if she's out of date ah'll need to pay a fine.

'Cos ye do. Ye'll be bored with me.'

'Erin?'

'What is it now?'

'Ah'm starvin.'

'Ten minutes. Ah'll get you somethin. Somethin really nice. Ah promise.'

'Gingerbread?'

'Wait an see.'

The woman behind the counter might have heard us. She watches me struggle with the metal bar that acts as a barrier, a smirk on her face.

'Excuse me; you are not leaving that wee lassie there by herself, are you?'

'Just for ten minutes. Ah've got messages to get. Only ten minutes. Just across the road.'

'Well, ten minutes. This is a library. Not a babysittin service.'

She lifts the specs up as if you emphasise, rests them back again on the edge of her nose.

Pressure's on. Better skedaddle.

It's a good time to go to Bairds, the biggest department store in the town. One o'clock. A lot of the staff will be away on their lunch. Ideal. The air inside is warm and stuffy, seems to long for rain: that freshness rain brings. Inside the shop, the aisles are piled with make up, different coloured lipstick, foundation and mascara and clothes to make ma heart ache. Seems lik ages since ah got something new. Dad does one big shop at Christmas now. We go to Glasgow to the warehouses. Aw the clothes set out on long tables. Great style. Ye can pick what ye like but it's hard thinkin what ye'll need for a whole year. Ah pick things ah can wear in the winter then remember there'll be summer comin too.

'This is your Christmas. Get what you need but don't be askin for anything else in a few months.'

At least we get to pick our own clothes.

At the school uniform section, a shop within a shop, its own door and a sign: 'Please enter.' A lady that used to talk to ma mum is hangin a skirt on a dummy. Oh naw. She'll start talkin about her dyin an it will be aw depression again.

The skirt is too big. Pins in her mouth, she's workin her way around the hem, takin up the length. Ah've stood like that dummy while ma mum did exactly that. She looks up and when she sees me, takes the pins out her mouth.

'Hiya, hen.'

The woman has perfect teeth for a woman her age. Always, notice other folks teeth cos of the big gaps in mine. But big gaps means ye're a good singer. Da....da....See.

'You're one of the McLaughlins, aren't you, hen?'

Don't put the money in a brass cylinder now, press a button to transport the container upstairs. Wheeeech. Along the rail like a bullet or a miniature ride at the fair.

'Where's it goin?'

'To the office for the change.' Ma mum's finger following the track upward to the level above, an arm reaching out for the cylinder wi notes inside.

'Aye. Ah'm Erin.'

'Ah'm lookin for a shirt for ma wee sister. She's startin school.'

All the wee sizes are in the big brown wooden drawers behind her.

'St. Brendan's, isn't it? That'll be a green an yellow tie so…'

Starts pullin out shirt after shirt, all of them wrapped in plastic, shirt folded over cardboard.

'Here's a green, aged five to six. Is she wee or big for her age?'

'She's wee but she's growin fast.'

'Somethin tae grow into. That's sensible.'

About to make an excuse that ah'll think about it or something but then a telephone rings from the next room that looks like the kitchen.

'Och, hen. Ah'm really sorry about this. You have a browse an if ye see anything take it to the check-out in the hall. If ye need any other sizes, ah'll no be a jiffy..'

As she moves into the back, rummage amongst a bundle of shirts until ah get ma hands on the best one, still keepin an eye on the door. When ah'm sure the woman is speakin on the phone, lift the package an drop it into ma shopper, slide the library book over it. When ah glance up again, a big two-way mirror in the corner catches ma eye. Because it's behind me, didn't notice the massive eye waitin to apprehend the criminal. The shape of the shop assistant turnin towards me, her hand still on the phone. Maybe, she didnae see me. At that moment the main door opens, a man comes in wi a tall, cheeky lookin boy.

Reach for the bag. Not knowin if the woman is still watchin, not knowin if the game is up.

Half wish somebody would put their hand on ma arm that someone would see through the eye of the big mirror, stop me and that it would all be over in one way. But it doesn't happen and ah walk out exactly as Donna an me agreed. Because ah'm good at this, good at not gettin caught.

Cos once a thief, always a thief.

Donna says later it's amazing how quickly ah'm takin to crime. For someone that's never been in trouble before. If ah get caught ah'll have had ma chips then. Ah really will.

132

TWO

1

On the bedroom wall, there's a crucifix with Jesus nailed to it; Jesus died for our sins; that's how much he loves me. Big long nails hammered into his wrists and feet by Roman soldiers and when he was thirsty, a sponge soaked in vinegar; ah've never drunk vinegar. Drops of blood painted on his feet; we used tae get the paint oan the doors in the house tae blister and then pick away the paint lik peelin loose skin off your feet when ye've had a bath. Could ah pick away blood fae the feet of Jesus? Cheeks sunken; crown of thorns, diggin into his head.

Who made you?

God made me.

Why did God make you?

Because he loves me. No matter what ah've done. God loves me.

This Sunday is Vocations' Sunday. After the gospel, Father O'Brien asks us to sit.

'Vocation' is from the Latin 'vocare.' That means 'to call.' God calls. Ye have to listen very hard, in case God is callin you.

Ah listen. Ah hear nothin, only ma own thoughts. There are different kinds of vocations; some people get married and have weans and that's a vocation; some become priests and nuns and that's a vocation as well. What if He's callin? Ah wonder what does it sound like ? Ah don't know what to listen for. Not a deep voice like in a film with Charles Heston so ask over and over how will ah know? In ma head there's silence, no voice, no vocare. Ah want to hear a voice; what

God sounds like but all ah hear is a voice like mine tellin me ah don't hear anything.

Ah wonder if a thief, can still me a nun. But that was ages ago when we were nine and ten an me and our Anna were fed up not getting pocket money to buy stuff so we started our stealin careers. We stole make-up tae start with, the bigger things were harder: a lifebelt, slippers for mum's birthday.

'These are just the boys. My feet are freezing in the winter.'

She was dead chuffed. Even Paul didnae know how ah afforded them. Paul hates not knowin things.

***

'Woolies is dead easy. Ye just nick it when nobody's lookin.'

Sandra showed us at interval: a necklace wi chunky stones.

'Come wi me the next time. Ah'll show ye how.'

The stones were lilac wi a wee black fleck. She let me try it on.

Ah was in a dream when ah stole, easy to be invisible and ah was the leader, everythin was ma idea: what we stole and where. Hid the lifebelt in the coal cellar out the back, hadnae used it since the Council renovated the house an gave us gas. For a while it was great but if nobody sees ye stealin, maybe, ye're not real. Ah wanted tae stop but couldnae; ah didn't know how far could ah go before they saw me.

One day it was ma turn to be the look-out, Anna was handlin the goods.

'Those sunglasses, get them.'

It was a sunny day wi a chill in the air. There was nobody about that part of the shop, except a woman in a raincoat turnin from the bags aisle into shoes. Made sure she was out the way. She lifted somethin, started movin towards the checkout. Gave Anna the nod, legged it tae the swing doors, turnin tae make sure she was with me but aw ah could see was an arm landin on her sleeve. The other sleeve was the sleeve of the raincoat.

There was no use me hangin about but Anna, Anna was nabbed.

An hour later, ran right intae John Thomson from our street.

'There's a meat wagon at your gate. It's been there for ages.'

'We got caught, me an Anna.'

No point tryin tae escape, knew they were waitin for me and ah'd need tae run too far to really escape. Felt sick but awright as well cos ah felt real again; wanted someone to stop me cos ah didnae know where ah'd end up. Ah should have known, our Anna's always been shite at runnin. If it was me the store detective caught, ah'd have run lik the clappers, maybe got away with it.

Turnin intae our street ye could feel everybody lookin through turned up slats in their venetian blinds even though the street was deserted except for the meat wagon parked at our gate.

'There she is now. Ah wonder what she's done?'

Inside the house, two polismen filled up the whole room. Ah felt dead wee same as when ah went tae the toilets in the senior school and ah was still in primary two an everything seemed so big: the sinks, the toilet pans, everythin.

'Now are you goin to tell the truth here or not? You're in big trouble, do you realise that?'

'Yes. Ah'm sorry.'

The door again. Mum.

She must have seen the meat wagon.

 She knows .

'She made me do it, mum. It was her.'

Anna, was nearly hysterical.

'I'm Constable So and So and this is Constable Such and Such.'

One was older and one was younger. The younger one was mortified.

He'd have let us go jist to avoid that look on ma mum's face.

The older one took a book out his top pocket.

'Would you like a cup of tea, officers?' mum said.

'No, no thanks, missis. We'll jist do this if you don't mind.'

Ah wouldnae have minded a cup ae tea. Tae break the tension but if ah

spoke then; anyway, ah didn't think it was a good idea.

'Tell us have you done this kind of thing before? Remember, ye'll be

in worse trouble if you tell lies.'

Anna's probably telt them.

Ah'm still waitin for them to say ah'm arrested. In the coal cellar, the

lifebelt's punctured and covered in coal dust. Tell them everythin. The

polis puts the lifebelt in a plastic bag, gettin bits ae coal on his hand.

'Anythin else?'

Our mum's dead quiet.

'Anythin else?'

'A pair of slippers,' ah say an ma voice sounds dead.

'Will I get them?' she asks the polisman.

'Aye, please.'

Goes tae the cupboard, bringin back the slippers still in their box. The polis looks sorry for her for havin us as daughters.

'Is there somewhere ah can have a word with her, in private?'

Me he means.

'In here, officer.'

She's pale, her voice quiet and ah've never seen her look so mortified but she'll kill me when they leave.

'The shop want to press charges,' he says, his hat in his hands.

Ma life is over. Ah'm goin tae borstal and everybody'll know ah'm a thief.

'But cos of your age they can't. You're one lucky lassie. It's their policy to charge anyone caught shoplifting. This is your last chance. If I ever have to come to this house again, you'll be charged. Do you understand? You come from a nice family, here. You've let them down. Don't do it again. The inspector'll write to you with a warning. We'll keep your name on record. Let this be a lesson. Understand?'

'Won't do it again.'

'Why did you do it in the first place?'

'Don't know.'

When they go mum sends Anna and me up the stairs wi a look that could kill.

'Get out ma sight. Ah can't bear to look at ye.'

'It's awright for you. Ah got shuved intae the back of that meat wagon. Everybody seen me gettin out.'

'What happened when they caught you?'

Sit on the bed lik convicts in their cell, Anna's mad at me as well.

'Took me tae a wee room: the manager's office. Asked me questions then sent for the polis.'

We smell the dinner downstairs.

After ages, Paul walks intae the room.

'Ye've tae come and collect your dinner. Ye've tae eat it up the stairs.'

Ah was thinkin she'd no give us any and at least then we'd know we'd been punished, this way we're just waitin for her tae decide the proper punishment.

'Ah've to take your plates. And ye've tae get ready for confession, mum says;'

Paul again, pure lovin this.

Must have been up here three hours; maybe, she's gonnae do us in after confession but then she'd need tae go again.

'Ye'd better go to the priest cos ah don't know what to do with ye.'

Can hardly look at us as we walk down tae chapel in silence except for the words she keeps sayin:

Once a thief always a thief.

 And it's even worse than gettin hit cos ye cannae hold your hands up tae protect yourself, the hate's sunk in before ye know it an from now on ah'm the thief of the family.

But it's really the slippers ah feel bad about. She used tae say she liked to know she'd somethin she'd no worn yet and those slippers in the box were lik havin money in the bank. Ah've robbed no jist the shop, ah've robbed her bank.

***

Father O'Brien, the parish priest, looks down from the pulpit right at me. His eyes are like Jesus' eyes in the picture of The Sacred Heart in our living-room, sees everythin. The two alter boys stare at the floor. Father's eyes scan the chapel for anyone not listenin.

'Inside us, there is evil. There's no point bein clean on the outside, if inside is evil.'

From the back of the chapel, one of the weans cries. Wish ah was sittin, nearer the back. Father O'Brien's voice is always the same way like he's gien ye a row for something ye didnae know ye'd done. He has a pin in his pocket; at primary, he used to jag us in the bum wi it.

'Run, run ye'll get jagged in the bum!'

Jesus got nails hammered in his feet and hands for me. And if people don't answer God's call there'll be nobody to go to go to the missions in Africa and there'll be no priests to say the mass for the black babies. Nuns don't say mass, so maybe if I don't become a nun it won't be that bad.

'Dear God, please give the Church vocations. Lord Hear Us.'

'Lord graciously hear us.'

'All stand .'

We all stand for the 'I believe in one God.'

Everyone looks at their missal, at the words, or stares ahead if they know it off by heart. Did God call someone right there? The man next to me is too old to be called. He's got his granddaughter with him, hittin her lightly on the hand, when she starts tae pick her nose. The altar boys could have been called but they still look the same.

Over at the statue of The Little Flower of Jesus, Auntie Maura is kneelin wi her pals. When ah was wee, ah used to stand wi her and

140

she'd gie me money for the plate; a cold, brown coin, the kind that went away when the new pence came in. She's no got red hair, but auburn. Auburn is a nice word; it's brown wi a sort of red through it.

After mass, if she disnae leave early we run over to walk up the road wi her but the day she leaves early, after communion, straight out the door. It's a pity cos ah'd like to have asked her about the sermon. Only old people and men are allowed to do that, leave early. That's so they can get a seat in the pub. No the old people. The men. But we're no allowed to leave until the singin stops. Some people stay till the priest goes off the alter; ma mum says we've to wait till the choir's finished singin so that sometimes me an ma brothers an sisters are the only people still in our seats.

All the way up the road, ah'm thinkin about what the priest said and ah'm listenin for the voice of God. But then maybe it's not a voice but a decision lik a leap of faith. That's why, ma R.E. teacher says, ye can't prove God exists. Ye make a leap of faith. How can ye leap inside yourself? Athletes on the telly leap. Ye must move from somethin to somethin else, from the ground to the sandpit: a long jump for God.

Ah think about it all day; if it's really a decision then there's no voice but your own.

Maybe ah'll jist say ah want to be one, and see what happens so that's what ah do.

When ah'm dryin the dishes for ma mum, after the dinner, ah tell her.

'Ah want to be a nun.'

She keeps washin, doesn't say anythin for a while. Thought she'd throw her arms around me. Isn't this every Catholic mother's dream?

141

She was dead chuffed when ma brother said he wanted to be a White Father and he was only twelve. Ah'm fourteen.

'Ye don't know what you're talkin about.'

No arms. Quite cheeky.

'Ah do. Ah want to be a nun; Ah've decided.'

'What's made you decide that? '

Her hands are stuck in the hot water; they'll be bright red when she takes them out.

'Ah heard a voice when ah wis at vocations' mass.'

'Whose voice ?'

'God's voice.'

'Jesus, Mary and Joseph.'

'No, God's voice.'

She takes her hands out the water, dries them wi the dry end of the dishtowel.

Half an hour later she's standin in the lobby wearin her coat, holdin ma duffel coat.

'Right. We're goin for a wee walk.'

'Where?'

'If ye want to be a nun, we better go and see the priest. To put yir name down'

There's somethin no right about it. She isn't pleased and there ah thought she'd be jumpin up and down, but she's gone dead quiet.

Sometimes, when we're walkin, she says things like, 'Don't slouch Erin, stand up straight or ye'll have round shoulders.' This evening she doesn't say these things. 'Do ye know ye won't be able to get married and have children of your own?'. Ah never thought about it like that.

142

Ah never expected a discussion just celebration. When ah think about Drew and the other boys that ah like at school ah get this feelin that somethin nice might happen but cannae put it into words and the doubts are already there when we get to the chapel house but ah'm no sayin anythin. By now feel sick cos once we put ma name down, maybe that's it. Signed on the dotted line. Forever.

Mum rings the bell; Father Reilly comes to the door. Usually, it's his housekeeper answers but no the night. Smell of chips, from behind him, must've had chips for their dinner.

'Hi there,' as if he was expectin us.

'Come in. Can ah get you both a coffee?'

'Oh no father, we're fine.'

Ah'm freezin.

'It's no trouble. Let me get you something. Milk and sugar?'

'That would be lovely, Father.'

Comes back wi two mugs: 'Hope mugs are okay,' to mum.

'Erin, ah'll just have a word wi your mum then ah'll speak to you.'

She goes into the wee room near the door where ye meet with the priest. Wait on a chair against the wall, wonderin what the rest of the house is like. It's a big house, the biggest house in the parish wi a lovely garden where ah got ma first communion photos taken. Pull the hood of ma duffel coat down; it wis really freezin outside but in here it's roastin. One time ah was in Father Reilly's room wi ma pals from the youth group, we were foldin leaflets for a folk mass. He had a guitar hangin from the wall, a poncho over a rockin chair and ah got a shot of the rockin chair. He put on music and ah sat on the floor wi headphones on listenin to somethin instrumental. Father Reilly disnae like the charts, disnae believe in them.

'Right Erin, in you come.'

On the desk, a mug of coffee and no dog collar on, as if he'd been watchin his favourite programme on telly an ah've disturbed him.

'Okay, Erin. What can I do for you?'

What if ah start tae speak an he pulls out a form an says, okay, sign here? But she wouldnae have brought me for that. Ah've only been in this room once before, the time Anna an me got caught stealin an that time the priest acted as if he didnae know why we were there but Father Reilly must know, otherwise what wis ma mum talkin to him about?

'Ah want to be a nun, father.'

He's wearin a creamy arran jumper, an the sleeves are pulled up to his elbows showin black hairs on his arms. Sits back in the chair, puts his hands behind his head.

'You're too young to make that kind of decision, Erin. You're life's just beginning. What's the big hurry?'

Is this a big joke to them? Did ma mum say, 'don't laugh'?

'Don't know now. Thought ah had a vocation.'

If it was the parish priest, he'd have signed me up by now. That's why she brought me to him, so he could talk me out of it.

'Don't you want to get married? Have your own children?'

Sometimes, ah don't know what ah'm allowed to want, they're always telling what ye should be and do, it's hard to know what ye really want for yourself.

'Suppose. Don't know.'

144

'I didn't join the priesthood until I was in my late twenties, Erin. You don't need to decide until you've lived a bit.'

First they tell ye, be a nun, be a priest, listen for the voice, then when ye say okay ah've heard the voice, then they talk ye out of it. Ah just don't understaun it.

Take a long drink of the coffee. Strong and hot. Nescafe. Better than the bottled stuff ma granny buys, like melted treacle. Mum loves coffee; she'll be enjoyin hers, sittin on the chair in the lobby. A wee bit of peace and quiet and a coffee. She'd probably have a fag if she could, but ma daddy won't let her cos his dad died wi lung cancer. 'Stinkin, dirty fags.' Disnae leave them a name, ma da.

'Look Erin, here's a suggestion.'

A'm already confused, havin doubts maself but if ma mum and Father Reilly don't think…

'Why don't ye finish your education, then if you still feel the same, then it would still be possible.'

Would it be possible or is this the time ah need to decide?

Outside mum's has finished her coffee.

'Thanks Father. That was lovely. '

'Anytime you need to talk, Erin, just come and visit, okay? '

'Okay Father, thanks. And thanks for the coffee.'

Goin up the road, it's bitter cold, that bad there's frost on the road.

'Put your hood up, Erin. It's cold enough for snow. Are ye alright now? What did Father Reilly say? Ye should listen to him, he's a good priest,' she says.

'Knows what it's all about.'

145

Somethin about the way she says it as if ah've jist been saved from a fate worse than death.

'Here put yir hand in ma pocket. Ye must be frozen.'

Inside the pocket is warm, a nice feelin lik lyin against a hot water bottle; havnae taken mum's hand since ah made ma first holy communion an we were walkin to the church, me wi ma veil over ma face, thinking ah was a bride, an her aw proud.

'What in Christ's name happened to you? Look at me for God's sake.'
Mum has me by the arm and ah'm doin ma usual, gettin ready tae
throw the other one up tae ma face but her grip isnae hard this time an
she lets go quickly. The school party starts in two hours an ah'm a
disaster. Drew won't fancy me after this, he'd be daft to fancy
somebody wi no eyebrows. And ah was in mum's room cos the razor
was there. She'll go mental about that as well.

'Let me see. I won't hit you. For God's sake.'

This is our dance now for years.

'What did you do to your eyebrows?'

On the upstairs landin, a sort of no man's land in our house, me about
to retreat intae the lassies' room, her, hearin a noise up the stairs,
investigatin who could be in the house so early, on a school day.

'Cannae go now. Look at the state of me. Ye cannae make me go.'

Everybody else in the class plucks their eyebrows, ah didnae even
know until today, just before the bell went when Sally said ah should
try it an that ma eyebrows would look nice, even volunteered tae pluck
mine at the bus-stop. No way hose. What a time for an experiment.

'Here, let me see.'

Mum rearranges ma partin, instead of it bein at the side, makes a
fringe.

'It's not so bad like that. What did you do, Erin, to make such a mess
of your eyes?'

'Ah shaved them off. Ah was tryin tae get rid of the bit in the middle For the party.'

She stops a smile with her hand. Why isn't she goin off her head the way she normally does?

'Come in here to our room. Let's see if I can fix it.'

All the dances wi fanciable boys disappearin before ma disappearin eyebrows but the way she says 'we' like it's happenin tae her as well. One day she might tell me what it was like when she was a teenager. What boys did she fancy? In the story of her life, she's only got to tellin us about when she was wee an it was Christmas in Ireland, they got an orange for a present. Sally's mum's always tellin Sally stuff. Ma family seem to have a silence disease when it comes tae talkin about themselves. Except ma granny Scottish. Cannae get her tae shut-up. She's a nervous disposition. Like ma da.

 Inside their room, curtains still closed, clothes lyin about the bed and floor because she was nightshift at the hospital last night. She lifts her cushion padded make-up bag from the top of the sideboard next to the new white wardrobe, ma daddy assembled. It bulges out at the back cos of too much stuff an him losing one of the screws. One day it'll spew all their things into the room, his black suit for weddins and funerals, the nice white shirts for nights out and her fur coat, her dresses and shoes. Hope she cannae tell that ah had sneaked intae her room when she wasn't there, the way she can tell if ah've stolen a biscuit or told a lie; ah know the secret feel of her foundation tube, soft velvety stuff gathered inside the lid, black clotted mascara on a brush and the colour of blood lipstick that sometimes gets on ma mum's teeth, especially when she's had a drink an she looks lik she's been drinkin blood.

'Here it is.'

How come other girls can pluck their eyebrows, so they look neat an trim but ma first go ah make a pure mess ae it, make maself half baldy?

She takes out a wee black pencil.

'You sit on the bed.'

As she pulls back the curtains and ah sit on their double bed, dust particles dance in front of ma eyes like a thousand Strip the Willows. Take your partner. Here we go, with a diddley die and a diddley doe. Feel for the bone above the eye socket: light pressure, down intae ma eyebrow wi the pencil.

'Ah'm no goin. Stop, it's too sore.'

'Shhh. Give me a chance.'

Everybody will take the Mick.

'There, you'd never notice it. Never in a thousand years. Go on, look for yourself.'

Ma hair's stickin up cos of the way she's lifted it but when ah put it back to a fringe position, she's right. You wouldn't notice that the black lines were pencilled an no real eyebrow hair.

'Okay?'

It might work. It just might work.

'Thanks.'

Liftin a pair of tights from the floor, already tidying.

'Away ye go an get ready or ye'll be late.'

And no slap comes. No slap comes.

149

One two three. One, one. The St. Bernard's Waltz.

My boots wi the heels make me taller.

Where is he, him wi the sallow skin an a bit of a moustache? Sally says bum fluff.

One, two

There he is. Surely tae God he cannae fancy her? That Veronica Connelly drinks Bucky; hair's pure bleached blonde, ye can see the black roots fae here. And she's done it before. Sally told me. She said her da found a Johnny in the waste paper bin. And a boy won't respect her. No way. Ah'm definitely waitin. Definitely.

In out lady goes

'Do you want to birl for a laugh?' The boy from ma physics class says aye awright.

Under.

One, two, three kick the person in front. Back, two, three, kick. Out two three CLAP. Run for four. Back for four. A wee jiggly bit when we turn around.

At primary it was the Igloo Song:

I see you

I see you

Tra la la la lA

I see you

You see me

150

I take you

You take me

I see you, I see you

Tra la, la la, la

A baby game; we don't do that now.

One, two, three, turn

Back, two, three, turn

Birl, birl , birl, birl. Dizzy bein a girl. Want to swap but can't be the man. In the small gym hall with five a sides lines on the floor, queue in a queue. Someone gives me a paper plate, a sausage roll with pink meat, a little cake, and a can of coke. Wait for Ladies Choice then ah'll ask him. Cannae really say no as long as ah get there first. That's the whole point. At rehearsals, the teachers made us line up: girls in one line, boys in another; go doon the middle, takin the hand of the boy ye meet. Sometimes count if there's talent you like; maybe he's number seven and ah'm number nine. Get somebody to change then pray to God and his holy mother nobody jumps in front.

At the party get to pick our own partners. The brainy boys ask me to dance but wish they'd go away, so him wi the sallow skin can ask me. He's in the fourth section for maths but don't care. Ah'm in the top section. Still, ah'll wait tae Ladies Choice. Better chance then.

It's aw the lassies at one side an the boys at the other. The lassies are sittin against the wall an the boys standin wi hands in their pockets, tryin to look casual. The teacher shouts: 'Choose your partners, boys;' lik CHARGE in a cowboy an Indian film; across the floor they come runnin and the main thing is bein glad ah'm no left standin; don't really care who asks me but at least with a boy from the top section ye know ye'll have a laugh. Ye can be yourself.

'Drew wants out wi you. Kevin asked me to ask ye. Please say yes.' Sally fancies James, Drew's pal. If ah winch Drew, she can winch him. Sally's got shoulder length blonde hair and long, lanky legs. The last time ah kissed a boy was at primary top class. His mouth was wet an he kept putting his tongue in ma mouth, ah thought ah would choke.

'Tell him okay.' Drew's in ma chemistry class, even nicer than him wi the sallow skin who gets the Pather bus. Drew gets the Motherwell bus. It's like livin on different planets, the way we all get buses and never see each other till school the next day. He's got blonde hair, blue eyes an the clearest white skin, more like a girl's skin than a boy's. They're waitin at the school gates but none of them makes a move until Kevin gies Drew a shuv; shrugs his shoulders, walks over; grinnin; out of sight of the other two, he takes ma hand. Ma feet are killin me cos the shoes are too tight from all the dancing, an the walk to the bus stop. Ma mum takes me ta Clarks to get ma feet measured before she'll pay for shoes but this time she agreed ah could buy them maself an now ah think ah might have bunions cos the side of ma feet are sore an they swell all the time. Out of the blue, ah'm holdin another person's hand an it feels dead weird. Should ah squeeze it back or stroke it with ma fingers; instead keep still, kind of rest it, as if ma hand is limp an asleep.

At the bus stop there are other couples wi arms roon each other. His mouth tastes wet, stay like that for a long time, his head movin an mine movin a wee bit. Never tries to slip the mitt; kissin some more then the bus comes and on the bus holds ma hand the whole time. Only ma mum an ma wee sisters have ever held ma hand before but ah've held lots of hands tonight: sweaty ones, cold ones, dry ones, coarse ones. Drew's hand's warm. Mine is cold. Cold blood, warm heart.

'Kevin's havin a party next Saturday. His mum and dad are in Spain. Will ye come?'

That's the day ah start my job in the chippie.

Promise you won't tell right?

That he asked me.

'Ah'll see. Probably will.'

When he gets off the bus, stare out the window, thinkin words up for when ah ask mum if ah can go. She's dead crabbit sometimes, no letting us out after eight during the week cos ae school but ye can get round her if ye play it right; the thing is to work it out, have a plan. If ah help wi the housework for the week, startin, Monday then ask around about Thursday. Sally's goin. It'll be easier if ma mum knows her mam's letin her go, it's mare pressure tae let me go. The light in the livin room's still on. Is she keekin out the windae? Need to talk about the party, what we had to eat, who was there and did anyone say they liked ma dress. The Maths teacher said she liked it. Ma mum'll be dead chuffed. She picked it.

Please God make it happen. This once. Make her say yes.

'Tell me about the dancing?' she asks, lookin up from her letter to ma gran.

'Was there any Alley Cat or The Slosh?'

Writing with ma dad's blue bookie pen, that's half the size of a proper pen.

'No, it was mostly disco. Abba, stuff like that.'

'As long as ye enjoyed yourself. Ye look nice. Did anyone say your dress was nice.'

The moment she'd been waitin for.

'Ma Maths teacher said it was the nicest at the party.'

'There. What did I tell you. You should listen to your old mother.'

She disnae look old. Her dark hair, still in a bee-hive from the weekend. Even with her piny on, she looks pretty, prettier than any of the teachers there tonight.

'You were right. You were right, Mum how does the Alley Cat go again?'

She's at my side, takes ma hand. Two steps to the right, two to the left, two back, bring in a wiggle and swagger...

'Sunday morning up with a lark. Think ah'll take a walk in the park. Hey, hey, hey, it's a beautiful day. Hey hey hey. It's a beautiful day.'

'Remember, Sunday, we're takin the wee ones to their dancin class,' she says, clapping her hands under her legs.

How could ah forget.

***

On Friday at school, in chemistry catch Drew starin at me, sittin at the far right of the lab, arm leanin on the desk, head restin in his cupped hand or sometimes chin leanin on a curled fist. Hopeless tryin to ignore him, cos he starts gien it this kidon coughin sound, until ye look back at him. Sometimes, look up to the corner of the ceilin, slowly slowly down tae his desk and those blue eyes waitin lik water in a swimmin pool. Splash.

154

One of his hands pretends tae write; a big hand, much bigger than mine. Imagin holding ma small hand against his wide-fingered one; that makes me look at him again.

'The periodic number of carbon is....'

Think. Carbon lik a big lump ae coal. Black. So blue as if he had a dimmer switch that made the blue bluer.

Two ones are two

Two twos are four

Here, we do The Periodic Table

Two atoms equal a molecule.

The periodic table has lots of squares with letters and figures on them. Those are elements. The periodic number of carbon is........When ah look at him get a tickly feelin in ma stomach like ah'm going to be sick but in a nice way if that's possible. Are ma eyes watery, full of the same kind of light as Drew's?

Carbon Dioxide is CO_2. Drew's lazy in class. He never ever puts his hand up tae answer a question. When the teacher asks:

'Drew. What is the periodic number of Sulphur Dioxide?'

He gets it wrong, hangs his heid a wee bit as if he's sorry but as soon as the teacher looks away, smirks at Kevin. Kevin's the second best player in the school football team. Our Paul's the best. Drew doesn't care about school. Says he's already got an apprenticeship lined up in the steel works. He's a thin, gangly boy. Cannae see him getting up at five in the mornin to go an work in the sweltering heat.

Next time Drew gets a question wrong, has tae stand up like a man accused of somethin in court. Ah 've never had to stand up in Chemistry. Sometimes, Drew and Kevin call me a swot but ah don't care. Everythin's made of atoms. Atoms join thigither to become molecules. On the front page of ma chemistry book, there's diagrams of two atoms meetin at a point lik when the Americans sent satellites into space an you saw the two bits seperatin on News At Ten, but the opposite. Drew's got this fancy calculator, really wee and dinky but he still manages tae get his sums wrong. Calculators are aw the rage but the teacher says ye've always to show your workin in case ye press the wrong button, get it wrong.

When the teacher leaves the room, we all gab. Drew throws a ball of rolled up paper at me; it hits ma head. Look over but he's pretendin to talk to Kevin.

Talkin to Drew, lean ma head in ma hand; look into his eyes.

'Erin, are you listening? What is the periodic number of mercury? '

'Yes, miss.'

Kevin says 'Voulez vous couchez avec moi ce soir?'

'Vous' for someone you don't know well or someone older. 'Tu' for someone familiar. French is ma worst subject. Mary, the only other girl in the class translates. Thinks he's smart sayin that.

'Voulez vous piss off.'

The chemistry teacher glares at our part of the room.

***

She won't let me go to parties in other people's houses. Ah'm to young for that she says but out the blue she asks to meet Drew. Think it's cos of Vocations Sunday an me sayin ah was goin to be a nun, she's worried ah might go through wi it an that would be worse somehow.

'What for?' Drew says.

'Cos she wants tae meet ye.'

'What for?' Drew says.

'Cos she says she wants tae meet ye.'

He laughs, a big space between his white front teeth. 'No problemo.'(After he's eats a sweetie, the bits stick between his teeth. Dead cute.) Drew's got a brass neck. Dead sure ae himself, that's why ah like him. Okay, his blonde hair and blue eyes help as well. At the door ma daddy shakes his hand.

'Come in, son. Fitbaw's jist startin. Do ye watch it?'

'Celtic, every time.' Drew's grinin at the boys aw lined up on the couch, waitin for Sunday Scotsport.

'Hi Paul.' Paul nods, movin up to gie him a space.

'Started yet?'

'No yet. Just in time, big man.'

'It's bad manners to have the telly on when ye've a visitor. Excuse our manners, Drew. And where do your people come from?' Mum's lookin at Drew as if she's interviewin him for a job.

'North Motherwell.'

Ah can tell Drew's dyin tae look at the telly, too scared in case ma mum catches him.

Mum always talks about 'your people' cos 'her people' come fae Ireland. You're nobody if ye don't know who your people are, at least that's what she thinks.

Most of the time ah'm wishin it would be over without them sayin anythin to affront me a bit like a horror that yir only kidon watchin but really ye've got a cushion ready tae hide at the scary bits especially when Pinkie and Simit are about. Drew watches the football while we make the dinner. Stew and steak an tatties. Ah've tae run out tae the Tally man wi a bowl for the ice-cream. 'Eleven scoops please.' The ice cream man wears a half-overall lik a jacket as if he's workin in a café. Everybody calls them 'The Tallies' cos their people come from Italy but they don't have Italian accents lik Mario in the chipper.

After dinner, Drew goes to play football wi the boys an don't see him for the rest of the afternoon.

'Well, he doesn't have much to say for himself, does he? Is he a bit slow or something?'

Mum throws me a teatowel in her way that means ah'll wash the dishes, you dry.

'No. Just shy.'

'Oh well. Still, if ye like him.'

Ah can hear the Tally van's jingle from another street, 'La cuccharracha, la chuccharracha.' And ah know she likes Drew even though she disnae say. Cos she can see he's alright, from respectable people. Nice, lik ourselves. But she's okay ma mum, to let me invite Drew home lik that. She says well if ye're gonnae go wi him, me an your daddy my as well get a right good look at the cut of him. Well, they did that. The whole family did.

3

Up early on Saturday mornin to walk to the bus on ma own. Hundreds of dry rolls in a plastic bag outside the shop. Start tae separate them. Me, Mario and Maria in the kitchen at the back. She has a long black hair growin on her chin. Mesmerisin. The smell of chips on ma clothes all night after a day workin. Mario leering at me. Catch maself in the mirror, dark haired, pale lassie wi big eyes. Wonder if ah'm like ma mum, really? Don't tell her about Mario. She'd stop me workin here. But at the end of the day, the feelin of money in ma pocket, especially the tips that ah'm allowed to keep. He sees ma mum collectin me. He knows she'd tear him limb from limb if he tried anything. Ah'm glad to see her when she comes even though ah have tae give her ma wages. Get tae keep the tips.

'Go you butter the rolls, lassie.'

Phssshttt, phssshttt! When Mario throws raw chips into the fryer, you have tae stand back or the fat'll spit. Maybe burn you. The chips are white and hard. ZZZZZZZZ. Watch them fry when there's nae customers. Promise ye won't tell. Mario pinches ma bum. Ah jump and look at his wife Maria but she just looks into the chip fat. She's got a brown spot on her chin with a long black hair growin out. Look at her but she looks away or looks at her husband. Shakes her heid.

'Go you butter the rolls, lassie.'

When she says 'lassie,' disnae sound Scottish. Sounds Italian. Mario and Maria are Italian. Sometimes they say, 'hen' and that's funny too. If ah'm a hen, you're a duck.

ah lay eggs, and you lay muck.

Don't say that but think it in ma heid when ah'm butterin the rolls.

One, two, three scoops a portion.

Salt and vinegar?

Sauce? Brown or red?

There are jars, lik sweetie jars, but instead of boiled sweets, there are pickled eggs and onions. We've a little metal ladle to scoop them out. Think of catchin black tadpoles wi ma brother's net: white egg tadpoles and there's a jar ae gerkins as well. Gerkins are green slimy lookin things wi ridges at the sides lik a crocodile's skin; no one ever asks for one. Ah'd be too scared to fish it out if they did. Ah'd die. How long has that jar been there? And those boxes of chocolates, wi bunches of flowers on their lids; no- one buys chocolates either. Jist as well cos Maria says the boxes are empty. And imagine some man buyin chocolates for his wife and when she opens them, there's nothin there but trays of empty holes, aw different shapes where chocolates should be. And a pickle's nice wi a bag of chips but a gerkin. Cannae figure out how someone could like that; chopped green fingers, floating in murky vinegar.

Ma overall is pink. 'Pink to make the boys wink,' ma Auntie Maura says. Sings when she's helpin ma mum wi the dishes;

    'Be baw babity, babity, babity.

    Be baw, babity,

    Ah woudnae hae a lassie Oh.

    a lassie Oh, a lassie Oh.

    Ah woudnae hae a lassie Oh.

    Ah'd rather have a wee lauddie.'

Lauddie is laddie. Ma mum disnae like us talking slang. Say 'boy.' Say. It's not, 'gonnae gie me' but, 'please give me.' It's not 'aye' but 'yes.' Nobody else says 'yes,' except the teacher.

Maura's ma da's aunt. She's lik a granny. Comes tae our hoose every day tae help ma mam. She's ancient, mare than sixty-five.

Fold the paper over like foldin a baby's nappy. One bit fae the right, one fae the left, triangles meeting at top and bottom. And wrap again in the Daily Record or The Sunday Post. The paper's soggy from the heat of the chips.

Pssssshhhttt!

Steam from the frier soaks ma face. Steam opens pores. If the steam's greasy will ah get plukes?

Maria hardly talks; disnae speak much English. Mario has this look that makes me glad ma mum's comin tae collect me the night, and every other night. And he won't pinch me again. Bet he won't.

'No too much. Look lika this.'

Maria says ah put too much margarine on the rolls.

'ScrAEEEEEP only. Okay?' Unscrapin marg fae one ae the rolls then butters three more dry rolls wi the marg on the knife.

Don't care aboot Mario pinchin me, an Maria an the marg, an people gettin annoyed when ah mix their orders up cos ah'll get two pounds pay and the rest in tips: half the jar. An maybe the night mum'll change her mind and let me go tae the party. If ah get home at seven, could get there for eight.

Two fish suppers

One pie and beans

One puddin supper

Four rounds of bread

Three teas

One coke.

At the counter forget an need tae go tae the table again.

'Would you like to see the menu?' a man, Lizabeth says works at the fair, laughs.

'Some menu. Very posh!'

Lizabeth's married and has weans and works afternoons an nights.

'Tell him sarcasm's the lowest form of wit,' she says. Write the meals on the back of the cardboard out a pair ae tights, to stop me forgettin. People ask ye the prices aw the time, even though they're in yellow letters on a big board on the wall, opposite the sweetie counter.

This mornin. Morning. Ma tights had a ladder an ah went tae the shop next door tae buy new ones. Pearl grey.

'I'll climb the ladder,' Mario said, grinnin.

'When are you comin tae see us at the shows?' One of the men from the fair crowd is leanin over the counter, talkin to me and Lizabeth. What a red neck. What a beamer. Ma face's burnin. He's lookin right at me.

'You've got come to bed eyes.'

Ah never did anythin and that's what he says. An all ah did was look at him.

Lizabeth laughs.

'Leave the wee lassie alane you, ya big pest.'

Talk to him Lizabeth. Please. So ma face can cool doon.

Hot fat in the fryer an those words, everythin sizzlin in ma head, the sounds and the heat. When ah go to the table wi their order, ma stomach's heavin like ah'm on the walzers or the big wheel; he's the big wheel and ah'm goin round and round. Sick in a nice way and want tae get off but when it stops ah want to go round again.

When he goes away, leaves a big tip. Twice the normal tip. Look at ma face in the aluminium side of the frier, tryin to see into ma eyes, tryin tae see what he meant but the fryer is misted lik hot breath on a bus window. Draw a circle wi ma finger. Cold and hot. Hot lik ma face. Him and the other people fae the fair aw laugh loudly as they walk out the door. Looks back and smiles, an ma face goes red again. Now he's laughin. These chips take ages. Gie them a shake lik Mario does. Never been at the shows when it's dark, maybe ah'll go the morra night. Go on the walzers.

The till has numbers and signs on big round keys like on a typewriter. And the tops of the keys are twice as big as ma fingers an when ah hit one, sometimes miss an the finger goes between them and it's sore. But don't say anythin cos ah want tae learn tae use the till an don't want them to laugh at me and say she's jist a wee lassie that cannae work a till. When ye get a five pound note, ye need tae shout somebody lik Lizabeth or Maria to come and watch ye count out the change, in case ye get it wrong. There are trays for every kind of money, small ones at the front for coins an long ones for notes like beds, an aw the money sleeps in the dark when Mario shuts the drawer.

***

163

Sunday afternoon comes an it's Simple Reel, Slip Jig, Lannigan's Ball; St Patrick's statue just newly painted, watchin the whole display, probably wonderin if this has anything to do wi him bringin Christianity to Ireland.

'Shoulders back. Arms in. And one -two -three, one-two -three. Erin McLaughlin don't slouch. Listen to the music. Sally Connor, stop leaping. You're dancin not runnin a marathon. Would the mothers please stay seated while the dancin's going on and would they please keep the children not dancing off the dance floor. Thank- you.'

The Irish dancin teacher, Mrs. Reilly, in her tan tights, has a voice that quietens the hall except for a wee boy runnin up and down. Stares at him till he stops. On the dance floor, the rest of us avoid her eyes in case we get a row. One day we'll drive her voice up that high that nothin will come out or only a sound that cats can hear.

'Beginners. Stay on the floor.'

She'll scrutinise our every move. Ah'm a Beginner, have to dance the lead round wi all the other Beginners. Ah've been a Beginner for a long time now. Our Anna's an Intermediate an she's younger than me. Dance a step at a time, everybody watches. Weird bein the only one on the floor cos in our family there's always at least three people beside ye so ye're no used to space, aw eyes on your legs. One day ah'll burst intae a run, run around the hall in circles tae the music. That would be better fun. Only the Champions dance a dance right to the end; a girl wi long black hair, big high kicks and a blonde girl that birls on her toes lik a ballet dancer. They go everywhere together. Ah'd love to see

164

them trippin up, just once. Ah'd love tae see them getting wound up in their own skinny high kickin legs.

'How come ye can't keep your shoulders back like those girls, Erin?'

Because they were born with pokers up their bums.

'Cos ah hate it.'

'How can ye hate it?'

'Ah just do.'

'Sure, it's lovely. Isn't it lovely, Anna?'

'Mrs. Reilly says ah'll win a medal at the competition. Mrs. Reilly says ma jump two threes are excellent.'

She's ma mum's pet at the dancin cos she likes it.

'There now, Erin. Why can't you enjoy the dancin the way Anna does? And you Irish as well.'

'Half- Irish. Anyway, ah'm Scottish.'

'It should be in your blood.'

There's that many things in ma blood, it's a wonder ah can take the weight.

'Why?'

'Your grandfather was a great step dancer. I thought ye'd take after him.'

One, two, three.

St. Patrick climbs down off the wall, takes me by the arm. We do a mad jig. He's waving the stick in the air.

'Ye know your trouble, Erin? Ye let your mind wander too much. Head Always in the Clouds. If ye concentrated ye'd learn the steps no bother.'

Ma mum disnae actually say 'ye're clumsy.'

165

'Look, girls. Watch me.' Mrs. Reilly does a lead round, her short legs seem to gain length as soon as she starts dancin. Suzanne, our Anna's pal's turn: long lanky legs takin her half way round the hall.

'Not this. Smaller steps, girl. Smaller steps.'

Does an impression of someone flappin their hands like the wings of a big crow. The champion wi the black hair whispers tae her pal:

'Skinny malinky long legs. Big banana feet. Went tae the pictures an couldnae find a seat. When the picture started skinny malinky farted. Skinny malinky long legs, big banana feet.'

Draw them a dirty look. It's one thing me thinkin it but another thing sayin it out loud.

'For the last time would the mothers please keep the younger children at their sides while the dancers are on the floor. Please. Thank-you.'

It's no fun havin to think all the time about your arms and shoulders.

It's no fun bein watched an gettin a row for no doin it right.

'Get our Lizzie and Annemarie. They're runnin about the hall like a couple of toe-rags.' See, even ma mum's scared of Mrs. Reilly.

Shut ma eyes; think about ma Irish grand-dad step dancin on a stone floor. Out the windae of his house, a cow and calf are runin down the field. Gien it laldie, nobody cares about his shoulders. And say into ma head Head in the Clouds, Head in the Clouds, the batter of feet stampin down on the floor, me an St. Patrick an ma gran-da havin a great time.

'Do you see your mammy, on the bike? She's goin round the aisle. Look…'

Sally's blue eyes are shining. She is at the top step and ah'm still inside the house.

'Naw.'

Lie cos actually me an our Anna have been watching her from behind the curtains since she took the new bike off me.

'C'mon, ye cannae miss it.'

'Aye, ah can.'

Pull the door closed behind me; walk down the five steps, going towards the gate.

'So, is it her bike, then?'

'No, stupid. It's mine.'

'Didnae know you had one.'

'Just got it.'

Three speed gears and a saddle- bag. Two girls' bikes advertised in the Wishy Press. Anna's is blue. We went to the seller's house with her, to collect them. Tried to hide our disappointment when we saw the bikes weren't Choppers. Mine's is The Pink Witch. Don't get many bikes called after your favourite colour but.

A bus pulls up at the bus stop outside our gate. People are lookin out the window at the woman going around the tarmac circle on the road on a pink girl's bike. Not many people round here have seen a grown woman on a bike even although it is nineteen seventy-eight but mum's always remindin us she used to go over a mountain on a bike to get to a dance.

Earlier the day we were wheeling them on the pavement towards home, after collectin them for the first time.

'Now, don't tell your dad how much they cost. Do you hear me?'

Mum was workin at nights so we could have bikes.

'I'll tell him myself when he's in a good mood,' she said.

Inside our gate, she'd taken the bike from me.

'Here, let me try this…'

Never even asked.

Then she'd stood up on the pedals, the whole weight of her.

'No, everyone'll see you…'

But she was already flying away from us, waving.

Me and Anna ran into the house and hid behind the curtains till Sally came to the door.

Now, we are at the gate, our Anna's still refusing to come out, watching it all from the safety of the window.

Mum sails past in cream flared trousers, her bum squashed into the seat, too big for it.

The second time around the aisle, she's puffing.

'She'll never make it,' Sally says.

'She won't give up,' ah say.

'No, her.'

She stands on the pedals again goin up the incline where even the buses struggle.

'Ah've never seen an adult on a bike before,' Sally says in admiration.

'Lucky you,' ah reply

She makes it up the brae. On the way down, stretches two legs out at the sides of the bike, free wheeling. We hear:

'Whhhheeeeeeeeeeeeee…'

Sometimes, ah want a normal mum that wears dowdy clothes an does housework and disnae go on bikes, other times it's great cos she's no lik anyone else, not anyone else's mum. Ma pals say they wish she was their mum cos she's got lovely clothes an looks nice but ah wish she'd stop havin weans. We keep havin tae move house when we're only just settled cos the house is too wee. But ah get to take them in their prams for walks, that's good an they're funny when they start walkin an talkin, an a whole new person starts to come alive in the house.

THREE

1

After her mum showed them how to make perfume wi flowers an water, Anna decided if she was going to work for Chanel then she'd need to get experience working in a shop sellin scent, first. A big shop in the town with a perfume counter. She could have strips of cardboard with special offer perfume sprayed, so she could put them under peoples' noses. She was only nine at the time of the roses recipe but at fourteen she still felt the same. When Erin got their mum's ring, the only thing Anna asked for was her half- full bottle of Coty L'Aimant. She couldn't wear it cos that would use it up but she liked to smell the scent in the mornings before she went to school or at night before Erin came into the room. It was inside a pink box and the bottle had the word 'Paris,' written on the front.

'What ye doin wi your nose in that bottle?' Erin said when she caught her.

'It looks lik weak tea.'

'No it disnae. Mind your own business.'

For her birthday the year before, their mum gave her money to buy a bottle of fragrance oil from the chemists and eau de toilette to dilute it with. She had to hide that from Erin as well cos she used it when she was goin to see Drew.

'It means 'toilet water,' Paul said when he was talkin.

'Why don't ye just put your hand down the toilet? Save everybody money.'

'It's flower water, eijit features.'

'Away an look at a crow.' That helped shut him up.

While Erin an her mum baked cakes in the kitchen together, upstairs, Anna mixed the oil with water, adding vanilla and cinnamon for the cakes, an cloves that they had in case of a tooth ache durin the night. It made the smell spicy. She daubed some on her wrists and behind her ears to see if anyone would notice.

'You smell of apple cakes,' Erin said.

'You smell nice,' their mum had said.

She looked up the word: 'L'Aimant,' when she was in second year French.

It meant 'loving her,' or 'the magnet.'

If she ever invented a scent, she would have to think of a name. Erin could help with that.

Lately, she didn't have the heart for messin about with daft bottles, there was too much to do in the house. Anyway, she wanted to go for a strawberry an vanilla flavour but their dad didnae ever buy strawberries, only bananas an whoever heard of a perfume that smelt lik them.

The roses kept coming in the summer, the same time of year. One day she hoped their dad or one of the neighbours would cut the rose bush away so she didn't have to ever see those roses again or listen to Erin askin:

'Do you remember that time we made perfume from the roses?'

'Nope,' she lied.

They talked less and less, her an Erin. Two girls at fourteen and fifteen, ye'd think they would have a lot to say but all Erin was interested in now was what their mum said and did and stuff about

172

getting Paul back as if that would happen. Anna was glad she had her pals at school, at least with them, she could forget the madness. One day six months after their mum died, the Coty started to smell fousty, lik somethin her granny would wear, not their mum. She buried the bottle at the very back of the MFI unit, underneath a pile of clothes that she would tidy up later. She would leave there for a while and in a few months, see what happened, if the perfume evaporated, just disappeared.

2

Pull the T-shirt with a picture of a black cat over my knees, makin two boobs. Ma mum gies me a dirty look when ah do that. She's no here. Make them booby even more. Donna sits on the bed, still in the tartan mini-skirt. She's kicked off the heavy black docks, tights are ripped at the toes.

Starts to pull the nylon back over the open toes

'Donna, do you know where Glasgow Royal is?'

Looks up from puttin the red nail varnish she stole from the bin bag.

'What?'

'You know where the infirmary is?'

'You're not up the spout are you?'

Ignore it.

'Could you show me the morra?'

Shakes her heid.

'What makes you mention that all of a sudden?'

'That's where ma gran was, when she passed away.'

'Well, she's not there, now, pal.'

Ah think it might help me.

See, what did I tell you.

Maybe, a nurse or a doctor that looked after her. They might talk about what happened. Remember her: the woman with all the children. That might help take the sick feelin in ma stomach away.

'Sorry but. You think they'll remember your gran in a big hospital. Honest to God. No chance. Anyway, they don't just let people,

174

especially young lassies, who, by the way, have absconded from home. Don't just let lassies walk into hospitals wi nobody to visit.'

'Could talk to a nurse. They might remember.'

'And start talkin to nurses about their gran an getting meetings with doctors.'

Ah'm beginin to think old lechy features at the station couldnae have been much worse than this. But ah'm here, anyway.

'Ah want to go.'

'Why? It's a big depressin, old buildin.'

'Want to see the place, that's all.'

Donna goes back to her nails and that seems to be the end of the conversation.

'Donna, will you?'

'And what about your bus?'

'That's in the afternoon. Could go first thing in the mornin.'

'Ah'm no jokin, can't just turn up at these places without an appointment. They'll throw you right back out. An they might phone social work or the polis.'

Maybe, she's right.

'Ah don't want anythin, only tae see the place. Maybe it's no there; maybe, they've knocked it down.'

'Knocked down Glasgow Royal? You're off your head. It's there.'

Now that ah'm in Glasgow ah may as well go. Might never get the chance again.

'Okay, but only if you promise we go to my old street after. Ah'd like to see if any of ma pals are there. Be time if we leave early enough, show you ma house.'

Maybe, ah'll get to meet her mum after all.

'Brilliant.'

Getting darker outside. Would be great if we were gettin ready for a night out wi Drew an ma pals from school now. The feel of new clothes, a wee bit of rouge and lipstick. Could introduce Donna as ma new pal from the city. We'd have a laugh. Ah'd wear those brown trousers ah bought wi ma chippie money.

Lyin in bed, feels itchy. Imagine the feel of fleas crawlin over me. In the mornin ah'll check for red bumps on ma skin. When ah look at the bed covers, think ah see a line of black things. Actually movin. Later, Donna thinks ah'm mad when ah run the whole way back from the bathroom, full of imaginary coachroaches, aw scurrying into cracks in the tiles. Next time ah go in there ah'm takin ma shoes off so ah can whallop them wi ma heels.

Under the covers, try to memorise the part of a poem:

> '*Oh! Yet a little while*
> *May I behold in thee what I was once*
> *My dear, dear Sister! And this prayer I make,...*'

When the poet is talkin to his sister, makes me think of our Annemarie, Lizzie an Elaine an that makes it too hard.

'Whit you up to? Donna shouts.

'Learnin ma poem.'

'Weirdo.'

Donna thinks ah'm mad to read ma Wordsworth book but readin takes ma mind off the noises, doors slamin, folk shoutin, the way it takes away the boredom of bein stuck when its rainin outside, or none of ma

176

pals are around. The book says Wordsworth tried to write about ordinary people lik a lassie he met when he was in Scotland: *To a Highland Girl*. It disnae sound lik a big deal but the book says it was a big deal then, when he was alive. Ah might make that ma interestin fact to tell ma class when this is all over, when ah go home an do ma talk to the class.

On our walk to the hospital, sky blue wi white school holiday clouds.
'Thoughts of more deep seclusion; and connect
The landscape with the quiet of the sky...'
The sky is quiet though the city is busy.

It could rain, don't take the good weather for granted. Even from here the sandstone looks black wi traffic fumes. Donna disnae notice, moanin about the walk up the hill but her long legs should take two steps for every one of mine. Still, she struggles. That racking cough, the fags have got to her. She stops twice to pick up fag doubts, examines them to see if there's any smokin left. Switch off; learned switchin off when mum was sick cos people are always talkin at you about how sorry they are an you have to look as if you're listenin, noddin your head, makin wee noises every now an then, while all the time, no really takin the words right in, for their meaning. That way it doesn't affect you as much. You've got enough wi your own sad thoughts. And it disnae get to you the same way. You've always got to be on guard. It can creep up on ye suddenly, turn ye from bein normal an happy tae starin intae space, forgetin what you're supposed to do next. It's like ma brain's made of water and other people's talk is a stone skiffin the surface, makes a ripple but then underneath everythin is still.

Up High Street, a long winding road, towards the hospital. Along the way, a pub that has a sign above the door that says 'Established in 1515. An old staging post.'

Maybe, Wordsworth came here when he was in Glasgow. The front door is locked but a side door opens to an alley.

'Wait a minute, Donna.'

'Where you off to?

Chews a nail, spits it out.

'Remember that book ah told you about?'

'No.'

'Well, ah think the poet guy might have been here.'

'Bit of an alkie, then?'

Leave her while ah go down the alley, through the open door. Inside, it's dark. A woman with curly hair and big earings is behind the bar at the far end of the room; there are two people sitting on stools at the bar.

They all look at me, don't speak.

This could be one of my useful facts for my introduction.

From the doorway, shout across to the bar:

'Have you ever heard of William Wordsworth?'

'Sorry, hen, he disnae drink here,' the curly headed woman shouts back.

Ah think ah can imagin him with his sister, Dorothy, sittin at one of the wooden tables.

'William Wordsworth, the poet. Cos this is the oldest pub in Glasgow, thought he might have been here.'

'Sorry, cannae help you. Try the Sarry Heid.'

Ah never came here to find Wordsworth, ah came to look for Paul.

'It's the oldest hotel in Glasgow. Listen, hen, we're actually no open.'

Have a quick look around the wall to check there's no a plaque cos she might no even know about it even if there was one; she might be somebody that disnae think it's that important that a famous poet was here. Nothin.

'Where is it?'

'Near The Barras.'

Donna has disappeared. At least don't have to put up with her moanin. Now ah'm away from home, maybe ah'll write a poem when ah'm older but instead of *Tintern Abbey* or that, it'll be the Craig ah'll be commin back to. It'll be the older me thinkin about the younger me and how everythin has changed, how ah loved the way the sky was pink at night but not the stink when the steel works farted.

Farther up the road, lots of shops that have closed down. Fumes from traffic. That's what ah remember, no bein able to breathe.

Ah don't like not tellin the truth, commin right out wi it. Ah will tell Donna when the time's right. But if ah don't do this now ah might never do it. And even if they don't let me past the front desk, at least ah've got to try. She was a nurse and they always look after their own don't they? That's what dad told us, anyway.

At the top of High Street, Donna is standin glaring in my direction.

'Look, Donna, you don't need to come any further. Ah can do this myself, now. Tell me where your street is and ah'll meet you there.'

The brown eyes flash back at me and ah half expect her to turn and walk down the hill. Half-hopin she will instead ae gien me aw the hassle.

'Ah've never known a lassie that close to her gran, she's checkin out the hospitals. Better places than here ah could show you.'

'Ah have a plan,' ah'd like to say but don't. And who asked her anyway?

Funny, how the nearer we get to the hospital, the more ah see it all from the back seat of ma dad's blue Cortina. His car turns from the busy road, towards the car park. What will we say? How will we look? How can ah play a game of bein happy and out loud, ma dad wonderin if he'll get a bloody parking place this time. The big hospital building, higher than other surrounding buildings. Butterflies in ma stomach lik when ye go over a bump in the road

Up close, ye have to lean back to see the top floors. Windows become smaller the higher up you go. And the outline of a statue, David Livingstone.

'What did Baxter say?' We knew the answer by heart.

'Doctor Livingstone, I presume.'

The gloom makes the sky seem grey like the blue is disappearin, more clouds but ah'm no sure if they're in ma head. Hundreds of wee windaes, lookin down into the street below. That was always the last thought that she'd be there, at one of those windows watchin us walk to the car when visitin was over. She could see us reversin out the space but we couldnae see her.

'I'll watch you from the window. Mind wave.'

180

Rapunzel in the fairy tale though her hair is short and grey after the chemo and we cannae make a ladder from pigtails to help her escape. If only it was that easy. And we couldnae wave cos we couldnae see her.

'Ah'm knackered,' Donna says.

'See that wee wall, ah'll have a seat an ah'll get you in that big mad church place when you're done.'

Donna's given up, walkin. The brick wall looks onto the road. At the other side, there's a tree wi white flowers, the brightest wee tree ah've ever seen. If it was me ah'd face the tree but Donna turns the other way lookin onto the traffic. She dangles her long legs, smokin her fag down to the brown bit.

She points in the direction of another building, older and grander lookin, set on out on its own. When ah look back, she's stretchin like a lazy cat after its afternoon nap. Settles down to a smoke and a sunbathe. She'll never have high blood pressure will Donna, the way she takes her time, the way she savours everything, even waitin in a busy city road. But don't clap her. Scratch you in a minute, claws from no-where. Ah'm learnin that. From the front of the hospital can't see the tree; maybe, she got out for a walk and saw it then.

Straighten your shoulders, Erin. Don't slouch.

Ah didnae know ah was.

Stick your chest out a bit, that'll help.

Okay, ah'll try.

It wasn't unusual for Erin to stay at Drew's but she'd never been away for more than a night before. Anna at first didnae think it was strange. She'd been awake but pretended to sleep the mornin Erin took Paul's bag out the wardrobe, stuffin in clothes, tryin not to make a noise. It was only when she went to curl her eyelashes that she saw that that the curler was missin. She checked the wardrobe for the bottle of perfume. Still there. At least she hadn't taken that as well. She meant to phone her to tell her to make sure an not lose the curler at Drew's. Anna didn't have Drew's number but she knew where he lived an decided to look the number up in the phone book. She stretched out in the bed. Great havin space for once.

'Keek a bossies an tallywallywossies…'

A voice at the door, her dad's.

She pulled the covers over her head.

'C'mon girls, rise an shine.'

'Erin's away,' she shouted back.

Pause.

'That's right so she is. Well. You get up, Anna. Let's get the show on the road.'

She liked when Erin went away. She got to be the eldest, his second in command. She jumped out of bed. Above the bed, a poster of The Police. They looked so good, especially Sting.

She went with their dad in the car to get the shoppin for the week. He let her put in all the foods she liked: baked beans an fish fingers, square sliced sausages an tins of creamed rice. After goin the messages, Anna walked about the streets all afternoon an then went to her pal's house for tea. That night they had their weekly treat of sweets from the shop, although there was no money for a comic each now. Still, the telly was good an the house was warm wi all of them in the livin-room. She forgot all about phonin Erin an the eyelash curlers until the followin day. It was the start of the afternoon when she finally sat down wi the phone book, looking up Drew's second name. She knew the area he lived so it was easy enough to narrow it down to a small number of possibilities. She couldn't phone when her dad was in cos he'd say it was a waste of money so she waited till he went out for his walk for his nerves. He'd put a lock of the phone, mainly cos Erin an Drew were always on the phone an he said it was costin him a bomb. Her pal at school had showed her how to tap out the numbers so you could still get through even wi the lock on. She got Drew on tryin the third number. Now she could hear his voice, she felt a bit daft. They'd only ever spoken lik this when he phoned their house an she answered an he asked was Erin in.

'Drew, is our Erin there?'

She'd quickly tell her she knew she had the eyelash curlers an that she needed them an to make sure she brought them back. End of…Erin would need to be nice on the phone cos the phone was probably sittin on a wee table in Drew's mum's house, his mum in a chair beside it.

'She's no here. She's away at your gran's in Ireland.'

She listened for giggles in the background, waited for Drew to crack.

'Look, ah need to speak to her. Ah can hear her.'

'No you can't. Ah'm tellin ye, she's not here. Is this some kind of joke? She phoned me from the train station yesterday on the way to the boat. She said you were goin as well. Look ah don't have time for daft wee lassies.'

Anna thought for a minute. If Erin wasn't with Drew then where was she? He sounded seriously pissed off wi her.

'Anna. You still there?'

She could see her dad's blue Ford Cortina pulling up at the gate.

'Aye, ah'm here.'

'So, what's this about? Is she at your gran's? What you on about?'

'April Fool,' she shouted and then she put the phone down just as her dad was walking up the stairs to the front door.

4

Paul thinks about how weird it is when ye don't speak; the way every sound seems to get louder, even the sounds inside your body, lik your own breathin. Ye seem to be listenin all the time. Then he tries to imagine what he must look like to others, a blank face always starin back at them. Everyone still talks at him even when he makes it clear, he isn't ever goin to answer. He can't explain it. Why he stopped talkin, it was like it was the end of somethin when their mum died an if he started talkin, that would start life up again, an that would be an insult to her. And she'd wanted him there at the hospital when she died, so it must be up to him, there had to be somethin he could do for her. Adults were always wanted him to be quiet, teachers at school, his mum an dad sometimes, when they were talkin or watchin the news on telly or talkin to other adults. So, he was only doin what they wanted him to do.

'Children should be seen and not heard,' their granny said.

Maybe, if he wasn't heard, he wouldn't be seen an then he could disappear too. Cos if she could disappear then so could he.

It's quiet livin wi his Aunt Mary an Uncle Jim. Oban is so different from their home, wi a shore where people constantly walk backwards an forwards, feedin big, noisy swans, a place tourists came to so they could get away from their own homes. It's a place people drive to then stand and look at views and take smiley photos of each other. He likes it there cos no one is in his face all the time askin him how he is or why he isn't talkin or why he's stopped playin football for the school team and when will he be goin back home. At the start, when he wasn't speakin, he could see they were worried about him but he knew he was okay cos he still had a voice in his head, that must have been his thoughts. Bein around his mum's sister helped him, made him feel close to his mum. At the time, he'd panicked when the funeral came an he realised all the family were goin back to Ireland; he couldn't stop himself throwin the big metal cross down, runnin away. Someone suggested he could stay there. He would go anywhere. He didn't care. He was the boy who chucked Jesus down the stairs so there was no hope for him.

That was six months ago. Now, he's started a new school, made pals wi a couple of boys in the same street. He isn't playin football, yet, not proper, only a wee kick-about himself, but maybe, soon, he could. They don't play football in the street up here the way they do at home wi everyone's jumpers for the goalposts an havin to lift the ball every time a bus comes; they don't need to. They play in big, open spaces, big as fields. He'd like to run about in all that space soon but not yet.

At first, Paul liked to be on his own more, to sit in the room he had to himself for the first time ever. He enjoyed havin every day of the week to the telly himself. He was Monday right through to Sunday, if he liked, not only Saturday. But lately, he'd wonder about Pinkie an Simmit's scribblin the football scores on their bedroom wall, if they still kept the league on the wall up to date or if their dad had put a stop to it. An if his posters of favourite players were still up or if the other two had different ones now; an he missed the noise of all of the family

186

watchin the telly at night, the place lik a cup of tea filled to the brim. And he missed their dad takin him to the games at the weekend, when Paul would be playin an he would be on the touchline wi the other dads.

'Ye played great, son,' he'd say, dead proud.

Then they'd go home in the cold, knowin the house would be warm an the dinner cookin. Not now.

Mary and Jim said in whispers that he was depressed but whoever heard of a depressed twelve year old boy? He just couldn't face goin back to the house bein empty of their mum, not yet. Only six months ago, so that wasn't a lot of time.

He saw his Uncle Jim's binoculars after his first month of not talkin. Jim noticed him lookin at them:

'Take them out of the case, son. Have a look out.'

'Och, Jim. Leave Paul alone. He's no interested in daft spyglasses,' Mary said. She was busy getting their dinner ready for Sunday afternoon, settin the table wi three places. It made it awkward at first when he wasn't talkin but they kept the telly on an let his chair face it when the football was on.

He lifted the binoculars from the windowsill. They were heavier than his had been, in a brown, leather lookin satchel. He didn't need to speak cos Jim was smilin at him, noddin his head.

Paul took them out to the front of the house, where the view of the sea was. When he looked through the glass, the scene was murky; lik the time he tried his dad's readin glasses on an couldnae see a thing. He worked out how to adjust the lens by turnin the front circle to clear the lens. It worked. He could see shore and hills in the distance, and up close, the heads of Jim's flowers were gigantic. He focused in on a bee. Bzzzzzzzzzzzzzzzzz. If Erin was here, or Anna, they'd jumpin about frightened they'd get stung. That made him laugh, the thought of the bee and their dance of fear.

The tree at the side of the house was full of leaves and cream coloured flowers like Dogs' Porridge, would be a great spot for birds when the weather was good.

'Paul, dinner's ready,' Mary's voice from the kitchen. As he went into the house again, the smell of roast almost him burst into a song. He didn't though, it wasn't that easy. It couldn't be that easy.

***

They're big brutes: Uncle Jim's binoculars, and heavy. Paul lifts them out from the brown case, goes and stands at the bay window at the front of the house.

Sometimes, birds don't stop long enough for him to look at them and are only shadows across the trees. Other times, when one takes a rest, he can focus in on it, the body becoming bigger and clearer to him like the a big crow carrying a clump of grass across the garden. There are certain times of the day, better than others; first thing in the morning when Jim and Mary are still sleeping; he can open the back door, sit on their wooden bench and listen to the birds chatting away until he goes back inside to open the cupboards in the kitchen to a choice of cereal. Early evenings are good too, the blackbirds going crazy, singing at the tops of their voices. When a bird senses him, it almost always fly off, so he tries to be still, even although he is behind a window. Could be anything being watched feels not right. At least, here, he doesn't feel everyone is always lookin at him, all the neighbours and teachers even his own friends. The gardens are more spaced out here, with hedges that hide the next door neighbours; at home, the houses are all crowded together: nowhere to hide.

This mornin, Uncle Jim finds him gazing at a magpie with turquoise tinged wings, in the bare tree out the front. The movement of Jim makes the bird fly away, flying right past the window. A racket of *marracha marracha.*

'It's a beauty, that one,' Jim says.

He's a few years younger than their dad; maybe not havin weans makes people look younger, Paul thinks; though Jim has hardly any hair, unlike their dad. He's never heard Jim shoutin, ever. He wonders if he gets mad about anythin, can't imagine it. Him an Mary talk quietly, their lives are so quiet compared to their lives at home: telly on in the background an all the voices talkin over each other, their da, the loudest voice of them all.

'My favourites are the robins in winter. They're so cheeky, the way they come right up to ye. Have ye ever seen that, Paul?'

Paul smiles. He has.

He feels more and more like talkin as the days go on. People are leavin him alone here an Paul likes that.

'Would you like to come a walk with me later an ah'll show a heron down by the shore?'

Paul isn't sure if Jim is havin him on that he likes to watch birds. Never heard him say it when he was at their house but right enough all his dad and Jim ever talked about was football when they were together.

Paul nods his head.

Later, when they finish havin breakfast they go down the front. All kinds of seabirds are already their havin their own bird breakfasts of bread that people have thrown down over the grey wall for them. Sometimes, he sees tourists snapping photographs with big cameras but the place is deserted this time of the morning. A few small boats bob up an down on the water, tied to buoys with frayed lookin rope. Two oystercatchers are screeching at the tops of their voices, their orange beaks pointing towards the seaweed covering the ground. When Paul and Jim start to walk away, the mayhem dies down.

'Must be nesting,' Jim whispers as if the birds can hear.

They can see the big round buildin that looks lik a picture of the coliseum, on a hill above the town. Must be great views from up there. He'd like to go up there one day.

'That's McCaig's Folly. C'mon. We'll need to walk out the road a bit to see ma pal,' Jim is smilin.

He doesn't want to complain that glasses are heavy cos Jim has given them to him in case the heron pops up unexpectedly. The road has pavement until the edge of the town and then they have to walk at the side of the road for a while. After that, there's a field leading down to the water's edge. They walk in single file, one if front of the other, on the grass. When they get to a bend in the road, traffic in both directions becomes lighter. Paul can see the heron ahead, even without looking

190

through the binoculars. Near a big boulder, not moving. Paul lifts the glasses to his eyes.

He has never seen a living thing be so still. To be able to not move for so long, that would be something. Its body is hunched up an ye've no idea really what its wings would look like spread out.

'What do ye think then?' Jim says in a low voice.

'Mazing,' Paul says.

Neither of them says anythin else even about this bein his first word for a long time.

After a while of looking, Jim nods to him that they should walk back. It would be easy to disturb the bird, make it fly away but they don't. Let it concentrate on the fish it's watchin beneath the water. It can fly in its own time.

***

After the day they saw the heron, Paul feels he could start to talk again, but it doesn't just happen. It's good they let him be quiet all he wants, that makes it easier. He feels he is decidin things for himself, when he will talk and what he will say. He notices stuff. Him an Jim watch football on the telly but he starts to miss that it isn't his dad. Doesn't tell Jim.

One day, a couple of weeks later, there is a box on his single bed with his name written in blue biro on the wrapping. It isn't his birthday or anythin but he opens the box, anyway. Inside, is a small set of binoculars. It says on the box, they are fully coated with ten times magnification. These are much smaller than Jim's, made of aluminium to make them lighter. Hardly any weight at all. Perfect for bein out an about.

When he comes downstairs to thank them, Uncle Jim is readin the paper and Aunt Mary doin dishes.

'Well, do ye like them? she asks.

'Aye, ta. They're bang on.'

She puts her hand to her chest as if she's got a pain.

'Och, son. It's great to hear your voice, again.'

He nods. He's not talkin full-time.

'Go an thank, Jim, son. Was his idea,' she whispers.

'He can hear ye,' Jim shouts from his chair in the corner of the room.

'Disnae need to thank me. Jist means he's got his own an won't be pinchin mine now.'

Paul takes the glasses outside, settles down to watch some sea birds that can't decide if they're landin in Oban or headin back to the cities and bigger towns for richer pickins. He wonders if the fact he has spoken at all, means he is sort of cured now and will they send him home, soon. He's not ready, doesn't know if he'll ever be ready to face all that. It's nice bein the only one. Too much to think about. He goes back to watchin the birds circlin the garden.

5

On the road outside the hospital, heavy traffic bedlam from slip roads coming off and going towards the M8. Three women wearin scruffy dressing gowns over their nightclothes sit on a low, mossy wall, smokin and drinking tea out of paper cups. It's a relief to get inside.

At the reception desk a woman is working in front of a computer. She's looking up from the key board to a man who is leaning over the desk and the way she looks to me then to him and him to me and him to her and both back to me, it's like all the looks are connected and one could never happen without the other. He's got the uniform of a security guard, a uniform ah don't remember from when we visited before. A new plaque at the door but could have been there. Ah wonder what else did ah score out. Maybe, it means every time you come back and look, it will be different cos you can't hold onto anythin.

When ah come through the revolving door, the man starts walkin towards me then the door spits you out in the lobby so ye've no choice even if ye want to keep goin around an around in your own heid.

'Hiya, can ah help you, hen?' He's much older than ma daddy, about sixty.

A folded up wheelchair leans against a wall, near a lift. Signs tell you the direction of wards. 'Isolation Unit.'

'Excuse me, hen. Can ah help you?'

The tone disnae make me feel he really wants to help me, more *what are you doin in here?* Ma mind is the back green covered in fresh, white snow and no footprints. Ah have no thoughts, no smart answers, no plan. Donna was right. What was ah thinking? Ah need to get to the third floor. Take the lift. Inside, a wee glass screen and above it another sign: 'In case of emergencies.' Behind is a phone, a voice like Sean Connery' says: 'Third floor. Doors opening.' The boys tried to imitate the voice. As ah leave the lift, look behind for the rest of ma family. It all happens before ah can stop myself.

'Can I help you, dear?' That's typical, no answer to a simple question and will it be like that the rest of ma life? Came here for answers, not more questions but the man is askin me a question, scrutinising me, head to toe: a stray teenager, hair a mess; the sandals, ripped and mucky like litter blown in from the road.

'Who are you lookin for?'

Maybe, he thinks ah'm in to steal drugs or murder a patient? Up to no good but he'll do his job, get rid of me quick. He keeps lookin at me, sort of rearranging his cap like he means business. The woman stops typin.

And it was going to be so easy. Ah would tell some person, this man, why ah was here and he would take me to someone who could help, a doctor, one of the nurses. Ah would explain what it was ah was lookin for and then everythin would be clear. But never expected this- that ah wouldnae be able to speak.

And ah turn, without speaking, without answering the man's question. Walk through the revolving door, again, as if ah was totally mad. Maybe ah am. Now, ah ask maself why can't ah be like other teenagers. It's the weekend. Ah know what other people in ma class will be doin an it won't be this, hangin about a hospital. They'll be lyin

194

about watchin telly or down the High Street, buyin records and make-up. Normal things. What would they make of me tryin to sneak into a hospital? Ah hope nobody phones the house in case ma daddy starts askin questions. He'll go mental if he finds out. He'll totally flip. And ah wonder what for. For nothin so far.

Sit on the wall and open ma bag and take out Wordsworth's poems. Ah scan the pages an try to find something that will help make me feel better cos sometimes the sound of the words when ah say then in ma head start to sound lik another voice an it helps. It's mostly about nature, as usual, nothing about somebody's mum dyin, that ah can find.

Therefore let the moon shine on thee in thy solitary walk.

Read it in the book.

It's pointless. Ah don't get it. If the moon shines or not, it disnae bring mum back.

Bring your brother home, that will help.

Okay, ah hear you. Do you promise?

Yes, it is the only thing to do…

Donna said to get her in the cathedral next to the hospital where the stone is black like the whole buildin's been covered in coal dust. The door is heavy bronze wi carvings all over it so have to lean ma whole weight to open it. Inside, stained glass windows give the place a darker feel, cutting down on the sunlight from outside, although towards the back, there are three windows wi the palest blue colour of glass ah've ever seen, apart from the actual sky when there are no clouds. A few

195

tourists, cameras slung across them, wander aimlessly as dust motes. They've got that look of not belonging as well as me. It's their voices ah'm aware of, Spanish and German accents and an English woman comparing the stone to Canterbury Cathedral. Down a dark stone staircase, there are doors to wee chapels on the floor below.

Sit at a bench for a minute. Rest ma feet. Ah'm sweatin from all the walkin.

After a silent prayer that ah'll be able to get our Paul home, get up and go towards a small alter with a lectern, open the book and start to read.

'Whit ye doin, ya daft bitch?'

Donna's gien me a real, you're off you're head look. Used to that now.

'Ah'm…Nothin…Ah couldnae find you.'

Prayin to God that you'll give me some peace, Donna. Just get off ma back for five minutes. Any chance?

'Cos ah was gettin fags at the wee shop down the road. Let's get out of this dump. It's freezin.'

She starts to scrape the surface of a wooden pew behind her wi her one nail that she hasn't bitten off.

'Ye shouldnae do that. The guy at the door will be over.'

'So? Let him come. Ah'm an atheist, anyway.'

No in the mood for a religious debate.

'Ye don't believe this shite, do you?' She won't give up.

More like ah've fallen out with God. Don't like her callin it 'shite' though, especially not out loud here.

'Shhh. Ye'll get us into trouble.'

'So. God's sake, lighten up, Erin.'

'This is the kind of crap you like ah bet.'

Peer over the open book, a gold coloured marker markin the pages. Ma legs don't shake this time behind the lectern.

It's a psalm. The paragraphs are a verse and a chorus. *The Song of Solomon.*

There's a gold cloth marker at the page that says:

'I am the rose of Sharon and the lily of the valleys. As the lily among thorns, so is my love among the daughters...' The words are strange, but ah like them. The last time ah read from a pulpit ma legs were shakin an ah thought the sound of ma knees would be picked up by the mike an that's what the people at the funeral would hear.

'Until the day break, and the shadows flee away, turn, my beloved, and be thou like a roe or a young hart upon the mouthains of Bether.'

Wonder what a roe is an if it's a kind of deer. Might ask our Paul when ah see him cos that's the kind of thing he would know.

'Where's Bether?' she asks, up at ma shoulder.

'Dunno.'

'Worse, than that Wordsworth shite.'

At least she remembered his name.

Slamming the door behind us, walk out into the sun-lit street.

6

The double decker bus takes ages, windin through grey, city streets, stoppin at bus stops for dribs an drabs of people to get on and off. Eventually, we're on a steep brae and the bus hovers at the middle lik bein in one of those high rise flats that move on windy days, about to topple; this engine might not make it. On either side of the road, long grass, a scheme built in the middle of a field with a view of sunshine on hills in the distance.

'Right, this is us,' Donna jumps up and runs down the stairs, takin two steps at a time.

'Are ye sure this is your stop?' the driver turns to ask, looks surprised people are still on the bus.

'There's nothin here, hen. These hooses at this end are aw comin doon. Next stop's the shoppin centre, ye'd be better off there.'

Donna's not havin it, she knows where we're goin, flicks her hair with her finger as an answer to the driver and takes me by the elbow off the bus right at the top of her street. Instead of goin down the road, the driver starts to reverse the bus backward onto the main road from where we've come from. We watch him with his head stuck out the window like this is a drivin test for bus drivers.

The street is part of a big housin scheme but no lik ours wi every house havin it's own gate with a back and front door. It's all flats here; wee bit ae garden at the front an washin lines at the back. At the front where there's grass instead of pavement paved over grass, it's long with a few front greens standin out cos of wild rose bushes still flowerin wi pink flowers. Windows are shuttered wi metal an the mouths of closes are sealed wi security doors. Quite a few of the metal doors are fallin off the hinges an they're covered in grafitti. The bus driver was right to ask the question; nobody's lived here for a long while.

Try to picture the place wi people livin in the houses, washed out towels on close lines, or worse, lines that never have a washin hangin on them, sound of the toilet next door bein flushed and at nights, the arguments, when you know there's been drink.

'This is dead spooky.'

'WHAT YOU WHISPERIN FOR?' Donna screams, birlin on one foot. Punk does pirouette.

'We're no in the pineapple now.'

She's Dorothy and ah'm the Straw Man out of The Wizard of Oz. We're off to see the Wizard, the wonderful Wizard of Oz because because because because becaaaause of the wonderful things he does. Annemarie loves that film, especially the Munchkins.

'Where's all the folk, Donna?'

'Somewhere better than this dump.'

So, why exactly are we here? Ah thought she was homesick for the street but disnae seem that bothered about it now we're actually at the place. She leads me to one of the close entrances with its security door hangin off.

'So, do you know here?'

'Course ah do. This is ma old home. Now, 'scuse the mess. If ah'd known you were commin.'

199

But before we can turn into the buildin, there's movement at the other end of the street where the houses stop.

Three figures, a tall wiry lookin boy wi brown hair an another boy that even from here walks wi a swagger that takes up the whole pavement and laggin behind is the third boy. All three are walkin towards us lik they're cowboys in a Western, hands in their pockets, the lanky boy, his body hunched the same way as Our Paul's. Are aw teenage boys never comfortable wi their growin bodies, the fact they're getting tall? The boys stop at one of the buildins. All three start crawlin around on the grass like they're lookin for somethin. Now, it's gone fae a Western tae a detective movie. Already, there's somethin familiar about the biggest of the boys, the slow one at the back. Wonder if they saw us dancin, really hope they didn't.

'Oh look company.'

She's smilin at first.

'My God, Tojo and Skelf ah've no seen them for ages.'

Donna's wavin at the backs of them but they're still busy wi lookin for the thing under the bushes in one ae the most overgrown gardens.

Her voice changes when we get a bit closer, whisperin not shoutin over rooftops.

'Christ, it's that eijit. The one ah owe the money to. Shite. That's aw ah need.'

Brow furrowed wi worry, she looks to either side of us as if she's checkin there are ways out of the street. Ah feel trapped.

'We could make a run for it, try an get a bus.'

But the boys are so interested in the grass, don't seem to have noticed us yet.

'No, he wouldnae touch me when the other two are here. We're good pals, listen. You wait here, ah'll go an speak to him. May as well face the music.'

'Ah'll come too. Don't want to stand here maself.'

Donna's hand is on ma arm, shuvs me backwards, towards the door.

Nearly trip over the ledge of the security door but she disnae bother. Recover ma balance as she's already goin down the path, leavin me in front of the door that's hangin from the hinges.

'But what will ah do?' Shout after her.

'Calm down. Don't be a baby. Just wait there.'

Don't have much choice since the bus has long disappeared an don't how to get out of this place.

It's kinda annoyin that Donna thinks she's got the right to tell me what to do an now that's happened a few times. She's no actually ma big sister.

Ah'm in a dwam for don't know how long until there's another movement near a bin at the next block. The gone folk who always lived here, must have put the bin out the front before they moved away, makin sure everythin was done right, up until the last minute, so that the strangers who did the demolition didn't talk about them. In this place, shared front greens, not lik our street were every house has its own wee square of green at the front wi a dug border for colourful flowers.

A magpie is makin a racket lik actual clackers, those two hard balls on one piece of string that you move up and down so the balls smash off each other makin a clack clack sound. But it's not me the bird's settin the alarm off about but a big dog; when ah peer closer, a fox, another fox in a couple of days. It looks up from what it's been eatin, gien me a long, long stare. The fox seems lost as if it's wandered off a mountain side, cannae find it's way back or could be the same fox ah saw from the train an it's walked all the way from a river bank in Lanarkshire, decanted same as the people who used to live here. This fox is old lookin, there's worn away patches on its side an it's amazin really as if it's walked right out a nature programme on telly into a street in a scheme outside a city.

Learn from the fox. See how the fox survives.

Ah'm not a fox. Ah'm a lassie.

When ah look over to the front green where Donna went, the boys are upright now, aw four of them starin at me lik ah'm the subject of conversation, lik ah'm the fox, afterall. It would be dead handy if Donna got some money off them because we need money badly now. Never realised livin was this expensive, money for food, money for buses. Ma dad's always sayin ah think money grows on trees an we think he has to go out and pick it off, that easy.

Waitin is so borin.

And now with dreams of half-extinguish'd thought

No, that's not right.

And now...

Gleams.

And now with gleams of half-extinguish'd thought

With many...many what?

Ah'd like to take ma book out an check the lines of the poem but if ah did that they all might see me. Hope that guy she owes money too isnae funny wi her about it. Ah've made a decision that ah'm gonnae

202

ask Donna to come wi me to Oban first to help me get Paul cos she can't live on the streets for long wi nae money. She's not a fox that can survive out of bins. If she comes to ma aunt's place, we can figure out how to get ma dad to agree to let her stay wi us in our house. Ah mean they're always sayin one less disnae make a difference so maybe one more won't make a difference either. Dad would never turn her away, if she didnae have a family. Knowin dad, he wouldnae notice cos he's always sayin there's so many of us, he can't remember our names an he calls us all Mary; well, Donna could be Mary Six. Obviously, ah'm Mary One.

'Waken up. Ah've brought the talent over to meet you. This is Tojo and this is Skelf. Tweedle Dee and Tweedle Dum, ah call them.'

The boys are grinnin at me then lookin away, always towards the grass they were lookin in.

'And what about me? Do ah no get a mention tight drawers?'

Have to search for the Fat Boy's face under the hood pulled over his big head, the tassles tied under the roll of fat for a chin.

'Oh, aye and that's Eijit Features.'

'Fuck you,' he lisps back but Donna does the flick thing with her hair, again. Wish ah had longer hair, could do that. It's the same to you back but much classier. She seems confident again so she must have sorted the money thing out wi him.

There's somethin not right about the way the tall guy says 'hiya.' He speaks wi a lisp, tryin to talk without slurrin but not succeedin. The third one is the good lookin one, the one wi the biggest swagger. He'd never move to the side of the pavement to let anyone past. Winks at me lik he knows me. Pure cheek. His eyes are light brown, the same brown as the kitchen units in our house but there's somethin weird about how he looks at me as if he can see right through me to the other side of me where it's only space. Ah feel the red risin from the tips of ma toes, right up through ma body to ma face an no matter how ah try ah cannae stop the blush. The other guys jist stare but Donna grins. The boy bends down and picks somethin from the ground, a big stone. Next minute, the sound of crashin glass as the window breaks and a streak of red brown lik fire jumpin as the fox scarpers in the other direction, big tail behind it. Poor fox, decanted, again. The rest of them clap lik a bunch of daft seals at a circus. You'd think the polis sirens would find their way here but no one stirs from any of the buildings. Ah'm the only one listenin. Did he do that for ma benefit?

Don't get a chance to dwell on it cos the others are talkin again, like he didn't just break a window.

'So, how's it goin, Skelf?' Donna digs her fist into the lanky boy's shoulder.

'Skelf an me went to the same school. Eh Skelf?'

'Aw aw rrrr….right.'

All the time, the good lookin one has this controlled toughness shinin out of him; he's all muscled shoulders and glarin eyes. Nothin lik Drew.

'What's been happenin, man? Are you awright?'

'Ye didnae he…ar.? About the slash…in'

Slashin. The word draws itself across the air lik a knife.

'Christ, no, big man. Did you…did you get slashed? God ah can see it now. Ah didnae notice. Did you, Erin?'

He turns the away side of his face towards us showin a raw, crooked line engraved in his skin. The line dips tae a curve where the knife slipped. You'd think they'd have had the decency to cut him in a straight line.

'No, ah never noticed, either.'

Ah've screwed ma face up before ah can stop it. Now the scar's all ah can see. Need tae find a distraction, stop starin.

Skelf gies us a poor excuse for a smile, makin me feel more sorry for him. The Fat Boy grunts an Skelf shrugs his shoulders. The slowly told story is that two guys came intae a chip shop an slashed him. No reason. Jist that he wasnae from that area. They didnae know him. Ah cannae imagine Drew wi a scar. He can be stupid when he's had a few cans, acts tough and stuff but it's all talk wi him. A big guy would blow him away; he's that skinny. Hope he's okay. Hope he never meets these three in a chip-shop even though they're bein nice enough to me.

'Do ye wan….wan…ttt a bottle of cider? Ah've got one spare.'

'Aye, we'll take it off ye're hands.' Donna takes the bottle.

Ah wonder where the fox is now. If it's okay.

'So, this is your new pal? Tojo's the name. What do you go by, hen?'

He looks me up an doon. Dead obvious.

'It's Erin, Tojo. Ah already told you.'

But even though Donna sounds lik she thinks he's a waste of space, she looks right intae the soft centre of his eyes. Obviously, she fancies him. First sign of weakness ah've ever seen from her and ah wonder if he knows. He's nice lookin, ah'll admit it but no in the same way Drew is nice-lookin. There's a daftness and innocence about Drew.

205

Tojo is dead sure ae himself. Is he from Donna's school? School of hard knocks. His button neck top is three buttons open an there are blonde hairs crawlin up to the V were the buttons start.

'Is that your real name or are you on the run after killin someone? Don't look at me like that, Donna. It happens.'

The way his eyes scrutinise me when he speaks and the takin the piss tone in his voice. Ah can feel myself bein twisted round his finger. Donna grabs his arm. Tries tae twist him around her but Tojo won't be twisted. No he won't. He pushes her away with hardly any force. Beams the big smile.

'Get off. Ah know ah'm irresistible. Ye cannae keep your hands off me.'

'Piss off, Tojo.'

Maybe it's because of the money, she's so narky. This is her way of lettin them know how mad she is havin to pay it back, or maybe she jist fancies Tojo that bad she disnae know how tae act. Ah feel sorry for Donna. Ah used tae hate it when ah took a beamer everytime Drew spoke tae me. Ye're tryin tae be cool, hide it. But the more ye try tae hide it the more ye gie yourself away.

'Where you from?'

'Wishy.'

'Really? Does ye're mammy know you' re this far away?'

This time Donna actually kicks him. Ouch.

He holds his knee, hoppin around but he's only actin.

'Christ, Donna. What the...'

'Well, actually, she does,' putting on a swagger that ah have to work hard at.

But ah'm enjoyin havin the upper hand. Irony. They don't know anything about me. Ma English teacher would be proud of me.

Now he disnae know whether ah'm kiddin or not cos shoe is on the other foot. See how it feels then.

'What were you lookin for in that garden?'

All of them, Donna included, stare at me lik ah've jist said the worst swear word ever but it's a simple question.

'You saw us?' the fat one jumps in wi a snarl to the question.

Tojo gies him a dirty look.

'Of course ah did, what do you think ah was doin but watchin you?'

'But she...'

'Ah don't know what you're talkin about, hen. Unless you mean Skelf's specs. Cannae find them an him blind as a bat...'

They all laugh, Donna as well, an the tension in the moment is air goin out a balloon but it's the 'hen,' that gets me more than the lie lik he's now a man and ah'm this wee lassie. Wish ah looked a bit older cos he'd no speak to me lik that then. Anyway, don't know why Donna's laughin lik they're suddenly aw best pals. A minute ago she was kickin him the shins.

'You're hilarious. To show there's no hard feelins, you two lassies are welcome to come and stay wi us at our pad. That's if you're lookin for accommodation.'

They aw snigger again cos of the way he says 'accommodation.' A breath in then the big word.

'Jeez Oh, Tojo. You're g g g reat wi the big words.' Poor Skelf. Ye cannae really be mad wi him for long.

'Where you stayin, in one of these?'

Donna looks scathingly at the empty flats.

'Naw, we're down the road in the Gorbals. Fancy place.'

The boys snigger.

'You can come visit if ye like.'

'Eh, thanks but no thanks. We're already booked into the Ritz.'

Now, it's actually good cos the four of us, even Skelf wi the sore mouth can laugh, though he flinches wi the pain of it. But the Fat Boy disnae join in, he scowls at us, spits on the pavement.

'Take the address in case ye need it, Donna. Have yeez a pen?'

Ah give Tojo a pen from the bottom of ma bag. He takes a bookie line out his pocket and writes on the back of it, hands the piece of paper to me. Put it in ma bag, in the zipped pocket.

'C'mon let's get out are here. Remember. We've business.'

The fat boy is pacin up an down, a wild lion in an invisible cage.

Show us your belly Fat Boy.

Tojo looks right into ma eyes when he says:

'Well, it would be nice to stand here talking to you lassies but we've places to go, people to see. Mind, don't let her lead you astray. An ye've got our address.'

At least he disnae say 'hen.' Now ah'm mixed up. Is he the big brother ah never had?

'And don't hang about here, too long. Ye never know what characters ye might meet.'

'Characcccctttters… Och, stop, man. Ye're ki…ki…llin me.' Skelf's away, again. Disnae take much.

They aw, Donna as well, start walkin away from me. By the way they turn their backs an Donna says

'A minute…' ah guess ah've not to go wi them, somethin to do with what they were lookin for in the grass or the money she owes Fat Boy. It's another secret conversation of nods an low whispers, leavin me standin lik a right tube. But to be honest ah'm glad to be away from Skelf. It's painful watchin him tryin to speak the words that don't come out right and then the terrible anxiety when you havnae a clue what he's on about.

Look around for the fox but it's well gone. There's a field to the back of the flats that ah can see the top of, tall grasses an bushes, would be a great place for a fox to live. It must be hard for the fox now the people have moved away cos it won't get the leftover dinners in the bins and nobody thinks to give a fox a forwardin address. There's probably a wee boy or girl in a better house now who used to watch the fox from their window.

Walk to down the path to the back of the flats; out the back of this one is a giant tree, a tree that's walked all the way from the real countryside, right into a back green in Castlemilk. Lookin for that fox, though the toes of the tree are dug so deep into the ground ye can tell it's been here a long time. The wind is up now so when ah close ma eyes, sounds lik the sea when we're on our holidays to Ireland on the boat. What mum would call a rough crossing when we spend most of the journey inside. Ah want the sea wind to sweep over me, take away ma worries, and take away ma thoughts. When ah open ma eyes, only the back greens with nothin but high grass and on the pavement, a yellow plastic cricket bat. The sun comes out suddenly an the leaves make a pattern lik water shimmerin on the grass and the whole back-green feels shimmery an watery and then the sun goes away so it's only tree and grass, again.

When ah go around to the street, the others are finishin their talk.

Ah've got the plastic bat in ma hand and Tojo throws a kid-on ball that ah kid-on hit. We all look into the air as if there's really a ball. Then Donna turns away from them, walks back to ma side of the street. Tojo and Skelf are linkin arms, doin the Off To See The Wizard walk. Fat Boy walkin behind them, shakin his big bum until he lets out a big roar. It's him, the burgundy doc martins with yellow laces, ah remember his voice shoutin into the old man's face, pourin pee over his head and those words: 'DIRTY OLD HOMELESS MAN. AREN'T YOU?'

***

When the laddies go, Donna an me move back towards the close entrance, this time easin our way through a gap in the door. It's dark inside and a horrible smell comes from the bottom of the step leadin down to the back door.

'Dog shite, most likely,'

Followin her up the first flight of stairs:

'Where did you live?' Your actual house?'

Donna stops at the flat on the right hand side at the top of the stairs.

'Here, sit down on the step. It's clean.'

But it's not. No wonder she left here, whatever happened. The buildin is fallin apart, the place stinks.

210

Now, the bottle of cider is on the step between us. Ah'm kind of scared of drink but Donna pets the bottle as if it's her baby. Ahhhhhh

Drink can take a hold of you.

As she screws off the lid, the top of it makes a whoosh sound. Shoooosh

'Want some?'

We're holdin on by our fingertips in our family; the last thing we ever need is drink cos it could loosen your grip and then you'd be free falling to God knows where. Ah'd be free fallin.

'You really are a novice. Here, gies it back, this stuff is wasted on you.'

She holds back her head and her Adam's apple goes gulp. When she's finished her eyes look brighter and her mouth is red from pressin on the rim of the bottle. Ah take the bottle when she offers it again to me. When ah take a drink, tip ma head back too far an it ends up shootin out ma nostrils, lukewarm, gassy cider.

'You're hilarious,' Donna says.

When ah've recovered from the first gulp, try again. A sort of warm feelin spreads fae ma chest outwards to ma whole body; takin away the sore bum feelin ah had when ah first sat down on the step. Ah'm smilin an ah don't know why. After a while of passin the bottle between us, Donna's voice seems to come from farther away an her face goes in an out of focus lik when ah got a Polaroid camera for Christmas an ah was learnin how to work it. Ah cannae find how to turn the thing in ma head that helps me see straight, makes everythin settle, not fuzzy cos things have lost their real shapes, the banister, the stairs, even Donna.

Gas of the cider makes me burp, we both burst out laughin as if it's hilarious.

'What will you do if your brother tells you to get stuffed?'

Ah have thought about that. Our Paul's not goin to suddenly change his mind it's unlikely ah can will him back home.

'One time ma brother Simmit got a pot stuck on his head.'

'What the…are you on about?'

'Our Simmit. He was playin that he was a soldier with ma other brothers and the pot got stuck. He had to go to hospital to get it cut off.'

Smells of beans in the pot lining.

'You're whole family must be nuts, same as you.'

'Gie me a drink,' ah reply.

7

Instead of tellin her dad what Drew said, Anna cleans the house. She starts wi the bedrooms, strips the sheets, and throws them in the washin machine, ready for the wash. She sweeps the kitchen an bathroom floors then mops them wi disinfectant.

Elaine bursts in, when she's nearly finished wipin down the stair banister.

'You'll never guess, what we saw?'

'Where's our Annemarie an Lizzie?'

The three of them were supposed to be playin together.

Elaine's shoulder length wavy hair is tied back in a blue, silky ribbon.

'Pull up your tights, for God sake.'

Her woollen tights are all gathered at the ankles lik Nora Batty out 'Last of the Summer Wine.'

'There's bodies,' she says.

'Where are the other two.? You were watchin them.'

'They're comin, look.'

Sure enough, from the window, she can see her five-year-old and six-year-old sisters, hand in hand runnin along the path, towards their house. They've got pieces of somethin in their hands. Anna wonders what they've been up to, wishes Erin was here so she could bugger off and let her worry about them.

'What do you mean bodies? Stop wi your stories. You're worse than our Erin, you.'

Elaine takes a deep breath.

'The Holy Family out the chapel in a man's garage down the road. Jill's next door neighbour.'

'What about The Holy Family?'

'He left his garage door open, an we saw them.'

Anna thinks she means like Bernadette seeing Our Lady.

'He disnae even have a car,' Elaine keeps goin.

'You mean statues, not bodies?' Anna replies while Elaine comes up for another gulp of air.

'There's Jesus, Mary an Joseph stuck in beside his lawn-mower an scabby tools.'

She holds out a chunk of pale blue painted chalk. Right away Anna recognises it as a bit of a fold of Our Lady's pale blue robe.

There was a break in last year. A big scandal about it, vandals nickin statues out the chapel.

'It must have been him. We're takin it aw back.'

'What do you mean?'

'The statues, the broke bits.'

She looks out the window and instead of coming through the gate, Lizzie and Annemarie are bending towards the pavement. She can see Lizzie's curls and Annemarie's bowl cut hair. At first it's not clear what they're doing but then she sees the white writing appearing. They can hardly write their names but they know all the numbers for peever. Bit by bit, from the neighbour's deadly store of bodies: pieces of Jesus, the colour of blood robes, an Joseph, the carpenter, dressed in brown; chalkin all the pavements for peever. Elaine says they've done the whole of their street an the next one too. Soon the whole place will be covered in numbers. An everytime that man sees those figures chalked on the ground, he'll wonder, what's this and this and this and then he'll run into his shed an Jesus' stomach will be missin, an Mary's head an Joseph's hands and then he'll know. He'll know they know. An in his dreams those numbers in the street will become holy numbers, hauntin him, gettin bigger until they multiply an they're everywhere. An it will be the worse curse ever; he'll be haunted by God and peever for the rest of his life.

'Anna, where's Erin?' Elaine says.

'You know where she is. At Drew's house. You better clean that chalk off your hands or ma da'll kill you.'

No need setting her off.

'Is she away away?'

It's easier for Erin, everybody expects her to be lik a mum, to know how to talk to Annemarie an the others about stuff.

'Look, ah'm busy, Elaine. Go an play wi the others.'

Elaine sits on the stair.

An eight year old on a protest. Her pink dress has white streaks of chalk dust.

Typical Erin as if things weren't bad enough now she's done a runner. That's the kind of selfish thing you'd expect from her; only, she wishes she didn't have to tell her dad cos he'll go mental wi worry. And she hates to admit it but she is worried too, about where Erin has got to and why and is she ever coming back?

'You'll no tell ma dad, will you?' Elaine pleads, forgettin about Erin.

'Of course ah won't.'

He'd go mad and they'd all be to blame.

'And not Erin, either. Cos she'll be mad ah took the other two.'

'But why are ye stealin them, you might get caught?'

Elaine gies Anna a look as if it's so obvious.

'Cos, it's our duty,' she says.

'What do you mean, Elaine.'

'It's our duty to free the Holy Family. Now, we know.'

'Well, he'll kill you if he catches you. You better be careful.'

She says deadly serious:

'Don't worry. We've got God on our side.'

8

After a while Donna looks at me on the step above her, leanin against the cold close wall.

'We better move if you're goin to catch that bus.'

This is the time to tell her about ma decision but hesitate cos it's Donna an ah know she'll have an answer why it can't happen so ah should think of answers back in ma head instead the cider's made ma brain dizzy an slow thinkin.

'Ah'm not goin. Not unless you say you're comin as well.'

Funny but now ah sound lik Donna's big sister: somebody flipped a coin that decided it.

She does her usual, ignores me.

'The forty-nine takes you right to the bus station.'

Why would ah think this lassie who's really a total stranger would come on a mad journey wi me for a boy she's never met, and then probably back to a house full of weans an ma dad? She's already made it clear that isnae her scene. But if ah leave her here, she'll go back to the station an sleepin on couches an surely what ah'm offerin is better than that.

'Seriously, ah'm not goin unless you say you're comin with me.'

That's the answer and the cider's helped me know it.

'Listen, pal, ah already explained. Aunts, Oban an that. No ma scene.'

She holds the bottle of cider upside down, a few dregs come out, make a puddle on the step.

'Well, ah'm not goin either.'

Ah can't just get on a bus an leave her. Ah'd always wonder what happened to her. And what if she disnae get the money to pay back Fat Boy? Maybe, he'll get rough wi her. He looks the type. We'll figure somethin out.

'We have within ourselves

Enough to fill the present day with joy...'

This is the best joy ah've had since mum died, ah'm doin somethin useful for ma family an ah could help this girl cos there's nobody else gonnae look after her.

'You mean you'll get a flat?'

If ah say ah won't, she'll stand up an ah'll stand up an we'll go an get the bus and then ah'll get the connection to Oban an ah'll never see her again. Even though we've only met, ah don't think that matters cos everybody should have a proper house and a proper bed no jist a couch, especially a young lassie lik Donna.

A white lie is all it will take. The colour of a lie is dead important. Ah can go along wi her for the day, sayin ah'll get a flat but work on a better reason to get her to come with me. There must be a way to persuade her.

'Aye, okay. We can get a flat. Ah won't go to Oban.'

There's a difference between a white lie and a proper lie and on the chart of lies, ah'll get less bad points for that.

They'll take the wee ones away.

No, they won't. Not now.

'That's fantastic, pal. Ah'm made up.'

218

Donna's pupils are larger cos ae the cider, she goes to hug me but it's more like a head but. When ah stand up, ground goes to the left an ma body to the right.

'Now, you've run away. They won't care, after a while.'

She says it to make me feel better but it doesn't, instead it's like a boot in the stomach. She's wrong about no one carin about me. Even though we argue an fight, dad an me, cannae imagine him not lookin for me, not even callin the polis. Really, she must mean about herself, she must mean that. And that's the real reason to stick with the white lie for now. Nobody should be left on their own lik Donna, even though she is dead cheeky and would be a terrible teenager for anybody to have.

'Comin let's get goin. Need to start planin gettin a flat. We've missed the appointment wi the stand -by people but can make a new one. We'll have points cos we're homeless together,'

Is that what dad means when he says drink makes people daft, makes them think impossible stuff can happen, lik him winnin a fortune at the horses an Donna an me startin some kind of new life? Somehow, even though ah've only had a few swigs of cider, ma mouth cannae connect wi ma brain even if ah wanted to take back the lie about the flat, the right words wouldn't come out.

'Will ye do me one last favour?'

'What?'

May as well, now ah'm here.

'Will ye take me to The Gallowgate, there's a place ah need to see?'

'Is to do with that mad eijit poet guy?'

'Sort of.'

'Okay, okay. Now, do you want to hear ma plan or not?'

'Come on then, tell me.'

Time and tide waits for no man.

Ah know. Ma da'll be expectin me back from Drew's.

You'll have lost the chance to get Paul back for good.

Cannae jist abandon her, please.

Charity begins at home, Erin.

It'll be fine cos ah'll still get Paul. Ah'll ring dad tomorrow, say ah'm goin straight to school from Drew's house. That gies me another night an day an ah promise ah'll still get Paul but it gies me time to talk Donna round to commin wi me.

9

Joe's out the back, hangin out some clothes. It's three months since Eve passed away an he's managing to keep things ticking along though he hates this, hangin out washin.

Better than that first week with the washin machine in the middle of the kitchen floor. He was puzzlin over it when Erin came in from school.

'Its no right, Erin. Have a look. What have ah done wrong? Ah jist cannae fathom it.'

No soapy bubbles, only a grey lookin skum for a surface.

'What did you put in the water, dad?'

He shook his heid lik it was rocket science an he'd never ever get it.

The kitchen floor was swimmin. His socks inside his shoes were getting wet.

He demonstrated where he'd put the stuff in the box that said 'Flash.'

'Dad, that's for the floors. Ye cannae put it in the washin machine,' Erin said.

Even though he'd put in half a box, no a bubble in sight.

'Christ, what difference does it make an how ah'm ah supposed to know. Ah've never used a washin machine before.'

They'd both stared into the grey water lik an answer would suddenly appear to this sorry state of affairs.

'Do you want me to do it?'

'Ye're too late it's done. You can do it from now on though.'

'Ah'll drain this bastard if you hang them out.'

There was a faint blueness about everythin.

'We can steep them in boiling water.'

He didn't know how come she knew that stuff.

For the whole of the week, the clothes were aw gritty an they smelt of clean floors.

Then auld hen pecked McKay is at his back step, smokin. Dirty auld habit.

'What you doin there, Joe?' He shouts.

Joe's a good mind to shout back:

'Mind you own fnnn business.'

'Hangin a few clothes out. While it's dry.'

The other man laughs to himself. Laughs.

He'd shouted it right from his top step, across the Poles' green so that anybody in their kitchen would hear. Joe notices he has braces on, not a belt like him. He's a good ten years older than Joe. Old fashioned, Joe thinks.

Next thing, he's walking down his stairs over to where Joe is standin with the washin basket. When he is opposite Joe, he looks down intae the basket. Nosy bastard, Joe nearly says it. Thinks twice.

'Aw they lassies, Joe. You shouldn't be doin that. That's wumin's work.'

Joe feels like he's letting all men down. He promised Eve though, that he'd do this.

'Well, it's only a few clothes and somebody's got to do it. So how's the strike goin?'

The steelworkers have been on strike for six weeks for a pay rise. Even though Joe's lookin after the weans, he feels guilty he's no not workin cos of the strike.

'The bastards have cut our strike pay in half,' spits on the ground; the spit sizzles.

Joe stands back, looking at the three towels he's pegged up. They look a bit grey. Shouldn't look like that but he can't work out what he's doin wrong. At least they're clean. Still, a bit higgeldy piggeldy, though. Now nosy features is here, making him more nervous.

Joe's scared to reach down and bring up any more clothes from the washin basket in case his neighbour has somethin else to say. Just to stick the boot in.

'She told me an Agnes she is stayin on at school, Joe. Next year. That big lassie of yours. Is that right? That cannae be right, Joe?'

Spits his yellow spit on the grass, again. Joe's fnn grass.

When a man stops workin people treat him differently.

'That would be Erin. Aye, she's smart. Her mammy was proud of her. Me too.'

'Aye, but Joe. Eve's no here now. Look at yourself, man.'

'Well…obviously…she's not…'

'Ah didnae mean…only sayin…'

'Aye ah know…'

'Ah'm sorry an that…only'

'It's fine. Ah know.'

'Ah'm only sayin, she could help you if she left school next year or that, instead of all this talk of stayin on. You could go back to work.'

Another world away: day shift, back-shift and night shift. He was always one sort of shift, had a pattern to his days. These days there was no routine.

He'd promised Eve, though.

Joe bends down to find the boys' football strips. The white of Simmit's Man U top is too grey as well. He'll need to talk to someone about the washin machine. Couldn't remember if you hung the clothes by the shoulders or not.

'She's stayin on. The young ones need an education these days. Ah want her to stay on. Wants to be a teacher, would you believe. A teacher from this place.'

They both gaze across the line of small back greens, each with four clothes poles in a sort of square. There is a pattern to it. He knows when he looks at the other lines the clothes were hung to a pattern too, that he can't get.

His neighbour coughs as if to sum up the conversation.

'Well, me an Agnes think it's a mistake. That you're makin a mistake.'

'Well, she's no your lassie, is she?'

With that Joe lifts the basket and walks back up the steps to his own open door. The basket is still half full. He'll put the rest of the stuff over the radiators. They can drip dry.

10

Donna's idea is to make a new appointment with the housing people for the morra. Cider makes me want to sleep but makes her dead excitable and more talkative than she's been. Cos she thinks we've a plan to get a flat she's excited about that as well. Donna says Mrs. Flowery Dress will let us stay at the hostel another night an there's always Tojo's place in the Gorbals, wherever that is, if she gets funny. Says it might be better to get a private let instead of a council flat. We're gonnae look in shop windows and the papers at those wee adverts for somethin small. Still disnae know the truth, that ah cannae stay longer than one more night. It's great seein Donna so happy. Donna says, maybe, one of us in the livin- room, just till we get on our feet. We really could do it, the start of new lives for us both. We could get jobs, in one of the big stores, a fashion store, discounts for staff and enough money for rent and a good night out at the weekend.

'Five years have past; five summers,with the length

Of five long winters'

The words of the poem come to me dead easy now. That would make me twenty. Ah'd love to be be five years older. Wordsworth was a right moany git, sometimes in *Tintern Abbey*. Ah'll need to learn ma useful facts and some good lines or Mrs Kelly won't let me go on the trip. Donna's right though, not to have to think of others aw the time; only to think of yourself an ah wouldn't need to learn any poems for school ever again in ma life. Only thing is ah quite like stuff lik that. Ah like school an ah like Mrs Kelly and her poetry class.

Can't help feelin that Donna's talkin about another lassie, not me. And she still doesn't understand how important getting Paul is to me.

Blood's thicker than water, Erin.

Time is an adventure: we've got nothin but time. Donna lifts tins from shelves in shops, turns them in her hands as if we've money to buy them: Beans means Heinz ...a lot of chocolate on your Club. P....p... pick up a Penguin. A finger of fudge is just enough to give the kids a treat. Enough! Enough!

Other customers gie us funny looks, one might phone the polis an that's aw we need. Ah'd have tae go home then. God knows what would become of Donna. Back to sit on the ground at the train station.

On the way out of the third shop, goin along to The Gallowgate, stop at a rail with a special offer on big bars of chocolate. Next to it, tins of sweetcorn in the canned vegetable section. Donna lifts a bar of chocolate; she's starin at the wrapper, a big crease of anxiety on her forehead.

'Month out of date.'

The man behind the counter has a beady eye on us.

'Let's go, c'mon.' But she ignores me. Instead Donna goes marchin up to the counter, hands on her hips: a middle- aged mum in a piny, goin up to the neighbour's door for a fight.

The man blanks her while he rearranges packets of fags on his display.

'Excuse me, mister,' Donna's right up in his face, almost on tiptoes, her long, gangly legs.

'See this chocolate?'

226

'What about it?' His finger are chubby. Fat chubby fingers that would squeeze intae the holes of the telephone an dial 999. Ah'm sendin Donna vibes tae shut-up an let's get out of here but she's immune to vibes.

'It's out of date. That could poison somebody.'

He bends over the counter, takes a big breath, suckin in air, makin this dead heavy sound an for a minute it looks like he might reach over and punch her.

'Beat it you, ya wee shite.'

Have to stifle a giggle, the way she stands up to him. Donna walks away in her own time. An when she's at the door, looks over her shoulder, dead serious look on her face.

'We could sue you, Mr.'

Gies me a look, sucks her cheeks right in, makin a pure fool of him but he cannae see me cos ah'm at the back aisle. Both engrossed in their head to head. That's when ah put a tin of sweetcorn under ma top.

'Toe Rag,' the man says about Donna, under his breath, rearrangin his papers. He's glad nobody saw it, skinny girl takin the Micky an him lettin her away wi it.

Outside, at the entrance, she leans against a Rupert Bear collection box with a slot for the money at the top of the yellow bear's head and a sign around his neck: 'I need you.' Along the black base the words: 'PLEASE HELP THE BLIND.' Rupert's eyes are stuck in an expression of cheery surprise.

'You watch, for a minute.'

'No, Donna. He'll kill us.'

Donna ignores me, picks a kirby grip out of her hair, droppin it through the coin slot: clinkin sound of metal against metal.

'Money in it.'

'But we cannae rob Rupert Bear?'

'That greedy man's Rupert, ye mean. He robs it at night for himself. You saw the chocolate he was trying sell.'

'But how will we get it up side down?'

Worse than stealin from the collection plate at mass but the man is sellin out of date chocolate and anyway, we need money from somewhere.

Donna has both her arms around Rupert's belly but it won't budge.

'Help me or what?'

Put the tin of sweetcorn ah lifted off a shelf on the ground.

Now, got ma arms around the bear's belly an she's grabbin the white head. He feels cold from bein in the draught too long, heavy too: not for moving. Rupert Rupert the Bear, everyone knows his name. Cannae stop laughin now, cannae help maself.

'Jesus, Erin, shut-it, will you? He'll hear you.'

'Who? Rupert?'

'Hey, you two.'

But she's started as well.

'Shite,' Donna says, startin to run even before ah've turned tae see the man who has come out from behind his counter.

'You, two, wait. Phone the polis, somebody, quick.'

Try to keep sight of Donna's blue, black hair. Fat man is out the door turnin to a lady in a raincoat an then the raincoat's runnin. Click of heels. Click…click.

'Stop them. Stop them. Thieves. Thieves.'

Wavin his fat arms about, Rupert the Bear himself.

Rupert Rupert the Bear everyone knows his name…

Ribbons of ma sandals are startin to loosen an they might fly off any minute an ah'll be one shoed or worse shoeless but Donna grabs me by the hand and pulls me along with her.

Raincoat woman is slowin down.

'She's not after us, Donna. Let me go.'

'Shut-up, Erin. Keep runin for another bit. C'mon, ye don't want to end up in the jail, do you? For robbbin Rupert Bear?'

The tin of sweetcorn is in ma hand; any minute the top might open leavin a trail of sweetcorn leadin the polis right to us: wee gold nuggets of evidence. Luckily, Donna knows the alleys between the four storey red sand-stoned building, flying ahead knockin a bin lid that clatters on the ground. This is great now, bein away from home, doing mad stuff like this. Donna's got her arms on her legs, leanin over, deep breathin, and nearly chokin. Alley is full ae empty lager cans; smells of dog dirt and the straps of my sandals are completely loosened, flapping about ma ankles, trailing in the dirt.

'God, that was close,' she says, still catchin her breath; still, get the feelin this happens to Donna a lot.

'Gonnae pour,' she says readin the weather from the clouds. There's a ridge of high pressure over the North.

'Ah know somewhere we can get cover,' she's already startin to move, no even checkin to see if ah'm followin.

 She's right, you can feel the rain before it starts; the way the blue sky gets grey, almost foggy. The street empties. Everybody senses it.

We're no dressed for heavy rain, in our light summer clothes, no jackets. It would be nice if someone cared that we had no warm coats.

'Erin, what are you doing out in the rain without a coat?' One of those people passing on the street that look right through you. When the splashes start to fall on our heads, we burst out laughing.

'Fuck sake. Ma hair'll be a mess after this,' Donna screams; finds a newspaper on the ground, double pages that cover our heads. Our wet tights start to stick to our legs, Donna's long sleeved black jumper soakin but she keeps it on.

Eventually, stop inside a shop door-way; take off ma black jumper; at least ma blouse is dry.

'Nice top,' says Donna.

'Wouldnae mind one that colour.'

  Don't wear wet clothes or ye'll get your death of cold.

Don't touch a light switch with wet hands or ye'll get electrocuted or

Don't walk on the kitchen floor in ye're bare feet.

Don't drink out a chipped cup.

All things not to do.

Donna's new smile would thaw a frost in winter when the windae ledges in our house are iced shut then the sun comes an makes water lie in puddles.

'In here, quick.'

Shop doorway is empty, takin us out the way of the rain. Donna's shiverin, her whole body shakin. Never noticed how really skinny she is. Nothin to her.

'Here, take this.'

Gie her the black jumper an she disnae argue for a change. Wait and watch the street, a few people running past, rain bouncin off the ground. Women find umbrellas at the bottom of their bags, hoods go up, everyone lik us runnin for cover from the downpour. It could be home but people don't know ma name an the signs in the shop windows say: *'No credit here.'*

While we're huddled together in the doorway, Donna notices the tin of sweetcorn.

'Let's have some then,' she says, grabbin it off me.

Not as if ah could bring it back to Annemarie an Lizzie so they would get to taste it.

Read the side of the tin when Donna holds it up to open it:

'France's favourite vegetables.'

'What you doin, Erin?'

'Nothin.'

Not tellin Donna ah've never had sweetcorn before in case she has and then she somehow thinks she's better than me. Inside the tin, hundreds of yellow eyeballs packed tight together, aw lookin out at ye. Breathe in the smell: sickly sweet.

Donna uses fingers to scoop out some then gies it to me.

Take one eyeball out then close ma eyes an swallow.

'That's wasted on you. Gies it back,' she grabs the tin again and wolfs down some more. Guess that means she likes sweetcorn then.

***

231

'Elaine can go to The Dohertys,' someone had said. Don't remember who cos everybody an their granny seems to have an opinion about where the three wee ones should go so they don't see any of the funeral stuff.

Denise Doherty is an only child an at one time or another; we aw wanted to be her. She gets everythin: new Raleigh bike, space hopper an even though she is a lot younger than me, ah'm pig-sick wi jealousy.

Adults say it lik it's dead sad:

'Aye, there's only her. Shame. They couldnae have any more.'

But when ye've seven brothers an sisters an ye've never had a bed to yourself, bein an only one sounds lik heaven on earth.

The night mum's body got taken to the church, Mrs Doherty phoned us to say Elaine had run away.

'Jesus, that's aw we need. And your mother goin to the church.'

It was to check if Elaine had come back home cos she'd been on about wantin to come home.

Dad was up at high doe anyway but Mrs Doherty told him not to worry that they'd find Elaine.

Loads of people came to the house that night to offer more condolences. Then we got ready for the walk to the church. Ah wis at the front of the crowd, behind the hearse. Ah felt ah was in a film, not really me. Ah looked up, as we turned out of our road, there was a figure standin over at the shop, separated by the grass aisle that the laddies play football on. It was our Elaine. Ah nearly never recognised her cos she was wearin a blue top, ah'd never seen. Ah wondered what she was doin, jist standin there, watchin and where did she get the blue top? She was too wee for a funeral everybody thought bein eight years old. Well, our Elaine made it anyway.

Ah wished she could have come in the house. She'd been sent away and then she'd run away from the Doherty's so ah didnae really know what to do about our Elaine.

When it started to rain, she didnae move, kept on watchin us. Think she knew ah'd seen her but ah couldnae go to her cos ah was at the front of the procession, tae tell her she'd catch a cold without a coat but ah heard the voice sayin that in ma head:

Elaine 'll catch a cold

Ah hoped she heard it too.

At the weekend, Elaine came back from the Doherty's when aw the Irish ones had gone back home.

'Was that you standin outside the shop the other night?' ah asked her.

'Aye, ah ran away. How come we never got to go?'

Wasnae really ma decision but that's no an answer.

'Cos ye're too young. Ye shouldnae have run away. Mrs. Doherty phoned ma da. Everybody was worried. Did ye not like it there?'

'Who were aw those people goin into our house?'

Thought about saying how lovely it must be at The Doherty's house. One time ah visited them wi mum. In their bathroom, the toilet seat had a wee cover on it; at first ah couldnae find the toilet roll but then ah noticed it under a doll wi a pink woollen skirt. Everythin was matchin pink even the toilet brush was in a pink container.

Elaine told us how they had their dinner sittin at a table in the kitchen an we aw tried to imagine a table big enough for us. Ah don't know what the rest of them thought but nobody said anythin, only a pause

233

when each imagined the table. Ah don't know what size of family was round any of their tables cos no one said a number out loud. My number was still ten. Every night, she got to play Kerplunk, which she thought was great cos she's only eight. In our house we get stuff for Christmas but we've usually lost a lot of the important pieces like the dice, for example, by New Year's Day.

Ah heard her tellin Joanie an Annemarie about sweet corn. Mum never gave us things out tins except peas an beans an aw the other veg was in the mince and stew: carrots, onions and turnip. That's why dad puts beans in the mince now cos he thinks it's a vegetable an disnae see the point in havin two pots to clean. Now, instead of brown, we have orange mince that tastes of tomato sauce. And it's runny as soup.

'Is sweetcorn a puddin?' Joannie asked.

'No, don't be daft.' Elaine is an expert on exotic foods since she came back from the Dohertys but ah'm curious as well cos ah've never had sweetcorn though ah'm no gonnae admit it to them. There are other things she got at the Doherty's: macaroni cheese, Angel Delight, tuna and pineapple chunks. Every time there's an advert on the telly now about some food we don't get, our Elaine says:

'We got that at the Doherty's house.'

Everybody's fnn sick of hearin it.

***

Donna an me seem to have been on the go for ages as we stoat about lookin in shop window after shop window. 'Ah've an idea,' she says outside a shop with three big, brass balls hanging above the doorway, surrounded by signs: 'Easy cash here. Instant, easy cash. Wages advance. Low deposits.'

The window is full of jewellery: diamond rings, bracelets, watches: 'a non-redeemed pledge,' written underneath most of them, whatever that means. ARBUCKLE and SWAN PAWNBROKERS Ltd written above the door.

'See that ring you've got, you could pawn it. We'll need a deposit for a flat, if we go private. Would really set us up, no chance with no deposit. Once we're workin or getting brew money, could get it back.'

Donna's lookin at me; her face full of *this is the best idea ever*. Ah can't tell her now ah'm not getting a flat wi her, so soon, an ah don't want to start a fight in here. That ring is all ah've got of mum an if ah give it away, there'll be nothin. But she's right as well. What good is a ring? It could help Donna wi the money she owes The Fat Boy. He might come lookin for it.

Why didn't she leave me a letter or somethin about how ah should carry on after she'd gone or money in a secret bank account for when ah turn eighteen? Ma Aunt Geraldine would say ah've got aw ma good memories an that should be enough but it's not.

'Ah'm far too young for a weddin ring, anyway.'

Donna's already got her hand on the door, pushin it open.

'Plenty time for the ball and chain.'

Inside the pawn shop, it's already decided without us speakin that Donna's doin aw the talkin.

A bell rings when we push open the door. Inside, the place is empty then the woman appears from the back of the shop.

'Whit you two after?'

The woman with the question is lookin right at us over the top of a glass counter. She's no other customers but we don't count as real customers, two young lassies in her shop. We're used to it. This time we're proper customers wi proper business here.

'Missus, how much would you gie ma pal for this ring? Pure gold.'

Donna's grabbed ma hand an she's holdin it over the counter, so the woman can see. Wouldn't put it past her to pawn me if she got a good price.

'Didnae steal it? Did she?'

'She didnae steal it. Sort of inherited it.'

'Let's have a look then.' The woman now takes ma hand, first she turns it palm upwards as if she's gonnae tell ma fortune then turns the hand the other way inspectin to see if the nails are clean.

'Ye'll need to take it off, hen.'

As usual, it takes a while tae get the ring off ma finger. As ah struggle wi it, the two of them watch me, don't say a word. Finally, the gold band rattles onto the glass counter. Thank God the shop's empty. It disnae feel right, it's not really mine to give away, it's Anna's an Elaine's an Annemarie's as well, it's ma dad's and all of theirs too. It was only cos ah'm the eldest ah got to keep it. The woman's nails are dirty an uneven and her teeth are too big for her mouth, pushin her lips up into a permanent smile. Puts the ring under a magnifying glass but when she turns it on one of her hands, ah have tae restrain maself from grabbin it back.

FIDELITY and their stamped initials inside the circle of gold.

'Gie ye twenty pounds. Ye can redeem it for thirty,' the woman says, holdin her smile for a long time.

'What does redeem it mean?'

Souls get redeemed by God.

Will ah redeem our Paul?

'It means you can buy it back for thirty pounds. You'll no get better anywhere else in the city.'

Easy.

Ten pounds profit for nothin. Don't know where ah'll get thirty pounds.

'Okay, then? Ah'm gien ye a great deal, hen. Ye'll no get any better.'

Donna nudges me wi an elbow in the side.

'Go on, Erin. We can always come back for it.'

Everythin is 'us,' an 'we,' now Donna's become desperate for the flat deposit.

'You've got ages to come back and get it. A week, we'll be on our feet. Ah'll help you get it back. Promise.'

It won't be easy to get the money to get the ring again. We're two young lassies wi no a penny to our names an no way of getting money; as soon as ah hand it over ah'll never see it again.

But ah never wanted it in the first place so shake ma head in a yes.

The woman gives me a slip of paper: one gold band wedding ring and a date two weeks from now.

Non-redeemable pledge.

Consumer Credit Agreement at the top of the page.

Disnae seem to care about ma age even though it says on the form ah should be at least eighteen.

It's weird cos ma hand feels bare without the ring, a sort of itchy feelin on ma finger an ma finger shiny were the ring has been.

237

'What do ah do with this?' ah ask Donna.

'Ye need to sign that. That's your proof that the ring's yours.'

Is the shiny finger not enough proof?

If ah sign this form, ah've signed away the only thing of her's that ah've got. Ah wish ah could have asked mum about when she got engaged and went wi ma dad to buy their rings for their weddin.

'Can't do it.'

Both breathe out heavily, ah can feel that shouts are comin next.

Donna's reaction is to kick the side of the counter then storm out of the shop, leavin me.

'She's wastin ma time, your pal,' the woman shouts after Donna but Donna's well away. Ah'm left wi her behind the counter who is glarin at me. She rips the form up, throws it in a waste paper bin.

'After me fillin it out, waste of ma bloody time. Ah've got better things to do wi ma time.'

The woman's voice is dead hard an there's no smile now as if ah stole the ring from her, no that she just tried to steal it from me.

'Don't come back here, again. You're barred.'

Shouts the words as she slams the ring on the counter. It's a wonder it disnae break but it's good gold, they didnae skimp.

Outside the shop, have to run to catch up wi Donna. At first she disnae look at me. Won't look at me when she does eventually talk.

'Don't know what we'll do now.'

More disappointed than angry an ah feel bad about it too but ah'm sure we'll think of somethin else.

We keep walkin for a while an Donna stays dead quiet.

'Right, it's Maureen, then,' she says, at last

Maureen's her aunt who works at The Barras an Donna thinks she'll gie us some money. After tellin me that, disnae speak again for the whole walk there. Not her pawning somethin. Try not to make it obvious when ah'm puttin the ring back on ma hand but gets stuck on the knuckle-bone at the middle of ma finger. Don't want tae make a big deal about it so slip it into ma pocket. Ah'll put it on later. There's a bar of soap in the room on the sink. Ah've done that before when it's too tight.

Donna still disnae speak so decide to let her stew in it for a while.

Keep checkin the ring's in ma zipped pocket, don't want to lose it after all that.

You should be on your way today.

The voice gets louder in ma head. Sometimes, have full-blown conversations. Mostly arguments.

Ah will go. Nothin's changed. But ah need to do this ma way. She's ma pal.

Time an tide, Erin. Remember.

But then there's the other voice.

Don't look back. Be free. Forget about duty, think of open spaces, the rest of your life.

But she always said look after people.

The longer Paul's away, the harder it'll be to get him back.

Ah know. Ah know ah have tae go.

You'll never escape if you don't grasp your freedom.

Ah'm so mixed up. Don't know what to do and who to listen to.

Back towards the direction of the hostel, goin past the shops at Trongate. A sign on the road advertises fish and fresh meat. Up the alley, a whole deer is lyin on the top of a coalbunker. It draws Donna an me the way an accident does, we don't even have to say let's go and take a look. Up close, the exact wound in its side were someone shot it; blood dried on the sticky hair, large brown eyes that saw trees and fields an maybe imagined itself safe, now closed tight. Still, ah'm glad ah can't see its expression. A man in a white apron covered in blood, stands at a doorway sharpenin two enormous knives. Ah've seen pictures of deer in magazines or on walls but this one looks so big and real, no paintin could ever prepare you for how beautiful they are in real life. Ah touch its skin, cannae help maself.

See into the life of things.

Even though it's dead, ye can imagine how alive it was runnin about the hills.

'Beat it you two,' he says but we're already turnin away.

The Saracen's Head pub is right across from a big archway with the words: *The Barras,* above it, a lot smaller that ah expected, a tiny doorway, one shop length. Shutters down when we get there, not much point hangin about till it opens.

'Satisfied?' is all Donna says.

Follow her under the archway along a road, past loads of wee shop fronts.

'Maureen's along here.'

Donna's still in a huff.

A young black man comes out of one of the doorway of a shop, dressed in workie overalls, coated in paint. There's people everywhere, no one lookin where they're goin.

A man is pushin an older man in a wheelchair; the man in the chair has only one leg and it's dead hard not to look at the place where a leg should be. Some older women are drinkin tea and eatin their own sandwiches on a bench on the paved part of the road. Nearly everybody looks old, even if they're not old. Donna and me must stand out. Really, The Barras is a small town, streets going off in all different directions so you'd easily get lost. It says in big writing 'established in 18 something.' Wordsworth wouldn't have seen it when he was in Glasgow; cannae imagine him lookin for bargains. Different here from further along the city centre, where we just came from; in this place, the way the two old women eatin their food say 'hiya,' and it's not just that, people look as if they are always on the verge of talkin; it's more like being at home.

A young guy walks past us carryin a scuffed lookin, white surfboard.

'Ye can get anythin here,' Donna says.

She's talkin again. It's a start.

We go further in to a section just stalls instead of shops. At first there's no people only all this stuff lyin about, makes me think somebody's fly-tipped aw their rubbish in the wee enclosed lanes; clothes on coat hangers rails, stalls, piled high. People are sellin everythin you can think of: cookin pots, knives and forks even dishes and cups. It's really a big jumble sale but not for charity.

Donna talks to a few of the stallholders; she's well known. Some of them have the gloves wi fingers cut out even though it's warm; around their waists are worn lookin money bags that rattle wi change when they walk.

'Donna, is that you?' A woman is shielding her eyes fae the glare wi her hand, to get a better look at us.

'Hiya, Auntie Maureen. How's it goin?'

Ah'm her old pal from school, Donna says roughly to me out the side of her mouth, far enough away so her aunt disnae hear.

Behind the woman there's a short piece of washin line wi ladies and children's' clothes aw hangin up. All the dresses are on their own hangers lik somebody's work clothes hangin up for work the next day. She's tall, stands out amongst the other women but has the same brown eyes as Donna. Ah wonder if Donna's mum looks lik Maureen. Her an her auntie talk together for a while. The longer they talk the more lonely ah feel. It's a relief when Maureen reaches into her pouch, gies Donna money.

'Now, go and get me a coffee, Donna. Ah'll have a wee blether wi your pal.'

Donna hesitates. Gies me one of her if you say a word looks. She takes the money.

'Erin can come wi me.'

'No, you go. Ah might need to go to the lavy and she can watch the stall for a wee bit, if that's okay wi you, hen?'

Although Donna wants me to go wi her, it seems rude not to let the woman go to the toilet, all for the sake of a few minutes.

'No, you go, Donna. Ah'll be fine.'

Donna disnae move.

'So, what's the big secret?'

'Ah really want that coffee, Donna.'

'Ah suppose….'

'Really.'

When we can't see the top of Donna's head any more, her aunt tells me to sit down on a beer bottle crate turned upside down. Doesn't seem to be desperate for the toilet, afterall.

 Could start a conversation about the weather. Ah could tell her about the man who wipes his sleeve along the top of all the walls where ah live. Maybe, ask her if she's ever seen anyone else do that but don't get the chance.

'Ah just wanted to ask, hen. How is she? How's she been, our Donna? She'll no talk to me.'

In a way it's disappointing that she disnae have any questions about me. It's Donna, she's worried about.

'She's fine, ah think.'

'And is she off the stuff? Is she clean?'

Trying to read ma face, starin at me while ma mind goes over what she just said. It must show that ah don't know what she's talkin about.

'What stuff?'

She looks at me lik ah'm havin a laugh.

'Drugs, hen. Whacky backy, whatever it gets called these days.'

'She disnae take drugs.'

She's made a mistake.

'Are ye sure? That's great. Ah'm glad, hen.'

'So, is she stayin wi you, hen? Where is it she lives? The Social Work were onto me. Askin about her. She'd never speak to me if ah said a word. Always gien me the run around when ah try to ask her. Has she seen her mum, do ye know? Ah'm sorry to ask, hen. Behind her back but it's the only way ah get to know she's awright.'

Ah'm beginning to wish ah'd gone wi Donna rather than go through the third degree.

'She's stayin at ma house until she gets a flat. She seems fine.'

She'd have enjoyed hearin about the man that wipes his sleeve but ah'm no tellin her in case ah end up getting the third degree about him.

'Well, if she ever goes off the rails again, could you let me know? Ah know her and ma sister don't get on, after what happened but ah'd like to be there if she needed any help.'

Ah say ah will though when ah go ah won't be able to deliver.

'What happened wi her and her mum? She never said.'

Ah know it's sneaky but ah told Donna about me.

'Well, our Sandra, that's ma sister. She met Colin about a couple of years ago. Ah think they worked thigither. He's a lovely man. A bit particular... about stuff. Big house in Bearsden. He's a quantity surveyor, whatever that is, hen. Anyway, Donna's dad's been off the scene since she was a baby. Donna never accepted it. For years it was just her an her mum. Caused ructions in the house. Drinking, all sorts. Made Sandra's life a misery. And then when the new baby came, well that was it. Donna did a runner. They brought her back a few times but the last time. They just gave up. She was stealin fae them, an they

244

were worried about the baby. Donna comes to mine every few weeks an ah keep in touch wi Sandra. Donna's no interested.'

When Donna appears back, she's carrying a white polystyrene cup and two cans of coke. We share the crate, drink the coke then there's an awkward silence.

'Would ye like to come to ma house for ye're teas? It wouldn't be any bother.'

'No thanks, Maureen, we've got plans,' Donna says. Ah've never heard a lassie ma age or nearly ma age call an adult by their first name. Ma dad would go mental if ah called any of ma aunts by their first names.

'Ah'll Maureen ye. Cheeky article,' but she's laughin when she says it.

'Can you loan me some money? Ah'll pay you back, promise.'

Her aunt shakes her head.

'Like the last time, Donna? Ah'm still waitin.'

'Please it's important.'

She gies her aunt a long beggin look lik butter wouldnae melt. Ah'm shocked when her aunt dips her hand into her money wallet.

'Ah've no got much spare but take this an promise me you won't do anything daft.'

She waits, restin her hand inside the wallet lik it's a glove. She won't gie her the money till she hears the words.

'Ah promise. It's for food an stuff till ah get ma first wage. Ah've got a job servin in a cafe.'

She takes out a couple of pound notes.

'That's great, hen. It really is.'

Her voice sounds as if she'd love to believe Donna. Then she gies her the money an Donna puts it in her pocket without lookin at me.

A customer comes to the stall, a woman who looks dead serious about one of the dresses hangin up, a bright red sleeveless wi black checked pattern; her aunt gets distracted and we take the chance to slip away.

11

'The romantic scent of rose, orchid and golden jasmine, softly embraced by sandalwood and vanilla.'

When she sniffs the perfume, it smells of talc. Anna sprays the air in front then walks through the mist of spray. Won't have much left if she keeps doin that, but it's irresistible, makes the room feel exotic and when she smells her skin, as if she's had a lovely bath.

'What you doin, up they stairs?' her dad, leanin over the banister.

He's unpacked the food, put everythin away, an now they'll need to make the dinner. Anna knows she'll have to tell him, but not yet. He's in a great mood an she doesn't want to spoil it.

'We'll try this mince, then…'

'Aye…be down in a minute.'

The words 'Coty,' and 'Paris,' are written in brown and 'L'Aimaint,' is pink.

Anna tries to think where Erin could have got to. She wouldn't have the money to go to Ireland to see their gran. Definitely not Paris. She's up to somethin, that's for sure.

To take her mind off it, she sprays two quick dashes on her wrists, rubbing them vigorously together, before bringing both to just below her nostrils. Ahhhhhh

Her dad wants to watch football on the telly after dinner, so he's in a hurry to get the show on the road. They only have their dinner in the afternoon on a Sunday. It's always a long night after that. Anna's head is sore wi him goin on about the mince an wonderin how ye cook it, aw the way home in the car that's all he talked about. He makes such a big deal of everythin an tryin to think of different things to cook is makin his nerves worse. Right enough, they're all sick of soup cos it disnae take away the after school hunger pangs.

When she goes down stairs, a pot of boilin potatoes, bubblin nicely away on the cooker. He's gettin good wi the mash, loads of margarine and milk, makin it creamy. It's all lookin good except Anna cannae see the mince.

'Dad, where's the mince?'

He looks at her.

'Under the grill, of course. Honestly, Anna, where else would it be?'

Opens the wee door of the grill proudly.

'Look, see.'

Sure enough the mince is in the grill part of the oven. He's laid it out nice an flat on the bakin tray across tin foil.

'What's up?'

Doubt has started to creep in cos the flame's on but the mince is reddish an raw lookin, an startin to burn at the top. No gravy, no vegetables. Mince.

'Eh, your auld da is gettin the hang of this.'

She doesn't have the heart to tell him.

Simmit an Pinkie arrive. Everybody's starvin. They stand in a semi-circle, starin at the mince.

'What's the mince doin in there?' Pinkie asks. Even Pinkie knows.

Only thing is she can't remember exactly how ye're supposed to cook it. They were never actually shown cos their mum thought children should be children an there was time enough time for housework an

248

cookin. So, all their pals were busy learnin how to make beds and use the hover but their mum said to Erin and Anna: 'They'll be old before their time.'

Erin would know. She watched stuff more.

'Ah wis sure ye grill it,' their dad says.

Everybody glares at him.

'That's toast ye're thinkin of, dad,' Pinkie says.

Anna would never get away wi that.

'Right, somebody go an ask Agnes for God sake, otherwise we'll be here aw day, waitin for it to go brown.'

Anna gets the job. It's humiliating, all the McKays laughin, when Anna asks for the recipe for mince.

'We need to put it in a pot of water, bring to the boil. Ah think she said add Bisto to cold water then add it to the mince.'

By now some of the mince is black lik sheep shite.

'When the Bisto is in, ye'll no notice that,' their dad says.

He opens a tin of beans an puts that in wi the mince at the end.

'No use, wastin pots,' he says.

The mince is crunchier than usual but the tomato taste of the beans gives it a new flavour. They eat it anyway.

'What's that smell?' he says when they're clearin the plates away.

'What smell, dad?'

'That perfumey smell. That's no the mince, is it?'

Doesn't say your mother's smell.

With all the trauma about the mince, she can't tell him about Erin now. Let him watch the football. Erin might appear. If she doesn't, then Anna decides she'll tell him then.

12

'Ah want to check if the pub's open.'

'Well, if you're goin in that dump, ah'm goin in there.' Donna points to a shop that sells wedding dresses.

'See if ah can nick a tiara.'

The shutters are off the front of the pub but it's hard to tell if it's opened or closed. Push open the door and walk in. Two old daytime drinkers look at me from their yellow lookin beer then to the bar. One of them has dyed black hair and a sheriff's badge on his jacket. As ah go towards the bar, ah'm all the time scanning for some memorabilia on the walls. Don't see an iota.

At the bar, a man with slicked down hair is cleaning tumblers. Above his head, there's Buckfast in the gantry and a selection of other tonic wines.

'Ye're too young to drink here, hen. Beat it.'

Behind the bar, right in the middle, above the till is a glass cabinet with a page of hand-written words.

'Have you heard of William Wordsworth?'

'Wullie who?'

We dipped our glass cups in a huge punch bowl.

'The poet, William Wordsworth. He might have been here. Doin a project at school; want to check for research.'

The two drinkers have stopped talking and are all ears for me.

'Naw, hen. Can you not do Rabbie Burns? See that writing up there? That's an actual poem by him.

Right then a door opens on the floor behind the bar and an older man climbs out of the hole. There are steps down to a basement and a bad stink of beer wafts up. He humphs up a barrel that the other man helps him with. Now, he sits on a stool catchin his breath.

'Who's the girlfriend?' to the other man.

They both grin.

'Seriously, don't serve her. Our licence, God sake.'

A tree with a blue bird and a bell
like a fruit on the branch
and a blue fish in the last of the punch,
where the bowl had been cracked in a fight.

'Naw, Ray. It's no drink she's after; it's some poet. What's his name, again, hen. You might know you've been here the last hundred years eh?'

'Fuck off, you. Who ye efter, hen?'

He adjusts his round specs like he means business.

'William Wordsworth.'

'Aye, he was here.'

At last.

'Actually here?'

'Well, in the old place across the road. The owners knocked it down years ago an built here. Wis fallin apart.

Ah find him and then ah go an lose him, again. Ah'm rubbish at this lookin for people.

'Ye should come back when the manager's in, she knows more than me.'

'Okay, ta.'

The man with the sheriff's badge winks as ah pass, lifts his glass in a *cheers*. The other one sniggers.

Outside, Donna is at the end of the road. She sees me an starts stormin away from me towards the direction of the hostel; disnae even wait.

When ah catch up on her, she turns around.

'That ring,' she says, a tone in her voice, the way she says 'that,' like the ring is a personality and clearly one she disnae have any time for.

'What about it?' try no to say anythin to start a fight.

'It's no your gran's ring, is it?'

Stares straight ahead, face steely lookin.

No point keepin the lie goin, an ah get the feelin she's known all along, that she's been waitin for me to tell her the truth. Maybe, if ah do tell her the truth we can start again; she'll tell me stuff about herself an her mum an what happened, what Maureen said, about drugs, she'll tell me about it. Ah can start to help her.

'Okay, it's ma mum's weddin ring.'

'Did she cop it or somethin, your mum?'

Ah don't think ah can handle it, not now.

'Look, we better hurry. The hostel might shut.'

She starts marching away, in the direction of the hostel, again; without me. Disnae even look back. Strides the whole distance in the biggest huff ever.

We're right outside when ah have to say it, though in ma head ah know ah should wait, there's a poundin in ma stomach. Ah mean she'll never handle a flat if she's been takin drugs even if it was a while ago. And even if whacky backy isnae the heavy stuff that's all ah need, to be landed wi Donna on drink or whatever an me stuck wi all the trouble. She's still not asked about how ah got on at the hospital earlier. She's makin it so hard for me but that's why ah need to try to help her cos who else will help her? She's so cheeky an annoyin an stubborn, no wonder she's on her own. Deep breath.

'Donna, do you want to come to Oban with me? Ma aunt is really nice; she'd help us both get started. She'd put you up too.'

Don't know how come ah feel ah owe her somethin. Maybe, that she's helped me up to now. Can't leave her all alone. What if?

What if they put you into a home? They'll take the wee ones away.

Can't get the voice out ma head, pushin me on even when ah want to give up.

Donna kicks the door of the hostel. Then she starts shoutin:

'Ah thought you'd given up that daft idea. Did you not say we could get a flat? Might have known you were at it. You know your aunt will put you on the first bus home, don't you? And your brother... Be surprised if he even speaks to you. You can't keep buggin him. You should leave him alone. Don't you get it, Erin? Nobody cares? Nobody's lookin for you, are they?'

'Just cos you've ruined your family, Donna. Ah'm no doin the same to mine.'

It would ruin mine, if ah disappeared. Ah've got to try to get Paul back, no matter what she thinks.

'What do you mean by that?'

Can't take it back.

'Your aunt told me about you and your mum. You're spoilt Donna. Jealous of a wee baby.'

Right up at ma face, close ma eyes for the punch but it disnae come. When ah do open ma eyes, she's lookin at me lik we're seein each other for the first time.

'You can talk. You lied about your ring. A pack of lies about your granny. What kind of lassie says that? Miss High and Mighty criticising everybody. Mrs Bloody Perfect. Not.'

'Ah'm goin, Donna. It's definite. We've got enough money to pay both our fares if we put ma money wi the money your aunt gave you and there's a bus leaves from Buchanan Street every day. Ah'm goin tomorrow at three o'clock. Ah've decided. Think about it. Think about comin. Will you?'

And we leave it at that. Her sulkin, walkin away ahead. Me, followin, ma head spinnin with what she's just said. She's right in a way. Me, that always wants the truth so much from everybody else. An ah took the easy way, so ah didnae have to admit to the whole story.

Tomorrow is another day.

That's right. Too much has happened today.

That night is the first night that we go to sleep without talkin. After a while go over and poke Donna in the ribs but she just sighs and turns onto her other side. She's not ma sister after all cos if she was then she'd want to go with me. Her mum's livin in Bearsden an she could

254

visit her any time. One day in the future, they might sort things out an she might get to call her mum by her first name.

That night, ah dream we lose each other amongst the stalls at Paddy's Market. There's loads of people with no fingers in their gloves. When ah ask a man if he's seen Donna, he turns into ma dad and ah end up runnin away. The rest of the dream ah'm looking for a lanky haired girl, ripped tights, a bad taste in clothes.

13

It's late on Sunday afternoon, Joe's about to settle down to football on the telly. There's somethin relaxin about the green grass of the pitch, the commentators' voices commin out the box. Simmit an Pinkie are out kickin a ball. They got up early, were away till dinner an now he'll no see them till suppertime. If Paul was here, they'd watch the football together. They all seem to have places to go durin the day but he has nowhere only the shops for the messages an then back to the house. Joe considers ringin Erin at Drew's to tell her to come home the night instead of the morra cos one night away from your own home is enough at her age. She's too young to be stayin away. That scent in the house. Must be their Anna wi Eve's good perfume. If it's no Erin talkin to herself bein head in the clouds, it's Anna sniffin wee bottles. Still, better than glue sniffin.

The wee ones are upstairs playin when the phone rings, only him an Anna downstairs. Anna answers.

'Who is it? For God sake fitbaw's about tae start.'

Joe is shoutin from his chair in front of the telly in the other room.

The theme tune for the football is on.

'Who is it? The game.'

'Drew's mum.'

Joe almost runs out the room towards the phone when Anna says it, that woman never phones there.

'Is that Mr. McLaughlin, Erin's dad.'

'Aye,' he replies. 'What's up, is our Erin okay?'

The wee ones are at the top of the steps.

'S'cuse me,' putting a hand over the receiver.

'Anna take them into one of the rooms while ah'm talkin, ah cannae hear a thing.'

Anna says:

'She's no there,' then turns up stairs an signals to the three wee ones to follow her.

'What's up?' Annemarie asks.

Anna draws her a dagger an she shuts up.

'No there, ah don't get it. She told me she was goin to Drew's look after your Karen's weans on account of her an her man goin to a weddin. She's been away since yesterday mornin. No there...'

It's hard to get off the phone cos Drew's mum has bad nerves as well an she's talkin machine gun rapid sayin where could she be, an she hopes nothin bad's happened.

'It'll be fine, ah'm sure. Ah'll check wi her other pals, of course, ah'll let ye know. Thanks again.'

Joe sits on the stairs, thinkin about what it means. Tries to puzzle it out in his head, how long she's been away an when he last spoke to her and what she said. Anna's back again.

'Whit did ye not say for? Drew said you phoned him askin for her an that's how they know? Eh? Whit's goin on Anna?'

'Ah was tryin to tell you, but ah never got the chance.'

His face is red an any minute now he'll explode.

'Ye're sister's missin. Did she say anythin to you about where she was goin?'

'Nope. She disnae tell me a thing. She's maybe at Sally's or one of her other pals.'

'Right, knowin her she'll be at Sally's, never bothered tae tell us. You look after the house an the wee ones. Ah'll get ma coat an start lookin.'

He's out the door, wi the coat over one shoulder, fixin it as he walks towards the gate.

Simit an Pinkie see him from the football field. When he tells them he's goin to try to find Erin, they say they can help, that they'll go to a couple of houses where her pals live, if their dad goes to Sally's.

'Tell her, when you see her that...'

'Aye, dad, that you'll kill her,' Pinkie shouts, punchin his fist into the palm of his hand.

'No, don't say that. Just tell her to come home.'

Later that night, when their dad comes back, Erin isn't with him, only Simit an Pinkie still kickin a ball outside on the grass.

He tells Anna not to say a word to the younger ones then lifts the phone, she watches as his face becomes pale and the phone falls out of his hand.

'But where...' then his voice tails off to silence. He hasn't dialled a number. Anna doesn't know who he's talking to.

'Dad, what you doin?' she asks.

'Polis, we need to phone the polis.'

He takes the dangling receiver that bounces up and down towards the carpet then puts the phone on the hook, again; he hesitates and Anna realises he's lookin waitin for someone else to pass the phone to, make the call. That's the kind of thing Erin would do for him: fill in his social security forms cos he said he couldnae write, talk to people on his behalf. Well, Anna can't do it. He'll need to learn to speak and learn now.

'But why would she do it? Run away?'

It's a daft question. She doesn't know.

He dials 999. They both listen to the ringing, waiting.

14

The first thing ah feel is how cold it is, that frosty feelin in the air when winter is only a few weeks away, and ye're shiverin for the first time in months. Soon, it'll be dark all the time, again. When ah say Donna's name, no answer comes.

No sounds come of the toilet bein flushed or the tap runnin in the bathroom; she must have gone off in a huff. Soon be back, tail between her legs. Ah stay on the bed for an hour waitin but she still doesn't appear. Instead it's Doris comes through the door.

'Hiya, hen. Where's that bitch of a pal of yours?'

She's carryin the black bin bag she seems to take everywhere. Imagine her walkin through the streets, heads turnin for aw the wrong reasons but Doris disnae care what people think.

'Have you seen her? She's maybe gone for a walk.'

Doris gies me a long long look.

'A walk? Ah'd check your pockets, hen.'

The next shock is when ah look inside ma zipped pocket. Ma money and the ring aren't there, only the folded pink bookie line wi Tojo's address. Crawl under the bed for the sixth time even though ah know it's just oose and hair grips. Where did ah put it? Did ah take it out ma pocket before goin to bed? All ah remember is leavin the ring there yesterday. Doris watches me. Disnae speak. Donna's no like that. Surely? Not after she knows what it means to me. Not after all the stuff ah told her and she told me.

Then ah remember what Donna's aunt said about Donna takin stuff and how it stopped and the way the aunt said it like it would be a miracle if it stayed that way. Ah can't believe she's takin mum's ring. She must know how much it means to me. Even after aw the bad stuff we said, ah cannae believe she would do that. That's what ah get for trustin a stranger.

Doesn't seem any point in gettin out of bed. Don't know what ma next move will be.

'When it comes down to it, hen, she's a thievin wee toe-rag. Well known for it. Ah should have warned you. Nice lassie lik you.'

Suddenly, it hits me. Ah've no money, no pal and no plan. Ah'm lost, really lost now. For the first time in ages ah start to cry, right there on the bed, in front of Doris. She gawks at me lik she's never seen anyone cryin in her life before.

'You're a runaway, aren't you? Ah can tell a mile. Too young to be on your own. Why don't you let the social work look after you? They're no that bad. They'll gie ye a proper home. No lik here. Ye cannae live lik this without Donna. You're too...too...innocent.'

'Ah don't want social workers. Promise, you won't say anythin, Doris.'

'Jesus Christ, hen, calm down. Ah understand, believe you me. Awright?'

Ah pour out everythin to Doris, how ah'm tryin to get to Oban to ma aunt's house and about our Paul. While ah'm talkin she gulps sips from a half bottle she takes out the bin bag. At first, when ah finish, ah think she hasnae been listenin. Her eyes are red and shiny from the drink already. She offers me some out the bottle:

'No, ta.'

After the cider, ah'm stayin away from drink. Ah felt sick after it.

'But what if he disnae want ye to bring him back? Have you thought about that?'

Same as Donna said.

Ah want to know what it was like when mum died. Paul will be able to tell me what happened and what she said. She must have said something to him cos she never got the chance to say anything to me. Paul will tell me everythin an he'll come back home an ma dad will have another man about the house. Let them live their lives and let me live mine. Ah don't need tae explain it to anyone. Tired tryin tae get people to understand.

Doris' hair is too black for her pale face. It makes her look sickly but ah can just about see the face of the young lassie she used to be. Wish ah could pray to a saint the way mum did, some picture of a bearded man dressed lik a monk or a lady wi blue rays comin out her palms.

Doris is quiet for a few minutes, looking out the window.

'Ah might know someone, a guy who goes up North a lot...he's got business there. Ah can ask him if he'd drive you, if you like?'

Doris is sittin on the bed, picking at the covers when she speaks. Donna didn't like her but she seems okay to me.

Ah could always go back home. Turn up at the nearest polis station and get them to phone ma dad. The polis would drive me back or he'd come for me. But then ah remember how ah felt that night when ah decided ah was leavin. Nothin has changed, ah'd go back and ah'd still have this big hole inside me that can only be filled if ah can get some answers. Only our Paul has the answers; anyway, ah don't have the ring.

Run, escape. Out into the world.

Remember what this is all about, Erin.

'Here,' she reaches into her jacket pocket and takes out two pound notes.

'That should keep ye goin, today, for food, ah mean. That'll mean you won't be tempted to do anythin daft, get in trouble wi the polis. Ah'll meet ye back here tomorrow about five. Ah'm spendin the night away from this place the night so ye won't see me. You make sure you get booked in here, again. Don't be wanderin the streets yourself. Promise?

'Aye, Doris.' Take the money.

'Ah'll speak to that friend of mine. We'll get ye on the road to your auntie one way or another.'

'Thanks, Doris. For helpin me.'

She pus a skinny hand on ma arm then takes it away quickly.

It's hard not to flinch.

Ma Aunt Mary will make it easier for me to take the next step. Find out what happened when they were in hospital that last time. We don't talk about stuff like that in our house. We act as if everythin is the same, only sometimes somethin catches the light, dust in the corner of a room that ye would never see only for the chance sunlight, at just the right angle. Like that day we left for Lourdes. For a wee while, only the three of us, mum, dad and me, had waited for the bus tae fill up. Funny how it was only three no ten. Couldnae remember it ever bein just me an them. Wish ah could remember what that was like. Bein an only one.

'Enjoy yirself, mind,' he kissed me on the cheek. Dad never kissed ye except at New Year, smellin of Bertola Cream sherry; he had looked thin that day, still the man in his weddin photo on the mantelpiece, but much older. Only one of us could go.

'Ah'm no religious. Never have been. Ah'd be a hypocrite to go now. No. Erin can go.'

He had put on his Sunday suit to see us off. Good deep pockets for stealin from if he'd won at the bookies, home with a few drinks in him. Everyone else was already seated when ah got on. It was well past the time when they were all fiddlin about wi cases, the time for starin out the windae, ready tae go but they stay holdin each other. Had to look away.

15

She liked catchin tadpoles, remember?' Simmit says.

'That was yonks ago.'

Pinkie thinks for a second.

'Well, she's always got her nose in books.'

'She's no at the library, daftie.'

'It's a perfect ruse.'

'Aye, but if she's in hidin, she'd go somewhere people won't guess an she'd been away aw night.'

'Wouldnae put it past Erin to be in the library all night.'

'We're missin somethin.'

'The bing?'

'Maybe, okay. Let's spread out. You take the grassy bit where the pond is, ah'll take the bing.'

'Right, Doyle, let's spread out. Good idea.

Pinkie says in his best English drawl.

Simmit is eleven, a whole year more mature. He shuvs Pinkly lightly but then takes up the voice himself, kid-on talks into a pretend radio inside his stripy jumper:

'C15 Agents Doyle and Bodie staking out area. Back up may be required.'

He's Doyle cos of his black, curly hair bein like Doyle's bubble perm. Pinkie is Bodie, younger, but tougher.

'C'mon. We better hurry up before the cops get here. This is our operation.'

Simmit leads the way, his younger, but taller, mousy haired brother behind him, who keeps checkin over his shoulder for imaginary meat wagons.

The bing is a piece of waste ground behind the housing scheme, with a hill that you can run down pretending Indians are chasin you, although Pinkie liked to be an Indian, rather than a cowboy when they played that game.

'Geronemoooooooooo…' was the cry as he charged down after Simmit, kid-on tomahawk in his hand. That was when they mostly watched The High Chaparral and old John Wayne films. Now, they watch The Professionals and American cop shows with big, fast cars.

The bing isn't far from the houses but when they get there it always feels like another world away, a part has only weeds growing, another part has the hill where they'd spent most summer holidays of their childhood playing games like Best Man Falls. Now, they hardly went there because there isn't any flat bit of ground you can play football and there are better places for that. After an hour of searching every corner of the place they meet up at the pond where Pinkie is on his hunkers, waiting.

He pokes a stick he picked up into a moving, greeny, black sludge that is frog- spawn.

'Checked the hill, top to bottom, Doyle. No sign of the missing agent.'

'She'll probably be at Drew's. You know what she's like.'

'Aye, probably.'

'If people keep escapin, we could as well.'

He has a point. First their mum, then Paul and now Erin.

266

'Paul an Erin'll be back. They cannae stay away, forever. Dad won't let them'

'He'd want to be Bodie. That's if he was in.'

'Well, he'd need to be 'The Cow.' He's the eldest. Ah'd tell him.'

'Would you?'

'Aye.'

'He probably wouldnae…'

'He might. Wonder if he's talkin again.'

Both boys stare into the pond at the surface that moves slowly like one large fish but never goes anywhere always connected to the banks. They'd spent so many summers scooping up tadpoles into jam jars, wee black commas always wriggling away.

'You know what we need?'

'What?'

'Fast cars to get around the place quicker. We can't cover Motherwell and Wishaw like this.'

'And The Ruskies might have the agent. She might not last.'

'That's right, ma man. We need wheels. Follow ma drift?'

'The bikes?'

Pinkie gets to his feet.

'Erin's old bike? But it says *The Pink Lady* on it. Ah'm no goin on that.'

'Look, this is an emergency. Anna's bike's okay. That's black. You can take it, ah'll take Erin's.'

'What a sacrifice, hope she preciates this.'

Pinkie throws the stick into the pond, it makes a sound lik *glug*. Then they turn and walk away from the desert of the bing, back towards the civilisation of their street.

16

From the hostel walk across the last of the big metal bridges ah saw from the train. The bridge is high and the water grey, same grey as the pavements. There's frost on the ground, an the water looks still and icy. Behind a rock, a big heron sticks out. Funny seein a sea bird in the city. Our Paul told me all about birds' names: heron and hawks, finches and sparrows: knows them off by heart. Maybe, that's why he loves Oban because of the swans at the sea wall, always scroungin for food from the tourists and at night how ye're always aware of their white shapes on the black water. Anna an me used to steal his binoculars and look through the window of the two Polish brothers next door but there was only ever them sittin in front of a television or a sad, empty livin room when they were at work.

For most of the day wander through shops, feelin lik a piece of blown in rubbish: empty packet of crisps, a sweetie wrapper. Fraser's perfume floor is a different world from the greyness of the streets: high open spaces and bright aisles wi white light shinin down from chandeliers; fat and thin shaped bottles, glass glinting in the light, all shades of amber, clear and rose pink. Guereline, Clinque, Chanelle. When ah say them in ma head they still sound hard and ah know that's just because of ma accent, that if ah was French they would sound soft and exotic. Women behind the counters have skin painted on perfectly; armed wi white strips of lightly sprayed scents, ready to thrust under the nose of any person who stops, catches their eye. They glance in the direction of the slightest movement lik the heron focused on the river, ready to jab a fish stirrin the surface, no me with no money and fousty smellin clothes. No exactly the fish they are after. Talkin of fish, the perfume women remind me of somethin trapped in a glass bowl wi their painted on smiles pressed against the sides lik ah was starin at them under our Pinkie's magnifying glass. Anna wants to work in a place like this. Sorry now, ah called her scent pee water. There's a line of wee testers. Reach out quickly, grab two for her then shuv in ma pocket.

That's when ah knock over a display of boxes of soap so then it's me under the magnifying glass. Run from the clatter the boxes falling makes to the ladies fashion floor, holdin dresses away from the smell and myself. That's what comes from havin the same clothes on for two days. But if ah stop then ah won't have a reason to be inside and ah'm not ready to walk the streets just yet. The only way to get a proper seat is to take a pair of jeans into one of the changin rooms. Hardly room to park your bum but manage it. Smile at maself in the mirror. Maself smiles back. The curtain is frayed at the hem. Maybe, someone will wonder why my feet are in this position. Who cares?

'It's too big,' a girl's voice from the next cubicle, so close ah have to check that it wasn't me that said it. Check maself in the mirror. She didnae speak either.

'Is it? Will ah get a smaller size?' A second voice.

'Yes, mum. You should see the colour. It's really nice.'

One day ah'll get to pick ma own clothes.

One day.

'Ah'll get you outside.'

'Okay,' the voice in the next cubicle replies.

Stay sitting on the bench, the pair of jeans lying on the floor. It's funny how ah'm noticin how mums and their daughters talk to each other all of a sudden. It's not somethin an ever noticed before. Why did they have to walk intae this shop? Swish of a curtain bein pulled back and the sound of feet and voices somewhere. Then silence. Sometimes it's hard to work out what's over, in the past. What's happenin now and what ah need to do next. There's probably a book explainin how tae cope wi stuff lik this. Next time ah'm in a library ah'm goin to check. Ye can request books. If it's no there ah'm goin to ask the librarian to order it. Read some of Wordsworth but not really read, the words swim in front of me an it's lik ah've forgotten how to read or there's something wrong wi ma eyes:

'The still sad music of...humanity..'

The sick stomach feelin has made me forget words. Put the book away. Sit for another while, until through the space between the hem and the floor there are feet waitin to get in. Ah stole everythin and anythin an God has got me back for it. God stole her from me.

It's a relief when ah find the art gallery in Nelson Mandela Square. Benches against walls, in front of modern paintings and other exhibits. People sittin down just starin at them. No one tries to move me on. Not yet. Must think ah'm appreciatin the art. A couple of times see lassies that look lik Donna but close up it isn't her. Don't know if ah want to find her or if ah'm better off on ma own. Still can't believe she stole the ring from me. Get the day in then Doris will help me get away. Her friend will drive or she'll get me the fare. Wonder what business he has in Oban. Her friend. Doris never said.

Resist the urge to curl up and fall sleep on one of those benches: *Lassie on a bench* written underneath. No one can admire me cos ah'm sittin on the admirin bench.

There's a timer inside ma head now, goin off lik an alarm clock that rings out: *Move move move.* Cos ye can only be in a place wi lots of people for a certain amount of time. Always somebody starts noticin ye, walks towards ye or worse towards the security guard an then they both look at you. Sometimes, ye only have tae be young tae seem suspicious tae some folk. Ah wonder if ah'll become like that man in our street who always wipes the wall on the main road wi the sleeve of his jacket like he has to keep it clean or will ah start shoutin swear words at total strangers? Ah could go back to the hostel place, try to get in there another night but somehow it feels lonely to think of stayin in one ae those rooms maself or wi strangers. Even though ah don't know that boy Tojo an his pals that well, at least ah've met them before an Tojo seems as if he could stand up to the Fat Boy, who would be the one to worry about. Skelf is a big eijit, he'd be okay as well. Ah don't even need to stay there for the night, could pass some time there, just to not have to keep walkin around the streets of the city lik a lost soul. Ah'll ask somebody for directions to the Gorbals from here, didnae sound too far. What if Donna's already there? Somehow don't think so. Don't think ah'll ever see Donna again.

***

The door of the pawnshop goes 'ping' when ah walk in. The woman behind the counter looks over the shoulder of the man she's servin, long enough to notice me then look away.

A different woman this time. She's younger, wi one side of her blonde hair shaved into the wood of her head. The ring's not in the window, amongst the chunky gold bracelets with charms of wee animals an star signs, an loads of gold an silver watches. It could be they've no put a price on it yet.

Scan the top of the counter but no sign of the ring but they could have it in the back shop.

'What ye after, hen?' she says to me as the man leaves wi a new watch on his wrist, checkin the time about six times before he finally closes the door.

'Ah wonder have ye got a weddin ring of mine? Ah think ma pal might have brought it in.'

She laughs.

'You're a bit young for a weddin ring.'

'It's ma mum's ring.'

She fusses about wipin the counter wi a cloth ye usually wipe windows with.

'Anyway, we don't take knock off here. This is a respectable place. '

'Could ye just check in the back. Please.'

She sighs as if there's a long queue of difficult customers an ah'm the first in line.

'Wait there. An don't touch anythin.'

Two minutes later, she comes back.

'Nope. Nothin new since yesterday. Aw the rings are in the window. If it's no there then ah don't have it. There's tons of other places. Why don't you try them?'

The way she says it there's no point arguin, explainin that it was her shop we were in before.

Look in the window, again, in case ah did miss it but it's not there.

Spend the whole afternoon in an out of pawnshops but still don't find the ring. People look at me suspiciously lik ah'm in their shop to steal somethin an the whole time ah'm talkin they're lookin behind me lik ah'm a decoy for the real thing.

All along was thinking collect the ring for good when ah had the full amount but put a deposit down wi the money Doris gave me. At least if they knew it was stolen, ah'd buy time till ah could ask dad for the money; at least we'd eventually get it back. Now, dad'll kill me when he finds out. One day he'll ask, whatever happened to your mum's ring an Anna will ask as well, cos she knows ah've got it. The one thing mum did leave us an ah've gone an as good as lost it. Definitely, cannae go home now.

17

Walk across one of the big bridges over the river, away from the city centre. Ah've got Tojo's address on the piece of paper. He said their place was in the red stone buildin next to the high flats. When ah get to the other side of the bridge ah can see the flats towerin above the streets, so head for them. Ma hands and feet are freezin wi the cold but at least ah'll get a heat soon.

At the flats, there's a bit of waste ground then a row of tenements that looks like they're about to fall down. There's either no curtains on windows or drawn curtains an the entry system doesn't work. Somebody's peed against the side of the main door an there are names in white, scrawled across the wall above and inside the close, insults: 'Johnny is a spazzz,' 'Gordy is a wanker.'

The address on the bit of paper says a number then: 'G/ Left.' No bell, only a name written on the wall to the side of the door, the same white paint, wearing away. Music from inside. No answer. Knock again. The music gets turned down and a voice behind the door goes:

'Who the fuck is it?'

Not sure if it's Tojo or the Fat Boy.

'Erin, Donna's pal.'

The Fat Boy opens the door.

'Hey, it's the wee lassie from the country. C'mon in, hen,' holds a can of lager towards me.

Don't go inside, Erin. Remember, about strangers.

It'll be fine, ah can't walk the streets aw day. This will be safer. Ah'll be careful. Can smell heat and lager from the doorway.

When ah'm through the door, he offers me the can:

'Want a slug?'

'No, ta.'

Pupils of his eyes too big, stinks of beer.

'Eh, where's Tojo?'

'Take it easy, hen. This is nice. Me an you.'

Big fat face too close to mine. Ah can see the marks that acne made, have to stop imaginin green puss and bits of cotton wool stuck where he's tried to wipe it.

'Wait an we'll see if your big pal is in. Tojo, ya bastard. Are ye in?'

No answer.

'No in, seems.'

'Do you know where he is?'

'Away to the shops for the messages. More BEER.' Ah have to wipe the spit off ma jumper.

'Ah'll wait for him.'

'It's fine wi me. You're a right laugh, the way you talk an that. C'mon in the livin room, for a seat an get a heat. Freezin, eh?'

'Aye, it's Baltic.'

He clears an armchair of dirty clothes, one swoop of the flabby arm, all the time watchin me like he doesn't know what to do wi me. The room has no carpet, only furniture is a couch, chair, a waste paper bin an the biggest telly ah've ever seen. The pile of dirty clothes lies in a heap on the floor.

'House-proud chaps, eh?'

That's when ah notice the fish tank in the corner of the room. A big lamp like a sun-bed lamp switched on.

There are clumps of bark inside the tank but no sign of any fish.

The big guy is still watchin me as he bends down into a bag on the floor. He comes up holding a dead mouse by the tail, swinging it into the tank. Its wee eyes catch mine as it flies through the air.

'That's for Trigger.'

'What kind of fish eats mice?'

'Fish? You mean snake. Reptile. Don't worry. Naptime. But ah'm just sayin, nice to be nice. Wouldnae like Trigger to get out and get lost in this place and maybe end up...'

He holds his belly pushin it up and down. *Ha ha ha.* The sight of the flesh of his belly on top of the thought of the snake in the corner and the mouse lyin lifeless as stone inside the tank. Ah'm heading back out the door. That's when the close door slams shut.

'That'll be Romeo. Do you no think ah'm nicer lookin than him, eh? What's he got that ah don't?' He's leering at me in a way that makes me Thank God Tojo's appeared. He's carrying two plastic bags, one rattling with cans.

'Yes, ye got served. Dancer,' the Fat Boy is over at the bags, mauling them.

'You, still thirsty? Fat bastard. Hiya, Erin. Nice to see you, pal. S'cuse the language. Hope this big eijit hasnae been botherin you?'

He remembered ma name.

'Ah decided ah'd take you up, on your offer. If it's still, okay?'

'Of course. Has He even offered you a drink?'

'Have you any tea?'

'Tea?' You'd think ah asked for champagne.

'Ah'm sure there must be some. Sit down, an ah'll make you a cup.'

Him an the Fat Boy both go into the kitchen. One of them closes the door behind them.

Tojo isn't drunk. If he was, ah'd definitely leave. Maybe, ah'll think about ma options after the tea. Tea will help me think. During the time mum was sick, ma dad an me were drinkin tea all the time. When ah think about ma dad an me drinkin tea an talkin about whether there's a God or not, a wee bubble of sorrow rises up inside but ah manage to quell it before Tojo puts the mug down on the floor at the side of my chair. Ah'm glad ah remembered about the tea. It made me not think about the snake in the room.

'Ta, that's great.' The tea looks weak lik Simmit makes it but hot. No milk and ah'm not askin for any.

'Well, drink up,' Tojo says.

One mouthful, there's a funny taste from it.

They gie each a look that ah don't like, the way they look at the mug then ma face.

Before ah can think straight, start to work it out the answer seems to be flying away from me, can't seem to hold onto thoughts.

Don't drink it, Erin. Don't...

Ah'm no drinkin another drop.

Try not to look nervous about the mug, about the tea.

'Is there really a snake in that tank?'

He nods towards it.

'Och, that's nothin to worry about. Ah've kept snakes for years. It's not dangerous. Anyway...'

The Fat One has moved, he's standin at the door, neither inside the room or outside. Keepin ma eye on his movements.

'Never mind that. When are we getting the gear?'

Ah don't know how can they say never mind a snake. Ah can't take ma eyes of the tank.

'You gonnae shut it? Everything's fixed. Ah'm talkin to Erin, now.'

If they've put somethin in ma drink then they'll expect me to be drowsy. But maybe ah'm too suspicious after bein away from ma family. Still, Tojo is so jumpy. One side of the mug has a dirty mark. Turn it away, pretend drink out the other end. Bring the mug to ma lips an tilt ma head but no tea goes down ma throat. From the kitchen sounds of bottles and cans being banged around then in comes the Fat Boy again. He watches me an Tojo, his belly hangin over the top of his trousers. When he drains the last from his lager can, chucks the can towards a wee plastic bin on the floor, missin it by ages, lager spillin out, spraying bits of wallpaper above the fireplace. Don't disturb the snake. Please. As long as ah don't see it.

'Haw, eijit features. Gonnae give it a rest?' Tojo on his feet, any minute now there'll be punches then sirens an ah'll be in the middle.

'Sit on your fat arse. You're givin me the creeps.' Tojo's fingers are right up at Fat Boy's face. Suddenly his hand takes the shape of a gun pointin but it's still only a hand. His voice changes, he becomes someone older, trying to fob off a wean.

'Take it easy, will you.'

'It's you makin me nervous. How long is this gonnae take? We've stuff to organise. People to see.'

279

The Fat One is less animated now. Still, Tojo seems to have a hold over him. He can change everythin by the tone of his voice.

'God, would you have some patience? We'll get there.'

Next time ah look up to where the other guy was, he's not there. Fat Boy. Is he in a huff? Try to listen for him moving in another part of the flat but no sound. Funny, that ah didnae hear him leavin. Around the same time Tojo goes out the room as well. There's a wee overflowin bin; lift some take away cartons from the top an pour the tea in. Disnae smell lik proper tea.

'Are you okay? You look a bit funny?' Tojo comes back in.

'Ah'm fine. Tired. On the go all day. Is the snake definitely not dangerous?'

'Aye, stop worryin about the snake. You must be knackered. Why don't you lie down for a while? We've things to do in the town. You'll have the place to yourself. We'll be back later. Ah'll bring some grub.'

He seems so kind when he says it, his voice softer than The Fat Boy's but then he goes as if to lift the mug on the floor but ah get there first:

'Ah'll take ma tea in wi me. Ah can sip it slowly.'

'Aye, that's a good idea. You'll probably want to sleep for a while. Don't worry. You'll be fine,' says Tojo.

It would only be for an hour. Tiredness can do funny things, make you think everybody is a threat but mum said never trust strangers.

'Don't trust anyone,' Donna said it as well.

'Tojo's into drugs. Makes him dangerous,' she said but she could talk.

'You'll be fine. Have a good long sleep and then we'll be back.'

He's using that voice he used with the Fat One, like he's hushing me to sleep, sly as an old snake. Hissssssssss.

'Ah do feel funny lik ah could fall asleep right now.'

'That's good, you'll be better for a rest. Here, go in there an lie down.'

He opens another door. There's a single bed. No carpet.

Next thing they're closing over the door of the flat.

18

'Look, Simit. Meat wagon.'

As the laddies come around the corner into their own street, a polis van is parked at their gate.

'It's no even serious. She's at it. She'll turn up.'

Lean the bikes against their fence.

'If they're no here then we should get their days of the week,' Pinkie says.

'Friday an Saturday, you mean?'

'Aye, best days of the week.'

'Ah like Monday. Anyway, we still watch the football on a Saturday so what's the problem?'

Pinkie kicks the tyre of Erin's bike.

'They get the good days then they go. It's us should have the days, cos we're here.'

'She could be back. The polis'll bring her back. She won't get to stay up late an go to Drew's then. Serves her right.'

'Aye, but Drew's awright.'

'Aye, Drew's bang on.'

'But she…she's always…'

'Causin trouble. Lassies, eh..'

At their gate, Tony from across the street is on his bike; his beady eyes on Simmit an Pinkie.

'Check youse out wi the lassies bike,' he points to *The Pink Witch,*
his whole self convulsin wi laughter but disnae take it too far cos
Pinkie is strong even though it's Simit on the pink bike. There's
millions ae the McLaughlins an if he starts a fight wi one, need to take
on the whole family, the da as well.

Pinkie grins. No harm done.

'Whit you to up to?'

'Nuthin. Jist lookin for our Erin.'

Tony looks away from them, to the last the house in the road and then
to the end of the road.

'How, where is she?'

'Dunno. Cannae find her. Have ye seen her?'

'Saw your Anna an Elaine but…'

'Aye, they're fine..we're no lookin for them.'

'An ah saw the two youngest lassies. What's their names…they were
chalkin the pavements.'

Simit an Pinkie notice the scrawled numbers on the pavement for the
first time.

'Naw, no them…'

'Is she in trouble?'

He points to the polis van parked on the road. Pinkie looks at Simmit,
shrugs his shoulders.

'Dunno…'

'Least it's no us, eh?'

Tony chuckles. He's been in trouble for fightin wi boys from the high
flats.

'Fancy a kick about…borin bein on holiday…'

Tony disnae have any brothers, only a younger sister. Ye would be bored the other two boys are thinking.

'Aye…better than school though…'

Simmit an Pinkie keep an eye on their front door in case it opens and the polis come out.

'Right enough.'

'So, do y'eez?'

'What?'

'Fancy a gem?'

'Maybe, later when…'

'Aye…okay…'

Tony lifts his feet off the ground, balances himself on his bike as if he's about to take off.

'Ah could help ye look for her, first. If ye like…'

Simit shakes his head.

'Aye, that would be good. If she's no back after supper, we'll gie ye a shout.'

Tony jumps onto the bike and starts to move.

'At least it'll be dark an folk won't see ye on your sister's bike, Simmit ma man. Whit ye thinkin there?'

He knows they know he only says it for a joke an that if he'd meant anythin he'd have said it when he wasnae peddlin away. The two brothers shake their heads.

'Desperate times…see ye later Tony,' Pinkie's glad it it isn't him on the bike cos no matter how friendly Tony is he'll tell some other boys about the pink bike and they'll slag Simmit lik mad.

19

Can't leave right away in case they're outside watchin but need to not be here when they come back. God knows what they're up to. Even ma breath seems too loud. No sound from the rest of the flat, the snake tank lit up like a tide drawn to the moon, ah'm movin towards it. The mouse is nowhere to be seen, the snake stayin hidden while ah peer into the tank. What if it's not in the tank and they've let it out to scare me? The Fat One threatened it. Turn the handle in the flat door. Nothing happens. Feel about for a key. Still nothing. The flat seems much smaller than when ah came in at first, like being in a cupboard wi the door locked. In the livin- room, light shines through the bottom of uneven curtains that hang baggy on the window. Across the road, most other flats are boarded up. Ah was in that much of a hurry to get here, ah never noticed that either.

At first the window won't budge. Stuck. Ah'm stuck. The windae's stuck. Push really hard, it gives way a wee bit. Final time put all ma strength into it as the window slides upwards, about a third of the way. Air, cold and fresh. Climb onto the sill, levering maself legs first through the gap, ma stomach gets stuck in the middle. If ah was the snake ah'd be able to slide through the gap, no trouble. Why did ah have tae think about that now. The thought of slithery features in the corner gies me strength from nowhere. Push hard again, moves slightly but enough for me to slide through into a messy garden, empty beer cans and broken glass at ma feet. About to push the window closed from the other side. But wait a minute. Now ah'm thinkin they did this deliberately and ah need to get as far away as ah can. Run, not looking back at the big snake eyes that get bigger behind the pile of bark, invisible red tongue still remembering the taste of the mouse, lickin its lips, eyeing up the open windae. Freedom for the snake. Freedom for me.

Now run run as fast as ye can, ye can't catch up wi the Ginger Bread Lassie. High flats peer down at me like grey giants, watchin my every move; not offerin any help: see no evil, hear no evil. Keep running, until can't run anymore. All the time, look out for Tojo and the Fat One in case they're coming in my direction. Donna was right, from now on, ah'll not trust anyone.

Streetlights are on by the time ah cross the nearest of the city bridges, moving further away from flats and houses, towards the outskirts of the buildings in the city. At the end of the bridge, in front of me, a man is eatin chips. The smell wafts past until ah'm nearly drunk wi it. He scrunches up the poke, throwin it into a yellow bin on a lamppost, smell lingerin above the bin, salt and vinegar perfume. Annemarie's face that day we got the chips and the warm feeling because ah'd made her happy. Feel sick at the thought of food but need to eat. Could find a polystyrene cup, kneel in the street, bow ma head, the way the man outside the café was doing, only the polis might see me. Ah'd get lifted, maybe end up lik Donna hangin about the station. If ah can hold on till mornin, go back to the Sal Army place for breakfast. Central Station is a five-minute walk away. The man with the liver spots will

286

be there. Ah know he'll be there, his snake eyes on all the young lassies.

No one sees me reach into the bin for the brown bag, still soggy with chip grease. Right in the corner, enough chips squashed up for a feed. Don't look at what else is there. Shuv them into ma mouth, still warm. As ah'm about to throw the poke away get that feelin in ma stomach when ye're in a car an ye go over a bump too fast but it passes quickly. Wonder how Tojo's snake's getting on. If it's windin its way along the pavements, lookin for a jungle.

Walkin to the street, facin the bridge, decide the important thing is to have a purpose so ah'm kid-on lookin for shops sellin the best deals in weans' clothes. Read prices in one set of windaes then take off to find somewhere to compare them with. At first, convince maself but after a while the balls of ma feet start tae hurt. Clock above a shoe shop near the station says it's only been a half an hour, ah've done the route of the shops twice. It's depressin how slow time goes when ye've nowhere to go an it feels a bit daft to be lookin in the same windae for the third time. There are less an less people on the streets of the city centre and lights inside buildings go off with the last person locking up, turning to check the door and that the alarm's been set. Too scared to stop an sit down in case somebody talks to me an ah cannae get rid of them. Cannae do this all night, need to find a place to sleep.

Later, footsteps in front are awright; footsteps behind are for listenin to. Never been on ma own in the city, now ah'm in the dark an ah'm scared of the dark.

Keep to the pavement in case someone pulls you into a car.

Whose car?

A couple are kissin on a bench, skirt around them, tryin not to look in their direction. She's only a couple of years older than me. Wonder what Drew's up to? Has he fallen out with me, yet? Not going to think about him, not his wide smile or the way his hair is a cow's lick at the front. Cos ah've got to keep goin now.

That's a good girl.

Be careful. Keep to the road.

Ah'm going to faint if ah don't sit down soon.

No. Don't stop. Keep going, remember?

Remember, remember, the fifth of November.

Walkin, walkin, till the soles of ma feet hurt, ah meet another man and woman kissin in the street, right on the pavement, in front of everyone. The woman sees me readin some lines of ma book under a street lamp. She starts laughin.

Two girls goin to a party, one dressed in only a bikini and fur boots, the other in shorts and wellingtons. One of them says:

'Hiya, hen, say a prayer for me,' smiles with amazingly white teeth for this part of Scotland. Out the telly teeth. They're both no much older than Donna. Hen. Cheek. If ah get called 'hen' again, ah'm gonnae start cluckin.

If ah'm right, ah'm quite near Marco's café. He could have seen Donna. He might let me sit inside his café for a bit. Wonder how long can a human body keep goin before it has to stop no matter where it is. It's the same as walkin a marathon except in circles. Need to be somewhere safe if ah get so tired, need to sleep. The light is good on the route. No sign of Tojo or Fat Boy; a game of rememberin details of buildins before ah see them next time around, a tenement with the crack on the side wall, lane wi an old pram; even remember types of curtains on windows: tie-backs, drop down blinds, venetian.

***

Marco looks up from the counter when he sees me.

'Hiya, hen.'

Marco disnae mean it in a bad way. Anyway, it's nice wi the Italian accent.

'What you doin out this time yourself?'

'Hiya, Marco. Have you seen Donna?'

Only makin conversation.

'No, no since the other day when she was in wi you. In trouble again is she? See that lassie. But you shouldnae be walkin about on your own, hen. Bloody freezin. Nearly eleven o'clock. Is there anybody ye want me to phone, come pick you up?'

'No, thanks, Marco. Ma dad's collectin me from the station. Ah wanted to say bye to Donna before ah went back home.'

'Ah'm glad you're goin home. Donna's a nice kid but you'll get in bother hangin about wi her. Those laddies.'

'Tojo?'

'Aye, bad news. Always polis in here askin for them.'

Donna never said her an Tojo went round thigither, she only said she knew him.

'Ah'm about to cash up but ah'll make you some tea to take away if you like. Keep you warm on the way to meet your dad. Ma wife's been on the phone. Says ah've tae hurry up, cannae wait to get ma money.'

Marco goes into the back shop to make the tea.

When he comes back, he's carrying an anorak, too small to belong to a man but too big for me.

'Here, this is my wife's. She'll no mind. It'll get cold out there. You can bring it back when you're done with it. Next time you're in the town shoppin wi your mum.'

Ah don't have the heart to refuse. The tea is hot, delicious. It works. Tea always works.

'Marco, how far is Oban from here?'

He looks up from the till.

'About two an a half hours ah'd say, if you know the road. Why do you ask that, hen?'

Everyone ah've told so far about ma plan ends up tellin me how daft it is.

'We might be goin there our holidays, that's all. Ma mum's sister lives there.'

And your brother.

'It's a nice place by all accounts. Ah'm a city man maself. Are you sure you're okay, hen? You look terrible.'

He takes the empty teacup, puts it on the counter.

Ah've been walkin all day an night what does he expect? Ma tights and clothes feel manky, ma hair is plastered onto ma face.

'Ah could go with you to the station, wait for your dad. We could phone him to come pick you up here. Ah'd jist need to phone the wife back. Ah don't think you should be walkin about the streets at this time of the night. What do you say?'

Ah'm so tired runnin, wish ah could take a rest from not feelin safe an go to Marco's even for the one night. He could phone ma dad, it would be okay. A hot water bottle for ma wee single bed in their spare room wi nice wallpaper an watch the telly and Marco's wife will make me a hot chocolate. Bet they've a cat stretched out in front of a gas fire, relaxin itself. Ah'd like to go there. Ah bet Marco's wife is pretty. We might get to know each other an ah can tell her about Fat Boy and Tojo. She'd say:

'Ah'm so glad Marco brought you back here.'

Maybe, it's okay for Paul to stay away an for Annemarie an Lizzie an Joannie to go to ma gran's in Ireland. Then ma daddy might be able to cope better, especially if ah go wi Marco an his wife. Ah'm too old to be adopted an ah've got a family anyway, but ah could still stay wi them for a while, if they let me. That would only leave Anna, Simmit an Pinkie.

And Paul.

Three's no too bad, easier than eight. Ah'd have ma own bed.

Stick together. You've all got to stick together.

At primary school, thick, white glue we plastered on our Japanese dolls wi masks made from wet newspapers that hardened like magic so we could paint on a face. Paper mache. The smell of glue used to make us dizzy, but nobody said it was illegal then cos the teacher gave ye it; couldnae help sniffin it if it was in your hand an ye needed glue to stick a cut out crepe tree to your project about the countryside. It would hang on coloured paper, rolled out across three desks then put up on the classroom wall for the whole term: The Countryside, for a title. Everybody is fallin off the coloured paper in our house lik we're bits of people that used to be a project.

They could put the wee ones in a home. When they split you up, ye'll never be a family again. What if that happens?

No, they cannae put them in a home. They'd hate that. Bein wi strangers, bein away from ma dad.

That's right.

Strangers, Erin. Remember, blood is thicker than water.

Thick and thin.

What if they put us into a home? What if they take the wee ones away? What if what if what if what if what if what if what if what if what if what if what if what if what if what if what if what

So ah need to keep goin. Ah need to get Paul.

That's right. You'd never see them again. So, you have to get the family, my family, back together. It will be fine then.

Okay. Okay. Take a deep breath for the lie.

'Thanks, Marco but ah'm fine, honest. Ah'll walk straight to the station. Ma dad's always early.'

He gies me a look, his brow wrinkled lik he's weighin it up. Then he writes down a number on a bit of paper:

'Look, here. Take this. It's our number, me an the wife. Ah want you to ring me if anythin happens, if your dad isnae there. Do you promise?'

Take the bit of paper an put it in his wife's jacket pocket that ah'm wearin now.

He's happy wi that, starts tidyin up the shop. Wipe the tops of the tables for him while he empties the till. Nice havin somethin to do apart from walkin, avoidin people. When ah put ma hand in the pocket of the jacket ah feel the papery feel of money. Ah don't know how to thank Marco but when the tables are done, offer to clean the floor.

Squeeze out the mop, do the job right.

'It's awright, hen. You better watch your time.'

Marco walks me to the door.

'Awright, pal, now any bother, if your dad's not there, gie us a phone. If you're ever passin again, come in an see me. Stay away from that Donna.'

Ah gie Marco a big wave as he closes over the door. Ah nearly shout back. Wait. Wait.

Don't give up now. Don't stumble at the last hurdle.

Ah need to just get through the night then ah can go an get Paul. That's it.

That's right, you're the eldest. It's up to you.

Ah wish ah could phone ma dad and he would come an meet me for real.

He'd be mad about the ring.

So he would. The ring.

Maybe, Donna's right, maybe after a while no one will care about me. If ah go back, anyway, it'll be a nightmare. Nothin's really any different.

Feel bad about lyin to Marco about meetin ma dad but couldnae tell him the truth. He'd phone his wife, end up takin me back home. Marco's nice, kind. Donna's lucky so many people care about her, Marco, her Aunt Maureen. One day she'll realise it.

An hour later, still walkin the streets. Ah'm exhausted. So much has happened in the last few hours, more than in ma entire life. Bein on the streets is exhaustin, always on your guard. Is this learinin the hard way? Haven't seen anyone for ages until this car passes, music blarin from inside, windows blacked out. It sits outside a tenement for what seems ages until a figure comes to one of the windows, not sure if it's male or female. Now ah'm permanently doin ma detective. What's goin on? Who is in the car and who is in the house? They stay in a deadlock like that, car not movin, person at the window staring down. When the car engine revs up, the figure retreats, pulls the curtains over. Maybe it's a husband and wife, she's chucked him out an he's back, lettin her know he'll always be in her life. Maybe, it's a feud that's been goin on for years, they never actually speak but transmit hatred from car to window then vice versa every night. Everybody seems to be angry at everybody in the city. Ah've seen at least two fights, people staggerin out pubs, shoutin abuse at total strangers. If they could see me they'd start shoutin at me but ah've made maself like a shadow. No one can catch hold of me. Still, don't feel safe. Ages to light time. Wish ah could imagine maself into a warm hotel room, clean sheets an a warm bath. It's Anna's fault, aw those years sharin a room, stories to scare each other, witches wi long nails, claw hands, reachin up between the gap between our bed and the wall. Wish ah could forget that, especially when humans are hard enough to deal

294

with, don't want to bring in ghouls an witches as well. It makes me more tired that ah have no place to go.

Ye have a place to go.

Cannae say keep goin ye'll soon be there cos ah don't know when ah can stop. Might need to walk the whole night, legs feel heavy an ma head feels light. At least now everythin is quieter, normal people wi normal lives, finally in proper houses wi proper beds. Gettin quicker doin the loop the loop, past Marco's café. This time the shop's closed, makes me feel sad. Maybe, ah should have went wi him but then ah'd never get Paul back. And no to see the others growin up every day would be terrible. We'd be whole different people by the time we met again. Wonder how could we cross the Irish sea to visit every summer holiday when we would still be weans an no have money.

So get your brother back before the rot sets in

20

'Will we go in?'

Simmit an Pinkie are still at their gate. Starlings startin to land on the telephone wires, makin a sound that will become a football stadium of noise.

'Naw, let's try one last lap before night. Ah thought ah saw somebody like her in Flaxmill Avenue.'

'We should try there then.'

Simmit shivers under his jumper.

'Ah cannae believe you've been through the whole of Wishaw on *The Pink Witch*. That's funny.'

'Ah know. Arrestable offence, ma man, arrestable offence.'

They both mount their bikes again, pedal away from the house.

In Flaxmill Avenue, the lights are on, and were curtains aren't drawn the two boys can see inside to living rooms. People are eatin dinner and watchin telly. The two go around the street three times but can't find the girl they thought might be Erin.

'Maybe, it was her an she's gone up the road now.'

'Ah'm starvin,' Pinkie says.

'Me too,' Simmit replies.

'Dad won't go will he?'

Pinkie is tying his shoe lace, as Simmit wheels the two bikes in front of them, going to the back of the house. He doesn't answer him.

Brodie is supposed to be the tougher one. That's why he gets to be him. He kids- on he never heard it. They go inside, one after the other, not speaking. They can hear the adult voices as they come through the door. The house feels warm and they can smell the dinner smells from the kitchen. They close the door behind them on the cold night, with the pink and blue bikes leaning against the back wall.

21

Ten minutes later, runnin back over the bridge. Smell of water, smell of city river water, river and sky: same black that ah cannae find anythin in. At the end of the bridge, an entrance to a park lit up inside. Along its wide walkway, lined with trees and fancy lampposts. No way can ah bed down inside the city centre, bad enough bein mobile, keep on the move an ah'll be safe. Have to last the next few hours, get to the hostel in the mornin, ah'm fast on ma feet, faster than ah realised. And parks have benches. Keep the statue of a stone needle in sight once ah've walked through the stone arch at the entrance. Once inside, grass to the sides, a wide paved path slices through the middle. Ahead, some men are unloadin from a green van. Smell of newly cut grass and rain. The needle is a five-minute walk from here wi a building beyond. Slow down to a normal pace. Take a deep breath, stay calm, everythin's gonnae be fine.

Close up, the same two men are fittin what looks lik metal barriers together, makin a fence, a piece at a time. One holds a section, lowerin it towards another bit of the fence, getting the hooks in line with holes. His yellow jacket says: '*Land Services.*' The jacket is filthy. The other guy is tryin to explain somethin with his hands, movin onto the pavement.

The younger one notices me; nods his head, lookin for support. The older one, whom ah've just noticed has grey hair stickin out the sides of his woollen hat still hasnae seen me. He looks towards the big glass buildin:

'Hey Stupid Heid. Did you lock that side door, properly? Ah'm sure ah just saw it bangin against the wall, there.'

The younger guy with dark, curly hair and a persecuted look, shakes his head:

'Aye, gonnae shut-it wi the 'Stupid Heid,' Davy. You're turnin intae a right nag.'

There's no other way, ah've got to pass them.

'God, hen, ah thought you were a ghost. Been at an all night party?'

If they get suspicious.

'Aye. On ma way home. Ah live over there,' point to the big flats ahead.

The older one gies me a long look.

'Ye shouldnae take this as a short cut, hen. No safe.'

Checkin out ma over-sized anorak, too long sleeves.

'Ah'm fine, ah know ma way. Ma dad's lookin out for me, he can see me when ah get to the end of the park.'

'Well, you better hurry up. This place is usually well locked up but we're gettin it ready for a concert the morra.'

'Whose playin?'

'Don't bloody know hen. Aw ah know is, we've got enough work to do without this on top our normal work.'

Turns away to lift another section of fence from the van.

'Mind, hen. We're lockin the last gate on our way out. You make sure you don't get locked in.'

The one called Stupid Heid makes a face behind his back. Good to smile again.

The stone needle says '*Nelson,*' on one side, '*Trafalgar,*' on the other. Names around the base: Scots who died in some great battle against the French and Spanish.

The glass buildin is a glass house for a giant from one of our Annemarie's storybooks. A sign reads: '*People's Palace.*' Ah'm one of the people so don't feel too bad about breakin in. Only takin what belongs to me. In front is a red stone fountain, heads of lions in a circle, mouths pourin out water. Right at the top lik the fairy on a Christmas tree, Queen Victoria. Never smilin. She seems so sure of everythin. She makes things tick. She's in charge of the empire an when she goes we're aw at a loss how we'll govern our countries.

'Britannia.'

Mum was lik a queen, wi aw her ways of dealin wi money lik that was the treasury an the way she ran our house lik a kingdom. Ah've inherited the crown. Ah don't want it an ah don't deserve it, either.

Other words on the fountain: 'Let Glasgow flourish.'

Queen Victoria's face is chubby as a hamster, soft lookin; her stone mouth, tightly shut:

'Go back to your father, young girl.'

Aye right.

Get me my son.

Ah don't know if ah can keep goin.

Say a prayer. Then ye'll get the answer.

Dear God ah'm so tired. Help me.

Nothin.

Typical.

The blue book and the black book. Remember what they're for.

The Queen stares down at me, steady gaze, never flinchin from her duty. So, ah shouldnae complain about mine.

Lamplight makes the surface of the water shimmer. Sweep a hand across. The water is icy. Under the surface, a layer of coins on the fountain's floor. They look ornamental, without value. Could soon put them to good use. Freezin, the water in the fountain comes up to ma knees. Need to keep checkin that the men in yellow jackets aren't moving towards me, that ah'm well hidden by the height of the fountain sides. Twenty pences mostly, a few tens and even a couple of fifties. Our Pinkie an the other boys would love this. They're always scavengin, ginger bottles mostly. Simit's great in water, fantastic for catchin netfuls of tadpoles.

Those people that threw the money, wonder what they wished for, aw their hands reachin out, as the money was launched. More money, or to be famous. Ask maself what's the difference between a dead queen and a God that does not answer. Well, at least ah'm not begging, ah'm bein resourceful like goin to the bank to draw out money, except, of course, it's no mine.

Stop shivering or someone will hear your bones rattlin.

Dry your clothes over a radiator or you'll get a chill.

Starts to rain. Drops of rain explodin on puddles, runnin down panes of glass in the glass palace. Definitely, need to get indoors now. Wait a minute. Think, think. Hide low down in a sheltered spot wi some trees. Glad now ah took ma jacket off before goin in the water. Rush of wind brings a bangin sound to the right, from the same direction, a small door, openin and closin. No thinkin about it just a decision by my body to be somewhere warm. Once inside the glass palace, moonlight switched on, makin everything feel lit up, brighter lik in another world until the sound of a car engine comes from no-where. Lie on the floor, away from the door, waitin.

There are two voices from outside, nearby.

'Fuckin wind. If that door smashes, it's me'll get the row. What did ah tell you, Stupid Heid? Always check the door.'

'Aye right, you said. That's the last night shift ah'm agreein to. Do you hear me? The last. You sort it. You're the foreman.'

'Here, gie me your jacket.'

Sleep under a tree, under the stars.

Aye, that'll be right. Get pneumonia, more like it.

Lock turnin, a hard push away to check the door is lock fast. Metal scraping the ground as somethin is moved against the door. If ah wanted to get out, no chance now. Silence then apart from wind and rain. In the darkness can make out a counter, some kind of shop.

Shadow of the truck drives across the words:

'Opening Hours: 9.00 am- 4.30pm.'

Box of vinegar crisps.

Surely, ah couldn't be this lucky?

Shelves under the counter filled wi white cups, matchin saucers, more boxes of crisps and biscuits: digestives and custard creams. Start wi a packet of crisps, washed down by a can of coke, wee biscuit for puddin. So bloated then, cannae move. Like when ah've starved maself of chocolate at Lent then eat two whole Easter eggs in one go on Easter Sunday mornin. Sick as a pig the rest ae the day. But ah wish Donna was here cos that would make this funny.

Beyond the counter, a jungle of trees, big exotic lookin plants ah've never seen before. Tojo's snake would be right at home. Any minute now, a lion out one ae our Annemarie's books'll appear.

Jungle heat generated from a band of black pipe startin under the windows, extendin round the entire room, makin steam rise from ma jacket as if ah'm cooking from the inside. Hate to think what ah smell like. The tree trunks are baldy wi branches like bigger versions of sticky out bits on pineapples. All the trees have plaques. Maybe this is a museum for trees. One says: 'Banana,' followed by a long word in Latin. Latin for banana, ah suppose.

Bright coloured flowers, reds, yellows, all planted in white coloured stone. One day ah'll bring the wee ones here because you'd never believe you could find real banana trees in Glasgow never mind Scotland.

The path around the trees and plants is made of rickety wood, wobbles when ah step on it like those connecting bits on trains goin to ma gran's in Ireland. Keep away from windows in case anyone sees me but it's hard when the whole place is made of glass. Roof even higher than a church roof. It's the People's Palace and ah'm the queen. Benches around the outer wall but keep to the middle, the trees are dense, ah can't be seen.

You'd expect hum of bees and flies in a place like this but no sound apart from the flow of water, pourin out the mouths of wee wooden structures that tip every-time the water gets heavy enough. Anorak for a pillow, lean against a banana tree near two Weeping Figs.

'...*The day is come when I again repose*
Here, under this dark sycamore...'

Wonder if there is a sycamore here, how you know one.

Easy to fall asleep against a tree when you're this tired, the free crisps, heat from the pipes and, at last, somewhere to lie down, without worrying that somebody's gonnae stab me or kick me in the head. Don't think ah can take another day of this. Rather turn maself in. How can you go from havin everythin, a proper family, a nice house to stealin money from a fountain, sleepin on a stone floor? Too tired to work it out.

Fall asleep to the smell of bananas and figs.

Ah really miss everybody, ma brothers and sisters, miss ma dad as well. Ah miss the way he makes us all laugh, makin up wee sayins, callin soup 'soup the loup, his track-suit bottoms, 'bombers. You never know what he's goin to say next but it's funny. Ah miss sittin at the other side of the gas fire listenin to his stories about when he went to school with no shoes on: girls in the mornins, boys in the afternoons. Ah miss the way no matter how bad it is, he's never made me leave school, no matter what anybody else says and that he does it cos that's what ma mum would have wanted. Ah miss ma mum. Ah miss her voice, not like any other mum's voice, her Irish accent that's got a bit Scottish from bein here so long. Ah miss her warmth, the clean smell of the floors when it's the holidays and food always cookin when ah come home from school Ah miss somebody lookin out for me, caring if ah wear wet tights and clean clothes. Because ah don't care. Ah really don't care now and ah don't know if ah ever will.

He's your own brother.

Okay, ah'll keep goin but ah need a rest. Ah need to sleep somewhere. Ah'm not givin up on us, on Paul, on you. Ah jist need to lie down somewhere safe till the mornin.

That night, dream of green an orange Lovebirds in a beautiful garden. Bright colours, ah never believed Paul that they were real. Maybe, when he said that time he saw them, it was a dream too. The green an orange colours are bright lik the colours of Opal Fruits: lime and orange flavours. Then the birds' faces are faces of people ah know: Donna, Marco, dad and Drew; all talkin in a language ah don't understand; all at the same time. Bird language. Dream of a boy with a hole in his heart that got shot by an Indian with a pot on his head, before he was even born.

22

'Christ, who are you?'

No a parrot voice but a human voice says it.

At first ah think ah've succeeded, that one of the birds in ma dream has decided to speak ma language. Then, instantly, the birds scatter to their secret branches inside ma head an ah'm in the middle of the wooded area, nowhere near were ah fell asleep, sleepwalkin. Somebody said at school that if ye wake a person when they're in a sleep walk, ye could damage them for the rest of their life. Maybe that's what happened to me earlier, that's why ma life is such a mess.

Anyway, this woman's glarin at me, holdin a sweepin brush towards me, plans hittin me wi it, any minute. An me only in ma underwear cos ah've put ma clothes to dry on the hot pipes. Out of the corner of ma eye, ah can see the clothes, lookin crisp an bone dry.

'Don't move or ah'll phone the polis. There's a phone, in the office an ah've got a key so don't think ah can't.'

Pointing her cigarette at me, another angry finger.

'Ah was only shelterin, no stealin, only crisps.'

'Who else is with you? Is your boyfriend here, where is he? Waitin to jump me? Ah'll hit him wi this brush wherever he is.'

If ah move she might think ah'm attackin her. Try to remember if ah've read anythin, seen anythin on the telly, how to deal wi a mad person intent on killin ye wi a brush.

'Please, don't hit me. There's no one else here. Only me.'

Gies me a long, scathin look.

Using her foot, stubs out the cigarette, lifts the doubt from the floor an throws it towards a metal bin against the wall. Then she gies me another long look as if everythin hangs in the balance. Wishin those birds wi faces would appear again, peck her on the body like in *The Birds* by Alfred Hitchcock, gie me some time to get away.

'Ah'd get the sack if anyone caught you. How did you get in anyway?'

Tell her about the open door.

'Stupid ejits, they two. Laurel an Hardy. Right comedians they two. 'S me would get the blame.'

Still clenchin the brush so danger not over but her voice isnae as threatenin. Her anger's turned onto the workmen an ah've got a reprieve. Gies me a chance to look at her in case she injures me an ah've got to describe her to the polis. Not old, about the same age as mum. She notices the coat on the radiator, ma tights rolled up in ma shoes.

When she lowers the brush, try movin to get ma coat. She disnae fly at me. Ah'm sore from lyin on the ground, an ma nose starts to run. That's what ah get for jumpin in the fountain. Put the anorak on, tryin to remember the direction of the door. Half the coins roll out the pocket, rattlin across the floor.

She looks at the money then at me.

'That better no be from ma till.'

'Naw, honest. Ah've been here all night. Ah've not been near your till.'

'Well, where do you think you're goin?'

'Nowhere. Ah mean, away.'

She does that clickin thing wi her tongue that mum used to do.

'God's sake, hen.'

And, this time, as soon as she says 'hen,' ah know it's going to be all right.

'Put your clothes on in the toilet then come back an sit on that bench. The kettle's on. You're no goin anywhere till you tell me how you got here. And then ah'm makin you some breakfast. Do you like ham and cheese toasties?'

Ah like cheese. Ah like ham. Ah like toast.

'Aye. Ah mean, yes.'

'Aye's, fine here. Now go and wash your face at the sink in the toilet. Take that towel on the counter. And there's soap. Ah've got some perfume in ma bag.'

The warm water feels great. The woman hums a tune to herself, the radio on, as she cuts a block of red cheese into slices. The white towel has '*City Council Property,*' written across it. She catches a glimpse of herself in a small mirror on the window ledge. It's one that magnifies everythin, makin your face seem enormous, a huge country of freckles and skin.

'State of ma hair,' she says to herself, tutting at the grey section near her left ear.

Can you do nothin right?

The kettle clicks off as the lid jumps off wi the heat of the steam.

'What time will folk arrive?'

Ah've found out her name is Francis. She works here in the mornin, doin some cleanin before the café opens; does some hours in the café

308

as well. Needs the money cos her man lost his job. Francis continues slatherin cheese between two slices of bread, placin the sandwich on a machine wi two triangle shapes engraved on the surfaces.

'Och, don't worry. Not for ages, hen. We'll have this then ah'll get the place spick and span. Won't be anybody for a few hours. There's a big concert so they're openin late an workin later.

'Where does your family live, hen?'

Here we go wi lies again. Ah'm in that deep now, got to find a way of gettin away, without Francis suspectin. Ah need to get to hostel to make sure ah get that lift from Doris' friend. Don't have time for the whole story.

'We fell out.'

'Fell out! Ma ones are always fallin out…fallin in. That's normal. But runnin away, hen. That's different. That's serious. Your poor mum's heart'll be roasted.'

It would be. She'd kill me if she knew. If dead people could kill, she'd murder me for this. Cannae bear to think what would happen if she knew ah'd run away, left the wee ones, left ma dad on his own.

The smell from the machine with triangles is unbearable. Cheese drizzles out the sides, running onto the worktop.

'Ah know. Ah've learned ma lesson.'

'It's no easy on the streets, is it?'

'Ah'm goin straight back.'

'What made you run away? That's a bit drastic, is it no?'

The house was fallin apart an he was that depressed he was bringin us all down with him, he wouldnae let me paint the livin room and he never gave us enough money for things and he didnae believe in birthdays or Christmas. None of this ah tell her though she is a person you could talk to.

Freedom and the possibilities.

'Clothes. Ah fell out wi ma mum about clothes.'

'The usual. Mines are always 'want want want.' They think money grows on trees.'

Really? Well, it doesn't. It's at the bottom of stone fountains.

'And what about your dad?'

What about him?

'He's dead hard to talk to. He never talks about stuff.'

'What stuff do ye mean, hen?'

Ah don't know.

'When bad things happen lik ma granny dyin, he acts as if everythin's the same. Stuff lik that.'

Ah hope ma granny disnae die cos ah said that.

'Och hen maybe, he disnae know how to talk about feelins an things lik that. Men are aw the same. Ma man's the same. But, listen, ma weans are older than you, aw leavin home. They never talk tae us now. It kills ma man. He misses them. One day, you're dad'll be the same. He'll be able to talk to you. Takes time, hen. It's no easy bringin weans up.'

'Ah've learned ma lesson.'

'Ah hope you have, hen, ah really do.'

Ah make tea in two white mugs, leavin the bag in mine for a while. She tells me to quick dip the bag in hers and add some cold water.

The toastie has wee lines across it, the triangle imprint of the machine. The edges are really hard, harder than normal crust but when ah bite

310

through the soft middle, cheese is burstin out, still stringy and hot. The breakfast is great and sets me up for the rest of the morning. It's a pity about the lies. And later ah know ah'll dream that ah tell the woman the truth and she feels sorry for me. That much we go back to her house, with all her family. With their family photos on the walls and their telly in the corner. Just like mine.

Charity begins at home.

That's right so it does. No use bein nice to everybody else if ye don't sort out your own family first. Ah'm glad ah thought that. When she goes to the toilet ah have to decide. Leave or stay. Leave or stay. No contest now. Ah've got this far. The next part is the easy part. Just get back to the hostel, meet Doris, get the money then catch ma bus.

Passin the fountain, one last look at Queen Victoria and the lions.

Hail, Your Majesty.

Hurry up, hurry up.

Off with her head.

The uniform fits, see me…

The statue has mum's tone of voice when she wants you to do somethin an it's a final final warnin. Floor of the fountain is bare, clear, after me. Cleaned it dry, worse than a crow fallin on stale bread. Even though ah don't believe it will come true, throw half the money back in the water.

That's for everybody's wishes. That's them again, Your Majesty. Gie them double luck. Ah wish you were back. Ah'll always wish that.

Above me a sea gull courses the wind, amazin how it seems made to be able to do that, the way it holds its own in the wind. Ah wish Paul was here that ah could say that to him. When ah think of the conversation, it disnae seem possible that me an our Paul would ever say those things now we're older.

The gull starts squawkin above me. That's aw ah need:

'Shut-up. Shhhhh.'

Goin over the bridge towards the hostel, mornin sky is red as if somebody is burnin their rubbish in a big fire out their back, in the distance; outlines of trees an buildins startin to take shape in the grey light of the mornin, an above me, clouds move in a journey to the city that never ends. But really, it makes me feel better to look at the sky. Ah feel lighter: a weight lifted.

Look to nature and you'll find strength.

Nature is your answer to everythin. It disnae bring people back.

But you feel better.

Ah do. At this moment though ah'm scared it won't last.

***

There's a phone box on the way to the hostel. One ring home to let them know ah'm on ma way back tonight. That'll buy the time ah need to get to Aunt Mary's. Then one ring to Paul. If he doesn't answer, ah'll leave it. Dial our number, hand is shakin, now.

You're wasting time. Time waits for no man.

'Hiya.'

They don't speak, probably Annemarie, she does that.

'It's Erin, Annemarie.'

Still, no answer. We're turnin into a family of silent callers.

'Annemarie, ah don't have time for this. Is dad in?'

'Have you runned away?'

'No, ah'm at Drew's house, didn't ah tell you. Ah'll be back tonight.

'We can play a game if ye like.'

'Yeees. Ring a Ring A Roses...'

'Anythin.'

'We found Jesus' body. See you.'

And she puts the phone down.

Dial again.

Anna this time.

'Is dad there?'

'No, you're in big trouble. Where are you? He's got the polis lookin for you?'

Think. Hurry up, think. Time, need a bit more time. Ah'm so close.

'Drew's mum phoned. Where are you? Dad's goin nuts.'

Ah've got to take a chance an tell her. They could easily trace this call an then they'd find me an ah'd never get to our Paul.

313

'Ah'm goin to see Paul. To try an get him to come home. It's the only way things can get better. Ah've thought about it.'

Put the telephone down. Don't let her talk you out of it.

'Will you just not say ah've phoned. Ah'm fine. Ah've got money to get there an everything. Will you do that?'

'Just bring ma eyelash curlers back wi you.'

And then she puts down the phone.

23

He shouldn't have picked up the phone but Aunt Mary and Jim were at work. He was havin his cornflakes and toast, gettin ready for school. Paul had been feelin much better, had even started to say things again, but he wasn't right, yet. Not back to his own self. So, when it was his sister at the other end of the phone, he froze.

'Hello, hello…' She sounded weird.

'Is that you, Paul. Is it? For God sake, Paul. Speak to me, will you. Ah know it's you.'

A long pause. The crackling of a bad line.

'Paul, you have to come back home. Do you hear me? You have to tell me what she said? You were there. You have to help.'

That's right, Erin. Tell him to come home. This charity is ridiculous. We don't use Shake and Vac. Why did you use it?

She won't give up.

'Ah'm sayin it once. Don't ask me again, ever.'

He was speaking at least, that was a big step.

'Look, ah'm commin to get you, you can tell me then.'

'No, don't come, ah don't want you to come. She said nothin. There was nothin. You have to stop this, now. You have to. The polis are lookin for you. Ah don't want you to come. Ah don't want to come home.'

Then he puts the phone down.

There's nothing else to be done; he doesn't know how to, even if he wants to.

Next day his dad is on the phone again to Mary and Jim. Paul hears them from another room, doesn't say Erin rang. He doesn't want a big conversation, doesn't want to have to talk to them about it. He takes the new binoculars and goes for a walk along the road to the shore front, to watch boats coming and going to islands he's never heard of, looking for a girl wi dark, curly hair an green eyes that he will know but she never appears.

Don't listen to him, Erin. It's the shock.

But what if he does mean it?

What does he know?

No, you're right. Ah have to keep goin.

That's right. No turnin back now.

24

Doris meets him in a café inside Central Station.

The black leather jacket with the polo underneath makes him seem to Doris lik someone out the telly. An he's got shoes wi a heel. Must be cos he's tryin to be taller but they make him look a bit of an eijit is all.

'Hiya, Andy. Still, wearin the flashy gear? That jacket must have cost a bomb. You never change.'

Doris smiles through her yellowing, squinty teeth and he grins back, his teeth perfectly white and straight. She hasn't had a fix today; feelin desperate. Her whole body craves for it and she'll not get any work till night. She's cursin herself for givin Erin any money. Maybe, guilt made her do it. Reminds herself, she can't afford guilt

'Hiya, doll,' he grins. They both do. She's not been 'doll,' for a long time. This is just chat. They have to do this.

Doris knows Andy is wearin better than she is. He's makin money from his line of work.

'What you drinking?'

'Only tea, in here,' she replies.

'You get them, will you,' he says throwing a tenner across the table.

'Sure. Sugar an milk or still sweet enough?'

'Just milk. Can you make it quick, I've somewhere else to go.'

That hurts. She's set all this up for him. Could have gone to someone else. It's not easy moving around these days. She feels a pain in her hip when she tries to move.

'Ah'll do ma best,' she says, looking at the queue.

When she comes back with tea, she goes to give him his change.

He says:

'Keep it,' looks away as she pockets the money.

'So, how's the wean?'

Andy looks at Doris, grinning.

She glares at him, her hand is shaking as she spoons sugar into the cup.

'Don't you dare ask me about her.'

'Take it easy. Still wi the social workers, then. She's better off, Doris. Face it.'

None of his business. 'Well, where's the lassie?' Andy asks.

'Doris stirs the sugar in her tea.

No right talking about her daughter. She's a good mind to call the whole thing off.

'Patience. Have you got the money?'

She considers doing him over. Taking the money and then disappearing. But when she thinks of it, she can't think of anywhere to go.

'Now, whose talkin.'

They'd agreed a figure on the phone.

'Ah'm not doin it here. Somebody might see us.'

'Still, frightened of the polis gettin a hold of you. How come everybody else gets the jail but you?'

Doris had known Andy nearly all her life.

'Cos ah'm careful, that's why. Now, where is she?'

'Shhhh. Keep your voice down. She's meetin me at the hostel tomorrow mornin, first thing.

She thinks you're takin her to Oban, to her relative.'

'Oban. Aye, that'll be right.'

'Look, ah'm only tellin ye what she thinks. To make it easier. Now, leave the money on your seat an get up.'

'You better not be screwin wi me, Doris. Ah swear to God ah'll…'

He takes an envelope out of his inside pocket, places it on the seat beside him then stands up.

'See ye tomorrow mornin then?'

She leans over the table, looks into his eyes.

'Don't hurt her. She's a nice wee thing.'

He grins.

'Cross ma heart,' he says.

'Mind the money. Don't lose it.'

As soon as he leaves, Doris lifts the envelope from the seat and shuvs it into a plastic bag.

25

True to her word, Doris is waitin for me outside the hostel.

'Where did you stay last night, hen? That bitch didn't let you in, did she?'

There's no point tellin Doris about Tojo and getting locked in the flat or about spendin the night in The Peoples' Palace.

'Ah stayed with a pal of mine. She's got a flat in the city centre. Ah know her from home.'

She isn't saying if she believes me or not.

Ah don't know why ah always have to depend on strangers to help. If ah was an adult everythin would be so much easier. Ah'd be able to work, get money for maself. But she's made the effort, ah can't say ah'm not going now.

'Where's your pal?'

'He'll be here soon, don't worry. He'll have you at your aunt's house in a few hours.'

Auntie Mary'll be angry about me lying to dad but once ah explain, she'll sit me down and we'll talk and everythin will be better. An Paul will be there; at last. Ah'll get Paul back. Things will be better. Better than it's been. It has to be today. Ma da'll start to wonder when ah'm not home this evenin. That's when he'll ring Drew's mum and then the trouble will really start. He'll get the polis. They'll all know: ma dad, Drew, his mum; everyone will know that ah've run away. The wee ones will know an they'll think ah've run away from them.

They're better off without you. You never washed the collars right for school.

You're an animal, you.

Aw the voices are getting mixed up in ma head. Maybe, ah'm goin mad. Pretend ah don't hear but know it's true.

He arrives at the hostel an hour later, driving a white sporty Capri, smelling of aftershave, not like Drew's, that you can detect from half a mile away.

Doris says she knows him from way back.

Don't go with strangers, remember.

Well, beggars can't be choosers and it's either this or another night here and then God only knows what. Donna told me that she's had her name down for a flat for ages but that ye need to have a wean yourself to be in priority need and she said that even when ah turn sixteen ah won't be entitled to any money in my own right.

'Are you ready for the road then, honey?' Ah don't like being called stuff like that, words right out of a pop song: 'Sugar de de de de de. Oh honey honey. You are ma Candy girl.'

'This is Andy,' Doris says.

'Mind you look after her.'

There's a spot light fixed to the back window, the kind that makes a car stand out when you meet it on the road and a black and white furry dice, suspended at the front; silver colour wheel trims. He's straight out the letters page of The Jackie, this guy, except he's a bit old, even for Sally's big sister who gets The Jackie every week. Mum got me

The Diana but there were no posters of pop stars to put on your wall. Sally and me used to read the letters pages for a laugh:

Dear Jackie,
There's this boy in the youth club that I fancy.
How can I get him to notice me?
Infatuated Manchester.

Jackie writes

Dear Infatuated from Manchester,
Boys don't like girls to be too obvious. You could find an excuse to talk to him:
Ask him the time or bump in to him, gently. Make good eye contact but be natural.
If he likes you back, he'll soon get the message.
Good Luck,
Jackie

Ah used to dream of writing to Jackie about Drew before we started going together but comics were kind of out of fashion by then. Still, it was nice thinkin Jackie would read your letter and put all that thought into your problem. When mum got sick ah wondered about writin for some advice but no one ever writes about people dying or stuff like that.

'If anybody asks, we'll say you're my niece, okay? And ah need to go somewhere else first. Won't be long though.'

Cheek. Tellin me to lie but under the circumstances ah don't have much choice.

'Will it take long to Oban?'

'Just relax. Ah'll keep you right.'

Pats me on the arm. Wish ah'd kept ma jumper on.

When we start off it's daylight. Trees take over from buildins. Never knew there were so many trees in Scotland. There's loads of rhode bushes as well, though the big flowers are not out full bloom. He switches on the radio attached to the walnut effect dashboard: Kate Bush singing Wuthering Heights. Drew thinks she's great. Haven't thought about Drew in a long time; wish he was here. Wonder if ma dad's phoned his house and if he knows ah've scampered.

Sink back into the leather upholstery. Better than our dad's Ford Cortina with us nine inside more like an endurance test than a pleasurable experience. The man asks me what music ah like and ah say mostly disco: Abba's Dancin Queen and The Bee Gees.

There's a big silence so ah tell him how at school some of the boys are getting into The Sex Pistols. He disnae say anythin back for a while.

'You're at school?'

'Aye, ah'm in third year.'

A tremor passes along the side of his face like the forerunner to an earthquake.

'And what does your family say about you travelling the country on your own? That's if you've got any family?'

Something in me wants to keep pleasing him until ah see a sign for Oban. Wish we were goin straight there, not first to his friend he has to see about a dog.

'Don't have family. Just ma aunt.'

Taps the side of the wheel.

'And does she know you're on you're way? Your aunt?'

'Aye, she's expectin me.'

'Oh, right. And what street does she live in? Ah know that area well.'

The spasm on the face, again.

'You can let me off at the shopping centre. Ma uncle'll collect me in his car.'

Pass a stretch of road with the biggest houses ah've seen. Hard to believe people live here when a few miles away Donna cannae get her own flat and ma dad and all the rest of them are squeezed into our house.

A sign says: *Loch Lomond 3 miles.* After a while of more trees the road widens to a view of water on the right hand side.

'Can we stop, please?'

He turns the radio down.

'Sorry, what?'

'Can we stop. Ah've never seen Loch Lomond. Look…'

He's got his two arms full stretched on the steering wheel.

'Whit for?'

'To see it, just.'

'Sorry, hen. Look at the queue. Must be the golf. Ah'll need to go another way.'

That's right, you don't have time.

A long line of cars, movin slowly.

The loch is a grey mirror that hills and green islands look into. There's nothin movin on the surface. In the distance, mist is commin down over the hills. The water says still, still, still. Wish ah could be still as a loch inside me.

Head in the clouds, head in the clouds. Remember.

He goes off the road we're on, around another twisty road. Every time he turns the wheel ma whole body lurches to one side, the same direction as the car but he stays straight the whole time as if he has somethin inside him that keeps him from flopping to the side. We take a turn as if we are doubling back on ourselves.

There's not been a road sign for a while but it is the country. Darkness falls quickly, so the trees and bushes and hills disappear into black. No street lights either on the twisty roads.

A sign says: *Trossachs,* not Oban.

Maybe, he knows a short cut.

Ah don't want to sleep. As the dark gets so he can only see the bit of the road the headlamps light up, this big boulder size shape makes the car swerve to the other side of the road. He steadies the car an we're okay again.

'What the fuck?' Unfastening his seat belt.

Ah'm not sittin here in the dark maself so unfasten ma seat belt to follow him out. But the door's locked. Ah'd forgotten he'd locked the door when ah got in before.

Hit on the window wi ma fist. He turns an look at me an shakes his heid. Keep hittin the window till he finally unlocks the passenger door.

'What's up wi you? Ye're safer in there.'

'Ah want to see,' ah reply.

It's dark outside even although he's put on his emergency lights. At first, don't see what he's lookin at cos the darkness of the road is

325

overwhelmin, no lights of houses, only the light from the car. At the other side of the road, a young deer is lying on its side. Looks as if it's takin a nap. Only other time ah've seen a real deer was the dead one on top of that shed, near Donna's auntie's stall. It's dangerous bein a deer in this part of Scotland. You can see it's chest goin up an down. It's still breathing.

'Fuckin, arsehole,' Andy says, kickin it in the side.

His boot gets bone. Ah hope the deer disnae feel it.

'No. Stop it. Stop it.'

Run between him and the deer.

He puts his two hands on either side of ma shoulders, almost lifting me away from the deer and round to the side of the car.

'Are you daft, hen?' But there's no softness to the way he says 'hen,' an ah can still feel pinched were his hands were.

'That was sore.'

'Get back in the car.'

He looks along the road, in both directions. Quiet apart from the breathing of the deer, that's like no sound ah've even heard.

'Ye cannae leave it there.'

'Hurry up or you'll be next if a car comes. Don't blame me then. This is a helluv a busy road sometimes.'

It's the most deserted road ah've ever seen.

It doesn't seem right leavin the deer like that but the force when he kicked it makes me scared. Ah wish we could carry it into the woods so it disnae get hit by another car or at least put it right in at the side of the road. He's not away for long. Ah wonder if he's had a change of heart and he'll move the deer but cannae hear any sound of draggin.

'Why didn't you move it off the road?' Ah can see the bulk lyin to the side of the car.

Ah wish ah had strength to move it myself.

Doe a deer a female deer.

'Fuckin nuisance. Ah was checkin ma bumper. Too dark to see if there's any mark. Don't know why they don't shoot them, anyway.'

'Please will you move it off the road.'

Ray. A drop of golden sun.

'Jesus. Okay but you get back in the car in case you get hit as well. Boy-racers are a nightmare up here.'

The light is going and ah'm scanning the road for a bus stop but this is the middle of no-where.

Don't understand how could someone hurt such a beautiful animal and for no reason. If ah ask the question out loud, he might hurt me. When he gets back into the car, he's breathing heavier from the effort of moving the deer. Ah wish ah was a man that ah could kick the shit out him. See how he likes it.

Maybe, the voice was right and this is a bad idea.

All can think of is the deer lyin in the muck, how it'll disintegrate. Ah wish ah could have whispered in its ear before it went onto the road: 'stay on the grass, always.'

You've got to stay strong.

As it gets darker, more shapes of tree line the sides of the road.

'Is the place we're goin to far?' ah ask again lik our Annemarie.

'No, not far.'

Try to forget the sound of his boot against bone.

Start to drift off again, but then the car slows down, instead of openin ma eyes to the shopping centre in Oban and the river with the boats on it, we're surrounded by even deeper silence and darker trees.

'Here, let me help you with that belt,' the man is sayin, leanin over me.

'Why've we stopped? Are we there?'

Ah'm so tired, ah want to be there.

There's nothing wrong with my belt. He starts….and then ah feel his hand on ma knee. Ah know ah should struggle, bite an kick him but it takes a few moments for it to dawn on me what's happenin. Cos ah believed him, ah believed he was takin me to ma aunt's.

'Everythin'll be fine. This is a good place, here.'

It's the side of the road, a dark lay-by, over-hangin trees.

Oh God no.

Maybe, if ah give him what he wants it will all be over an he'll still take me to ma aunt's house.

Ah've probably got one chance so ah say ah'll unbuckle ma own belt an he says that's good. Ma bag is on ma lap so put ma hand around the handles. He's still pawin at ma legs. Just as he bends his face towards mine, ah slip ma hand towards the door lock and push the door open. He never locked it again after the deer. Turn towards him as he leans over to pull me back, hit him once wi all ma strength, across the face wi the bag.

'Fuckin little bitch. Fuck. Fuck.'

But the hardback poetry book gets him right in the face. Wordsworth whallops him.

He reaches to grab me again but manage to scramble out the car and back onto solid ground. Ah'm already runnin when he gets out the car.

328

He's still tangled in the bag handles an it gies me a few seconds but then ah hear him shoutin:

'Ah'll find you. Wee bitch. Ah want ma money's worth.'

'Ah want want ah paid for,' he shouts.

Now, Mr. Wordsworth is face down in the bag that's around that maniac's feet.

Run like the clappers, what ah'm good at until ah can hear the car movin, the lights are turned off. There's pavement but narrow, keep stumbling into bracken, only managing to keep ma feet. Close like he's used to driving like this in the dark, and ah'm trapped at the side of the road, when ah put a foot out and the pavement ends. Sound of a car coming in the opposite direction, and when ah look up the full glare of lights comes around a sharp bend, straight into Andy's line of vision.

He has to put his lights on but does it too quickly, blinding the other driver. An argument of car horns. Crouch behind a wall, near the road. Wet to touch smells of green moss and grass. There's another car coming in this direction so he has to pick up speed. If he sees me, ah'm done for and he will, if ah stay near the road. Start to run through the bracken, nettles sting ma legs but ah keep low, almost crawling, onwards.

You're the thief of the house, you.

That's right ah am the thief of the house.

The voice isn't helpin me now. Try to shut it out.

Don't know where to look; the ground is boggy underfoot and the bracken scratches ma face; after a while, make out shapes of things, trees and a wall off the road. Need to make ma way away from the roadside and follow the wall. Been quiet for a while but Andy could be playing a game of hide and seek. Grab a fist of the top of a barbed wire fence and have to stifle a big ahhhh in case he hears me. An ah don't see the root of the tree stickin out above the ground. Before ah know, ah'm fallin into darkness, towards a floor of leaves and muck. Ah quickly start to get up again, disentangling ma ankle from the tree root. When ah look up, Andy's standin right in front of me.

You'll make your bed and lie in it.

At first ah can hardly see his face but ah know it's him.

'Ah just want what ah paid for,' he growls.

'Ah won't hurt you or anythin.'

All brains an no common sense.

Whatever happens ah'm stuck wi it. Oh God, no. Please help me. Ah'm too scared to fight.

You've got to defrost the turkey the night before.

That's right, ah forgot. That's why the turkey never cooked for the dinner.

Red cells an white cells aw gone tae fuck.

Love nature. You will find peace in the sky and the woods. Be free.

Shut-up. Please. Ah can't think.

Burnin plastic bags full of sanitary towels, months of blood.

What are you doin?

Never you mind, get back inside and close the back door.

If ah can focus on his face.

Right…this is the form

Fill it in for me. You're good at that, fillin in forms.

Stop, ah can't think.

You made me die. You wished me dead.

26

Come out, Erin. Please.'

Drew gets to go wherever he wants and when. Nobody's on his back, lookin fir him tae be home at eight o'clock. He disnae get it when ah say ah cannae go out at night, that ah'm no always allowed.

'Ah'll try.'

'You better.'

'Mum ah'm goin up tae Sally's for an hour.'

She likes Sally. She says Sally comes fae a respectable family. She says we're respectable people and we should mix wi respectable peoples' children. She sent me tae Sally's big sister tae learn elocution. Sally's big sister's studyin tae be a speech therapist. Ye've tae stand wi one foot in front of the other and say 'peter piper picked a peck of pickled pepper.' And ye've tae keep yir arms clapped in at yir sides just lik getting ready tae jump aff a dale at the baths. Ah'm that worried about ma arms an ma legs, cannae hear the instructions about what ah'm supposed to say. But Sally keeps interruptin; her an me burst out laughin whenever her sister says a thing in a really hoitey toitey voice. She's really nice, her sister. It's just her job.

After a few weeks she gives up on Sally an me. We sit on Sally's bed, listenin to their Osmonds L.P.

'Crazy Horses.Whhhaaaaaa Whhhaaaaaa.'

'What did you learn today?' mum asks.

Show her how ah stand: one foot in front of the other.

' How does that help your voice?'

' Don't ask me, but it must.'

'Jesus, is that what ah'm payin good money for?'

 Practise in front of the mirror:

She sells seashells on the seashore.

Red leather yellow leather, black soap and sloda.

Black soap and soda.

What did ye learn the day?

'On a hill there stood a dookit it's no there noo cos somebody took it. '

'Very funny.'

A   EEEE EYE OHHHH YOUUUU

Elocution is the world's worst thing ah've ever did. Done.

Doe a deer a female deer. Ray a drop of golden shite. What chance have a got wi ma mum always tellin me to speak proper and these elocution lessons? Ma pals already suspect ah might be posh; if they find this out it'll be little left out lassie. But ah act daft. Waste time, kid on ah don't know how to stand the right way; Sally's sister can spend a whole hour showin me that. Finally, she tells ma mum she can't have a class wi just one person. One peck of pickled person.

Drew and the crowd are goin to the site of the old primary school. There's a bing there now; we go there for a lumber; us, goin steady couples. Drew looks relieved when ah arrive. Thought he might get a knockback.

There's Sally, Rose-Ann our three boyfriends, me and the rest are pan watchers. They're the lowest of the low, jist standin watchin us kissin. Only thing they're good for is bein lookouts. Nosey parkers extraordinaire. If ye let a boy slip the mitt or that they'd tell everybody next day at school.

Drew's mouth's nice and wet. He moves his hand up and down ma back. He knows if he makes one wrong move, ah'll tell him where tae go. He likes me for that. So he says. Ah wouldnae make a show of him; jist move his hand where it should be.

We stay like that for ages our heads goin round in circles, stoppin for a breath every now and then. Ah close ma eyes cos when they're open ah can see the pan watchers lookin right at us. Dirty buggers.

Everythin's fine until ah look up and there's our Anna.

'You better get home. Ma mam went up tae Sally's lookin fir you. She knows you're up here wi boys.'

'And how does she know that? You told her, didn't you?'

Anna just turns and walks away. That means she did. Bitch.

Drew doesn't want to stop.

'Ah've had enough air; one last time then ah'll let you go.'

Ah feel grown up with him; there's no way ah'm runnin home lik a wee lassie.

This time he puts his tongue in ma mouth again. Jesus. What do ah do? Did he mean it?

Walkin home, ah ask Sally.

'Has a boy ever put his tongue in your mouth?'

'French kissin. That's French kissin.'

'What do ye do?'

'Ah don't like it so ah accidentally on purpose bite them. They get the message.'

'And what if ye like it?'

'Put your tongue in his mouth and jist see what happens.'

'Isn't that your mum?'

334

Look back, Drew's at the other side of the road wi the other boys.

The purple pinny; that means she left in a rush. Arms are swingin lik a sergeant major. She wouldnae dare do anythin in front of ma pals. But the closer she gets, the more scared ah start tae feel but ah'm still tryin tae look cool. Lookin cool an getting ready for the off at the same time. And see when she's next tae me she slaps me right across the face.

'Get home you little B. Where the hell have ye been? Lyin B. Ah'll show you.'

Ah know Drew's watchin and so's everybody else but ah just take off; run. She'll kill me if she gets a hold of me. Nobody's laughin; everybody jist stands there watchin me runnin away an her runnin behind me. Ma face is sore where she hit me but ah'll get worse if she catches me. The only safe place is a place wi a lock on the door: the bathroom. Thank God ah thought of it. Run run as fast as ye can ye can't catch me ah'm the gingerbread man. She's the wolf an ah'm the gingerbread man. Our gate. Our gate. She's no a fast runner but fear slows me down and anger gies her wings. Through the front door an up they stairs like a hare at a dog track. But this hare stumbles on a step. She grabs ma leg, briefly. Ah didnae think she wis that close. Ah pull the leg away; she stumbles. Ah'll git hit worse for that. When ah'm inside the bathroom, ah nearly get the door closed but she jams her foot to stop me and that's that. Ah'm done for then.

Might as well gie in. One day ah'll run faster, be stronger. Then she'll see.

'Don't hit me. Don't hit me.'

Pleadin. Pathetic. It would make her want to hit me. Ah always get it wrong. Always. Then ah put ma hand over ma face cos she's kickin and punchin me and ah want to protect ma head. Why's that? Why do the hands go up lik that? That makes her angry.

'Get your hands away.'

But ah don't. Ah won't let her near ma face. She hates that. That's me fightin back. That's why ah get hit. Nothin to do but wait for it to finish. Cos ah'm a thief, cos ah talk back. She disnae lose it often but when she does she does big time and the one thing ah want to do then is hit her back; gie her a taste of her own medicine. That'd make it worse, to kick her. So ah take it, gettin her back wi the hate ah feel.

'Ah hate you,' ah shout back.

'Ah wish you were dead.'

What will you do if I never come back?

You'll never leave. You can't leave. You're our mum.

It was me. Ah made her die. Ah wished for it and it happened. And ah can never wish her back again for real. Ah never meant it. Ah never thought she would actually die. Ah thought if ah get Paul somehow it would make it up to her. Somehow. But now it's too late. There's nothin to make it better an there's nobody can help dad, especially not me.

FOUR

1

'ERIN.'

Finish rubbin orange lip-gloss on ma cheeks, tae gie them a bit of a glow cos ma mum won't let me buy blusher, says ah'm too young. Lip-gloss is sticky and shiny no lik powder, never mind, better than peely wally.

'WHAT?'

'Don't shout lik a banshee.'

'What?'

'Ye'll need to come to the doctor's with me. I've a got an appointment. I'll give you a note for the teacher.'

'But mam, it's English.'

'I'm not your mam or your maw. Don't use that Scottish slang on me. I'm your mum Now, don't argue. Ye can go back to bed for an hour if you like, the appointment's not till half ten. And what've ye done to your tie? Jesus Christ, where's the rest of it? Ye made me swear. Tell your sister to hurry up or she'll be late.'

The fashion's tae tuck the long part of yir tie inside your shirt, so's only a short, stubby bit shows. Everybody has their ties like that except the snobs who have big thick knots and long parts to their bellies. Like pickin aw the chocolate off a Club biscuit, linin the pieces on a silver wrapper, so ye can eat the chocolate last, wait for the right moment tae tell our Anna that ah'm gettin the mornin off school, no her.

The reaction's better than expected; she pure runs down the stairs gien it:

'How come SHE gets to stay off school, how come?'

Mum's at the cooker makin toast for the three wee ones, half watchin the grill, half gien us a row.

'Ah only need one of ye. Get to school and stop moanin.'

Pick up yesterday's Daily Record, have a wee read while drinkin a luxurious, second cup of tea. Paul's last up, cannae find his tie. As usual. Ah hid mine the night before like treasure. Anyway, this isnae the three musketeers, that all for one and one for all crap. It's brilliant bein able to sicken him, stayin off school an that but when he leaves and she goes up the stairs to get ready, ah'm left maself in the livin-room. Don't think ah've ever ever been in the livin- room maself. It's funny, cos ah can still imagine the others even though they're no here. And see when ah look at the picture of The Sacred Heart of Jesus, above the fireplace. Well, he's lookin in ma direction, like a big glass mirror in a supermarket. God is supposed to be the picture but the God in my head has no face. Sometimes, God's a voice saying do this and do that and other times God is just there listenin to my troubles, helpin me sort it all out. It's funny, sittin in a room myself, not doin anything, just sittin. Ah'm aware of me as a body and ma thoughts as thoughts but it's weird, as if the family's another body, an ah'm part of it, without them, ah'm no whole.

'Ready?'

'Is it your migraines, mum?' She's sometimes gets sore heids, especially after work.

'Aye. And I don't have any energy. Probably need a blood test. A good tonic.'

339

Her answer to everything is a tonic, if ye're pale or that. Tonics have a busy life pickin people up. There's gin and tonic that people drink on the telly with ice cubes clinkin in a glass. Tonics put colour in your cheeks.

'The doctor'll sort me out.'

'Here, take my arm, will you? Ah feel a bit weak.' Ye take old people's arms to help them cross the road and ye take a boy's arm at the Dashing White Sergeant when it's the school Christmas party. Ah've never taken ma mum's arm before, not to help her.

Outside pure dreich and peltin down wi rain. February's a miserable time ae the year wi Christmas and New Year past, the summer holidays ages away but maybe we'll go to Ireland on holiday.

'Stop a wee minute. Till ah get ma breath.'

God sake. Worse than ma gran.

At the bus stop, this workie guy turns tae her.

'Hiya, gorgeous.'

Men still look at her. Disgustin. Don't know where tae look. When will it be ma turn? When will she start bein invisible like everybody else's mum?

At first she disnae say anythin. Hope this appointment disnae take long.

'Ah said, hiya gorgeous,' he says it lik she's supposed tae say somethin back. S'cuse me for bein here but what happened tae her no bein well? Where's ma invisible ink?

'You need your eyes tested,' she says back. Nae bother wi the breath now. Tug her arm tae remind her ah'm here. But ma dad disnae need tae worry. Ah'll keep an eye.

'Hen, ye're obviously married an don't get telt enough.'

She laughs lik ah laugh when Drew's gien me aw the patter in Chemistry an auld Eggie Heid isnae lookin. Maybe for ma daddy's sake it's a good job ah'm here. It's always the same. Even ma History teacher Randy Rooney fancies ma mum. Ah think even Drew's got a thing for her.

Thank God, the number twenty-five. It's muscle man's bus. Winks at her, before he gets on, his builder's bum showin at top of his trousers. White Y's. Ah mean really.

'Don't mention that to ye're dad. Just a bit of fun.'

Aye right. But this is good cos now she owes me.

'Mum?'

'What?'

See at the parent's night next week, gonnae wear ye're fawn rain-coat wi the big buckle.'

'But what if it's not rainin?'

'It's what the other mums wear. Ye really suit it.'

Ah know they must do it, otherwise there wouldnae be us. Sometimes, on Saturday mornins, ye cannae get intae their room cos they must push the sideboard against the door. Cannae sit in the livin room, knowin they're at it. Ye have tae put the telly up dead loud or get out the house. Ye shouldnae need tae put wi that in your own house.

'Shhh. Here's Agnes commin. Let go of me for a bit, till ah straighten up. Ye know what she's like and for Jesus sake don't mention the doctor. Say we're goin messages.'

'Hello there, Eve. Ah'm just away tae mass. Prayed like Billy Oh for our John tae get that job. He got it. Imagine. Ma prayers always seem tae get answered. It's like ah've got a hot line to God. Ah'm away tae give thanks tae Jesus.'

A sore nip on ma arm.

'We're away to get this one school shoes. Better run or we'll miss the bus. Mind say a prayer for me. God always listens to you, Agnes.'

When Agnes is out of sight we burst out laughin.

'Christ, a hot line to God.'

Ma mum never says Christ unless it's really important. Agnes is kind to us but she's on another planet when it comes to religion. Planet Virgin Mary.

Maybe, mum's havin another wean, that's why she's tired. A bun in the oven, Drew calls it. Last time wi our Lizzie, ah guessed cos her chest got dead big. We were doin the garden an she must have seen me noticin cos she telt me that night. What ah was wonderin was would ma chest get that big when ah got older? Och well, as if we've no enough. But she always says another one won't make any difference. That's another person tae fight wi for any attention, another bed to squeeze into one of our rooms. It's dead nice though, at the start: the smell of talcum, white nappies, the fresh skin of the baby and its dead cute smiles. Ah'll get tae take it for walks, right enough. That's good. Ah'll have tae change shitey nappies. No so good.

Off the bus, she leans into me as if she might lose her balance and in ma heid can see her fallin an me not bein able to stop her both of us hittin the ground at the same time like a bad dream when ye're fallin off a cliff and ye watch yourself puttin a foot over the edge. Ye cannae stop it even though it's your own foot. And for the first time in ma life, ah'm stronger than her. Funny how ah'm always readin her face, workin out her moods whether ah should duck cos there's a slap commin or whether she's in a happy singin in the kitchen mood.

'Now hold on to me again.'

'Won't be long now.' Above her top lip, the red lipstick's smudged.

In the waitin room, there's a picture of a body on the wall: ye can see all the parts, liver, lungs and heart, red lines for blood vessels. The intestines are like a long pink rope, all curled and twisted. We don't speak. She's in another world but not in her dirty look way, as though you're the cause of every misery she ever had but in a anxious way as if she's worried about somethin that we didnae cause. It's nice bein here, with her on ma own, only ah wish this bit was over quickly now and we could go for a coffee. Coffee is nice, such a treat. A green light comes on above the reception desk.

'Eve McLaughlin,' the woman behind the desk says, a bit like a teacher callin the register.

'Erin McLaughlin.'

'Here, miss.'

'What?'

'Present, miss.'

'Be good,' mum says as if there was any scope for bein bad.

Mrs. Simmons from Ritchie Road appears through the swing doors.

'Hiya hen. What ye in here for?'

'Ah'm waitin for ma mum. She's in with the doctor.'

'Is she, hen? What's up wi her?'

343

'A headache.' She nods but doesn't say 'Aye, no wonder wi you lot,' out loud.

'Och well. Tell her ah wis askin for her. Will ye, hen?'

'Aye, Mrs. Simmons.'

She hovers for a wee while, looks towards the doctor's closed door.

'See ye, hen.'

The Scots Magazine on the table has a picture of a mountain and a stag at the top. Inside, there's nothin about pop music, only cures for arthritis, findin your family tartan. There's other people come in, sitting behind me, like we're at a concert. The man on the wall is the actor. Any minute now, he'll come ta life, start singin: Ah did it my way.

The door opens.

'What did the doctor say, mum?' She disnae answer until we pass the desk and all the other people can't hear.

'Said ah probably need a tonic, right enough. Took blood for a test. Ah feel better already. I'm desperate for a coffee. Let's go.'

Ah'd like to go back tae school now; see ma pals but the coffee would be nice.

Ah tell her about Mrs. Simmons.

'God, they they're nosy, round here, aren't they?' Like it's a shock every time.

'Aye or they've got a hot line to God.'

In the wee Tally café, next door to the Co-Op the woman who serves us has jet black hair lik Maria in the chip shop.

'How you doin?' she says to ma mum, wipin the table.

'Fine, Maria. Just fine. This is my eldest.'

'Aye, right enough. Your double.' Funny how all Italian women seem to be called Maria. There's a picture of green hills, lookin down to a blue sea and wee white houses on hillsides that look like they might slide into the water.

'What'll you have. Usual? '

'A milky coffee, Maria. And Erin, what'll ye have?'

'Irn Bru, please.'

Maria brings the milky coffee first. Lovely and creamy lookin.

'Mum, can ah change ma mind? Can ah have coffee?' Because if ah'm old enough to hold her arm then ah can have coffee as well. A perk of bein fifteen.

'Course ye can.'

When mine does come there's a skin on the surface of her's because she waited for me.

'The Pope's hat,' she says, liftin the skin expertly with a tea- spoon. Well, the Pope's head must be roasting because the coffee's steamin hot. Ah drink mine quick cos ah don't want one on ma chin.

'Mum?'

'See that painting? Where is that?'

'Don't know. We'll ask Maria.'

Maria brings two teacakes on a wee plate.

'Maria, where is that place in the picture?'

Maria claps her hands, puts them to her chest but smiles like she's got a pleasant kind of pain.

'That Barga. Where I an Luigi come from. Beautiful. Sunshine. Sunshine every day.'

'Maria, ye must miss it.'

'Aye. Miss it sore but go ma holidays there at the Fair. Lookin forwards.'

She leaves to serve someone else, leavin us wi the teacakes and thoughts of Barga were it's sunny all the time. Ma mum disnae speak.

'It's like Ireland, isn't it? In the picture. Green, an the hills are like Kerry?'

'I was thinking that.'

Don't say that most holidays involve us starin out the window at the rain. That would waste the feelin that Maria and both of us share a memory of a warm, green place. Ireland is always like that a longing for a place that only lasts for a few weeks after the holiday and then it's as if it never existed, once we go back to school.

Play wi the paper from the teacake, tryin to think of something to say.

'Ye like school don't you?'

'I like English the best.'

'Did ye know I was best in my class at the Irish, when I was at school? I must show you my certificates. Remind me.'

She's told me that before. Bein at the doctor has made her more talkative. It's nice. Wonder what's happenin at school.

'Ah can count to ten in Irish: an, doch, tri.....Uncle Micky showed me.'

Forgot, she doesn't like it when ye show off but don't know what else to say when she's brought the subject up.

'My, you're good,' she says lookin at the paintin.

Later the same night when we're all sittin in front of telly havin our dinner there's a chap at the door. It's the doctor who asks to speak to mum an dad in another room, only problem is we've no spare rooms so he has to speak to them in the lobby. Mum's all annoyed cos he's not had his dinner an ah've to make him a cup of tea in one of their wedding china cups.

All we know is she has to go to hospital tomorrow for tests cos of the blood test.

'Away an give me peace, Simit.There'll be no ice- cream the night. Erin and Anna get the dishes done. The rest of ye get your school things ready for the mornin. Ye heard the doctor, ah'll no be here when ye get up.'

Switches off the telly. This time the house goes dead quite but too early for that kind of quiet, the street lights just on and the ice-cream van in the street.

'Why didn't you go, when ah told ye?' But he's no shoutin, they won't fight if she's goin into hospital. They definitely won't fight. Sometimes, when they have an argument, ah lie in bed; push ma fingers as far inside ma ears as ah can. Maybe, one day ah'll burst an eardrum. It'll be their fault if ah do.

Paul appears at the door wi his binoculars. He's no had them out the box for years. 'You'll get a slaggin if any of your pals see you,' ah say, hopin to get rid of him.

He ignores me, lifts the glasses to his eyes, aimin them in the direction of the gooseberry bushes. There's a bird singing sound, a sound like a squeaky bike wheel but ah cannae see anythin.

'Honestly, Paul. The neighbours'll report you for bein a peepin Tom.'

'You mean, a twitcher. Now, shhh. You'll frighten it away.'

A wee grey bird flies out of the bushes, hovers a bit then heads off across the tops of houses.

'Swift,' he says like it's a miracle that there is such a bird in Scotland. Ah'd understand it if it was one of the exotic birds he showed me in one of his library books ages ago.

'That's if you're interested,' he says gien me a wee dunt on ma shoulder when he walks back into the house.

Starin oot the back windae, half-listenin to them talkin but then the telly starts up again, so cannae hear. It starts to rain, drizzlin at first then really teamin; at the back door, watch the rain pourin doon. One minute's it's dry then this. On the grass a leaf moves; jump up wi the fright, throwin the teatowel doon the stairs. But when ah look again, there's a green frog hoppin over the grass, no a leaf at all. Better git that teatowel or ma mum'll kill me.

'Help me pull out the twin tub, so ah can show ye how to work it.'

Everyone else gettin ready for bed when she shouts from the kitchen; she's wearin the black padded dressin gown wi the big exotic flowers in the background, the one she got for goin into the maternity to have Annemarie. Thigither, wheel out the machine fae under the work surface.

'First ye take this tube and connect it to the hot tap. Are ye watchin?'

The number of times ah've done that maself; don't know why we're goin through this rigmarole the night.

'Now for God's sake, don't put your hand in the spin drier while the thing's goin round, otherwise it'll take off your hand.' Once it's full of soapy water, she turns an orange dial to '*on;*' the water starts tae churns in the tub lik the sea when we're on a ferry goin to see ma granny in Ireland. All ah can see is a torn hand and blood mixin wi the creamy liquid. Upstairs the rest ae them are goin mad, jumpin on beds, playin tig.

'Shut up, or ah'll belt the lot ae ye.' Ma da's in bed. Stayin off work the morra, to put us out to school. He'll go mad if they don't quieten down. She disnae let him hit us in case he really hurts us so she usually gets in first to keep him away. She does no bad tae but the night he's shoutin from the bed, and once he's in bed and the light's out, he'll no get up again.

Ah like puttin ma hand in the wash part of the tub when the spinner goes round dead fast makin ripples on the soapy surface, lik milky coffee at the top, underneath, grey used water. Scoop some froth: liquid snow.

'Christ, what'll you do if I never come back?'

The smack across the face comes fae nowhere. The spinner's roar gettin louder an louder lik her anger; the machine vibratin an movin on the floor as if the twin tub might explode in a climax of sound.

'Erin, are ye listenin? After a few minutes lift up the lid like this, for God sake wait till it stops goin around. Do ye hear me?'

Ah wonder what she means never come back? A few days the doctor said. Just for some tests. Anyway, it's always me gets hit. Push the machine back into place. Ah hate bein the eldest.

'Do ye want some milky coffee, Erin?'

'You hit me for nothin.'

'Sometimes ye're head's in the clouds, Erin. Ye're the eldest, ye need to look after the younger ones when I'm away.'

'Aye but ye didnae need to hit me.'

'I'm sorry for hittin ye but can ye not waken up a bit? You need to get your feet on the ground more.'

Bubbles in the milk. To get a good froth she lets the milk rise to the top runnin from the cooker to the cups, as the milk threatens to boil over.

'Now drink this in the livin room. Don't tell the others or they'll all want some. We'll have no milk for a cup of tea in the mornin.'

Ah'm quite pleased ah got 'sorry' out of her cos she never said that to me before; ah'm sorry as well for thinkin earlier ah was glad she was goin tae hospital.

'When will ye be back, mum?'

'A few days, I hope.'

'Will it be like when you went intae the maternity to have Annemarie?'

'Aye, it'll be like that. Ah hope anyway. Now ye better get to bed Erin otherwise the hoards'll be down. That ambulance is commin at the back ae seven, so ah'll likely be away when ye all rise. Mind and help the wee ones get ready for school. Make a few rounds of toast for ye all.'

350

'Is yer mother still up? Tell her the doctor said she'd to get some rest.' Ma da shouts fae their room, still wakened, directin everythin fae their bed.

'She's comin in a minute. She's just puttin out the lights.'

The next day durin Geography Mr.McKenna says the quarter ae tongue our mums buy from the Co-Op is made of ox's tongue. When ye get it from the Co-Op it's flat as if the tongue's been ironed, bits ae jelly in between an served up on a piece of grease proofed paper, no a moooo comin from it then. Ah'm still goin home even though she's away in to Law Hospital for her tests. She'll be back tomorrow an we can get back to normal. She said she'd leave me the key of the door wi Agnes an there'll be somethin on the worktop for me to eat. She was gonnae put it out before the ambulance came.

All the way to the bus stop ah can feel ma tongue inside ma mouth, wonder what's for lunch. Wonder what else do we eat, that's actually disgustin? Ah hope Mr. McKenna disnae tell us about sausage rolls the morra, cos ah'll die if there's a terrible history tae them.

Everybody else is at school dinners. Ah don't like school dinners even though we're Free Dinners. Mum says it's okay for me to come home at dinner- time every day for company for her but no the rest cos that would be too much. Breaks up the day. Aw big families are Free Dinners. The ones fae the children's home are Free Dinners as well but some of them sell their dinner tickets for crisps an a bottle ae ginger from the wee van outside school. One nutritious meal of the day. Mix that wi the smoke inhaled from the smoker's corner and that's a three-course meal.

Ah'm in a dream about ox tongues from the bus-stop till when ah go up our path to our door so ah forget about gettin the key from Agnes but the door's open, anyway. That's when ah remember. In the livin-room, ma daddy's sittin in front of the gas fire, looks up an starts tae speak but looks away an ah cannae hear him for his mutterin. Ah wonder what's he doin here? That's all ah can think while he's talkin, that he should be at work.

'She's been rushed to the Infirmary from the Law. In Glasgow,' he says 'Glasgow,' lik that's enough tae explain it. Then somethin about tests. More tests.

'You'll need to stay off school the day anyway, right? The doctors want to speak to me this afternoon. In Glasgow. Ah'll need to get a bus, it'll take aw day but. Ah mean somebody has to be here for the ones comin in from the wee school. You're the Woman of the House today, right?'

And that's the first time ah get ma new Red Indian name. That's when the clouds drift away an there's the new person called Woman of the House. Ma mum'll kill him for sayin ah'm Woman of the House cos she's still Women of the House even if she is in Glasgow. Don't argue though.

French, first two periods in the afternoon, then geography. The geography class on the fifth floor full of big windows and light. Ye can see right across Motherwell, tae Tinto hill from up there. Said ah'd see Drew and ah've done ma homework. It's always a good class when ye've done ye're homework.

Ah don't know if ma dad wants me to see him cryin or no but how can ah stand in the middle of the room wi closed eyes? Want tae say somethin, to make him feel better but don't know why ah have to stay off school.

'Christ, ah wish ah had brothers or sisters, ah really do,' he says slamin the front door.

When he leaves for the hospital, it's the end of the lunch- time news on the telly and the weather forecast is startin, a map of the UK and high high up where Scotland is; the weather man sticks a cloud wi a trail of stars. The stars are snow. 'Rain to follow.' The stars turn to tears. He says there'll be westerly winds the night.

'Gales and heavy snow in the North.'

'Have a nice afternoon,' dazzlin teeth and a sun-bed tan.

The Scottish news starts off wi a story aboot a climber lost in the hills: a thirty -five-year-old dentist. Rescue teams trudge through knee deep snow like a documentary about people tryin to get to the North Pole. The people are in the distance and the camera makes them look toaty compared to the mountains. A rescue man says they'll keep tryin but a helicopter in the background drowns him out as it lands. Every ten minutes, ah'm at the door, lookin for Annemarie. Ah heard the school bell. She should be home.

'Hiya, hen.' Agnes stops at the gate. 'How's your mum? Your poor dad. Is he still at the hospital?'

God, Agnes knows everythin. She's telepathic when it comes to news.

'Aye.'

'Tell him tae gie me a chap when he gets home. Cheerio, hen.'

Ma mum would go dolally if she thought Agnes knew her business. Ma dad cannae keep his mouth shut right enough.

Maybe, the lost dentist is trapped under snow wi no oxygen. Hope they find him.

Hours pass until school's out an there's an avalanche of bodies, ma brothers rushin for spaces in front ae the telly, castin school skins: coats, bags, even their shoes. Four pies and four sausage rolls. Eight disnae fit the grill. Shifts of three. The wee ones first. Three sausage rolls. Decisions, decisions.

'Ah want a pie.'

'Shut up! Ye'll take what ye get.'

The night the boys do the dishes without an argie bargie.

Sally comes tae the door.

'Commin for a walk?'

'Cannae. Need tae watch Them.'

'See ye then.'

'Aye, see ye.'

Maybe, the test'll be good and they'll both come back thegither. He'll go back to work an ah'll come home for ma lunch the morra the way always do.

After dinner, in the livin room, it's warm wi aw the bodies and the fire on, two panels. Later that night when ma da comes back, the rest are in bed.

'What's up? What happened?'

Everytime he goes to speak his eyes fill up.

It's shockin. Ah don't know where to look, what to say. But he knows the answers so he has to start to speak.

'Da, what's up?'

It's too quiet up they stairs. Ma brothers an sisters are awfie quiet for this time of night.

Ah can imagine them in their beds, aw listenin; each one of us waitin all night, secretly frettin. The tests. Results. Did she pass or fail? Part of me waits, gettin ready for THE NEWS and another part of me separates from the me that's there and becomes a me that watches; watchin him and watchin me. Ah see him disintegrate before ma eyes: a mosaic, wee pieces stuck thigither, flyin apart or a mirror that's broken into shards.

'They weren't good, the tests.

She's got a

She's got a

She's got a blood disorder.'

'Don't ask me aboot it. White cell count isnae right. Christ, if you'd had to listen tae what ah had tae listen to. They doctors.

'Joseph, it's not looking good.'

This is another mosaic: white cells, red cells an doctors in white coats; mum bein kept in hospital. Put the pieces together and make an answer. What's the answer?

'Is there a cup of tea?'

Two mugs. Will ah need to stay off school?

'We'll no tell them. Okay?' nods towards the ceilin.

'Okay.' Don't even know what there is not tae not tell them. White cells, red cells, what the doctors said. Listen for hints, somethin that might make sense again.

'Why did it happen tae her, eh? Forty-two years of age. They doctors, eh. Ah walked onto that main road right in front of a double decker bus. Ah wish. Never mind.'

356

After a while it's as if ah was inside his head, hearin his thoughts but that's better than listenin to mine cos when ah turn to mine there's just space where thoughts should be. Must be freezin on a mountain, wind howlin in your ears, the loneliness of all that snow. The last shot on the late news is the dentist's uncollected car in a deserted car park.

What is it that's happening? Make it not be true, God. Make it not be true.

A couple of weeks later when we stop at the yellow box on the road, a red double decker flashes him tae go but this black BMW races right through just missin us. It's Saturday visitin time at the Royal Infirmary, the first time we can all go in together. Six weans in the back seat, an me an our Paul in the front. If the polis catch us we'll get done for car over-crowdin but, maybe, one look at us lot, they'll wave us on.

That would be aw we needed, ma dad in jail.

'Concentrate, dad.'

'It was him, did ye see it?'

'Shut it, you,' Paul says to me.

Well then.

'How are ye, hen?'

The car park attendant wi the capped hat turns a blind eye tae ma dad's blue Cortina, lookin half-cut as he winks at me. Dad tells him about mum's illness like it is a bit of gossip for everybody else. No somebody's actual life. But it gets us a parkin space. Although, sometimes, wish he'd shut- up cos when ye feel sad the last thing ye want is people lookin intae your face, askin ye how ye are. A parkin space isnae worth it, nothin really is worth that.

Rectangular windaes look out tae the short-stay car park from the hospital. Wonder can she see the rigmarole we have to go through.

'Would ye believe that? Ye wouldnae believe it, would ye?'

Dad's is still goin on about the near miss but thank God, he's moved away towards the entrance, otherwise, we'll be here aw day. Have to keep the wee ones by the hand, otherwise, they might walk into a car. Like herdin cats. Ma dad has his eyes on the boys an Anna is helpin me. We're lik somethin out The Sound of Music, a big line of weans, walkin across the car park:

Raindrops and roses...

Climb every mountain...

The second attendant is starin at us, face covered in red pimples. He's a laddie dressed up in a uniform for the day. Two workies in overalls are ab-sailin down the wall ae the hospital, must be somethin up wi the roof.

But the traffic is mad on the main road. It's a relief tae get inside the grounds.

'Fancy a shot?' says the one on the ground.

'No, ta.'

Annemarie giggles, starts to pull away. No chance.

As soon as you breathe near the main door, it opens. Everythin happens too quickly, automatic pilot. Sometimes, ah wish ah could stand in the middle of the road and scream at the traffic: Stop! Slow down! But everythin is the same for everyone else, even though our lives are changed, forever. Dad says the first day he went there, the day they telt him she was really sick, he didnae have a car, walked out onto the busy main road, no lookin where he was goin: a thin, red haired man standin in the yellow box, aw the drivers hootin, callin him a daft bastard. He didnae care. He wanted somethin tae happen that would get him off the hook.

After that, he got the Ford Cortina, second hand as if getting the car would save him from near misses.

The Infection Control Unit is on the top floor. We aren't allowed in the cubicle aw at the same time. Ma dad takes the boys first and ah have tae stay wi the wee ones who are fightin about the radio head- phones on the wall in the waitin room. Lizzie has them in her ears, Annemarie wants a shot. Annemarie is wearin her special occasion dark green velvet skirt. Petted lip starts to appear.

'Aye, stand still. Tell me if ye hear anythin.'

Lizzie is pullin the head- phones off her-self, puttin one headphone in Annemarie's ear. She has on her satin dress wi the white lace trim that she inherited from Lizzie, makin her lik a pale blue angel. Ah wish we could all have wings to fly away from here or that ah could fly away maself. But it's borin lookin after them, borin lookin after weans.

'Gimmee a turn. A real turn.'

Annemarie starts to greet.

Oh God gie me patience.

'Shhhh, the two of ye. Or we'll get thrown out. Do ye not want to see mum, do ye?'

Hear maself and wonder were words come from. Like ah'm an old woman and all the threats adults have ever said to me ah can call up now against ma brothers and sisters. It happens when ye're no lookin. It comes up on ye. Ah should be at the library, the boys should be playin football an dad should be been pickin a horse out the papers for later that's probably gonnae lose. Mum should be cleanin the house or shoppin or goin to the hairdressers for the whole of Saturday afternoon. Comin home lik a woman out a film wi her hairpiece piled

360

high in a bun, all ready for a night at the club. And the wee ones should be out the back, playin or watchin afternoon cartoons before the racin starts. Ah used to be bored wi that routine, always the same. But there's always been a door to slip through. You can be invisible when ye want. In the hospital, we're stuck. She's stuck an we're stuck.

When the boys come back, dad takes Annemarie, Elaine and Lizzie. We do this in shifts.

'Are you no commin as well, Erin?' More of an order than a question. What can ah say that would help? There is nothin ah can say. If they cannnae think of it, how could ah?

'Ah'll watch the laddies. Somebody needs tae watch them.'

Dad gies me a look. Don't leave this to me, it says. Well, why are they leavin it to me? Ah don't want it, either.

The boys settle down tae watch football on the big telly in the ward. That should keep them occupied for a while. At least it disnae kept cuttin out like ours does and ma dad disnae need to hit the top wi his fist. One of these days, he'll put his fist right through the ten o'clock news, knock out Trevor McDonald or Anna Ford. That'll be a laugh. Nee naw nee naw…

He's still standin there.

'Erin, she says ye've to come. Wants tae talk to ye about bills. You come. Ah cannae remember everythin.'

God, dad it's no a general knowledge quiz.

And no matter how much ah try to avoid it, ah have to go and speak to her. It should be enough to be there in the building, doing stuff. They didnae need tae speak to me when nobody was ill, happy to let me live, be a normal invisible teenager, now everybody wants to talk to me as if ah've suddenly become interested in adult conversation or they've suddenly found ma conversation interestin. Well, ah havnae. Ah might look lik ah have. Appearances can be deceptive.

Anyway, there's no point arguing. No point, gettin a petted lip.

The cubicle she is in has only a bed an a few chairs. The bed has metal sides, a bit lik a fence that folds up and down. Need tae wear these masks that ye pull out fae a box attached to the door lik a paper towel holder, the kind ye get in the toilets at school. Ah hate those masks, can hardly breathe wi one on; after a while the elastic is diggin intae ma ears but ye cannae take it off cos there are germs in our mouths that could gie her an infection. Ye can feel ye're tongue against the paper. It's wet an ye've only put it on. But ye have to keep it on. Have to. Ma dad says most people have immune systems that protect their bodies lik an army but her army's deserted, he says. He always explains things as if life's one big war film. At least it's no a Western. And that's why ah'm scared to breathe in case some of the germs manage tae sneak through.

Mum is in a kind of a box too: a glass box and when ye're walkin towards her, she can already see ye from her bed; sittin up in bed wi her arm round Annemarie. Lizzie is eatin the chocolate we brought. Typical. She's an eatin machine, these days.

'So you're here. Are ye hidin from me?'

Hide an seek. Chance would be a fine thing.

'Ah wasnae hidin. Ah was watchin the wee ones.'

Silence. It's too much. Like a big piece of stone you trip over. Fallin. Fallin into a fast flowing river of anxiety.

'Ye never paid the furniture place with the right book. Did I not say the blue book?'

Black and blue bruises on her legs. Black and blue books. Everything goes blank.

'Are you listenin, Erin?'

Her hair is grey aw over because she isn't gettin to the hairdressers on Saturdays. Black hair shows grey. Grey roots.

'Ah thought ye said black.'

'Sure, haven't you been with me many a time and I've handed over the blue book. You'll have to concentrate. While I'm in here you're the woman of the house.'

The black book is for the carpets. Ye have to tell the women in the shop that, or they'll mark the wrong amounts in. The carpet place is the floor above the furniture show room.

'Do ye not mind?'

'Ah thought ye said black.'

He had given me a wee list that she'd written down:

Co- Operative	*£3 a week*
Jean's Place	*£2 a week*

'So ye'll need to go back an tell them to change the figures. Tell them the money ye've been payin should be scored out the black book and written in the blue book. Bring it here the next time so I can check myself that it's been done right. Are ye listenin, Erin?'

Nod, cos ae the mask cannae really talk back, no properly. Ah have to lift it away fae ma mouth; ma tongue is makin the paper more wet an soft as if it might tear, as if ma tongue might stick right through and that will be awful cos aw the germs will come rushin towards her an ma tongue will peek out, gien her cheek for what she said. She catches me tuggin it.

'Ye'll tear it, if ye keep doin that.'

As if ah'm goin to tell those women in the shop they've made a mistake that it was their fault. They were starin at me as soon as ah'd walked in, too young to have any place there. It had taken me all ma time to open ma mouth; it could have been me. Ah could have said the wrong thing, ah was so nervous. Ye could see them wonderin, what kind of woman sends her lassie to pay the bills?

And we keep goin lik that, me fidgetin, ma daddy rememberin bits ae news, Annemarie and Lizzie on top ae the bed, gigglin until the nurse brings ma daddy's birthday cake. The cake is yellow wi ten candles but ma dad isn't ten, obviously. Ah like 'obviously.' Ah used to like 'basically.' Simit's favourite word's 'marbles' but that's another story. We sing 'happy birthday,' wi the masks on, keepin our voices quiet so we don't disturb the other patients cos their curtains have been drawn back again an they can see us and we can see them. Ma daddy is watchin the racin on the telly. It feels lik the Sound of Music again. Singin an that. Like we were in a film cos ma daddy says he'd never had a birthday cake in his life even when he was a boy. Our mum must have be Maria but she is in bed instead of teachin us how to climb trees and 'Doe, ray, me, fah, so, la, tea.'

And that makes me think even more that this is a film about us and one day we'll wake up and the story will be over and the old story will start again.

'Ah'll go an ask the nurse for a knife, will ah?'

'Blow your candles out first.'

Don't remember ever havin candles except big white ones in the Three-Day Week when aw the lights went out at night an we were too scared to go to the toilet up the stairs.

It was ma mum's idea, the cake.

'Let the girls do it.'

When he goes for the knife we look at the other visitors but she looks right at us.

'Ye're bein good girls for your dad?'

Ma mind goes blank.

The three wee ones nod their heads lik it was rehearsed.

'Good. Keep it up. Keep up the good work.'

'Mum, what's nil by mouth?'

Lizzie is over at the empty bed next to mum's and a sign above the bed that says:

'nil by mouth.'

'The person can't eat anything so everythin's fed through a drip.'

She takes the young ones' hands cos they're still young. The older you get, the farther you become from all that.

Thank God mum isn't nil by mouth otherwise she wouldnae get any cake. The knife is gigantic. He slices a wee bit for himself, two big bits for us, another wee bit for her; we read our comics for a while. Ah got The Jackie, Anna's got The Diana. Ma daddy reads the paper, startin fae the back, sports page first. He has a small shavin cut at the side ae his face that ah only noticed. Ah don't like to think of him wi the razor so close to his chin and it slippin. He is all over the place without that. It's a wonder he hasnae a whole face of cuts. But ah can't take charge of that as well, can't take charge of everythin.

'Erin. Go and get me a coffee from the machine. There's change in that top drawer. Mind don't spill it. Mind don't burn yourself.'

Have to move the cards tae open the drawer but cannae move them for our Anna cos she was up at the vase, smellin the flowers. One day she's gonnae get lost inside one, nose first. It would be great if there was a big fat bee an she got stung. For a laugh. Tae break the tension.

'Carnations. Gypsopheli.'

'Ye're a real scholar at the flowers, Anna. Pity ye don't know your sums as well.'

Mum never lets ye off the hook. She's always on the ball when it comes to schoolwork.

'Put sugar in mine.'

'What? Ah cannae hear ye.'

'Two sugar.' She disnae take it usually. Gave it up for Lent but maybe it isn't that important now.. Maybe, it helps build her up. She's always goin on about certain things building ye up. Certain things lik liver. Things that have iron in them.

Milk and sugar. Milk and sugar. Ah hope ah don't forget.

4

Before ah know it ah'm getting fitted into one of mum's nurse's uniforms. She got it altered for me so that ah can go with her to Lourdes, to the baths at the Grotto.

We have to pray from the minute we get on the bus. Pray. Pray. Pray. Aw the time. First, we have to pray for a safe bus journey so we give it Hail Mary for ages then we have to pray for a safe flight. More Hail Mary's. Some holiday this is going to be. No wonder dad had sent me. What about ye cannae shuv your granny aff the bus? The priest stands in the aisle of the bus, holdin his rosary. More like ye cannae even look out the windae but he'll catch you. It's a bad start that we're prayin the bus disnae crash and then when ye're just off the bus you start worryin about the plane. Must be very dangerous, goin to Lourdes. Ah'm mainly goin cos ah want a tan. France is hot, bound to get one there. We must have said a hundred thousand Hail Mary's. Where do they go- those Hail Mary's? After a while becomes a drone in the background. Mmmmmmmmmm. Lips are movin, sayin words, missin the beat a few times but catchin up easy.

The priest says a bit; we say a bit. For five decades. Ten Hail Mary's in a decade, that's ten times five, that's fifty followed by the 'I remember Oh most gracious Virgin Mary,' and then 'Hail Holy Queen.' Sometimes, Mary asks God to cure people because God's too busy, maybe stoppin a war or sortin out starvation in Africa. That's why we pray to Our Lady. Intercession.

Wonder what mum prays for? Ah'm not prayin for a miracle, no way. If ye think the worst, ye won't be hurt when it happens. Move ma lips wi the rest of them but ah'm not countin on it cos dad wouldnae be depressed and mum wouldnae be sad if they thought it was that easy. It isn't that easy. The bus jerks to a stop all of a sudden, the priest has to hold on to the rail to stop himself goin flyin.

Ah'm so sick of sadness, it's funny that the priest nearly goes flying.

At meal times in the hotel, mum and me sit wi an elderly woman, Cathy, an her daughter, Maggie, who's a nurse. There are two knives and two forks at dinnertime so copy mum; she shows me what to do. For breakfast we get croissants and when ye put butter and jam on them they crumble in your fingers and gigantic cups of coffee, big as soup bowls. You don't get tea in Lourdes. Folk smuggle their own tea from Scotland and at night drink it in their rooms along with duty free Bacardi and vodka.

Every day we get the same pea green soup for lunch.

'They jist add water,' Cathy says.

The meat looks lik chicken but disnae taste lik it. Cathy an ma mum say it's either horse or rabbit, a big race- horse out ae Grand- stand on the telly, an we're eatin it. Mum says,

'If ye're father wis here, he'd put a fiver on it.'

Really, really an truly hope it's rabbit cos horse sounds horrible an in Scotland we're no allowed to eat horses, jist as ye cannae eat dogs or cats in Scotland cos they're pets.

'Don't listen to them, hen; they're kidon on. It's venison or somethin lik it,' Cathy says, but still ah look at ma plate, suspiciously. If ye're not allowed to eat horse an ye do then what happens?

'Mum, why don't we eat rabbit in Scotland?'

'Myxomatosis,' she says, then ah remember we got that at school. Wait for the frogs' legs. Every plate ah get, think this'll be it but they never bring them.

Every day we go to the grotto, push mum in her wheelchair. There are three tall young laddies. No really laddies, really they're men. They help out at the hospital durin the holidays for free board and they're tall, taller than any ae the boys at school. One's fae near me but ah don't know him, one's from Glasgow an one's from Dumfries. The one from Dumfries has reddish hair an he goes all freckly when the weather's hot. Ah like him the best because he never slags me off, no lik the other two. They're always teasin, tryin to make me take a beamer. But Pete disnae talk to me lik ah'm a wean and sometimes, he'll offer tae push mum to gie me a break, an we walk thegither, the three of us talkin and him shuvin the wheelchair.

To get to the grotto, walk over a bridge, along a road then past shops wi tacky souvenirs. Never been in Blackpool but it must be lik here: instead of 'kiss me quick hats' and plastic necklaces that light up wi green light at night, there's holy water fonts, plastic grottoes that spurt real water; all sorts of holy things crowdin entrances and when ye go inside ye need to duck or ye walk right into a suspended Our Lady or maybe a crucifix and get whacked on the head.

On the way back from the grotto on the second day, a sudden heavy shower, wi the rain hard on ma bare shoulders. Take off ma cardigan as soon as we got out the grotto cos as a sign of respect ye're no supposed to be in to a holy place wi bare shoulders, same as ye used to have to cover your head with a mantilla, white or black. In our church only The Children of Mary wear mantillas. They have to go to novenas every Sunday, sit at the front with mantillas on lik nuns. They know all the words of The Memorare and sing in Latin sometimes. Thank God ah'm not Children of Mary.

We're a bit away from the shops, without shelter, so we have to run. The red haired helper takes a short cut across the courtyard of the hospital, a gloomy lookin buildin wi bars on the windows. No wonder the helpers spent so much time in our hotel.

The rain in Lourdes rains mainly on the pilgrims de, de, de dum. Pushes mum's wheelchair through puddles like havin a trolley race back home.

Never thought ah'd be so glad to see those wee crowded shops wi all the holy paraphernalia. But it's weird cos ah'm not cold, the way rain makes you freezin in Scotland. No it's warm rain. Even ma clothes are dry in seconds and that is the really strange thing, that French rain isn't like Wishaw rain where ye would need to get a change of clothes or stand in front of a fire to heat up.

'Ah'm dry mum. Are you?'

'Yes, this is a warm country. The rain never lasts long. Do you like Lourdes, Erin?'

'Aye mum, ah do. Ah like the warm rain.'

'It's not like home. Ye'd get your death of cold.'

At the shrine where the Virgin Mother appeared to Bernadette, dead quiet like bein up the street in Wishaw when the shops are all shut. Some of the crutches had been covered in cobwebs and the wood looks rotten.

Cathy says that some people don't know they're cured until they go back home. Maybe it's years later, crippled people can suddenly walk. Ah don't know. God was always doin miracles in the olden days of the bible but ye wouldnae put a crutch up there for a joke.

Saturday night, it is the torch-lit procession so the whole of Lourdes goes to the grotto, carrying candles made into torches; ye line up to kiss the stone underneath where Our Lady appeared. Usually me an mum are in our beds by eleven, but the night we need to stay up late cos the procession disnae start till after ten.

'It's beautiful,' Cathy says. 'You'll love all the wee lights, hen.'

When we leave it's still light outside but Pete wants to get us to the startin point before it gets dark. The nearer we get to the Grotto, the busier it is and instead of goin in, the way we've been doin every day, we turn left at the gates, climb a steep hill at the top, there's people standin beside big boxes, givin out torches.

'You all need five franks,' says Pete.

Everythin costs money in Lourdes, it's no a place for poor people. Hand over a ten-franc note; ask for two, one for mum and me. It's a candle on a stick thing, a wee paper lampshade covering the candle.

From here we can see the thousands of lights in front and below. Now it's half dark, half-light, and the darker it gets, the more the lights stand out, until ah cannae see people, just lights. The line moves. Within minutes, we're in pitch-blackness, apart from candles lightin up our faces and below the procession winds a way through the grotto, a big snake of white light.

Ave , Ave, Ave Maria.
Ave, Ave, Ave, Maria.

At first, don't feel the drip, drip. The lights and the singin carry me away to another world but then feel a burnin sensation on ma hand.
'Look out, hen.'
The candle's drippin like an ice-cream cone meltin in the sun except it's hot. Maggie grabs ma lampshade just as it collapses fae around the candle.
'Here, take mine. Yours is ruined. Ah've done this so many times.'
Ma hand is covered wi wax blisters but there isnae time to pick them.

Ave, Ave, Ave, Maria.
Ave, Ave, Ave, Maria.

Never seen so many people in wheelchairs, aw bein pushed in the dark and we've been walkin for ages, about an hour an a half. Nearly fallin asleep but when we get inside the grotto, ah waken up. And the nearer we get tae the shrine, the more ah feel this is it and if there's gonnae be a miracle then it's the night. That's the unspoken thought in every head, the unexpressed hope. But ye can feel it, the expectation, here in this dark wi the candles and hymns and everythin seems so sad, all these sick people wantin a cure. Ah watch them one by one goin to the shrine; everybody's hopes brought to this ugly piece of wet rock.

Before ah know it, it's nearly ma turn. Don't know where she is. Ah think she's behind me, a wee bit back. A middle-aged man wheels a young guy up to the rock. He lifts him out, holds him towards it; he kisses.

And then it's me.

There's water pourin down, feelin spray as ah'm walkin towards it and the rock's aw black an shiny; lean forward and ma lips are full of water. And ah jist lie ma heid against it. Ah could lie here on the ground wi water pourin doon on top of me. But then the water's ma own tears and everythin ah've been holdin in, comes pourin out. Jist when ah'm supposed tae ask God for a cure, ah think God doesn't have a heart to make sick people beg for mercy like this, in a big queue in the dark, in a foreign country and ah can't bring myself to ask. Ah know the laddie in front won't get better and neither will she, none of them will. And the miracle is them, their courage and their faith in spite of their sickness. And ah'm sad too because ah wish ah had the faith ah had a few months ago, that's gone lik the water pourin on ma head, away into the soil, so ah don't know if ah'll ever feel it again.

Somebody puts hands on ma shoulders, eases me away.

'Ah'm sorry. Ah didnae mean tae cry.'

Nobody in the group complains. None ae the sick. No one cries. Have faith. Hope.

Maggie gies me a hankie.

'Don't worry, hen. Here, wipe yir eyes. Ah felt like greetin myself, the first time ah was here.'

373

'Did ye, Maggie?'

'Aye, hen. Now here's your mammy comin, dry your eyes.'

'Don't tell her Cathy, eh no?'

'Of course. But listen, hen, it's nothin to be ashamed of. You probably needed it.'

'Mum's illness brings neighbours to the door. Everyone wants to do something. Agnes is in and out the house wi pots ae soup, a smell of home made Cocka Leekie comin up the path in front of her. Mum disnae know; she'd go mad. We're not that badly off that we need other women doin our work, her work, an bringin us soup. There's somethin weird about havin the neighbour's pot in the house: it's no our food smells on it, it's no brown at the bottom an sides from our gas cooker. But we learn not to tell her. We learn how to keep the peace. Another neighbour gathers up all our washin to take to the launderette where she works. Everythin seems funny, different. Fabric softener. We don't use that.

'Don't tell your mother about the soup,' dad says, the way she used to say, 'don't tell your father about the new dress.' Hide the bag at the back of the wardrobe. He'll never guess. We don't mention the soup that it's tasty and that Agnes brings lovely home baked apple cakes as well. Mum's a great apple cake maker, so no way do we mention the cakes. But she can smell the clothes are different. She's no daft. Mum thinks Agnes is bein nosy but ah think she's only bein nice. Lyin in bed in the hospital, she thinks too much. Is her pastry better than mine? She liked Agnes a few months ago. Her best pal. It's bein sick, makes her think up stuff, that sometimes disnae make sense. As if she thinks people are tryin to steal her family by bakin a cake or makin soup. We're no that greedy. But it's not people; it's the illness.

People offer tae take the wee ones for a night or two making the house so quiet, you can hear noises you never heard before like the central heating coming on and a buzz in the air that the quietness makes if you really listen hard. And it's scary how people can agree to take away your three sisters. You might wish they were quieter but you never wish them away. Wish somebody would take me away sometimes but it passes. Bad enough mum bein away most of the time. But it's kind of a relief as well, not to have to think about how they're taking it and how do we entertain them. There's more space than we've had before and that's weird as well, rooms being empty. You can walk from one room to another and there isn't anyone in the whole upstairs. Ah don't ever remember that except when the parish priest came to bless the house when we first moved in and he said one of the rooms was haunted. For ages, we avoided bein up there ourselves, especially in the dark. Now, the thought of a ghost doesn't even frighten me as ah wander though the house, getting used to the new set up. If a ghost appeared ah'd gie it one of they books for the bills. Tell it to go and pay it instead ae scarin people in their own house.

Ma da makes up for the quiet though, gies up work, sittin in front ae the fire, yappin lik a budgie on speed cos of his nerves. Nerves get blamed for everythin. Nerves cause people not to sleep, cause them to shout. Nerves are a disease. He joins Alcoholics Anonymous like he's been thinkin about hitting the drink and this will help him. His pal from A.A comes to the house every night, tellin us stories about terrible things he did when he was on the sauce. He would go tae funerals of people he didnae know for the free bevy and the steak-pie dinner but maistly for the drink; he told us how he'd help people gie it up, pouring one woman's vodka down the sink while she cried. He goes tae help at the Mat Talbot Centre in Glasgow. Ma daddy calls it the Nat King Cole Centre. Ah don't know if he's bein funny or if it's him gettin his words mixed up. Ah'll never ever take a drink when ah'm older if it makes ye spend your days lecturing people about how bad it was when ye have to give it up.

On Saturday's when mum's in hospital, we still watch Scotsport, waiting for ma dad to come back from the hospital.

Dirrrrinnggggggg The big black phone's rings on the telly but Archie McPherson disnae pick it up, more interested in the Celtic v Aberdeen game. He keeps talkin away about the likely team selection and stuff like that.

'Erin, get the phone, ye're nearest,'

'It's no our phone. It's His.'

'It's that…Get it for God's sake. Jesus.'

He would never get away with that if mum was here.

We've a new cream phone in our alcove. Instead of a cure or a miracle mum got a phone and a part-time home help. The first home help's resigned because ma dad kept movin the hands of our livin room clock backwards. He took off all the time she spent drinkin his tea and eatin his biscuits. But she said that was part of the service. Counselling cos he's depressed. We got the phone for free cos mum's in the hospital and there might be an emergency. We've a phone box at the end of our street but the vandals are always at it and it's either jammed with 10p bits or the glass is smashed to dangerous tiny pieces that get everywhere. Never been in the house when the new phone's gone off before and it's kind of disappointing cos ah thought it would be like in a Tom and Jerry cartoon when the receiver levitates from the phone and there's the words on the screen: DRING DRING like ye cannae hear the sound.

'It willnae stop ringin till ye pick it up.' Our Paul's a right smart arse sometimes but there's no way he's moving from a football game.

'Hello.'

Breathin down the phone. It's Mum. Seems funny that she's phoning her own house.

Aw the things ye didnae have before: a car and a phone. Ye've got them now.

'What took ye so long?'

She was counting the rings.

'We're watchin Scotsport. No dad isnae back yet. How are you? Annemarie, mum wants tae speak tae ye.'

Quick, pass the phone to someone else. Annemarie's hasnae been on the phone before. Not even in a phone box. She wouldnae be able to reach up. Disnae realise ye can talk an the other person hears. Have to hold the phone to her ear and mouth and tell her exactly what to do. Ah've been on the phone loads ae times: in phone boxes, dialin the operator and screamin: 'GET AFF THE LINE THERE'S A TRAIN COMMIN.'

Nearly better than chap the door and run away.

The phone's funny cos it separates the other person's voice fae their eyes an mouth; imagine a machine ye could just dial tae get the expression in somebody's eyes or the smell of somethin. Wonder how would her face look now.

Paul's next in the big rush for it to be your turn but shy as well as if we're speakin to a stranger.

'Aye, ah mean yes. An ah scored two goals for the school team the day. Sitters.'

Turn and turn about. Like everything we do. You won't get long but your turn will always come. You wait and your turn always comes. And then the phone is back to me. Wish ma dad was here so he could have a conversation that sounds right, sounds adult, not like mine.

'We thought it was the phone on the telly ringin. On Scotsport.'

'You must have had the volume up too loud.'

'You know our Paul an fitbaw.'

'Your dad should be home soon. Left here half an hour ago. I gave him some fruit to take back. I'm sick lookin at fruit.'

'Was that the big basket Agnes sent ye?'

'Maybe, I don't know. What's she doin sendin me fruit anyway? Ah'm not an invalid. Ah don't want anythin from her. Is she at the door a lot?'

'No, not a lot. She just asks about you, how you are.'

And you are in hospital. A kind of invalid. In valid. Is that how it makes her feel?

'Well, tell her nothing.'

'Okay.'

'Mind ye share the fruit between ye.'

Hope there are grapes and pears and tangerines.

'Okay.'

'The wee ones should be in bed. Make sure they're in bed by the time your dad gets home. He's bound to be tired with the travellin in an out.'

'Aye.'

'How's your father getting on with the new home help?

'Same. He hates her.'

She talks too much as well, same as the other one.

The other day he looked up 'home-help,' in ma dictionary just to make his point.

'Someone- usually paid by the local authority to assist, usually elderly or disabled people with their household tasks.'

'Telt ye,' he says.

'See that woman. She'll be the first home-help to make her client worse.'

'Is he still changin the clock?'

We're both enjoyin this.

He takes the clock fae the mantelpiece an puts the hands back fifteen minutes. This one's worked it out an now she wears her husband's wristwatch on her hand, keeps checkin our clock against the watch wi a puzzled expression on her face. Ma dad just keeps eats his roll and cheese an disane crack a light. He says she leaves the place worse than when she arrived but ah think he'd miss her if they took her away. He needs somthin tae complain about.

'Any more news? Where's Anna?'

'Up the stairs. Somebody gave her patchouli oil an she's experimentin.'

'Oh…good. Tell her not to touch my good scent.'

'GOAAALLLLL

'They scored.'

'That's good. Tell the boys to keep the noise down. Next door'll be chappin through.'

'How are ye feelin? Are ye commin home soon?'

'Wish ah was home just now. The days are long in here. Please God, ah'll be out next week. Say a prayer.'

If you closed your eyes it's like when she used to whisper things in your ear if you'd had a bad dream or were frightened of the dark.

'That's great.'

'How's school?'

'Fine.'

'Ah didnae know ye had a phone in the hospital, is it the nurses' phone?'

'It's a portable one; they hurl it to your bed if ye want to make a call.'

Is there a plastic bit for puttin your head under? Probably no, that's daft.

'That's nice.'

Silence. The daft phone even picks up silence. You'd think they'd invent somethin that would cancel out the awkwardness of not knowing what to say but the phone catches it as the long pause and then a cough.

'And what did ye make for the dinner? '

'Tatties, fish fingers and beans.'

'Did the wee ones eat theirs?'

'Aye, ah checked their plates.'

'The food's okay in here. We had a salad, nice cold meat as well. I've put in two more 10p's, so keep talkin to me.'

'Ah've no more news but mum.'

'Och. Can ye not spare a few more minutes for your auld Irish mother?'

'Passed ma French test.'

'That's a good girl. You stick in at school. Get out that dump of a place. See the world.'

Drrrrrinnnnnng.Drrrrrinnngggg.

'Mum. Ye'll never guess what's happened?'

'What?'

'Archie MacPherson's phone's ringin. It jist rang there.'

She laughs. It's nice to hear her laugh.

Pip.Pip.Pip.Pip

'That's the money runin out. Tell everybody'

When the pips come there's a mad rush tae say everythin; ye realise there's no time; time's runnin out, aw the words you want to say, that come from nowhere. And the sound of the line goin dead and your own voice, sayin the words in your head.

But we'll laugh about Archie's phone when she gets better. That was gas.

6

Agnes' back door is open even though it's pourin. Got the note in ma pocket:

'Your daddy's at the hospital. Chap ma door.'

Biro ink already runnin on the note.

Last thing ah want is to have to talk to anyone but should be glad dad's got somebody to leave the key with, only it's as if everybody else knows stuff before us. If they'd tell us what was goin on, what it means but there's certain things we can't ask, certain things they won't tell us like how long will it be, will it ever be over. Stuff lik that. Maybe, they don't really know. We've had six months now of notes on the door cos dad's had to go in visitin in the afternoon or a consultant wants to talk to him about mum. Sometimes, we come home an she's there on the couch as if it's the most normal thing. But not today. Whatever's happenin, things have changed an nobody's sayin they won't be the same again, everybody's just prayin and hopin for a cure. Wish they'd just cut me a key instead ae aw this rigmarole.

Grass soakin, and gooseberry bushes heavy wi rain. Agnes disnae have a washin out. She usually always has a washin out. The trees have shed flowers all along the path lik some sad confetti, after a rained out weddin when everybody gets pure soaked an aw the photos have a man wi a white umbrella in the back-ground. Anyway, that's the trees bare for another year. Don't last very long. Skinny finches sing and drip…sing and drip.

Our other neighbours have their curtains still drawn in the afternoon. Night shift, probably. The two brothers who live there don't hang anythin out on their washin line even in summer. They're called 'The Poles,' even though they're Lithuanians. Their mum and da came to Scotland when Stalin was persecutin the Catholics. Mum said they're a great people for prayin and there's a Pole takes the choir in the church. Dad says they only came here because they thought it was New York. Scour their washin for hints: a few yellowy vests and pairs ae socks; everythin grey, a bit lik them; sad beside our full lines wi weans' clothes and women's' things, cotton clean sheets and towels rough to the face, all blowin full in the wind. They must have a pulley in the kitchen but. And it's great cos me and the boys play badminton over their line, the grass cold underfoot when our shoes are off. But as per usual right when we're gettin intae the gem, wan ae them chaps the windae, huntin us.

'They should get a life,' mum always says but then she says it's their grass so we've tae keep away.

One of them is wee an stocky an the other is tall an thin; they work night shifts in the steel works, sleep aw day.

'That's their lives,' dad says.

Most ah've ever seen of them is as outlines standin at their back door; they smoke fags, starin at us lik they're aliens. They're wonderin how they ever got stuck amongst aw these weans or maybe how they got old so fast, thinkin about their own dead mother an father an how it used tae be them runnin wild. Though ye'd never guess it, the sullen way they look at ye. Throw their fag-ends over the railin an go back inside like creatures who can never stay long in daylight, who need to check every now an then that there's a place with grass an a tree an people livin other lives. Never had the nerve to stare at them close up to know if they really look like brothers: the way their lips curl or their jaw sits or if they have the same eyes. People say it's a scandal takin up a five apartment, just the two of them, neither chick nor child but no one can shift them, and they've the same right as us to be here. Dad says the only way they'll go is out in a box. Seems lik another world, when ye're their age an the only thing that matters is holdin on tae some house ye never even owned but it's sad as well because they left Russia to be free and they don't seem that free to me.

Next door tae the Poles are the Duffys, the McKays, and at the end of the block, the McGonigals. There's nine McKays, countin the mam an dad. Five apartments. It's a street of big families here except for the Poles. The council don't gie ye a bigger house no matter how many weans there are, ye've to keep squeezing closer and closer together. We're the biggest family in the street, a record so far.

Beyond their bit ae green's some bushes wi goosegogs an blackberries. Ye need tae wait for the right time tae pick the goosegogs; no when they're green and spiky cos they're dead sour but see when they turn red and soft, pure melt in your mouth. Sometimes, ah can see the brothers watchin us an they don't chap ye away. One time they said tae me: 'Ye can pick the fruit if ye want.' That done ma nut in. Started me thinking, maybe they'd poisoned them.

In summer Agnes gets a great tan fae sittin out the back. All year round, even September and April when there's a chill in the air and ye're shiverin inside, she sits out the back, facin her green wi the folded down red parasol wobbling around in a hole right in the middle of their plastic picnic table. When ah'm at school stuck in a class-room, ah think about her readin her paper or maybe doin a crossword, the doors of the house and the windows open, a delicious freedom: sittin on a step, not closed in by teachers an four white walls.

'What's the secret of your tan, Agnes?'

Mum's too busy for a tan. 'Rub coconut oil on yir skin; great fir a tan.'

There's coconut in macaroon bars, coconut and potatoes.

Anna, ma sister, and me tried it. Ye heard oil sizzlin on your skin an ye could fry sausages on it but the smell was great an made me want tae lick ma own arms.

'Away ye go big ears,' mum said.

'But mum,'

'Erin, ah'll give ye your dinner first, if ye do.'

That time needed to step over Lizzie and Annemarie, at the bottom of the stairs, playin cafes, pourin water into two holes were railings used tae be:

'And would ye like a milky coffee, hen?'

A big black crow goin grey at the edges, landed nearby.

There's stuff ah remember dead clear but there's stuff ah forget as well.

Stir the mucky water wi a lollipop stick, so ye get a nice froth at the top and when Lizzie takes the stick out it's startin to dissolve. If ma pals could see me playin wi weans.

There's moss growin through the cracks, an weeds all around the bottom one. In the summer, she'd make me pull the weeds out with ma bare hands cos it'd be too dangerous wi the shears an ma fingers would be pure muck ingrained. Buds on the rose bush haven't opened yet but there's the start of a scent and the promise of bloom.

'Aye, so as ah was sayin Eve, ah lost three; one after the other; that's why ma nerves are so bad. But the Valium's great. Calms me right doon. Ah'd have been lost without it.'

In the kitchen asked ma mum what Agnes lost three of.

'Jesus, can you not mind your own business? Children should be seen and not heard. Now where's the pot?'

'Mum, what was it please? Ah'm not a child. Ah'm thirteen. Muuuuum. What?'

'Don't craic on about it. Ah'm warnin you.'

Next time ah'm talkin to Veronica Duffy, asked her.

'Babies,' she said.

'How? Ah mean how can ye lose babies?' Visions of weans left in a box an nobody can remember were they put them.

'They died.'

And there was me always rubbin it in that there were more of us than Veronica's family cos sometimes she pure gets oan ma goat and that shuts her up. From then on, ah was gonnae count those three weans, and that'd mean there'd be more ae them than us. But ah really hoped ma mum didnae have any more weans after this one. The house was too wee. Things were upside down when there's a new one: ma mum in hospital, ma da off work, tryin tae make breakfast then it's nappies an ma mum hidin up the stairs, breast feedin the wean.

'Hard luck,' Veronica said when ah telt her about the last arrival, three years ago.

'Ah know.'

Sat on the back step for ages, wonderin if ah'd ever get a room tae maself.

***

Agnes' kitchen is empty an warm. We're no allowed to walk into other people's houses even wi a note. Ah'm used tae standin at the door, waitin to pass a message tae her, gien her back the sugar she borrowed or sayin there's an extra apple cake cos mum baked too much.

'Agnes!'

Need to shout above the tumble drier. It's dead noisy an it's movin away from the corner the way they do when it's a fast cycle. Any minute now, aw the clothes will spill out across the blue tiles.

'Agnes.'

'Aye. Who's that?' She appears through the inside door, wearin her apron, a yellow duster in her hand.

'Hiya, hen. ' She appears through the inside door, wearin her apron, a yellow duster in her hand.

'Hiya, hen. C'mon in. Ye're soakin standin there.'

Inside, the blue floor tiles are spotless. The place smells of bleach. Same as ours when ma mum isnae in hospital. Ah cannae get them that clean. Ah always get bits ae grit and stuff piled up in the corners. That's cos ah don't pay attention when ma mum's doin the floor. Housework's borin. Anyway, she hates us under her feet.

'Don't worry. You can take your shoes off. Gie me your jacket. Och, hen. See this weather. They've got a drought down in England an we've got this.'

Ah saw the drought on the telly.

Here at the door, ah can breathe.

'Did ma dad leave a key?'

Agnes is shakin ma kagool over the sink. There are pots and dishes dryin on the plastic rack, a bottle of Fairy Liquid behind the tap and a used tea bag on a teaspoon. How many times will she use the tea bag? She better no get any left over bits ae food on ma kagool.

'No, hen. He said ye've to wait here. Shouldnae be long. He knows ye're off this afternoon. And he'll definitely be back for the wee ones. Somethin about a meetin at the hospital. Your poor mum.'

Shakes her head. Poor Agnes, ah bet she misses mum an their chats on the back steps.

Och naw. Ah could put the heatin on, get the house dead cosy for the rest ae them comin in. And ah'd get peace. Now, ah'll need to talk. Ah'll need tae listen. That's the way mum takes ma coat, when she's home, always makes us take off our wet things in case we get a cold, right down to our knickers.

Agnes puts ma jacket across the radiator. We'll be able tae smell the nylon mixin wi the heat soon. She better no burn it.

Outside, at the bottom of the stairs, the black bin bag inside their wire bin has collapsed inside itself. Ah keep meanin to tell Agnes but she keeps talkin an the words don't come out. Ah cannae find a space were the words can go so they get stuck somewhere between ma brain an ma mouth, the way a piece of paper gets trapped in the wire ae the bin. That happens to me. Ah wait to speak but the time never comes so ah give up and think what the hell or ah forget or ah'm too bored to bother.

'Ah'll put the kettle on. Wee cuppa, eh?'

Her worktops are clean, not like ours: bits of this mornin's breakfast, jam and margarine for toast. Ah'll detol it for ma mum comin back from the hospital.

This is a pain. Ah should be studyin for the exam but how can ah now? If ma daddy came back, ah could get in a few hours.

'How come you're off, hen?'

The Daily Record folded over on the worktop. The headline: 'Cop's Kinky Secret.'

'Exams. Shedules.'

The rain's really batterin the ground but there's a peace about it, the way it takes over everythin. Ma hair's soakin, rain runnin down ma face, in ma eyes and mouth. Tasteless. The plastic bin lid's like a drum and there's water pourin through the holes, in the mesh and lyin in the creases of the plastic bag.

'C'mon in, Ah'll need to shut that door. Ah hate the door bein closed, feels depressin, don't ye think?'

Ma mum keeps our back door closed, especially when she's washed the floors and wants to keep us out.

Ah'm shivery but it's nice.

'God, you're worse than me. At least come in a wee bit an we'll sit on these chairs.'

She pulls over a couple of kitchen chairs, leavin the door open so we can still see out.

She gives me a fresh tea bag from the box but takes the used, yellowing one for herself. The tea is hot and weak. Mum's tea's dead strong. 'Irish tea,' she calls it. This must be Wishaw tea.

Even the doorsill is clean. Might ask Agnes if ah can move in.

'Did ah tell ye we were goin to Spain on holiday? Ah've been before. Ah tried to get ye're mum to go but ye know what she's like about goin to Ireland.'

Why does she have to remind me? Ma mum won't be fit for Ireland this year.

'Does your David not have his exams?'

She laughs back. Right enough.

'Him. He's no looked at a book since primary school. '

He's in ma year so he must have exams. Ah see him sometimes at the bus stop but he's no in any of ma classes. Their David was the nicest lookin boy at primary. It's a pity.

'Ah think he's got French today and Chemistry tomorrow.'

'Aye, hen. Ye could be right. He did say something but he disnae study. No interested. Cannae wait to leave.'

From the front of the house there's the sound of another door openin.

'Christ, it's our John. Home early. Ah forgot about him. Here, hen shut that door, will ye. He'll think ah'm daft, sittin lookin out at the rain. Away you go into the fire now. Ah'll get the tea on for him.'

Closin over the door, Agnes is right. The kitchen does get smaller, shrinks to jist a wee room, same as ours.

The sound of a toilet gettin flushed then boots or somethin gettin thrown across a floor upstairs.

Sit on one of the sofa seats, near the coal fire. They didnae get gas lik we did when the Council renovated the houses. Ma daddy was the only one could light the fire in the mornin, an we were freezin when he was at work. Ma mum says gas is cleaner but ah miss the coal fire. That lovely warmth. Heats ye right through to your bones.

Yellow cloth flowers in a glass vase, drops of clear sugary stuff on petals, supposed to be rain. No water, ah check. They've had the room artexed, white circles inside other circles lik white cream bein stirred. Everythin in the room is green: sofa and chairs, swirly patterned carpet an even the curtains.

Ah'm holdin the wee card Agnes pressed into ma hand: '*Miracle Prayer*' '*Jesus, I trust in you of divine mercy.*' Ah'll keep it for mum. There's a photo of Jesus, the same as ours above the fire and to the right.

The door opens. Mr. McKay in his work clothes.

'Hi, hen. Where's Agnes?'

'Hi, Mr. McKay. She's in the kitchen, makin tea.'

'Agnes. Are you there?'

He closes over the kitchen door. Now ah'm shut in here ma self wi their Colin's weddin photo and Jesus.

Wonder if dad's back. That's two hours ah could have left tae study.

The door opens again, making flames blow about a bit from the draught.

Mr McKay sits down right across from me. He looks at me an the chair, it's his chair.

A mortal sin.

'Do you want to sit here, Mr. McKay?'

Ah've never said two words to him before.

'No, ye're awright, hen. Ah'm fine here.'

He lifts the paper and starts to read, leavin me to wait for Agnes and watch the fire.

His hands are like shovels and his fingers are yellow at the tips from the fags.

'Here's ye're tea, John. Are ye all right, hen. Would ye like a top up?'

Agnes is hovering between the kitchen and the livin room. Ah wish she'd sit down.

'No, thanks. Ah'm fine.'

Eventually, she sits on the couch between the two chairs. The swirly red carpet is like ours but they've got artex on the walls an that makes their livin room seem different. Ma mum disnae believe in artex. She says ye're stuck wi it and then it goes out of fashion and ye cannae get rid of it.

'How come ye're home early the day, hen?'

Mr.McKay's blue eyes are on me quickly but back towards the fire before ah can meet them.

'Exams. It's the schedules. French today and chemistry tomorrow.'

'She's brainy, John. Aren't you, hen? Better than our David.'

He spits into the fire and we have tae wait for a reply.

'What goods are brains tae her now, wi her mother sick'

The words are a spit right in ma face. Ah don't know where tae look.

'Surely, ye'll be leavin school to help your father?'

It's as if he's been savin up the questions cos they keep comin lik he's thought about it over and over again. And when ah look up, his blue eyes don't drift from ma face.

393

Coal rages in the fire now, the heat burnin ma face. At least ah think it's the heat. Ah cannae move, cannae get up an say it's too warm in here.

'No, ah want to stay on.'

Right back in his face. Now, he looks lik ah've spat on him.

'For God's sake, John, shut-up. Leave the wee lassie alone. Times are different. There's nothin better than a good education. Quite right, hen.'

'That lassie's place is in the house. Let her father go back to work.'

Ma dad's been off for months now, he's right an ah'd love ma him tae go back tae work but does that mean ah cannae stay on at school? What's one got tae do wi the other? Ah'm no the reason. It's no up tae me. Reflected in the fire, his skin seems grey lik he's been inside aw his life lik somebody who's never been young or maybe, just, ah cannae remember it. He takes a draw from the fag.

'Ah'm goin to university.'

Ma voice shakes lik when ah'm doin a readin at mass in front of the whole parish, the word 'university,' sounds long an foreign, disnae even mean anythin to me. Mrs. Kelly said ah could there, if ah work hard an ah hate that it sounds lik ah'm showin off but ah cannae help it.

Why do ah have tae say it? Why do ah have tae talk?

'University?'

Shakes his head, glowerin into the fire; flames curl an lick the air, above the burnin red coal.

He lifts the metal poker from the hearth, shakes it underneath embers, makin a sound that rustles downwards into the ash pan. Ah imagine the poker bein in ma hand. What ah'd do.

'You're a bit too big for your boots, hen. Know your place or ye'll learn the hard way.'

'Jesus, John.'

'Well, Agnes, ah'm tryin to help the lassie. Somebody needs to tell her.'

She's still here.

'When John's father died, hen, he took over and looked after the mother and his brothers. He didnae leave home till the rest were away is that no right, John?'

Agnes is leanin over towards him, nearly touchin the side of the chair. Maybe she knows if ah get the poker, then we'll see.

'Aye, that's right. Did ma duty. Stick by ye're family, hen. Nothin else matters in life. You listen to me.'

His eyes are wide and he seems to not be lookin at me but starin at the wall behind. What has it got to do with him? Why is it so bad wantin to stay on at school? Suddenly cos mum's sick everybody's tellin me how ah should live the whole of the rest of ma life.

The heat's gettin more intense in the room. There's no air to breathe. Ma mum's here, she's no like his dad. But what if he's right? There's no signs of mum getting better. People hardly ever get better from her sort of Leukaemia an ma dad cannae stay at home lookin after us for much longer, he'll go mad. Madder. If ah left school, he could go back to work. It might make everythin tick over more, if ah was at home. In a way, it would be easier, no havin to go somewhere lik Glasgow, away from home. Ah don't know if ah could bear it. An it would only be for a few years until the wee ones were older. Ma mum must want him to go back to work. Ah think. Ah think she would want things to be normal again. Not everybody mopin about the house bein sad. Ah could always go to university later. Ah cannae ask them though, they'll go mental. Ah don't have to ask them, it's ma life. Okay, that's decided. That night ah pray for an answer but only silence. Maybe silence means it's okay that's the answer cos if the answer was no then ah would know. That's it then ah'm leavin school next year when ah'm sixteen. Ah'll tell ma dad when the moment's right. It's a relief, to have made the decision. It's the right thing to do. Don't think about tellin mum cos ah know she'll never allow it; well, she cannae really stop me from hospital, she cannae make it happen over a hospital pay phone. Ma dad can tell her.

7

After months of bein in an out hospital, we get used to her bein away for a week then bein back, the talkin on the phone and the visits an part of ye thinks that's the way it will stay. Then the day comes when she's not up the whole the day. Niggle at the back of your mind, lik dust in a corner of a room ye never dust. Well into the day and she's still in bed. Not even come down to the kitchen for a cup of tea. That would be enough, for a cup of tea. It's happened before that she's stayed in bed but never this, never all day.

We're watchin 'The Doubledeckers.' Ah used to be Billie, wi the long brown hair tied back in a pony tail but Elaine's her now. Our Annemarie is Tiger. She even has her own fur tiger that she carries around.

Ma dad is up and down the stairs. Ma dad is nobody in a programme. He's himself.

'Don't disturb her. She's no well. Leave her alone.'

Can we not peek our heads around the door?

Four o'clock, says he's phonin the hospital.

'They're sendin an ambulance. Ah've tae bring her in.'

Sometimes, he talks an ah don't know if he's talking to me or himself. Don't know if ah'm supposed to say something back.

'Only one of you can come. Erin, ye'll need tae look after this lot. She wants Paul tae come.'

Thank God, it's no me. Never said ah wanted to go. Ah'm pure sick of that hospital so Paul can go if he likes.

Time drags until ah have tae bar the door wi ma foot cos the wee ones are at the livin room door, they don't see him carryin mum down the stairs.

'Phone ye fae the hospital. You look after them, mind?'

Have to look anyway, glad ah've got the excuse not to go with him. Carried down the stairs.

Lizzie's pullin ma jumper but the ambulance is waitin at the gate.

'Ah want ma mum. Let me past.'

It's a vicious circle. Ma dad's keeping us away from ma mum cos she's sick and now ah'm keeping the younger ones away. We're building a circle of space around her wi no weans, no us. Hold the door so tight, hurt ma fingers. Lizzie isn't givin in without a fight, she's usin all her strength to pull the door in the other direction. It would be a scene, if ah let the door go, let the flood-gates open, all the children runnin towards them, remindin them there are dinners to be cooked later, school-uniforms to be sorted: tantrums. Ah think ah'll let it go, join the queue.

What about us?

Final push wrenches the door away from Lizzie and Annemarie's hands.

The wee ones go tae the windae to see the ambulance drivin away; wish the rain would go off so the house would empty but settle down an wait for the phone tae ring. They sit on the carpet watchin Double-deckers on t.v. Ah wonder why all the kids are smiling, it seems false, pure white perfect teeth, all that American t.v happiness. Even Doughnut stuffin his face, isnae funny. It finishes.

'One banana, two banana, three banana four. Five banana, six banana, seven banana more.'

Nobody can be bothered wi The Banana Splits. Usually wolf our dinners so we can watch it but it's the school holidays an rainin outside. Soon all four dancin girls are dancin to 'Doin the Banana Split,' at the end of the show. Ah'm starin at the screen. Don't ask me what happened: the usual note from the Sour Grape Messenger Girls then a lot of daft stuff in between. But Annemarie and Lizzie are settled again. That's good.

The hours drag until the door goes, early evening.

'Who is it?

'Me, hen. Sally's mum.'

'Your dad phoned me from the hospital.'

Dark outside when ah open the door. She has a big bag of tatties, sausages an two tins of beans. At least ah don't have to make the dinner. Bits ae breadcrumbs on the grill from ma mum's fish last night so need tae clean it. Wi her own time zone she'd been in bed all evening, then when we were gettin ready for bed, there she was, at the cooker waitin for a single piece of fish to be ready on one side. Crumbly sofy white fish, easy to digest. Nothing to it. That won't fill her up.

After dinner Sally's mum starts cleanin the house. How come aw the women that come here want tae clean our house? It's still our house. It's still ma mum's house.

Away an clean your own house.

Nine o'clock put the rest tae bed. Everyone's exhausted, waitin for the phone to ring, keepin busy. The wee ones are normal exhausted. They cheered up about four o'clock.

'Mum'll be back later tonight.'

That keeps them happy.

Agnes arrives fae nowhere. She starts cleanin as well.

'Ma mum disnae use that.'

Puttin Shake and Vac on the carpet, go up the stairs tae get away fae the smell. It's as if they're all expectin a big visit. Someone from Ireland is comin or the priest? Why doesn't the phone ring? Maybe, if Agnes stopped hoverin, ah could hear it. Maybe it did ring. Now ma dad'll think we never bothered answerin. He'll think the telly's up full bung. He'll ring again. Cannae sleep so go back down to the livin room again.

He might not ring. He might think it's quicker getting on the road. Waitin for us to answer the phone, that might go on all night. That's probably it.

And the phone rings just as ah reach the lobby. Sally's mam's already got it.

'Okay, son. Okay. That's fine. No problem. Look after yourself.'

The bitch puts the phone down.

'Was that our dad? Was it?'

'Aye, hen. That was him.'

Well, it's our house, it's our phone. Away an answer your own phone.

'What did he say? Did he say how our mum was?'

'She's still no well, hen. He didnae say much.'

'Is he commin home? When is he commin home?'

'He didnae say. He'll stay another wee while. Could ye no sleep?'

'No. Ah'll sleep when ma dad gets back. Ah never sleep when me da's at the hospital.'

Anna's awake, leanin over the banister.

'What's up? Did ma da phone?'

'Aye. Ah never spoke tae him. She disnae know when he'll be back.'

Ah'm sorry ah said SHE but don't know how to take it back.

'What time is it?'

'Half eleven.'

'Will everybody stop hoverin and talkin loud? Ah cannae sleep.'

'Shhh you'll waken the rest.'

This time when the phone goes ah'm down the stairs lik a shot. Ah get it.

'Hello da?'

'Hello is Joe there?' a woman's voice. Very polite. Ah'm just about to put the phone down on her but she keeps talking. Ma dad could be tryin to get through. What a nightmare.

'He's at the hospital.'

'I'm just phonin to say we're so sorry about, Eve. We phoned the hospital and they told us. They told us the news. Will you tell him we're sorry. Will you? Will you tell Joe we phoned.'

Who does she think she's speakin to? What's 'the news?' And then it dawns on me; it seems slowly like the whole of the rest of ma life it takes to dawn. Actually, its seconds.

Didn't realise when ah was holdin the door away from them, keeping them away from her, that they'd never see her again. That ah'd never see her again. If ah'd known it, ah'd have tried to keep her wi us, if ah'd known what was goin to happen. But nobody knew an we never had the talk about me leavin school cos ah knew all along she'd never allow it, not while she was breathin, no way, no way.

8

Usually, the coffin's in the house at the wake but he says we've tae remember her as she was, says we wouldnae recognise her anyway. She might repulse us. Repulse is a good word for disgust, the way 'pulse' bulges out at ye lik a big toad's throat. Her face might be purple; purple lik the hair-dye she put on her grey hair. Instead ae the coffin there's a space on the carpet in the wee room beside the phone. Three nights in a row, the rosary's at our house Loads ae people. Mare prayers.

She'd be mortified at no bein allowed into the house at her own wake, itchin tae know if we made the tea with the best cups. Did we put sugar in a bowl like she showed us and clean the rooms, skirtin boards as well? The St.Vincent De Paul men put Our Lady on the fridge freezer. It's always cheaper to bulk buy when ye've a crowd but it's empty cos Simmit ate the last choc ice for breakfast. Our Lady's feet are creamy; the snake's painted gold. Her face is too white lik a dead person. Ah wonder why are we kneelin in front ae her? Ah should be prayin but aw ah can think is what good did Our Lady ever do us? Worry durin the rosary what if the phone rings? We should have taken it off the hook. Should ah answer it?

'Our father who art in heaven.

Hallowed be thy name.'

People in the livin room, in the lobby, on the inside stairs and right out tae the gate but we're in the wee room, Anna, dad and me. Above the statue are scribbles on the wallpaper and the paper's ripped so ye can see a layer underneath. Aw the time, thinkin who'll paper the rooms now? It's wood-chip wi somethin flowery underneath.

The priest's black shoes stick out under the purple vestments. Purple is for death. White is for Easter and risin fae the dead. Red is for blood. Like when ye speak intae a tape recorder, play it back an ye sound dead Scottish. The me in ma head tells the me whose legs are shakin. Be calm. But the me that has legs disnae hear. Try to be carved fae stone lik the statue of Our Lady. The chapel ceilin, high and arched; ye get the feelin that if there is a God, he starts up there. Say the words but they don't mean anything.

Across the words to the end of the paragraph and

'THIS IS THE WORD OF THE LORD'

But a statue's legs don't shake.

Congregation : THANKS BE TO GOD

Me: ALL STAND

'Alleluia, Alleluia. Give thanks to the risen Lord

Alleluia, Alleluia. Give thanks to His name.'

How come the Lord gets tae rise but no real people?

Down the altar steps, turn at the rails, genuflect, walk to ma seat in the front row, aw the relatives behind us.

'That was good. Are you okay?' Anna whispers, smellin of Aunt Geraldine's perfume.

We stole some, a wee sqoosh each. This mornin, Aunt Geraldine was so mad about Aunt Mary not comin, she never noticed the smell of perfume was hers.

Nod to Anna, but ma legs keep shakin right through the offertory procession. Wearin the darkest clothes in their wardrobe, people stand at the back cos the place is full. Maybe, she isn't in the box. How do ah really know? They told me she was, but the lid has been closed the whole time. Simmit is swinging the casket full of black powder that our Paul spooned in; the creak ae the swingin chain is the only sound then... Anna smells it first. She knows. Ah catch it from her. Butterflies in ma stomach. The smell of incense signallin the end of mass; Frankincense one of the wise men brought to a manger, Myrrh for the dyin, daft present for a new-born wean. Me an Anna looked up the meaning of the scents.

'In Egypt, they bathed the dead body in myrrh.'

It was me got Anna the book out the library.

When the tomb of Tutankhamen was opened, that's what they smelt.

On the altar, the boys walk beside the priest, but their faces are the faces of statues. Paul looks the worse as if he might vomit aw over the white altar cloth, bits of his breakfast stainin it. Steps down the stairs in front of the coffin, holdin a big, bronze crucifix. Our uncles an our dad move tae the front, gettin ready to lift the coffin; first, they support its weight, puttin an arm round each other's shoulder. Ah'm glad ah'm not dad or any other man, that has to lift someone he loves on his shoulder, the heaviness of the wood and the body, along athe aisle, hundreds ae faces starin at ye. Glad that will never be me.

The holy water font is dry, green stuff at the bottom, ashes at Lent. At the Passover, a mark on every door to save the eldest child but the mark was the blood of a lamb, no green dust.

Big, black cars outside. One of them had opens at the back. People across the road are watchin, and behind us everybody comin out of chapel. No one moves down the steps until we do, nearest relatives at the front, second cousins an family friends behind, then neighbours and the people who knew her to say ' hello' in the Co-Op. Across the road, a big crowd. A blur.

Out of no-where Paul throws the crucifix on the ground then takes off down the steps, runnin into people, the big cross clatterin after him.

'Jesus, someone. Go after him,' ma aunt shouts.

'Poor laddie,' another woman whispers near me.

'He was there when she passed away. Never been right since.'

Paul's hasn't even bothered to hitch up the white altar gown as he's flown down the stairs, away up the road, towards home. And after it, our Paul never says a word about mum or the funeral, in fact, Paul won't speak to anyone.

'He'll be fine,' Uncle Tom says to ma dad.

'I've bought him a new football strip and some lovely boots. Once he's back at the training, he'll get over it.'

'Thanks Tom, you're right.'

We can't even talk about normal things like what telly programme to watch without fightin so how we gonnae ever find words for this?

FIVE

1

When ah focus on Andy, it's pure ugliness: his whole face raging.

What did I say?

Ah should never have trusted Doris or him. Don't know what's the truth any more. Maybe, if ah gie him what he wants, it will be over; he'll still take me to ma aunt's. Ah'll still get Paul.

Ah don't think ah can do it, beat him.

He lunges at me an ah move the opposite way. He slips now.

'Bastard, fuck, fuck.'

Nettles, pee-the-beds an sticky willies.

There's no point, ah can't do it. He'll get me in the end.

RUN You can still do it.

Ah can't. That's the problem. Ah'm no her. Ah'm no you.

You can't give up now.

Ah can. Ah can give up.

And what will that do to your father? You're a selfish girl, Erin.

How dad would feel and how the others would feel then with another one of us gone and it would be ma fault. Clear the jaggy nettles in one go lik a long jumper, the nettles scrape ma arms an scald ma hands, can't stop cos Andy is chasin after me but his heels keep him back. He'll never be able to jump wi heels or if he does he'll go over in his ankle. And ah'm fast for a girl, no longer only a girl. Ah've only got this strength in me for so long. Andy's lik a wasp that's dyin an he has to sting me wi his poison, before he dies but if he can be a wasp then ah'm a butterfly, feet for wings. Ah'm terrified everytime ah think of how ugly he looked lik he hated me and the way he spat out the words: 'Ah want what ah paid for.'

After ah've cleared the patch of nettles, keep runnin, only turnin back to see him crawlin along the ground tryin to get his footing again, then he's up an runnin lik a wild man, again, wi sticky willies in his hair an clingin to his good suit. His voice is farther away this time. Ah'm runnin faster than ah've ever run.

'Wee bitch, bitch.'

This is same as sleep walkin, bein in a dream someone is lookin for me, trees calling my name but how do they know my name? Willing who it is to stop in case Andy hears. Like after mum died when ah kept hearing this woman's voice, calling her wean in for dinner. Used to think, she was calling me: all ah had to do was find that street and there'd be ma real house and at the top of the stairs, she'd be there.

Don't know the difference between real life and dreams anymore. After ah've been goin for what feels lik ages, there's no sound of him runnin behind me but ah don't know if he's got in the car and gone ahead of me. Keep goin along bumpy ground that make ma feet hurt until ah can't go any further. The rain has started an a wind is pickin up. It's harder to run an not fall cos of the rain makin the ground slippy. Put on the kagool Maro gave me and at least ah've got a hood to protect me from the wind and rain. When ah'm sure Andy is not behind me ah stop under a group of big trees,whose branches fan out makin a roof of leaves. Catch ma breath, tryin to keep quiet but ma breathin won't let me.

After a bit when ah look out from ma den, it's rainin heavy an the wind's howlin, a high-pitched scream of its own. Ah start tae run again, through the eerie sound of the whisling wind, until ah've out run darkness and into the start of light, until ah can't run anymore. Ma legs are so tired; they buckle beneath me but ah feel safer with the light comin. Ah've nothin else left now. Nothin. The plan to get Paul seems daft and not worth all this an ah don't know what drives me, what makes me run away. It's as if ah just needed an excuse. It's as if ah've put maself through all of this, lik ah'm punishin maself for somethin an ah don't even know what it is.

An ah'm not selfish. Ah tried. Ah tried. You're the selfish one. You died.

When ah waken up, ah'm in a big double bed, with a hot water bottle at ma feet. On a wee cabinet beside the bed, a nightlight glows although it's daylight. Two dogs are lying on the floor, as if this is their bed and ah've made them homeless for the night. Remember a burnt out log on the ground, a tin of Forest Green paint at the side of the cabin. Birds break the silence, a bee drones like a motor bike on the main road. The ridge of a gate was cutting into ma back. Ah was lying on the ground, lookin at a pair of muddy Wellingtons. That's all ah remember.

Once again I see

Something something... *little lines*

Of sportive wood run wild: these something farms,

Green to the very door;'

Wish ah could remember useful stuff stead of lines from a poem though they're hard to forget when ye get them into your head. The sound of the words of the poem stick with you. Mrs. Kelly says that's what the poet intended but when ye read it, sometimes, it's as if he's talkin to you right into your ear, but in a different way from normal words; ah can't explain how it sounds lik everyday but lik a prayer as well. Or a song; anyway, somethin ye remember once ye've read even if it is only a tune or a couple of words. An the person speakin is desperate to tell you the thing, has to tell ye the truth, no lik everybody else who goes silent when any hard subject comes up. Ah don't really really get all of *Tintern Abbey,* an ah don't know if what ah say will make any sense to the class but ah'll tell them what ah read, that he was tryin to make poetry more lik real life, not highfalutin, the way it had been before; he wanted to write about ordinary folk an that's why he went on his journeys. Ah wonder if he would have taken me with him, if ah'd asked. Probably not. He'd have listened to me askin then got on his jaunting cart and maybe, written a poem about a scraggy wee lassie who tried to hitch a lift for free.

Someone in the next room is moving around. Wonder could it be her? Maybe, the whole thing was a dream and she didn't die and she's here, makin herself a cup of tea? But the room is not ma gran's or our house and the photo of the family on the wall is not ma family. On a table next to me, there's a wee candle nearly burnt out.

'Hiya, hen. You're awake' says a woman, who appears at the door, her short hair tousled by sleep and one of her front teeth missing.

411

She puts a hand to her mouth.

'Don't mind me, hen. Ah'm gumsy. Ma tooth came out in a cake last night. Just before you arrived.'

The dogs start to bark, running out of the bedroom towards the front door.

'That'll be our Charlie. Shut it, Buster.'

It's like being in hospital that time ah got ma tonsils out, the bed really high up.

'You take your time, hen. The kettle's on.'

'Where am ah?'

The woman laughs.

'Carbeth, hen. Our own wee heaven.'

'How did ah get here? Ah don't remember. Ah was high up...trees.'

'Did you shelter in the wood from the rain? God knows how you found your way to here. Charlie, that's ma man, he went to take the dogs for a walk, opened the door of the hut and saw you leanin against the gate. What a fright. Couldnae get over it: how you were there and the dogs not barking. They bark at the slightest thing. You were in some state, hen. What on earth happened? Your clothes covered in muck. We couldnae get over it, how you found your way here in the middle of the night.'

'Don't know. Ah remember bein lost, an ah think ah hit ma head but ah don't remember much.'

A man appears at the door, stocky with bright blue eyes, as if his eyes know a joke that he is just about to tell.

'Well, Maggie, it's the ghost from the forest,' he says to the woman.

412

'Och, leave the wee lassie alone you. C'mon, hen, ah'll pour you a nice cup of tea.'

The way the man and woman talk to each other feels so easy. The place with its walls full of photographs and paintings of what looks like the cabin, all different seasons, covered in snow, with no path, or surrounded by leaves from the big trees ah don't remember seeing outside. It's like a house in a fairy tale, the one that Hansel and Gretel found. Climbin out the bed, find ma shoes from last night. Someone has cleaned them, scraped all the muck away and my tights have been washed and lie folded, waiting for me.

The couple are talking in a whisper when ah enter the room. There's a wee stove with a glass door, coal and some logs burning inside, right in the centre, against a back wall. The smell reminds me of when we had the coal fire and mum or dad got up early to light it for us going to school. One of the dogs is stretched out in front of the fire. The woman goes to the coal bucket, puts some fresh coal in the stove and when she opens the door, the smell is a mix of the all the scents of the forest, dampness, bracken, grass and trees. She pours steaming hot tea into three plastic mugs and places a pile of toast on a plate. The mugs make it seem like a picnic.

'Your daddy's been lookin for you, hen. It's Erin, isn't it?'

She's got her legs crossed, looks into the fire then at Charlie. The door of the stove is open but you can see that the glass doors are blackened from the smoke.

'The polis announced it on the radio. That you'd gone missing. They've been searching everywhere.'

'Have they? Didnae know.'

413

'Aye, hen. Your dad made a special appeal. He's been worried sick.'

'Has he?'

'He has. Lucky, Charlie remembered hearing it after the news last night. He helped you up an brought ye here.'

'Don't remember that.'

'The shock. Probably, the shock.'

Charlie puts his mug on the table, as he stands up.

'Anyway, ah'll need to go, ah've got stuff to get on with. Ah'll see you both later.'

Opening the door, he lets in the view of hills and sky.

While he's gone, his wife keeps the fire goin so ah fall asleep to the sound of wood spitting in an open hearth and outside, birds singing.

When the door goes again, it could be hours later; ah've been sleeping; ah hear voices but not what they say.

The front door is open. Ah can feel the breeze from the bedroom. They couldn't stop me if ah made a run for it. Ah could easily get past them. Ah'd be faster than them. Ah'm sure of it.

Leave or stay. Leave or stay. So exhausted. Ah fall asleep on the couch to the sound of rain on a tin roof.

***

This time when ah waken ah get the shock of ma life. Dad is at the door of the hut, comin inside wi the man that lives here. He looks

414

drowned in his sheepskin coat as if he's shrunk since a few days ago. He comes towards me his arms held out, and when ah rush to him, there's a smell of suede from the coat.

'You gave us such a bloody fright. How....' But then he hugs me tight again, both of us sobbin and cryin, not able to say the words.

Through ma tears ah see another figure behind him but it's all a blur. When it clears up, it's our Paul standin there wi the polis-woman.

'Hi.'

'Hiya, sis,' our Paul says back. Paul's talkin again.

Later, when dad's had some tea ask him:

'How did you find me?'

The poliswoman who brought him here is outside talkin into her radio. She'll want to shine a lamp in ma face, ask me questions.

'The polis spoke to a woman called Doris, at that place. What a place for you to end up in. What were you thinkin, Erin? How could you take a lift from some man you didnae know? Did your mum an me no always tell ye that was the last thing you should do. Anythin could have happened, Erin. It was stupid.'

Two lines between his eyebrows seem deeper. Maybe, he put his worries for me in that ditch.

Ah'm sick being out in the world without ma family. Nothing's perfect, not at home, not anywhere. But ah'm not goin back to be shouted at. Ah'd rather be on my own than frightened in ma own house.

415

'Sorry, hen, about the paintin. Ah shouldnae have painted over it,' he says.

The words sit between us for a while. Neither of us speaks.

Ah've never heard ma dad say he's sorry about anythin to anybody. Cannae look me in the eye. Ah know if ah look away, he'll look at me then.

When dad goes to speak to the polis it's only me an our Paul.

Ah know ah should leave it but cannae help maself.

'What was it like Paul when you went to the hospital the night ma mum was sick, do you remember?'

Paul rubs his forehead, rememberin is hurtin his head.

'It's okay, Paul.'

'What do you mean like?'

'Did she say anythin else? Did she tell you, what we should do now?'

He shakes his head in a no.

That's it then.

2

In the summer, before school breaks up for the holidays, Mrs. Kelly takes us on the trip to New Lanark. Ah was worried they'd cancel it cos of the rain of the last three days but the forecast for today is for light showers only, so the school says we can go. It's a funny mornin, end of June warm but the air feels heavy an the sky is grey wi clouds. The road goin there is twisty and seems to take for ages although it's only a forty-five minute drive. Some of the boys at the front are eggin on the driver to go faster around the bends but Mrs. Kelly's got her beady eye on them and so has Mr. Naughton, who is a bear of a PE teacher. Mrs Kelly is massive wi her baby now.

'Bet it's twins,' Sally whispers near the back of the bus. Tell her to shush cos don't want any more trouble after runnin away. The history teacher, Mr. Twaddle is here as well but he's keepin a low profile, still sittin, leavin Mr. Naughton to lay down the law.

When the big door opens with a whoosh, the people at the front go to rush forward.

'Hey, you lot, back in your seats.' Mr. Naughton has his arms across the bus, barrin everybody's way.

We get the talk.

We've to stay in pairs.

We've not to wander off the beaten track.

We've to be nice to the staff at the centre and anyone we meet.

We're here representin the school and we've no to gie the teachers a showin up.

The first sight of New Lanark is from the top of a high path, beyond the car park. The village is lik one big old-fashioned factory with tall, clean lookin buildins.

Sally's only interested in the talent: what boys are where an how we can be amongst them.

Mrs. Kelly is stayin up near the bus wi her flask an magazines cos she's too big to make it down the hill but Naughton is with us every step of the way. Some of the boys go into a run down the hill an when they start can hardly stop themselves. It's a strain on calves goin down. The grassy bits are still soggy but the pavement through the village is dry.

When we get to the bottom of the path, the teachers lead us in to a grim lookin buildin that used to be the old school house. Ah'm here at last, somewhere, where ah could actually find a sign of Wordsworth and ah'm stuck inside learnin about Robert Owen. He's no ma project even though the educational tour is £2 a head. There's ages of listenin to the woman tour guide who talks to us lik we're our Annemarie's age, about how great everythin was for children here cos they actually got to go to school. Ah suppose in those days it wis a big deal. Naughton, at last, says we've got some free time but we've to remember and meet back at the bus in an hour.

There's a sign that says 'Falls of Clyde,' pointin away from the visitor centre, towards trees an a path goin up a hill.

'Sir, can ah go there?'

He gies me a look that says he thinks ah'm up to no good.

'What for?'

'Well, that's where the waterfalls are, up along that path.'

If Mrs Kelly was here, she'd have made the whole class go.

'Och, that's right. That's where the poet went, wasn't it?'

'Yes, sir.'

'Who else wants to see the waterfalls?' He shouts to the class who're already dispersing to picnic tables or back into the visitor centre to buy nic nacs for their families.

'Not very popular is he?'

'No, sir.'

'Ah'll go wi her, sir,' Sally does history with Mr. Twaddle. She's a prize pupil.

'Coffee, Mr Naughton?' Mr. Twaddle says; he looks too hot in his tweed jacket.

The teachers nod their heads at each other then Naughton says:

'Right, well, stay on the path the two of you. Be back in good time.'

We get only a small distance from the mill village with its picnic tables and visitor centre; suddenly, the roar of water drowns out the sounds of birds an draws me an Sally to it. We stand inside a buildin without a front, a lookin area that's undercover, right where the bottom of the Falls run in full spate over flat rocks. Two geese skite across the smooth surface of water landin lik two water skiers. The water is white where it cascades over rocks an soupy green where it's still as a slab of glass. A big black crow flies across lookin for its tea.

All along the path that skirts the water's edge, following it up to The Falls, are wee bits of cardboard with labels for names of plants. The smell that's everywhere is 'wild garlic.' Another card says 'pink campion,' beside a star of pink.

The path cuts right through a wood, all along the side of the water. The wee labels say 'anemone,' and 'bluebells.' Sally an me sit on a bench that has 'Billy an Lizzie,' carved into the wood.

We walk farther along, until we see a sign with an arrow that says:

'Corra Linn.' The name of the waterfall.

Now, the walk is steep. Ye need to really climb.

Eventually, Sally gies up.

'What's up?'

'Ah'm knackered. It's too hard.'

Ah just want to see what he saw.

'We're late, Erin. We'll need to turn back.'

'Ah'm no goin back after comin all this way.'

'Naughton'll kill us. '

'Naw, you're Mr. Twaddle's star pupil, we'll be fine.'

But she means it.

Ah cannae explain how important it is.

Ye can smell the rain before it starts, trees seem to be listenin for it, know what we hear as a breeze are already raindrops fallin on the highest branches. And then the rain begins.

'Aw naw, Erin, we'll get soaked up here. C'mon, we better head back.'

Rain's good. Rain will make it even better.

Sally has her hand out as if she cannae believe the rain is real from the sound of it on trees.

'You go back. Ah promise ah'll only take a quick look then come straight after you. You can tell the teachers ah'm on the way.'

'Ye're no goin to run away again, are you?'

'It's just to do with the English project.'

Sally shakes her head.

'You need to lighten up, Erin, that's your problem.'

But she doesn't mean it in a bad way.

Nearly there.

Another twenty minutes goin up before ah see the ground stickin out to a platform with the sign 'Cora Linn.' The Falls are white across rocks and ah can just make out someone's fishin gear. The river below slices an soars through a forest of tall trees that seem to be singin wi the sound of water as well. It's so high and far away but feels near too cos ah can actually see it as real, not a book, not a film. Ah sit on a bench that overlooks the drop down. When ah close ma eyes, there's only the on-goin pounding sound of water and a feelin in ma blood lik ma blood is poundin as well, as if ma blood an the water sound are the same. The rain is heavier, ma face is wet but keep ma eyes closed an only hear the roar in ma blindness.

When ah open ma eyes, there's no William Wordsworth appears, not even his name carved on the bench. What did ah expect?

'William Wordsworth was here,' and rubbish attempt at a quill.

There's only sky and trees and water.

Shit, the time.

On the way back down the steep hill, along the wooden path, this time ah run to the sound of the water: the feelin of it inside me.

The sounding cataract…

Like a waterfall. Haunted.

Let me go. If you let me go, ah'll let you go.

Ah can't stop maself runnin, keep goin, no brakes, past the visitor centre and up the steep hilly path to the car park as if ah'm racin maself to see how fast ah can go. Now, the rain is a proper downpour, somethin is happenin, no jist an everyday shower.

At the bus, Mr Naughton has his arms crossed.

'Look at you Missy, you're soaked. Hope you don't think you're getting on this bus lik that?'

Right enough, ma hair's plastered to ma face; ma kagool is drippin.

Ah'm in big trouble. Mrs Kelly appears. She looks hot and exhausted. Won't be long till the baby, now. She says somethin to Naughton. He shakes his head, then ducks back into the bus. All the faces of the class are lookin at us through rain-soaked windows.

'So, Erin, did you find our Mr. Wordsworth up there?'

She reaches out to take ma wet kagool.

Ah found the sky and trees and the roaring sound of water.

'Ah saw the waterfall. Ah saw Cora Linn, miss.'

She smiles at me.

'Good girl,' she says.

The driver shakes his head at me as if bein wet an late is a personal affront to him; his windae wipers are goin backwards an forwards, makin a racket an inside the bus smells of left-over packed lunches at the bottom of bags; apart from him worryin about drips on the bus, everyone else has lost interest except Sally whose pointin to a seat beside her. There's already a plastic bag on it for me. When ah sit down, the bus goes into gear as we start to move away.

Lightning Source UK Ltd.
Milton Keynes UK
UKOW03f2258141014

240098UK00005B/665/P